"Compulsively readable, *Walking on Hidden Wings* has all the twists and turns of an aviation act, with all the intrigue too. Rachel Scott McDaniel proves herself once again as a master of her genre in this story that's filled with romance, history, and dangerous secrets. The witty banter between characters is guaranteed to make you swoon. I couldn't put it down!"

—Ashley Clark, acclaimed author of the
Heirloom Secrets series

RACHEL SCOTT McDANIEL

WALKING ON HIDDEN WINGS

A NOVEL *of the*
ROARING TWENTIES

KREGEL
PUBLICATIONS

Walking on Hidden Wings: A Novel of the Roaring Twenties
© 2024 by Rachel Scott McDaniel

Published by Kregel Publications, a division of Kregel Inc., 2450 Oak Industrial Dr. NE, Grand Rapids, MI 49505. www.kregel.com.

The persons and events portrayed in this work are the creations of the author, and any resemblance to persons living or dead is purely coincidental.

Scripture quotations are from the King James Version.

Cover design by Faceout Studio, Elisha Zepeda.

Library of Congress Cataloging-in-Publication Data
Names: McDaniel, Rachel Scott, author.
Title: Walking on hidden wings : a novel / Rachel Scott McDaniel.
Description: Grand Rapids, MI : Kregel Publications, a division of Kregel Inc., 2024.
Identifiers: LCCN 2023042954 (print) | LCCN 2023042955 (ebook)
Subjects: LCGFT: Christian fiction. | Romance fiction. | Detective and mystery fiction. | Novels.
Classification: LCC PS3613.C38576 W35 2024 (print) | LCC PS3613. C38576 (ebook) | DDC 813/.6—dc23/eng/20230929
LC record available at https://lccn.loc.gov/2023042954
LC ebook record available at https://lccn.loc.gov/2023042955

ISBN 978-0-8254-4813-3, print
ISBN 978-0-8254-7093-6, epub
ISBN 978-0-8254-6992-3, Kindle

Printed in the United States of America
24 25 26 27 28 29 30 31 32 33 / 5 4 3 2 1

Dear reader, this one's for you.

PART 1

Chapter 1 ————————————————————————————

September 1, 1922
Stella

MY GLOVED HAND STRETCHED HIGH as if to skim my fingers along the fringe of heaven, but one wrong move would send me careening eight hundred feet to unforgiving earth. Spectators huddled below on a broad field, their necks craning, eyes no doubt squinting against the fiery afternoon sun. All to glimpse the crazy dame who batted her lashes at danger and wooed risk atop the wing of a Curtiss Jenny biplane.

The custom Hisso engine roared its powerful song and muted the crowd's gasps and hollers, but even from this height I sensed the thrum of their excitement. I was no fool. They'd come to see if my blood would stain the sun-bleached grass. Sensation seekers. Every one of them. From farmer to mayor, the citizens of Columbia County, New York, had paid hard-earned cash to watch me challenge death.

With my boots planted on the wing, I leaned and swayed with the plane's movement, becoming one with the machine as it inclined.

We cut through the sky at sixty-five miles per hour, a dizzying speed on solid ground, let alone at this altitude.

Stella! You're crazy! Tex mouthed from the safety of the open cockpit.

While the mustached pilot was probably miffed that I'd climbed out of my seat before reaching peak elevation, he hadn't known me long enough to make such an assessment. He didn't even know my true name. The lanky man had approached me after this morning's flight show, tugging his worn suspenders and claiming he was the best aviator to ever sit behind the controls.

He'd lied.

Because I'd married the best flier. Only to become a widow before my wedding gown could fade. I pushed past the stab of grief and forced myself to focus. Thankfully, Tex *did* seem to have a good handle on the Jenny, or else I wouldn't have ventured onto the wing. Or maybe I would've anyway.

If things got shaky, all I had to do was drop to my knees and cling to the spar bar within my reach. The plane climbed higher, nearing fifteen hundred feet.

My heartbeat drummed at the base of my throat. I pried my resolve from the murky depths of my mind and took a step forward. Then another. A tremor rocked the plane. I defied the instinct to stoop and brace myself. Instead I stilled, adjusting to the new angle as if the wing were an extension of my feet. Good thing Tex hadn't jerked the controls. One panicked jolt could've knocked me off-balance and into the slicing blades of the propeller.

I strode two remaining paces, positioning close to the wing's edge, and my gaze swept over the crowd.

Those below had no idea whom they stared at. My stunt in the air wasn't my only performance. Nor my most dangerous one. *That* particular act had begun the moment I'd run away from the glitter. For I'd shed the vulnerable identity of golden-haired Geneva Ashcroft Hayes, society's angel, to become raven-locked Stella Starling, showman of the skies.

I glanced at Tex. He signaled to pull the rip cord, then pointed at my vacated cockpit. Basically he wanted me to either open the chute or climb back into my seat. As if those were my only options.

I stretched out my arms and flared my fingers. The wind pulsed against me like fevered breath. My eyes slid closed. Darkness invaded, but I wasn't terrified of it. Not anymore. I'd been wrestling the shadows ever since darkness had the nerve to snatch Warren from my arms.

Being this close to the clouds meant being closer to him. If only I could reach up and draw back the velvety blue curtain of sky to see my husband's face, the tease of his smirk when he called me Eva. The hints of amber in his dark eyes when the light hit just right. The thrill that rumbled through me at his touch.

And there it was.

The familiar pang. It tore into me, and I clung with a desperate grip, allowing the scoring force to numb me to the rest of the world. This was the precise amount of dulling needed for me to pursue a third option. One Tex hadn't considered.

My temples throbbed against my leather helmet.

A prayer left my lips.

I fell back, giving myself to the sky.

● ● ●

A man slumped against my door.

I froze at the top of the stairs leading to my rented room. My accommodations weren't wired for electric lamps, inside or out. The waning moon and the dim lantern in my right hand were my only light sources.

The man sat motionless, his folded arms stacked atop drawn knees. A hat slung low on his face, but the straw boater didn't muffle the gruff snores ripping from his lips.

Of all the places for this fellow to fall asleep.

I hated the idea of disturbing the landlords below, but I wasn't about to wake a male stranger at night. The alternative would be returning to Mr. Ewing's farm and bunking with livestock. Not only had the generous farmer given me use of his field for the flight shows, but he'd also stowed my plane behind his barn, all for no fee.

My aching muscles protested the mile trek to the Ewing property when a comfortable bed stood only yards away. A bed in a room I'd paid two dollars to call mine for the next twelve hours.

Unlike Mr. Ewing, the middle-aged couple who leased the room above their own humble lodgings had inflated the going rate by a dollar and fifty cents upon my arrival—if the rumor was to be believed.

Once upon a time, all I had to do was tug a braided bellpull, and attendants would flock to do my bidding. But like all memorable stories, a severe plot twist had changed the course of my fairy tale. I hadn't even reached the coveted "The End" and had already amassed complaints—I never encountered talking woodland creatures and most definitely had been robbed of my happily ever after.

So now I flipped the figurative page, turned to fetch the landlord, and nearly tripped on the uneven planks. I grasped the railing, which was wobbly at best, and prayed it didn't crumble into splinters beneath my weight.

"Huh? What?" The dozer startled upright, then skittered to his feet, his hat tumbling to the floorboards.

Oh for the love . . . "Tex? What are you doing here?" From the dark-blond hair and copper-hued mustache to the spindly arms capped with stubby hands, his entire person consisted of mismatched parts strung together on a gangly frame.

He wiped the slobber from his mouth with the frayed cuff of his sleeve. "Waiting for you. Must've fallen asleep." He yawned. "What time is it?"

I remained a safe distance from him and strengthened my grip on the lantern. Not the best choice of weapon, but it was something. Tex didn't seem the kind who'd force himself on a woman. Then again, I'd known him for less than a day. "Around ten."

"And you just now arrived? What were you doing?"

"Nothing of your concern." There was no way I'd confide in Tex the true reason behind my not-so-casual interest in this town. Or the reason why I'd selected this dot on the map for a flight show.

Notes hidden in a cigarette case had dictated each stop on my itinerary. The silver-plated container would appear rather plain to any onlooker, but stashed within were scribbled secrets by a private investigator. The detective had been my husband's best friend. He had also disappeared a few weeks after Warren's death. Coincidence? I didn't believe in those anymore. Which was why I'd taken the case from Brisbane's deserted apartment.

His notes were the only clues I had. But like the past spots I'd visited in search of truth, this town hadn't coughed up any answers—and neither had the resident gossip, Mrs. Felicia Turnbell, proprietor of the busy drugstore. I'd emptied my pockets on chocolate sodas, lingering past closing time and encouraging Mrs. Turnbell to divulge any and all gossip. Apparently the town committee was at odds about the possibility of some kind of factory opening the following year. The schoolteacher was getting married next month, and the board still hadn't hired a replacement for the fall. Oh, and the doctor's elderly mother had a habit of switching price tags at the church rummage sale.

Nothing that involved the murder of my husband. Or his missing friend.

Exhaustion seeped into my bones. "C'mon, Tex. What are you doing here? I already paid you a swell sum for your flying services."

"I came to see if you're okay."

From my parachute jump? "I landed perfectly." Free-falling a hundred feet before opening my chute wasn't my finest decision. All to silence, if only for a second, the tug of grief and the push of guilt, the tormenting twins of my existence since the day Warren was killed. "I'll be sore tomorrow, but the crowd loved it."

"That's not what I meant." He scooped his hat from the dusty floor and brushed it off. "Remember I served in the war. I recognize a pair of haunted eyes when I see them, Stella."

Shame poked my conscience for lying about my identity. But if this man knew who I was—or rather, who my family was—his concern for my haunted eyes would shift to padding his pockets.

A five-thousand-dollar reward belonged to the person who safely returned me to Ashcroft grounds. "I'm fine. Just tired. Now if you don't mind stepping aside from my door—"

"I wanna work for you." He held his hat over his heart and fidgeted with the brim. "With me as your flier, you can expand your show. Do that whole wingwalking bit." There were traces of something in his voice. Something that'd blazed in me the moment I'd first set eyes on a flying machine—desperation. That jolt of longing to climb into the cockpit and escape into the heavens.

How much more difficult was it for aviators to be sentenced to land? Flying coursed through their blood. Even with two feet planted on the ground, their sights were forever on the sky. Today I'd mistakenly given Tex a drop of adventure's milk, but not enough to nourish his starved soul. In my efforts to be gracious, I'd been cruel. "I'm sorry. I work alone."

"Why? I can help—"

"I have an appointment at noon tomorrow, then I'm leaving the area after that." That was the plan, anyway. I had no idea who Kent Brisbane had made this meeting with before he'd gone missing. Attending in his place could get me answers . . . or get me killed.

Tex's arms wilted to his sides. "I understand."

"Several families have been asking for rides in the Jenny. My engagement is in the next township over, but if you want, you can fly folks around. Just charge two bucks a passenger and limit their jaunts to fifteen minutes. Keep all the profits minus what's needed for fuel."

His head jerked up. "Really?"

"Be sure to finish up by three and tack her to the fence post. I need to head out as soon as I return."

"Thank you, Stella." He slapped his hat on his head.

I offered a friendly smile. "Don't do anything stupid with my plane."

"Like allowing 'em to parachute off the wings at low altitude?" he teased with a grin.

"Off with you now." I set down the lantern, which had burned out during our conversation, and fished the door key from my purse. "You've kept me from sleep long enough."

"Yes, ma'am." He gave a two-fingered salute, then his face sobered. "If you . . . uh . . . change your mind down the road, I hope you'll consider me for a partner."

I nodded but kept my lips pinched. I'd no intention of joining forces with anyone.

Tex bounded down the steps with the grace of a hundred elephants as I unlocked my door. The room smelled like stale cigar smoke and unwashed feet. A newspaper had been slid beneath my door. Probably yesterday's edition from another town, considering this rural community had no local press.

Moonlight shone through the gap of the tattered curtains, running a silvering finger on the front page, highlighting a familiar face. Mine. Since my disappearance, my family had plastered my likeness on every times and gazette from Philadelphia to Seattle. Hardly surprising, considering my marriage to Warren had shoved a dozen of the nation's leading newspapers under my father's powerful thumb. I'd inherited Warren's publishing empire after his declared death, and now with my absence, I could almost guarantee Father had pushed his way into command.

This picture was the one taken from my debutante season. My smile was so prim and innocent, my light hair in a perfect coiffure. How different I looked now. No one would place Stella Starling as Geneva Ashcroft Hayes. But still, I should move with caution. The more flamboyant I acted, the less likely the connection to the reserved socialite.

I snatched the offending paper from the floor so I wouldn't trip over it come morning.

I relit the lantern, and my gaze drifted to the paper's headline. I froze. My shaky fingers crinkled the edges as I reread those bold words, hoping—no, praying—my exhausted mind had tricked me. No. The words were there in stark contrast of black on white.

Missing Socialite Confesses to Husband's Murder

Chapter 2 ————————————————————————————————————

I LOST COUNT OF HOW many times I'd read over the headline and the subsequent article, each condemning phrase leaping out and twisting into me like fiery thorns.

"The police department has a letter by Mrs. Hayes."

"In her own words, she confesses her guilt."

"Takes blame for her husband's murder."

"Wanted for questioning."

Yes, I'd written to Kent Brisbane, but my words had been utterly misinterpreted. And how had my letter slipped into the hands of the authorities when I couldn't recall ever sending it?

I remembered addressing the envelope and placing it in my desk drawer, but . . . then what? I squeezed my eyes shut, willing those faded moments to return. Had I mailed it? I must have, and in my muddled emotional state, not realized what I'd done.

How foolish. Also, how trusting. I had penned my fears and shame for Brisbane's eyes only. Him being a private detective, I'd thought he could help. That was why I'd visited him, only to find he'd disappeared. So I'd taken the cigarette case and decided to conduct my own investigation.

Hair rising on my neck, I scanned the article again. Not one mention of Brisbane. But how else would anyone have possession of my letter if not from him? Maybe he'd turned it in anonymously. Maybe Brisbane's vanishing had nothing to do with the danger I'd left home to escape, but for another reason altogether. What if he was purposely hiding? Did he have something to do with Warren's death? What if he had set me up?

So many questions piled on my soul without any hope of being answered.

A sigh pushed past my lips. I was wanted for murder. The fairy tale shifted yet again—the princess had become the villain.

I glanced at my New Testament propped against my bag on the bed. God had never promised a life of fabled bliss. The Scriptures warned of tests and trials, but this? It was more than I could bear.

Nausea flooded my gut, crashing against the stony edges of my heart. Should I continue my hunt for the elusive private detective even while the world hunted me? What other choice did I have?

Ignoring my pounding temples, I dug out Brisbane's cigarette case from my bag. With a soft click, I opened the rectangular trinket and withdrew the small notepad. My heart raced as I set the opened pad beside the glaring article.

I'd studied Brisbane's choppy scrawl a thousand times, but at this moment I hoped something new would emerge from the uneven ink strokes. I knew this was foolish, was like staring at splattered paint on a canvas for days and expecting the mess to blend to create a clear picture. All I had were disordered snatches of clues with no assurance of them leading to anything.

Brisbane had jotted down ten towns—all rural communities, all threaded throughout New York State. Why were these locations important enough to be in his treasured notepad? Why had he left said notepad behind when he'd never gone anywhere without it? When I'd gone to his studio apartment, utilizing Warren's key, it was obvious the man had left in a hurried state, his wardrobe left open, drawers askew—though the cigarette case had remained on his nightstand. Had he left it on purpose? Or had he been in such a rush he'd forgotten it?

I asked myself these questions over and over. Whether the idea was irrational or remarkable, I had used the information within the case as a map of sorts. Under the guise of barnstorming, I had visited the first four towns on Brisbane's list. I intended to go through with this charade until I visited every location.

Something else was within his notes, an inscription that didn't gel with the other entries—a date and an address. An appointment that happened to be tomorrow in the next township. I was determined to investigate. Heaven only knew if it would direct me to Brisbane or something more sinister.

• • •

I hadn't prepared for this.

When I'd given the cabbie the address, he'd flashed a smile with a hearty "Sure thing, dollface." But I never imagined the appointment Brisbane had made months ago was at a gin joint in the middle of nowhere.

I'd never stepped a T-strap shoe into a speakeasy before. Of course, I'd inclined my ear to the gossip about these establishments. How they brimmed with all sorts of glitz and glamour. How gorgeous flappers danced the foxtrot with men styled in the finest garb.

This, however, was not that kind of place.

The structure—if it even deserved that title—seemed nothing but warped boards and rotted beams melded together by the putrid, hot breath of drunks. Cigarette smoke clogged the air, adding a haze to the already shadowed space.

Judging by the number of fedora-capped heads, it was evident I was the only female in the room.

Swell.

My hot plan of remaining unobserved fizzled like a wet firecracker. Maybe I should've worn my trousers and flight jacket. But that would have made me stand out more—if that were possible. I ran a damp palm down the skirt of my dress. When packing for this trip, I'd only had time to shove a few frocks into my traveling bag. This one was dark blue with ivory trim. Hardly remarkable. But it appeared as though I were competing for the popular Most Beautiful Bathing Girl in America for all the stares I garnered. But I wasn't pageant material, and this joint wasn't the Atlantic City Boardwalk.

"Hiya, baby." That slurred voice did not belong to Kent Brisbane. Nor did the weathered face stretched into a large smile with an even larger knot on the nose. The man staggered toward me, his eyes glossed over.

I gave him a wide berth only to collide into a billiard table. The impact disrupted the game in progress, sending a striped ball into the side pocket.

"Why, thank you." A shorter gentleman removed his hat and bent forward in a sweeping bow. "You just earned me a buck."

His opponent yelled an unsavory term and commenced to argue.

This wasn't going as I'd imagined. The only thing keeping me within these seedy walls was the hope of meeting Kent Brisbane. My eyes swept the space in search of his tall, sturdy frame. It was early yet. The time on the paper said noon. It was ten till the hour.

He wasn't lingering by the pool tables. Nor seated at the smattering of tables. That left the bar. Several men had their backs toward me, heads bowed over, no doubt nursing drinks. My heels clicked loud and choppy—just like my heartbeat—as I approached the long stretch of counter, stained with who knew what.

The men at the billiards table continued their shouting match. To add more chaos, the bartender dropped a tray of dirty glasses. Amber liquid splashed on a boot belonging to a man who possessed keg-sized arms. Those massive limbs shoved the bartender, flinging him into a group of rummed-up patrons.

Cackles and curses erupted. Some jumped from their seats, while others pounded meaty fists on the tables. My lands. A brawl was sure to erupt.

Panic punched my heart. I needed out of here.

Masculine hands slid over my waist from behind. Possessive and way too intimate.

No way I was getting assaulted in a speakeasy. I jerked my elbow back and connected with a muscled abdomen. The man's hold didn't lessen, but his fingers tightened in almost . . . a protective gesture?

"Easy now, Geneva."

That voice. Deep and soulful.

Again, not Brisbane's.

I braved a look over my shoulder and peered into the eyes of my dead husband.

Only he was very much alive.

Chapter 3 ————————————————————

Approximately five months earlier—April 7, 1922
Geneva

"YOU'RE SACRIFICING ME ON THE matrimonial altar." All for the sake of politics and power. I tugged the silver-plated brush through my long golden hair, wincing when it tugged a snarl.

"What a notion, Geneva." Mother's laugh was forced, her mouth pinching at the edges. "You always have a flair for the dramatic, my love."

Love.

Even though that particular topic terrified me, it'd be nice to be given a choice. But that sort of pettiness appeared to be last on my parents' list of requirements in pawning off their child. Only it wasn't to the highest bidder. No, my family didn't need to fatten their already gorged bank accounts. They craved influence. And apparently Warren Hayes, with his newspaper empire, held the golden key to Father's political hopes.

Mother's pale features seemed almost ghostly in the mirror's reflection. She stood like a porcelain sentinel beside my open oak bookcase. I never knew what version of Mother to expect. Sometimes she assumed the role of dutiful parent, instructing me in long-winded monologues of the unbending ways of society. Other days she remained tight-lipped and begrudging, as if she felt obligated to visit me. Another task on her lengthy list. The only other time Mother approached, and my least favorite, was on assignment from Father.

I presumed today would be a blend of all three.

She touched the Bible my grandmother had gifted me years ago, the slow creep of her bony finger along the spine almost mocking. Helena Ashcroft quoted society pages more readily than Scripture, but she knew enough verses to wield them to her advantage. And to Father's control. As in the Scripture about children obeying their parents. Years of such forced guidance had left me questioning if Mother was friend or foe. Same went for God.

She padded across the carpet to where I sat on the plush vanity stool. "You don't have to encourage a proposal tonight. There's plenty of time to get to know each other."

Not according to Father. He needed this union between Mr. Hayes and me last year. I had dug in my heels, claiming I needed to see Lilith through her debut season. My parents had relented but only because Lilith was shy and needed a buffer from society's wolves. But now I must align myself with a *worthy* spouse because that was what one did when situated on the highest rung of the social ladder.

I wanted nothing more than to kick the infernal ladder over. "If Father wasn't running for the senate"—with his hungry eyes on the presidency—"I wouldn't have to be the bait to lure in a man I've never met." And knew nothing about. The gentleman could have a secret life as a bootlegger for all I knew.

"Another ill-placed analogy." The hollowness in Mother's brown eyes wasn't comforting. "You're simply helping advance your family."

From what I could assume, the Hayes Publishing Company sought financial backing to keep their newspapers rolling, and the Ashcroft family sought favorable publicity for Father's senatorial campaign. Everyone benefited.

Except me.

"It's just for a little while." Mother placed her hand on my shoulder, and I recoiled as if her slender fingers were snakes. A little while? Last time I checked, marriage was a forever thing.

How could Mother say the situation would only be temporary? Unless . . . "Are the rumors true?"

"Narrow it down, dear." Her voice struggled for lightness. "There are, indeed, several."

Yes, which was why Father needed the papers to soften his tycoon image. To use the power of the Hayes family's ink on paper to paint him a hero. My future husband had his work cut out for him. "The rumors about Howard Yater's passing." The unfortunate fellow had betrayed Father in some business dealings. Father had invited him to dinner to discuss the issue, and not two days later Mr. Yater was dead.

"You think your father had a role in that cruel man's death?" She shook her head, as if I were an ignorant child. "Mr. Yater succumbed to a stomach illness. Your Father had nothing to do with it." Her cold fingers squeezed my shoulder, not in affection but to emphasize her words. "I meant only that you need to entertain Mr. Hayes for a little while. He'll certainly fall for your charms. And Father will be pleased."

And not punish Lilith. I could almost hear those words drip from her thin mouth. No, Father wouldn't ruin my sister's life if I allowed him to rule mine.

"Now, no more talk of this, Geneva." Mother tucked a loose hairpin back into place. "We have the ball to get ready for. Cecily will be up shortly to start your beauty treatments."

Mother inspected my gown hanging on the dressing screen, then exited in a flourish of lavender and grace.

The ball began at eight. I had six more hours of freedom. And I wouldn't squander them. After hastily arranging my hair in a low chignon, I bounded out the door, not half as elegant as Mother but wholly more determined.

Quick glances ensured all was clear in the hall. I fled down the staff stairway and exited the back door.

I usually favored our country manor over our town house in Manhattan, but not today. The walls seemed to close in. I needed away. My feet carried me swiftly through the garden and out of sight of the opulent estate. The familiar dusty lane stretched before me, and I paused to catch my breath. In my haste, I hadn't changed from my satin slippers, which by now were ruined. But I couldn't bring myself to care. I pushed on, putting more and more distance between myself and the manor.

My parents regarded me like I viewed my slippers. I used these shoes to get me where I needed but didn't care about their well-being—only placing all my weight on them, forcing them to move where I pleased. I'd use them until they broke. Such was my existence as an Ashcroft—used until broken.

I would marry a man I'd never seen to save a sister I did see. And adored more than anything. A fact Father often used to his twisted advantage.

Starlings winged overhead, their sable bodies warping the steady rays of sun. What I wouldn't give to join their ranks. I envied their freedom. Oh, to be able to fly far away from scheming parents and an inevitable wedding to a stranger.

Lilith.

My spine straightened. I would do this for Lilith. I passed a derelict barn, my usual marker for returning home.

"All better, darling. Now you'll sing pretty for me." A masculine voice floated on the breeze, drawing my attention to the nearby field on the other side of the paint-stripped structure.

A man stood in front of a . . . flying machine?

My mouth hung open. I'd seen photos of airplanes, heard tales of their brilliancy, but never actually glimpsed one. Mother labeled them death traps. Father declared them a foolish means of transportation. I called them fascinating.

I gravitated toward the small fence separating me from the field. In a move that would send Mother to the fainting couch, I climbed over the wooden barrier, careful not to snag my stockings. I dodged shallow ditches and piles of cow manure. My poor slippers. What was I doing? I didn't know this stranger, but the airplane tugged me unshakably toward it. Oh, to rest my eyes upon something that tasted the sky.

"Hello." My tentative voice made the man flinch.

"Afternoon, miss." He lifted his hand to tip his hat, only to realize he had no hat. What he *did* have was a fascinating display of artfully mussed brown curls that the rays of afternoon sun took as their personal playground. Being accustomed to seeing men's hair waxed stiff from tubs of pomade, I was enamored how the tips of his masculine locks lifted in the gentle breeze. How the—

A throat cleared.

I jolted. What was I doing staring at a complete stranger? I took a step away from him and toward the airplane. "Is that your flying machine?"

He nodded, still not pulling his gaze from me.

"It's magnificent." The propeller was wooden. The body was a curious blend of painted fabric and thin metal. "I've never been this close. Honestly, I've never seen one."

"She had a bit of a fit during the barrel rolls. But there was some debris in her fuselage. Her engine should purr pretty now." He spoke aloud, as if I understood what in the world he was talking about. He took in my face, which must've betrayed my confusion, for the corner of his mouth lifted along with a casual shrug. "Sorry. Mechanic's jargon."

"Oh." I lowered my brows. "I assumed you were the pilot."

"I'm that too." His grin broke free. "Jenny can be temperamental. You have to understand how she moves so you can keep her gliding."

I allowed a small smile. "You call your plane Jenny?"

His curious gaze squinted against the sunlight. "If you want to go by the model name, she's a Curtiss JN-4. But us fliers just say Jenny."

I stepped forward and ran my hand along the Jenny's silver body. The frame was warm, but my palm seemed to sizzle, as if it could absorb the adventures this plane had encountered. Meanwhile, I had been confined to this soiled earth. "What escapades you've known."

"You sound jealous." The man came up beside me.

"I am." My confession was more to myself than to this stranger. "It's only metal and wood and fuel. It has no heart or soul, but it's traveled places I've never been." With all the wealth in my life, I could never buy that experience. Or could I? I faced him, raising my chin with fresh purpose. "How much?"

His brows spiked. "For the plane? Sorry. She's not for sale."

"No, I noticed there are two seats. Take me on your next run?" It was my last window of freedom before stepping into the bleak plans everyone so effortlessly set for me. I needed this more than anything. "I can pay you any amount. Name the price." I pulled my attention from the enormous contraption and focused on its owner.

I had a lot of practice observing gentlemen while not exuding any interest. I'd survived my debut season, accumulating several marriage proposals, none of which my family approved of. But with all that came an ability to quickly assess people, take in their measure in the span of a few heartbeats.

With a swift glance at the man, I noted the confident slash of his dark brows. He'd had some sort of schooling—higher education if I were to guess. Intelligence marked his dark-brown eyes. But what impacted me the most was the strong line of his jaw. There was a hardness to it, as if naturally locked in determination. In his open-collared shirt and dusty trousers, he embodied ruggedness, something unsuited for the ballroom but far more intriguing.

The mystery pilot was quiet for a moment, studying me in return. His mouth pressed together, then relaxed into an easy smile. "Sorry, miss. I can't do that."

I blinked at his casual dismissal. He couldn't give me one lousy jaunt through the sky? Couldn't the man see how much it meant to me? Defeat taunted. So much was being stripped from my hands. My choice of husband. My last name. My future. Something snapped in me, and I clutched his arm. "Please? I'll make it worth your while."

As soon as the words were out, I wished them back. I didn't know this man. Sure, the way he carried himself spoke of assurance and smarts, but he could be low principled. And here I was, in an abandoned field, far from civilization, uttering words that could be taken in the worst possible way. I straightened and adopted a cool tone. "Let me repeat my offer. I can pay any monetary fee."

His arms crossed in a tight fold over his chest. With his shirtsleeves rolled to his elbows, it made for an impressive display of brawn and strength. "You make it sound as if anything can be bought."

"In my world, that's the way of life."

His head tilted, and something marked his eyes. It looked suspiciously like compassion. He braved a step toward me, caution saturating his movements, as if approaching a delicate creature. "In *my* world, all you have to do is ask."

"But you told me a second ago you couldn't."

"As in, I couldn't accept anything from you. But I'll freely take you up there." He nodded toward the sky. "If that's what you want."

What a refreshing—and scarce!—thought. Someone existed who didn't want to take from me, but to give. Emotion clogged my throat at this stranger's kindness. "Well then." I couldn't help the smile breaking loose. "Would you be so kind as to give me a turn in your flying machine?"

He snatched a leather jacket from the ground and slipped it on. "It would be my honor." He paused. "Miss?"

Oh. *Oh.* I hadn't introduced myself. My manners were abominable, but I was glad of it. Because at the moment, I didn't want to be Geneva Ashcroft, heiress to countless lumber mills and paper factories. I longed to be like the starling.

"Pardon?"

I blinked. Had I just said that aloud? Gracious, I was a million miles out of my mind. "I said St-. . . Stella. You may call me Stella."

If I expected the man to scowl at my informal prattling of my fake name, I'd been wrong.

A reckless grin split his tan face. "Nice to meet you, Stella."

"Likewise." I dipped my chin. "And you are?"

"Your pilot for this afternoon."

• • •

I had almost died. Well, it had felt that way. Several times. But it'd been nothing like I'd ever experienced. The thrashing of the propeller, the growl of the engine, the way my stomach had rolled into my throat when the wheels had lifted from the ground. The journey into the skies had made it difficult to draw a patchy breath into my squeezing lungs. My skin had prickled beneath the battering of the air current. Good thing my maid, Cecily, hadn't already arranged my hair for the evening's event, or else I would've been in deep trouble. For my golden locks were stuffed beneath a helmet, but some tendrils had broken free, whipping wildly about my face, even as my heart soared beyond the gilded earthly cage.

The goggles secured over my eyes hadn't limited my vision of the glories around me. My pilot had proven skilled in handling the airplane and had given me an exciting jaunt as near to heaven as one could possibly get.

All thrilling. All over way too soon.

The field, pitted with ruts and ditches, seemed the worst place for a smooth landing, but the experienced flier set the wheels on what had to be the only stretch of even ground.

Knowing Cecily had probably sent out search parties by now, I thanked the handsome aviator, patted the plane one last time, and scurried home.

A few hours later I found myself in the boring ballroom. Glittering dresses donned by those with sparkling smiles surrounded me, pressing in on every side. Yet everything was insipid compared to my memorable flight. Sighing, I took a sip of lemonade. It was bland.

My parents had organized this country house party, tonight being the first evening of a two-week-long event to celebrate spring. Though truly this had been planned to schmooze political powerhouses for their support this fall. Since Father had announced his senatorial run last November, it'd been nothing but a string of societal gatherings to boost my parents' image. And this one had the markings of being the dullest one yet.

I wanted nothing more than to be back with my mystery pilot. I'd never gotten his true name in fear he'd call me out on my own lie. But it was better that way. For I'd always remember him for his scent of leather, flash of smile, and air of secrets.

"Geneva." Father's voice carried over my shoulder.

Perhaps I should pretend I hadn't heard him and walk away in search of a darkened alcove to disappear in. I knew the reason Father sought me out. The only reason he *ever* sought me out in a ballroom—to make an introduction. And tonight the impending new acquaintance lying in wait could only be Mr. Hayes. My future husband.

For Lilith.

My jaw tightened. My sister was in her room tonight, recovering from a spring cold. Last month the youngest Ashcroft had turned twenty, three years younger than me and far more fragile. Which was why my parents had delayed her society debut, thinking an extra couple of years would see her through her shyness stage. Though it hadn't been a phase. Lilith was more comfortable away from crowds and strangers. And yet Father had a worse alliance arranged for Lilith if I refused to marry Mr. Hayes. With a calming breath, I inclined my chin and pivoted on my heel toward the men who'd agreed to make my life miserable. "Yes, Father?"

I almost dropped my lemonade.

For standing beside Father was my mystery pilot. The man who'd escorted me into the skies. The man who currently had a knowing smirk lining his handsome mouth.

"Mr. Hayes, may I present my daughter."

Warren Hayes, newspaper king, pilot extraordinaire, stepped forward. His appearance was so different from hours earlier. His curls had been tamed into submission. He no longer filled out a crisp leather flight jacket but a tailored tuxedo. His eyes fixed on me with exhilarating intensity. "Miss Ashcroft." He bowed over my gloved hand. "I'm charmed."

He straightened to full height with a lithe movement, reminding me of a panther. Powerful and dangerous. And yet I wasn't intimidated in the least but rather jolted with thrilling energy.

His lips tilted into an amused smile. "You put me in mind of another local beauty I've had the pleasure of meeting. Perhaps you're acquainted with Stella Fibberstale?"

I'd never given him a fake surname. And if I had, it certainly wouldn't

have been Fibberstale. No, he was calling me out for my earlier deception, my telling of a fib. A smile tickled my lips, but I wouldn't succumb.
Not while Father watched on. "I've heard wonderful things about that
elegant young lady." Hiding any hint of mirth lent a throatiness to my
voice. Not exactly the tone I intended. "I'm honored to be likened to
her."

"And I'd be honored if you'd dance with me." His request was so
smoothly placed, it'd taken a second to gather my wits. He outstretched
his gloved hand, beckoning mine. "That is, if you're not already engaged."

I swallowed so hard I almost choked. *Engaged.* Of all the things to
say. But the twinkle in his eyes betrayed his deliberate word choice. As
if we shared a secret joke. Which . . . we did. But now was a test to see
where his allegiance lay. Would he reveal to Father our afternoon escapade? Though it seemed Mr. Hayes had forgotten about the Ashcroft
patriarch. The newspaper mogul looked at me as if whatever rolled off
my lips next was of the utmost importance to him.

Too bad my mouth couldn't move. Nor the rest of me. If John Ashcroft was anywhere in the vicinity, all attention fixed on him. Not so
now. I glanced at Father. Not that I expected any reaction from him.
There was a reason why people cowered in his presence. And a fiery
temper couldn't be blamed.

If he had one, he'd never shown it. No shaking fists. No vein-bulged
forehead over bent brows. Never a sharp tone. In all my twenty-three
years, he'd never adopted a severe expression.

Or any other expression. His countenance was one of perpetual
emptiness. As if there'd been a leak in his emotion tank, draining the
ability to express any kind of feeling from his system.

Such a coolness terrified those around him, me included. Father's
frosty blond hair and glacial blue eyes, along with his regal bearing,
made him appear less like a lumber mill tycoon and more like some
mythical ice king ripped from the pages of a storybook.

But now the left corner of Father's mouth curled even as he divested
me of the lemonade glass. Someone could pluck that ridiculous plume

from Mother's gaudy headpiece and knock me over with it. Maybe I'd imagined Father's smile. Or a bored guest had laced the beverage bowl.

Meanwhile, Mr. Hayes awaited my answer.

With a single nod, I slid my fingers into Mr. Hayes's, and he led me onto the dance floor. My stomach roiled as it had hours ago, but this time I couldn't fault the turbulent air rocking the flying machine.

His hand settled on my waist, and I inhaled a sharp breath at the fire leaping inside me.

My previous ball gowns had been heavily beaded in the torso, but tonight's chiffon dress was most assuredly lacking in studded ornamentation. With the thick barrier removed and my secret rebellion to forego wearing a corset, the flowy layers of cloth were thin beneath his hand, making his touch intimate.

"Did you know who I was the entire time?" All the blinding shimmer of the chandeliers, the soft chatter of the surrounding couples, and the floral-scented air in the room narrowed until there was nothing but him and me.

His lips twitched. "I thought you were familiar, but I couldn't place you. Not until you refused to tell me your full name." He leaned in and lowered his voice. "How about you? Did you purposefully seek me out this afternoon?"

I scoffed. "Hardly. Until today I hadn't a clue as to what you even looked like. Now I see I misjudged you."

His eyes gleamed with mischief. "In a good way or bad?"

"I can see you're far too amused by this. Perhaps I'll withhold my answer and leave you captive by suspense."

His scorching gaze stretched into me, melting the frosty spots of my defenses. "I'm held captive. But suspense has nothing to do with it."

Oh, I'd been wrong earlier. The man *was* ballroom handsome. If I was mistaken in my assessment of Warren Hayes, I could also have been in error about our future. Perhaps this thing between us . . . could work.

Chapter 4 ————————————————————————————

SHOUTS ECHOED OFF THE DECAYING walls of the gin joint. Bodies shuffled and launched at each other. Glass shattered. The cry of broken things. My vision, a chaotic blur of dizziness and tears, must have deceived me. The man beside me couldn't be my husband. Warren was dead. I'd wept at his memorial service. Felt his loss every moment since I'd been told of his crash.

But there he stood.

My mind couldn't grasp what my eyes took in. I lingered in a peculiar shifting of disbelief and what felt like . . . happiness. But I couldn't allow myself to give in to the swell of relief. Because this man couldn't be him.

"Let's go." The gruff command spurted from his mouth.

But my feet, along with the rest of my stunned body, couldn't move. How was this possible? Was I imagining it all? A warped result of too much grief and too little sleep? I reached out, fingers shaking, half expecting him to disappear. I hesitated, unsure of reality. If this was all some cruel twist of my mind, I'd rather linger in this state, where I could at least see him, if only a moment longer.

My hand moved, as if in alliance with my heart, and touched his face. My thumb stroked his lower lip, my hand spanning across his jaw, now lined with a beard. He didn't vanish. He remained. Stiff. Unresponsive to my touch.

"Is it really you?" The words were breathy, but the voice belonged to me. Something about hearing it aloud broke my trance. "Warren, you're alive." A sob wrenched my chest, and I fell into him, gripping his broad shoulders.

He was here. Real.

"It's not safe, Geneva."

I leaned into him, determined never to let go, but he took an abrupt step back, disentangling from my arms.

"We need to leave." He wrapped his large fingers around my wrist with a gentle but decided grip. His gaze darted, landing everywhere but my face.

The brawl had intensified. But I couldn't scrape enough sense to care. My husband had returned to me. Only . . . he hadn't. It was I who'd come here. And why wouldn't he look at me?

Warren led me around upended tables, broken bottles, and two unconscious gentlemen. The numbness, so overpowering a few seconds ago, eased with my rushed steps. Yet as more clarity came to my mind, the more confusion pressed in.

Warren had been alive all this time. How had he survived the crash? Why hadn't he reached out to me? My gaze fixed on the back of his head. His curly hair was overgrown, but that wasn't what stole my attention. His neck muscles were taut. His usually lithe body moved with the rigidity of forged iron. Of course, we *were* picking our way through a riot.

Warren kicked an overturned chair from our path, even as I almost tripped over a discarded hat. We skirted a pair of men exchanging punches. A rogue elbow shot back, and Warren shielded me, taking the impact in his spine.

He grunted but kept moving. We reached the door, and Warren fell behind to let me pass first. The afternoon sun pierced my vision, such a sharp contrast to the imposing shadows I'd just emerged from.

Warren shut the door and set off toward a grove of trees to our right. I didn't know where he was leading me, but I hustled to keep up with his long strides.

The humid air made it impossible to draw anything but shallow breaths. He slowed and glanced about as if searching for someone. A Model T was parked in the shade alongside a narrow road. Warren jogged to the passenger door and opened it. Was this his vehicle? I had so many questions, but his gaze locked with mine, and I stumbled to a halt.

Something flashed in his eyes. It wasn't affection. Nor any trace of warmth. The gold flecks stood out from the brown, like darts of fire.

"Warren, what is it?" I closed the distance between us, yearning for a proper reunion after a month and a half separation. I latched on to his neck, thankful the drunken brawl could no longer distract us.

His hands came around my back, then slid to my waist. But it wasn't in tenderness. His fingers roamed about me in swift, deliberate movements.

"No weapons at least," he muttered.

I drew back. "Weapons? What do you mean?" I peered into his face. Warren had never looked at me with anything but admiration. Even when we'd first met, I had recognized it. But now he regarded me with an edge of irritation. The truth sliced into me with the precision of a rusty blade, cutting painfully slow, corroding my hope—he wasn't pleased to see me.

"Thought you were here to follow through."

Follow through . . .

My gaze moved past him to the newspaper on the passenger side of the bench, the exact one I'd seen last night. All those awful words smeared about me. Accusing and painful. Shock wrapped its powerful fist around my vocal cords, but I managed a weak response. "It's not true."

"No?" He had an arsenal of severe glares, but it was his lone word that disarmed me.

Truly he couldn't believe I'd sabotaged his plane. I could endure the world thinking such rubbish, but him? "It's all lies. I didn't go to the hangar that morning. The last thing I'd ever want is something to happen to you." I bit my lower lip hard, trapping the rising confession. No, it must remain buried. At least for now. My tendons tightened, joints grinding, as if my body locked away the scarring truth—I wasn't responsible for the plane crash, but I was guilty elsewhere. The accusation in Warren's eyes revealed he wouldn't understand.

His fingers curled over the top of the open auto door, his gaze wandering to my hair. How different I must look to him. My hair, once golden as the sun overhead, was now as dark as the night sky. Or was it the bobbed length that caused him to stare? I waited for him to remark on it, but instead he cast a glance behind me.

"Is he with you?"

I blinked. "Who?"

"Brisbane. I assume he sent you here." He released his grip on the door and motioned me inside. "Tell him he's fired."

What was he talking about? I lowered onto the car's bench, the sunbaked cushion searing into my thighs. Why would he believe Kent Brisbane was with me? And why was he acting this way? So harsh, so different than I'd ever known him? But from all the tangled questions, one answer surfaced. "Brisbane knows you're alive?"

He grunted. "Of course. I hired him after the crash to investigate you."

What? Brisbane had been at Warren's memorial service. The man had offered his condolences with such somberness and sincerity. Had he known Warren had survived the crash then? Or after? But wait. "You hired him to investigate . . . me? You truly believe I tried to kill you?"

"Yes."

• • •

We rode in tense silence. I didn't know where Warren was taking me. I couldn't bring myself to say anything. Not even to deny his vicious claim. Warren believed me a killer. That at least explained his detached treatment, the icy glint in his eyes.

When Warren's plane crashed, every flare of life extinguished within me. He'd been the torch that thawed my frozen world. The element of fire that always made me want to pull my heart close and draw warmth. That was Warren. Heat. Energy.

But now . . . he was cold.

"Did Brisbane tell you I was here?" He raised his voice over the rattling floorboards.

"No."

"Then how did you find me?" He cut a quick look over. "I'm sure discovering I'm alive eases your conscience. But know I don't intend to let you get away with it."

My fingers dug into the seat cushion. How could I respond? I couldn't defend myself, because anything I could add about my role in that awful day would only strengthen his case against me.

He kept driving, his mouth pressed into a tight line. After a handful of strained seconds, he flicked a glance at me. "I assume you're lodging somewhere." It wasn't a question, but he waited, expecting my answer.

Was he going to drop me off? Leave me? "I have a rented room in Greenford. My airplane is there too."

He jolted. "You flew the Jenny here?"

"Yes."

"*Your* plane?"

Did he not believe anything I said? This verbal sparring snapped whatever nerve I had left. Being accused of murder, being talked to as if I were a villain, seeing my warm and affectionate husband behaving aloof and surly, all rubbed together like kindling, igniting a fire in me. "Of course I took my plane. Yours is at the bottom of the lake. And just so you know, I'm not going to let you just drop me off at the edge of town and drive off. Whether you like it or not, we're still married."

His brows furrowed, but he said nothing. It was obvious my words bothered him. And I couldn't deny the fresh wave of pain coursing through me. This was Warren. The man I'd pledged my life to. To have and to hold. Till death do us part. I'd mourned, thinking death had parted us. But now we were together again, and yet . . . somehow we remained severed.

"Let's get your things."

An hour later Warren had driven us into the woods to a rustic A-frame cabin. I followed him up a set of paint-stripped stairs. He held the bag we'd retrieved from town in one hand and unlocked the front door with the other.

"Is this where you've been hiding this entire time?" I asked.

He stepped aside, letting me enter first. The firm clamp of his mouth told me I wasn't getting any information out of him.

Sighing, I moved to brush past but paused on the threshold. His hand flexed as he held open the door for me, though it was his left finger that stole my attention. "You're still wearing your wedding band," I said softly. If he'd been so determined against me, wouldn't he have removed it?

"I noticed you're not."

In response to his chilling remark, I lifted my gold chain from underneath the neckline of my dress and displayed both rings. "I couldn't show anything that identified me. My engagement ring is one of a kind. But I wear them this way. Keeping them close to my heart." I gently let the necklace fall to my collarbone, his gaze a slow descent to the base of my throat. Did he remember how he would press a kiss to the hollow spot there?

His chest visibly rose and fell, the only hint my nearness affected him. I flattened my hand over his heart, absorbing its thudding beat against my palm, the pulsing of life. A life I'd thought was taken from me. Overcome, I lifted on my toes and leaned in, purposing to erase the distance.

"Don't."

I froze, sliding my eyes closed. I couldn't bear to glimpse the revulsion I'd heard in his voice. Like the day before on the Jenny's wing, my limbs were frozen. I forced myself to take a step and then another, opening space between his rejection and my heart.

He closed the door with an ominous thud. Inhaling a calming breath, I took in the one-room cabin. The late-afternoon light filtered through narrow gaps in the curtains. Along the back wall stood a stone fireplace, the charred rocks framing a blackened hearth. Beside it, a small potbelly stove, also darkened with soot. In the corner was a sink with a pump faucet. One sweeping glance told me the cabin wasn't wired for electricity, considering the oil lamps strategically placed about.

Warren tossed his hat on the small table and strode to the other side of the room, where he set my bag on the floor beside the . . . cot. There was no other furniture except two wooden chairs tucked beneath a tiny table. Were we sleeping here?

I stepped in farther but stopped when my gaze landed on a rifle tucked into a nook behind the cot. I would've missed it had I not been so awkwardly staring at the only bed in the cabin.

Warren followed my gaze and snatched the gun from its hiding spot. "It's not loaded." He pumped it, the noise echoing off the dark paneled walls, then released the trigger, as if to prove his point. "Just in case you were wondering."

"In case I planned to use it on you? Is that what you mean?" My voice strained thin, my fingers twitching at my sides.

He returned the gun, blatantly ignoring my irritation. "Why did you fly your plane to Greenford?" He shrugged out of his tweed coat, one I hadn't seen before. The fit had been snug across the broad line of his shoulders, making me wonder where exactly he had acquired it. As well as the rest of his suit. The quality wasn't as fine as his others. He hung the coat on a wooden rack and regarded me with a raised brow.

"I held a barnstorming event there."

If I expected him to be surprised at the realization that his high-society wife had been hosting an air circus, he didn't show it.

He only jerked loose his tie knot. "So for the past weeks, instead of being a grieving widow, you run out for a thirst of adventure. I'm touched by your staunch devotion."

Who needed a loaded rifle when each of his words punctured like a bullet? I bit the inside of my cheek to keep my chin from quivering, but there was nothing I could do about the tears burning my eyes, blurring his stoic face. "I've mourned you these *past weeks*." Yet mourned didn't seem strong enough to depict the agony that ravaged me. "Nightmares and loneliness have been my companions, driving me to the point of running away. Barnstorming and this"—I motioned to my hair—"are my cover."

"Because you're wanted for murder?"

"No, because I was searching for clues about your death." I met his eyes. "And I was looking for Brisbane, hoping he could help me discover what had happened."

"What do you mean?" He peered at me as if he could pick me apart secret by secret but then turned away like I wasn't worth the effort. "Have a seat." He motioned toward one of the two wooden chairs beside the table.

I lowered on the seat closest to him. My fingers trembled, and I folded them in my lap. "Brisbane's missing."

He yanked a wool blanket from the cot, then strode toward me and tossed the heavy cloth onto my lap.

It was September, but I was shaking fiercely, as if it were February. Shock was at fault. One didn't expect to stumble upon one's dead husband, only to have what could be a happy reunion spoiled by a bothersome accusation of murder.

He stepped back, and I felt his distance. We were only a yard apart, but it seemed like a canyon separated us. Our gazes locked, yet he said nothing.

"It doesn't bother you?" I asked. "That your close friend has disappeared?"

He turned the other chair around and straddled it. "He's always ducking out for a spell. It's part of his job. Not absurd for him to leave town on a whim without telling anyone."

I felt a mild swirl of accomplishment. He'd spoken more than three words without scorn fused to each syllable.

"I wouldn't blame him for making himself scarce around you. Especially since I'm paying the man to look into your activities."

My fingers twisted the edges of the blanket. All these weeks my husband had been building resentment against me. If I could get him to open up, to explain why he believed the absolute worst of me, then maybe we could work together to figure out the truth behind the crash. Voicing my sincerity for him hadn't worked. I'd have to take a different approach. "I didn't realize that Brisbane disappeared often. But would he have left his cigarette case behind?"

He jolted. We both knew Kent Brisbane guarded that cigarette case as if it were crammed with diamonds instead of personal notes. It was his most treasured possession. His book of secrets.

Warren paced the small space, then stilled. "He left it? Did you bring it with you?"

I nodded, then moved to stand, but my legs quaked. What on earth was wrong? I no doubt looked like a clumsy fawn learning to walk.

"Stay." Warren's command came out gruff, but I could detect concern in his eyes. It was a flicker. Gone too quickly. But there nonetheless. "Is it in your bag? I'll fetch it." He reached for it, then stilled. "Unless there's something you'd rather me not see?"

And just like that the frost returned to his voice with a resounding bite.

"No." Heat rose in my chest. "Unless searching through my underthings would now make you blush."

He shot me a look, but there was something in it. Something I couldn't quite understand. If there wasn't this awkward hostility between us, I would've named it longing. But given his rejection at the door, I knew I was mistaken.

He brought me the bag instead of rummaging through it. I quickly located the case and handed it to him.

He opened the lid and withdrew the small notepad. "Most of the entries have been ripped out." He scowled at the torn pages.

"I noticed. Toward the back you'll find your name." I observed him flipping through, stilling on the entry I mentioned.

His coffee-brown eyes scanned the list. "What are these? Newborn. Hartshire. Hanover."

"Towns scattered throughout New York. All country towns."

He glanced over. "Yes, but Greenford's listed. That's right here."

"That's why I came." I lowered my lashes, disconnecting from his piercing gaze. "I've been to Newborn, Hartshire, and Dalton. But I didn't discover anything. Here is the first place I found something . . . remarkable." I had found *him*. "I started all this because I thought maybe I could locate Brisbane or something that could give me more insight on who and why someone wanted to hurt you."

He listened and watched me with astute soberness, as if sifting through my words to determine the sincerity.

"I was going to Hanover next to host a barnstorming event and search for clues. But . . ."

"But what?"

"I'm not sure it's necessary." I picked at a loose strand in the blanket. "The entire reason behind these shows was to find information about my dead husband." I looked up and found him watching me. "But that's no longer needed. And since you make light of Brisbane's disappearance, then what's the point of continuing?"

"I think we should go there tomorrow."

I blinked. "Why? You're okay. We can just go—"

"Go where? Home?" He released an ill-humored scoff. "Someone tried to murder me, Geneva. I can't just walk back into that life knowing very well that person could try it again." He handed me back Brisbane's cigarette case. "Unless there's something you'd like to confess."

I jumped to my feet, the blanket wilting to the floor. A retort pressed heavy against my lips, poised and ready to launch, but then . . . my bluster withered. I did have something to confess, several things actually. Which was why I hadn't yet asked about how he'd survived the crash. My question would prompt a crucial one from him. About the parachute. My stomach clenched. Perhaps he already knew. There was only one way to find out.

"Why do you believe I tried to kill you?"

"I have many reasons." He shot me a heated look, but I refused to cower. "Our argument the night before the crash. Your behavior the entire week previous." He ran a hand through his hair in frustration. "What you said and what you purposely *didn't* say."

I winced, but he continued.

"Not to mention your charming confession printed in the papers. Who'd you send that letter to? Your father?"

My jaw slacked. "No. Brisbane." I shook my head. "My words got twisted. I felt ashamed because you and I fought that night. I hated our last words had been ones of anger. And also because of—" My mouth clamped shut. I couldn't tell him about the parachute. That would condemn me on the spot. But Warren's stare seemed only to intensify, making my thoughts scramble. "Because I . . . I wasn't at the hangar that morning."

"Exactly," he abruptly said, and I caught my blunder. I'd fallen into his trap like a skittish rodent. "We planned to meet, and you never showed. Then what happens? My plane is sabotaged. How could you, Geneva?"

"Just because I wasn't there doesn't mean—"

"Where were you?" His gaze fastened on me. "Tell me where you were that day." His features softened a fraction, giving me the smallest glimpse of the man I'd married. "Please?"

Pain sliced through me. He didn't understand what he was asking. I shrank into myself, reaching deep to the icy wells of my soul. If only to numb the memories. The anguish. The destruction I'd caused. I met his gaze with a sorrowful shake of my head. "I can't."

Chapter 5

Approximately five months earlier—April 8, 1922
Geneva

"Sh." My eyes widened, and I tipped my head toward my chaperone several yards away.

Cecily leaned against a tree at the edge of the garden reading a book, but I had my suspicions she was eavesdropping.

Having an escort was about as old-fashioned as a hoopskirt and just as ridiculous. But Father had said so, and his word was law. And if Cecily had heard Mr. Hayes's last remark and subsequently reported it to Father, I very well could be placed in solitary confinement—bound to my room until my wedding day. "You can't say such things. Not with her around."

Amusement brightened his eyes. "I guarantee your maid can't hear us."

"Cecily has a keen sense of hearing," I mock whispered. "It's quite impressive."

He leaned in closer. "But there's nothing scandalous about talking of my airplane."

"There is when you talk about me inside it." My scold didn't have the effect I intended, for I couldn't quite keep the corners of my mouth from arcing into a smile. "Maybe we can keep that a secret between us."

"I take it your parents wouldn't approve?"

I shook my head, the early afternoon breeze stirring my hair against my temple. "There isn't much my father approves of. But he specifically dislikes anything with heights." My gaze floated to the clouds. "He wouldn't be pleased to know I was up there." Not because of any paternal love on his part but because I was his bargaining chip. I was Father's key to influence. My marrying Warren Hayes meant Father would have a say-so in what was printed about him.

Mr. Hayes offered me his arm. "I'd bet every paper I've ever sold that you enjoyed your trip into the sky."

I held my finger to my lips before slipping my hand through the crook of his elbow. "I didn't enjoy it, sir." One swift look to Cecily had me lowering my tone. "I adored it."

His laughter coaxed my full smile.

We strolled farther from my chaperone, and I was more comfortable to speak freely. "That was one of the greatest experiences of my life, and I have you to thank for it."

"Glad to do it." He looked at me as if I'd said something in a foreign language. Perhaps he hadn't expected me to be so grateful. Mother had once said a woman shouldn't be overly appreciative to a gentleman, for they would consider it forward and might press their own advances. But I hadn't sensed any malicious intent with Mr. Hayes. If there were any ulterior motives, it all rested on Father's side.

"Perhaps I will make a pilot out of you."

I faltered at his words, and he wrapped his other hand around my arm, steadying me. Surely I had misheard. "You'll teach me to fly?"

"If you want."

Want. Such a peculiar word. Dreams, passions, and wishes all curled up in four simple letters. Yet it could also be a gift. I'd rarely been asked what I wanted. Though I'd surely given it a lot of thought. What about the man before me? I studied him openly and without reservation, just as I'd done with his plane yesterday. "Do you truly *want* to marry me?"

His brows winged north in obvious surprise. But I wouldn't retract it. I needed to know where he stood. Was he a pawn in Father's scheme? Or did he actually have a choice in the matter?

"Your father seems eager for the match."

"That's an understatement." The shuffling of footsteps prompted a glance over my shoulder. Cecily shadowed us yet again. Though she was only doing what she'd been commanded. She was completely at the mercy of Father. She and I were not so much different. I offered her a smile before returning my attention to Mr. Hayes. "That's not answering my question. Goodness knows my father wants us together."

What was Warren getting out of this union? The Hayeses weren't by any means paupers, but the newspaper world as a whole had taken a hit with the introduction of radio. With the expediency of broadcasting, the masses didn't have to wait for news anymore. Were my assumptions correct? Had Father given him an incentive? Offered him a deal on paper from our several mills? Maybe I didn't need to know the particulars. But one thing I was most curious about. "I'm asking if *you* want this."

"Yes."

"Why?" We set off down the stone path leading to the flower trellis. "You never met me before yesterday. Is the newspaper industry that important to you that you'd pledge your life to a stranger?" There. I'd hinted around the business side of our union rather than ask plainly. That should give me ample points in the etiquette game.

"My family's business is important to me, but my father raised me to understand the value of priority. My career is only one facet of who I am. It doesn't come before faith and family."

I didn't know how to respond. All the men I knew placed their livelihood above all else.

"You're not exactly a stranger." He quirked a smile. "I've long heard of the Ashcroft Angel."

A laugh burst from my lips. "Oh, the Ashcroft Angel." That infernal nickname. "The shy, taciturn heiress, etcetera, etcetera." If this was Mr. Hayes's perception of me, the poor soul was in for a colossal disappointment. Perhaps it'd be best to disillusion him now. "You shouldn't believe everything you read in the papers, Mr. Hayes." My voice dropped to a conspiratorial whisper. "Publicity can be bought as easily as my new frock here." My free hand tugged at the side of my chiffon gown.

"I only print truth in my papers."

"That so?" I probably shouldn't goad him, but if he wanted the truth, then he would get all the pitiful facts. It seemed Father hadn't divulged his standards of operation. "Father paid a very nice sum for my image of quietness and reservation." Though I wasn't certain if he'd bribed my intended or just other newspaper publishers. "He preferred the world to believe a fantasy rather than reality."

His mouth quirked. "So you're not ethereal sweetness?"

I paused under the trellis, frowning at the blooms twisted to conform to manmade boundaries. At least my flowers grew wild. "To my father I have a tart tongue." I faced him with a smirk. "To my mother I'm more opinionated than a suffragette. She thinks that's a dirty word, by the way. Suffragette."

"What do you think?"

"I'd join them if I could. They advocate for a voice in the world. There's something freeing about such a thing." The wistfulness in my tone faded. "But I promised Father I'd be the very picture he so amply paid for." I wrinkled my nose. "The consequences weren't to my liking."

He seemed entertained by my remarks. "Which were?"

"If I didn't comply, Father said he'd send me away to be a cook at the lumber camp in Minnesota." I gave him a dry look.

"He wouldn't." His appalled expression made me like him even more.

Lumber camps were comprised of solely men. No loving papa would willingly send their daughter to such a place. But Father was not loving. "I chose to play the part because I didn't want to be accused of murder."

He teasingly played along. "Of your father?"

"No, the poor lumberjacks. I'm a terrible cook."

His chuckle surrounded me, infusing warmth. The deep tone was genuine, and authenticity was hard to come by in my sphere.

"So there you have it, Mr. Hayes. I'm forever bound to be boring and saintlike." And more polished than our finest silver. While the rest of the world progressed into jazz slang and modern lingo, I was forced to speak like a woman plucked from the Regency era, only without the enchanting accent. Unfortunately, proper language had been so ingrained in me, I didn't know how to converse any other way.

"Please call me Warren. And I have proof that you're saintlike." He shot me a wink and held out his arm again, as if he hadn't just uttered the vaguest statement I'd ever heard.

He had proof? Of what? I opened my mouth to question him, but he spoke first.

"Last evening, when dancing, you said you'd misjudged me. Care to tell me how?"

"Let's go sit on that bench." I motioned with my head to the seat, which was most assuredly designed for ornamental purposes rather than comfort. "To answer your question, I honestly don't know what I was expecting, but it wasn't you." We reached the bench, and I lowered onto it. "Most powerful men have a superiority about them. Where I'm expected to be besotted if they give me a passing look. It's irritating. But when you looked at me yesterday, it was . . ."

He claimed the spot beside me. "Yes?"

"It was as if you were the one besotted."

He laughed. "Because I was." He reached for my hand, his eyes taking on a sudden interest. "I am."

I stared at our hands locked together. "Because of my fortune? My family? My social status? Take your pick. I've received proposals based on all of them."

"No."

"If all I had to my name was a hundred acres of swampland, would you still marry me?"

"I would."

My lips curled into a smile. "Liar."

He nudged my shoulder playfully. "I'll prove it to you. Somehow. But the true question is, why do *you* want to marry me?"

My good spirits sank like a stone in the lake behind me. His gaze swept over me, questions filling his handsome face.

"Oh, there's Lilith." I left his side and walked with swift steps to greet my sister.

Her demure smile put all my practiced ones to shame. "Hello, my dear."

"How are you? Truly?" I studied her thoroughly to be certain she looked well enough to be outdoors. Her complexion had always been fair, but there seemed to be some color in her cheeks. Was she flushed? Had the fever returned? That familiar panic gripped my throat. Lilith had been the only one in the family to contract the Spanish flu during the outbreak almost four years ago. Though her case had been mild compared to most, her health hadn't been the same since. Before I could question her, Mr. Hayes—rather, Warren—joined my side. "Mr. Hayes, may I introduce you to my sister and the most beautiful soul alive, Miss Lilith Ashcroft."

Warren tipped his hat to her, a friendly smile on his lips. "Very pleased to meet you."

"And I, you." Her head dipped with a certain elegance I could never replicate.

"I'm sorry to have missed you at last night's ball. I hope you're feeling better."

She smiled at his thoughtfulness. "I'm very well, thank you."

I quietly exhaled my relief and caught Warren's attention on me. Had he noticed my discomfort? Or was he comparing our appearances? Lilith and I were almost complete opposites in our looks. Where my hair was golden as sunshine, Lilith's was red like fire. My heart-shaped face framed lean cheeks, where Lilith's were gently rounded, leading to a soft jutted jaw and thinner mouth. She was a delicate vision of grace, and I was not. The only trait we shared was our blue eyes.

"Geneva tells me you're a pilot, Mr. Hayes. Did you fly in the war?"

"No. I was an aviator instructor." He scratched the back of his neck, and I wondered if he was uncomfortable. Most men didn't fancy discussing the war, especially with women. "I taught people how to fly." His gaze met mine, and there was a newness to his expression. One I hadn't glimpsed before. It reminded me of how one looked when making a promise. A vow.

Ah, he'd offered to make a pilot out of me. His eyes now confirmed just how serious he'd been.

A rustling noise snagged my attention. Lilith fussed with her pocket, where the edges of an envelope poked out.

That explained her rosy cheeks. My dear sister had received a letter from her sweetheart. I smiled at her. "Good news, I hope."

"The best." She grinned. "The plan's in motion starting next month." But then the brightness dimmed. "Which means we don't have much time to convince Boreas."

According to Greek mythology, Boreas was the ruler of winter. Seemed the perfect code name for Father.

"Tut-tut." My gentle reprimand seemed to stir Lilith from a haze. "Leave it all to me." I waved her away. "Be a darling and collect Cecily on your way back to the house so I can have a private moment with Warren." My sister and I didn't always share a maid. We each had our own until several years ago when Lilith's maid, Marta, made the unfortunate mistake of supplying Lilith with books outside of Mother's approved list of titles. Marta had challenged Mother, arguing that young women should have a right to read more than etiquette manuals. The poor woman had been dismissed, and Cecily assumed her duties.

Lilith now shot a hopeful smile, and I renewed my purpose not to fail her. I'd stick to the plan and keep my sister from ruin. I shifted my focus back to Warren, only to find him watching me with a mischievous grin.

"What?" I asked.

"You just called me Warren." He took my hand and lifted it to his lips. "I liked it." He pressed a kiss to my knuckles, and that exhilaration— that rush I'd experienced in the biplane—swept through me. Warren Hayes's touch was a thrilling force, and it made me crave more of it. And that terrified me.

• • •

The birdsong in the distance had a weariness to it, as if the winged creature was tired of singing the same tune again and again. I could commiserate. Since the ball, I'd been forced into nearly a week full of

garden parties. All afternoon I'd behaved as the prim and poised socialite to the point of getting a crick in my neck. Smiling when necessary, laughing at dull jokes, and pretending to hold a keen interest in
the same topics on a tiresome rotation.

An escape was in order.

With quick looks to my left and right, I slipped into the crack between the branches of the massive Camperdown tree and ducked beneath its blossoming canopy. Cloaked in delicate white flowers, the
sweeping limbs stretched to the ground, feathering the carpet of lawn
like the lacy train of a wedding gown. Other than being beautiful, the
tree provided the most effective hiding spot. I could walk beneath its
sheltering limbs, concealed from the rest of the world.

"Am I late to the party?" A deep voice as unfamiliar as it was masculine spoke from beyond the wall of branches. "Or haven't the festivities
started yet?"

"Brisbane." That was Warren's voice. "I wasn't sure you received the
invitation. Or if you would want to spend an afternoon with us high-
falutin snobs."

I moved closer. Brisbane? I didn't remember that name on the guest
list. Though Mother might have granted her future son-in-law an al-
lowance to add friends or family as he wished.

"What makes you think I didn't come for the marriage mart?" He
paused, and I wished I could see this gentleman's face. "Hmm, maybe I
can snag the Ashcroft Angel dame. I heard from the men at my club her
gams are legendary."

I swallowed the rising gasp. Gams? So this was what men spoke of in
private? Women's legs? I leaned in further, wanting to catch Warren's
response. Would he indulge in vulgar conversation?

"Careful, Brisbane."

I breathed relief at the scolding edge in Warren's tone.

The gentleman acknowledged Warren's warning with a good-
natured chuckle. "I'm only teasing. I know how you feel about the girl.
Though I have to say, it isn't very sportish of you, since I saw her first."

This man knew me? I didn't recognize his name or voice. If only I could peek through the branches and nab a good glimpse of the fellow, but I couldn't risk getting caught.

"Have you proposed to her yet?" This again from Mr. Brisbane.

Warren groaned. "I haven't been alone with her to get any question in, let alone that one."

I smiled at his frustration. It was comforting to know I wasn't the only one who missed our conversations. Since that stroll in the garden a few days back, I'd hardly spoken to him. The house party guests had commandeered our moments.

"Shame." Mr. Brisbane tsked. "Are the general partygoers aware of your arrangement with Miss Ashcroft?"

"I have no idea. Why?"

"Because in the full minute I've been here, that lovely brunette by the trellis has been staring at you with interest in her eyes."

My fingers twitched at my sides. I was fully certain of the lady he referenced. If one could call her that.

"Ah, that would be Miss Reinholt." Warren confirmed what I already knew. "I danced with her at the house party's opening ball."

He certainly had. And Beatrice Reinholt had pressed herself against him at least twice during said dance, all while maintaining a picture of innocence. I'd detected her fascination with Warren but was unsure if her nauseating attentions stemmed from Warren's charm or her dislike of me. I suspected a mixture of both. We'd debuted the same year, and I'd been foolish enough to try to befriend her. It turned out she'd chosen me as competition rather than confidante.

"Might work in your favor, Hayes. Especially if Miss Ashcroft notices. Women can be very territorial, you know. A little jealousy could motivate your intended to be more affectionate toward you. Claim you as the matrimonial prize that you are."

And this was my punishment for hiding under a tree—an undiluted education of the workings of gentlemen's minds.

"I know what you're doing, Brisbane. You're testing me, and it won't work. I refuse to toy with her affections. And I'll make certain she's convinced of mine."

"Well done, friend." Approval marked his tone, and I sensed this was the first time Mr. Brisbane had been sincere the entire conversation. "I only wanted to be certain you were worthy of her."

My jaw slacked. Who was this man? And what was his claim on me that he'd act as my protector?

Warren muttered something I couldn't catch.

"So how about you introduce me to her. Formally this time."

I panicked. These men would soon be searching for me. Yet here I was, prancing about under tree limbs like some kind of forest fairy. With quick steps, I emerged from the back of the tree, hoping they moved toward the center of the garden where most of the guests were. I went left instead of right and nearly collapsed in relief to find Lilith approaching.

I reached her in time to spot both men rounding the side of the enormous tree.

"Act like I said something charming," I said quietly.

She met my eyes and laughed. Apparently she found me more humorous than charming.

"Forgive me for interrupting your conversation." Warren approached, a warm smile in place. "But I would like to introduce you to my longtime friend Mr. Kent Brisbane."

I turned my attention to the well-dressed man. He was about the same height as Warren, only with wavy black hair. I waited for any sort of recognition to strike, but nothing. "Nice to meet you, sir."

"Believe me, the pleasure's all mine. I've been long hoping to catch a glimpse of the famous Ashcroft Angel." Mr. Brisbane smiled a bit roguishly, and a small scar puckered to the right of his mouth.

Wait. That scar. The memory was foggy, but I'd seen that scar before. Seen *him* before. But from where? "Yet this wasn't your first glimpse of me." I delighted in his perplexed expression. "I believe our paths have crossed before, but I'm struggling to place where."

Warren's brows lifted, and Lilith gave me a gentle nudge. I didn't want to make our guest uncomfortable, but something told me I hadn't.

He only smiled. "I doubt you'd remember meeting someone like me, miss."

And yet he hadn't denied it. Interesting. I rattled off introductions between Lilith and Mr. Brisbane, who struck up an easy conversation with her, leaving Warren and me a few moments to ourselves.

He embraced the opportunity as much as I. His hand caught mine with such finesse, I wondered how often he'd employed the tactic on other ladies.

I smiled. "You seemed surprised that I admitted to meeting your friend before."

He chuckled. "I was more surprised you openly confessed it."

"There's no shame in admitting I've seen him before." But from where?

"Of course he seemed familiar." He paused and faced me. "You heard him only seconds before when you were hiding under that tree."

I gasped, and he unleashed a wicked grin.

He leaned close, his face near mine. Surely he wouldn't kiss me in front of all our guests. His hand lifted and stroked my hair. Only to withdraw something, his fingers pinching a blossom petal.

Oh. "Women wear flowers in their hair all the time, Mr. Hayes."

"I'm not done." His fingers dug into my locks again, and to my mortification, he extracted a twig.

Heat swarmed my cheeks, and I resisted the urge to press my palm to my face. "Did you know I was there the entire time?"

He retook my hand. "No, only when I saw you."

Might as well address what I'd heard. "You told Mr. Brisbane you'll make certain I'm convinced of your affections. Did you mean that?"

His face softened. "I did."

"How will you accomplish it?"

"You'll see." He smiled. "I'm very much looking forward to it."

I flashed a saucy look. "As am I."

Chapter 6 ————————————————————————————

SLEEP LESSENED ITS HAZY HOLD, and biting reality replaced it. Warren was dead.

The cruel voice of grief cut through me like it had every morning for the past weeks.

Except . . .

My fingers clutched my blanket, its coarse threads itching my palms. Yesterday's events rolled through my mind like a nickelodeon. Going to the speakeasy. Finding Warren alive. My eyelids twitched. I feared opening them. What if it'd all been a dream?

My lashes lifted. The morning light streamed through the window behind my bed, illuminating dust motes floating around the one-room cabin. The cabin Warren had brought me to. My breath leaked from my chest, and a rush of sweet joy echoed through me. It was true! Yesterday *had* happened. I pushed to sitting, the blanket dropping to my lap.

I reached for my brush and worked it through the tangles, my gaze scanning the space for my husband. Only he wasn't there. The pallet Warren had slept on last night had been stowed. Which wouldn't alarm me, except his bag was gone. My eyes flew to the door. His suit coat no longer draped the wooden rack.

My brain emptied every thought but one—he'd left me.

Heart racing, I kneeled on my bed and peered out the window. No sign of him. But Warren wouldn't abandon me. It was against his nature. Protectiveness and loyalty were the bedrock of his existence.

Then again, he also believed the unimaginable about me. If he embraced one irrational thought, who was to say he wouldn't act upon another, such as leaving his wife in the middle of nowhere? Panic clawed. I had to catch him. Perhaps he hadn't gone far.

I dashed to the front of the cabin, my bare feet slapping against the wooden planks. With jerky movements, I yanked open the door. "Warren!" My vocal cords were full throttle. "Warren!"

Gaze swiveling in all directions, I rushed toward the porch steps. My legs collided into something bulky. My upper body dove forward. My eyes screwed shut, and my hands shot out, bracing for impact.

"Got you." Warren's voice pressed into my ears even as his arms caught my waist.

I smacked my chin on his expansive chest, but it was a welcome sting. He held me against him, and everything in me relished his embrace. Not only because he'd rescued me from nosediving into the stone walkway but because this moment, wrapped in his sturdiness, the spiraling had finally stopped. I'd been falling since the news of his crash.

How I needed this. Needed him.

He eased back and studied my face, concern etching his brow. His stare dipped, as if to make sure the rest of me was unharmed. But then he stiffened, ripping away his touch and angling to the side. "You're okay." His voice was deep and raspy, like *he'd* just woken from heavy slumber. But I knew those husky tones. They only surfaced when he buried his passion, be it anger, curiosity, desire, or some other nameless emotion. He harnessed it to the point that his brown eyes smoldered.

My own eyes lowered, and at once I grasped the reason for his abruptness. My nightgown had shifted during my tumble, revealing an ample amount of cleavage. I looked positively scandalous. I glanced at Warren, who took a sudden interest in the toe of his boot, and pressed my lips together, taming a smile.

Perhaps he wasn't as indifferent as he'd led me to believe yesterday.

I shifted toward the door to adjust my faulty wardrobe—we were out-side, after all—but any amusement vanished at the sight of his bag on the porch, the reason for my stumble.

I whirled, pointing an accusing finger. "You were leaving me."

His gaze drifted over my shoulder. "Is that what you thought? Why you came running out here like the cabin's on fire?"

"Can you blame me?"

His stare penetrated mine for a long second, then he brushed past and up the steps. "I'm not leaving you," he called over his shoulder. "I can't take my eyes off you."

Not long ago I would've taken those words as some romantic dec-laration. But such as our situation was, I knew better. Especially since those words ripped from his mouth like a poisoned dart.

"Oh that's right." I chased him up the stairs and into the cabin. "Be-cause you think I'm a coldhearted killer. I'm surprised you slept at all last night. Weren't you concerned I'd gouge you with my hatpins? Or shove my stockings down your airways?"

He turned and regarded me with a long-suffering look. "More like tease me out of my sanity." His eyes roamed my form again, and he groaned. "Here." He shrugged out of his coat and held it out. "Put this on."

It seemed my only weapon at the moment was a thin, lacy night-gown. Since he was my husband, it wasn't like morality was on the line. "No, thank you. It's excessively warm in here." I inclined my chin. "Why is your bag outside if you don't intend to leave me behind?"

He sighed and tossed his jacket on the cot. "I went into town while you were sleeping and arranged for a hired car to pick us up. I can't put your things out there until you get dressed." His tone brimmed with exasperation, as if I were the one being difficult. "I suggest you do so soon, unless you intend to travel in your nightgown."

I ignored his complaint. "Why can't you drive us to get the Jenny?" Hopefully, my plane was still tacked to Farmer Ewing's fence.

Warren grabbed a glass and pumped water into it. "Because Bris-bane wouldn't appreciate it if I stole his car." He offered me the drink, and I shook my head in refusal. He shrugged and downed the water in three long gulps.

"So this is Brisbane's place." Finally I was getting information out of him. I took in the cabin with fresh eyes.

He gave a brisk nod. "His hunting lodge. His car." He tugged the lapel of his jacket. "His clothes."

"So he knows you're here?" I moved toward my bag and withdrew two frocks, uncertain which to wear. After setting them on the cot, I angled to Warren. "I'm assuming you were supposed to meet Brisbane yesterday."

"You assume right."

At least he was kind enough not to repeat his previous words. That he, in essence, had recruited Brisbane to investigate me.

Warren stepped closer and bent. One of my dresses had slipped off the bed without my knowing. He grabbed it from the floor, and the unmistakable sound of ripping fabric made me cringe. The hem—or what was left of it—was trapped beneath his boot. "Sorry."

He'd torn the gown I'd worn the day he'd proposed. I'd brought that dress along because of that sentimental reason. He held it out, and I ran my fingers along the tattered edge. I shouldn't feel this much sorrow over ripped clothes. But to me it seemed to stretch further, to the brokenness between us. I bit back the emotion and returned the dress to the bag and my thoughts to this conversation. "You say Brisbane was supposed to meet you, but he didn't show at all yesterday."

"I've noticed."

I grabbed the other frock, along with fresh underthings, and stood. Warren, realizing what came next, turned around, giving me unnecessary privacy.

"You don't have to look away, you know. We are married."

"I'm aware."

Sighing, I slipped out of my nightgown and into my undergarments. "Why didn't Brisbane show up? And why did he agree to meet you at the speakeasy when he could've easily come here? It makes no sense." My nose wrinkled as I slid on my stockings.

"As long as I've known him, Kent Brisbane never made any sense."

"You don't think . . ." I reached for my gown. "What if Brisbane had something to do with your accident?"

"Never." He shook his head. "He wouldn't stoop to such a thing. Even if it meant getting the prize."

I yanked my gown over my head and shrugged it in place, inhaling a fortifying breath to combat the prick of betrayal. Warren had dismissed any suspicion about his best friend, all the while throwing accusations like spears at his own wife.

"The prize?" I shifted to reach the buttons on the back of the dress. "What's that mean?" I huffed. "I can't fasten this. Can you help?" A part of me hated asking anything of him, but my unsteady hands weren't capable of the task.

He faced me and nodded.

Not wanting him to glimpse any residue of hurt in my expression, I spun around. My fingers went to the base of my neck to lift my hair out of the way, but then I remembered.

"Your hair's short now." He voiced my thoughts.

"Yes."

"And very dark." His hands deftly worked the buttons, moving up my back. "You look so different, Geneva." His voice had softened to a coarse whisper, and warm fingers lingered on my neck, my eyes sliding closed at his familiar touch. "There." He took a step back. "You're all put together."

I turned. "Thank you."

His mask of indifference slipped firmly in place again. "Let's get your things. The car should be here soon."

I responded by packing my nightgown. My gaze searched for anything else that was mine. "Since we're heading to town, you should know I've been going by another name." Satisfied I wouldn't leave anything behind, I secured my bag and stood.

"Which is?" He snatched my bag from the floor, a bit too abruptly, and tossed it over his shoulder.

"Stella."

His jaw tightened. "Seems a favorite name of yours." He turned on his heel and strode outside. His voice had undertones of . . . hurt? No doubt he remembered I'd introduced myself as Stella when we'd first met. It was something special between us. Had he thought I cheapened the memory by using the same name now? But it was for that very reason—because I missed him so much!—that I'd chosen that disguise.

With a heavy exhale, I followed him, snatching my hat along the way. "I couldn't go by Geneva Hayes. My parents are offering a nice sum for my return. The authorities are—"

He paused, half-raised from setting my bag beside his. "Your parents." Eyes on mine, he straightened. "Are you saying they don't know where you are?"

It appeared my husband wasn't as schooled in what was being printed about me as I'd thought. "My parents offered a five-thousand-dollar reward to anyone who returns me safely to them."

"And you've had no contact with them all this time?"

"No."

"But now you know I'm alive."

"And?"

"What's keeping you from reporting it to your daddy?"

I took a step closer, shrinking the distance between us, taking in the familiar and the not. His eyelashes burned a reddish hue in the sunlight, and there was still a small gap at the edge of his lower left lid where two or three lashes refused to grow. But it wasn't his lashes I needed to inspect so thoroughly, but the eyes they framed. Was there affection in there, somewhere, for me? Or only a detached coldness? "Who are you?"

He didn't turn away but accepted my challenge with such an intense expression that my breath pinched in my chest. His gaze roamed my face in an excruciatingly slow manner, the tension between us so real it could have its own shadow alongside ours. His attention slid to my hair, his eyes narrowing at the corners as he studied me. He drew closer, as if my own body had called to his. His hand lifted, then stilled only inches from my face. He blinked. The moment vanished. With a shake of his head, his arm collapsed to his side. "I could ask the same of you."

I swallowed back my disappointment. "You're obviously not the same man I married." Though he was outwardly, his severe mannerisms, his unfeeling words, were so much altered. "Because *that* Warren Hayes would know I never called John Ashcroft *Daddy* and would never volunteer information to him."

An engine roared in the distance. Our car had arrived to take us to fetch my plane.

Warren broke eye contact with me first, shouldering away and scooping up our bags.

I hadn't applied any cosmetics, a crucial part of my disguise. Had I even finished brushing my hair? I tugged my hat onto my head. Our heated conversation had distracted me to the extreme. I must look as exhausted and disheveled as I felt, yet I couldn't bring myself to care. "Warren, what did you mean about Brisbane not hurting you even if it meant getting the prize? What's the prize?"

His gaze flickered to the approaching automobile and then back to me. "You."

Chapter 7 ————————————————————————

Four and a half months earlier—April 14, 1922
Geneva

LILITH SPREAD JAM ONTO HER toast while impaling me with her sharp stare. "You're upset, Geneva. I can tell. What's going on?"

I gave my sister a subtle nod toward the housemaid stepping cautiously into the breakfast nook, the tray in her white-knuckled grip rattling precariously. "Thank you, Iris." I reached for the silver platter before it ended in my lap. "We'll take it from here. Perhaps you can grab some breakfast before the other guests awaken."

Lilith and I had risen early, taking a private morning meal in this forgotten room off the kitchen. Our nanny had brought us here when we were young. As little girls, this had been a place where we could be loud with our giggles, sloppy with our meals, and act like normal children, not heiresses. It was the only luxury the nanny afforded us, and Lilith and I had been grateful for the gesture. Upon every visit to this estate, we continued the tradition of breakfasting here. No houseguests, no domineering parents. Just the two of us and the warmth of the sunshine filtering through the expansive windows. A space to breathe.

Iris's blond brow twitched, as if unsure whether to raise in surprise or furrow in confusion at my remark. "Thank you, miss." She executed the tiniest curtsy, the lace on her mobcap swinging as if waving farewell, and she fled the room.

"Mother hired her for the house party." I set the tray on the table between us, and my stomach gave a ravenous plea for the blueberry scones. "I think she's nervous."

"You should see her around Father. She almost conked his head with a teapot when she stumbled on the study rug."

My fingers made quick work of filling Lilith's teacup, then mine. "Father has that talent of rattling everyone in his presence."

"We aren't supposed to mention our parents in this room." Lilith recited our favorite rule.

"You asked why I was upset." I grabbed a scone and took an un-ladylike bite of flaky sweetness, then frowned. Probably should employ some manners since I was wearing my favorite blush-colored frock with ivory lace accents. "I received a summons on my way here." I rolled my eyes. "I have to meet Father in his study before the guests' breakfast. Ruined my day before it even started."

Lilith gave a sympathetic smile. "Perhaps it won't be as awful as you think."

"Let's not speak of him. As you said, no parent rule." I forced a bright arc to my lips. "I want to hear more about Lieutenant Cameron."

"I have something to show you." Her eyes sparkled as she reached inside her pocket, withdrawing the envelope.

Curiosity rising, I poured cream into my tea until I was convinced it was lukewarm, exactly how I loved it. Lilith had never shared his letters with me. Why now? Her dainty fingers didn't ease out an ink-scrawled paper though, but a photograph.

I let my spoon clink against my cup. "He sent you a picture?"

She bit her lip, but not before a smile poked through. "He included one with his letter." She passed it over as if handling our great-grandmother's heirloom crystal goblet rather than a bent snapshot.

I studied the photo. Lieutenant Cameron was lankier than I'd envisioned. He had a carefree smile framed by deep dimples, his breezy expression contrasting the rigidness of his army uniform. He held his cap in front of him with both hands, indicating this must have been taken before the battles of the Meuse-Argonne. "He's good-looking," I surmised with a growing smile.

Lilith blushed.

I handed it back to her. "Have you written him back yet?"

She took her time returning the photo to the envelope. Then she stirred her tea, her gaze lowering with each passing second. "Not yet."

"How come?"

"I'm not certain." She ran her finger over her spoon handle. Back and forth. "He's different than what he once was, you know, during the war."

"War changes people. And the lieutenant certainly had his share of . . ." *Misfortune? Hardship?* "He's had a lot to adjust to." Lieutenant Cameron had lost his right arm in battle. "You know his struggles. Do you love him less for it?" I would never believe my kindhearted sister would change her affections due to such a thing. But then . . . "How has he changed? He hasn't been cold to you? Or worse, like Father?"

Her eyes rounded. "No, no. Not in the least. If anything he's more affectionate in his letters. But he's also more insecure. And I admit I'm still saddened it took him three years to renew our correspondences." Her mouth flattened. Lilith had thought the lieutenant had died in battle. For having never set eyes on the young man, she had experienced a bond so deep. Their hearts had united through their inked words. When those letters stopped, her grief had been severe.

"I don't believe he meant to hurt you. After all, you were very young when you began writing him." Our parents had no idea a sixteen-year-old Lilith had exchanged letters with a young army officer during the war.

It had started innocent enough—a former maid had mentioned a young man from her church was overseas and wondered if she could send him some of Lilith's sketches of Central Park since he missed home. Lilith had quickly drawn up a letter with some of her favorite drawings and given it to our maid to send. He'd written Lilith back, and they'd continued their correspondence. Over time they'd developed feelings for each other. Lilith's heart had been so crushed by Lieutenant Cameron's supposed death that she'd withdrawn, and her societal debut had been a misery. For all of us.

She'd always had a shy personality. In writing, her thoughts had been released, and she'd expressed herself more easily. It was no wonder she'd fallen in love via the pen. She'd refused every other suitor. I'd protected her as much as I could, convincing our parents to pin their hopes on me for a good match.

Abandoning my teacup, I grasped Lilith's pale hand. "Lieutenant Cameron probably thought he was doing you a favor at the time. Men are strange like that. They have this ingrained instinct to protect, to provide, and he probably felt stripped of that having lost the use of his arm."

"But it doesn't matter to me. I've told Paul as much."

"Well, when he arrives, you'll get the opportunity to show him." I smiled and gave her fingers a gentle squeeze. "It wasn't right for him to allow you to believe he was dead, only to shock you by writing you again. But we don't always make good decisions when in pain."

I couldn't help but wonder, though, how well matched they were, considering they both struggled with low confidence. With Lilith's fair looks and sweet temper, she could have her pick of any gentleman. And she'd chosen the lieutenant. Meanwhile, I'd sacrificed my choice to bestow on her that freedom. Though I had no regrets. More and more of her bloom returned with each of his letters. I could never deny her this happiness.

"Paul hinted about returning to the city next month, but I'm concerned Father will forbid this."

The "no talk of parents" rule had been violated more times than the prohibition this morning. But really, what better time to address our circumstances than in our private sanctuary, where no one could eavesdrop and then splatter the gossip through the vapid ears of society.

"Father won't interfere. Not when I marry Warren."

I could do this.

I *would* do this.

Perhaps I even wanted to do this.

Warren Hayes was a fascinating contradiction. I glimpsed adventure in his eyes. He welcomed danger. One only had to see his biplane to gather that knowledge. But while he embraced risk, he didn't appear careless. Those same hands that wrangled an airplane into the skies also stroked my own with aching gentleness. Brushed my fingers with the most reverent of touches.

"Are you really going through with it?" Lilith set down her tea and looked squarely into my eyes. "You don't have to."

Oh yes, yes I did. Lilith didn't know the extent of the consequences. Or how *she* would be punished if I refused Warren's hand. "Write to Lieutenant Cameron and invite him home to New York." From what Lilith had told me, he'd been born and raised in the city, though in a different sphere than Lilith and me. "Things should be set in motion soon between Warren and me. Since we'll be back at the town house by then, maybe you and your officer can meet for the first time in Central Park where you made those sketches."

That seemed to speak to her romantic heart, for she wistfully smiled. I finished off my scone and stood, bracing myself for my meeting with Father. My mind raced, but my feet took hesitant strides down several halls to the study. It wasn't often I was summoned to this part of the house. What could Father demand this time? What else could he possibly need? Perhaps he'd inform me what gender my future children should be and proceed to name them as well.

I'd worked myself into a foul mood by the time I reached the final hall leading to the ornately carved wooden door. I paused to collect myself, peering out the window, steadying my breaths. My fingers ran along the curtains as my gaze roamed the outside scene. The sun washed the manicured lawn with golden light. Springtime in the country had always been my favorite. The newness of a season. Where the earth shed its dull gray cloak and wrapped itself in vibrant greens.

"Thinking about hiding behind the drapes?"

I recognized Warren's voice even before I turned and found him approaching. His playful eyes lit on me, his mouth tipping in a crooked smile. He was dressed in a tan suit and brown waistcoat—a color I found drab on most men. But Warren Hayes wasn't most men. He could wear a burlap suit, and I'd no doubt find him handsome.

My smile proved genuine, a small miracle considering my annoyed state. "I only duck behind curtains at balls and soirees."

His brow quirked. "For rendezvous with gentlemen?"

"No. For rendezvous with desserts."

He chuckled, and I enjoyed the sound of it.

"Father never allows me to indulge in sweets in public. Drapes and large potted plants are perfect for covert dessert consumption."

"I'm honored you entrust me with such a secret." He slipped his hand in mine. Something he'd often been doing. "Am I to assume you're here for the same reason I am?" He inclined his head toward the study door. "A meeting with your father?"

"Yes." My deep sigh couldn't be stopped. "Though I didn't know you were invited too."

"Shall we go in together?"

Together. That one word wrapped around my heart with surprising strength. This past year I'd had to brave these meetings alone. No ally. No one championing my cause. Mother never inserted herself in anything of relevance. Lilith, by my own instructions, had avoided Father, allowing me to face him by myself. Having Warren beside me was an unexpected comfort.

My smile broke free, and he returned the gesture. With joined hands, we entered the study with high wood-paneled walls, an imposing mahogany desk, and a multimillionaire with a passive look of boredom.

John Ashcroft acknowledged us with a slow nod. Unsurprising, but still irksome. As if our presence wasn't worthy enough to voice a few simple words of greeting.

I lowered onto the chair, and Warren claimed the matching seat adjacent to mine.

As usual, my hands braced the armrests. My fingers brushed over the wood, which had been scarred by my digging nails. Each tiny trench was a result of entering battle with John Ashcroft over many years. From when he'd told me he'd fired my favorite nanny. Or had enrolled me in boarding school away from Lilith. Or most recently when he'd informed me of my nonnegotiable role in marrying Warren. There was a similar piece of furniture bearing my marks at our Manhattan home. It was a wonder I had any fingernails left.

Father aimed his hooded gaze at Warren. "Have you proposed to my daughter yet?"

My gut knotted so hard I feared the reemergence of my breakfast along with a vital organ or two. I'd known this was coming. Expected it. Father hadn't the patience. But to be so blunt and businesslike about something as important as a marriage proposal? Heat suffused my face.

Warren, however, didn't flinch. Instead he cast me a reassuring look, then locked stares with Father. "Not yet, sir."

"Why not?" Father never sounded forceful. Or even intense. His tone was quiet, which alarmed me more than anything else. "She's already agreed to it."

Not only was there the mortification of being talked about as if my presence wasn't in the room, but I had the horrible imagining of Warren succumbing to Father's unvoiced demands and proposing to me right here in this study. I hadn't expected anything grandiose or even romantic, but I'd hoped to have this pivotal conversation away from John Ashcroft's probing eyes.

Warren turned in his chair, facing me, and my heart catapulted into my throat. "I was hoping to spend more time with you. Please know I'd never pressure you to marry me."

He hadn't withered beneath Father's insistence. My face warmed again, but not from embarrassment. He acted like I had a choice. What a thoughtful, beautiful man. A foolish man, but thoughtful nonetheless. I offered a smile with my nod.

Father, on the other hand, sat silently in his chair, studying us over his steepled hands. "I'll admit that I hoped an engagement would be announced in order to have the ceremony within a month."

One month. Married. Numbness spread through me. Exactly what I needed to feel—nothing. I could rally forward with my campaign to help my sister. Marching right into my own possible prison meant freeing Lilith of hers.

Wait. One month? Wasn't that the time Lieutenant Cameron hinted about returning to the city? It would work. It had to. There was no better opportunity to advance their relationship than when Father was preoccupied overseeing everything he wanted through my marriage to Warren.

"Sir." Warren leaned forward as if ready to challenge. "One month seems—"

"I accept." My voice sounded sure and smooth, and I congratulated myself at the success. Especially when my insides quaked hard enough that I was certain my spleen and heart had changed places. "We can marry within the month."

Warren jolted beside me, his brows lowering in a deep V.

Father nodded. "Wise choice, Geneva. We'll announce it at luncheon and will host an engagement reception this evening. I see no reason to wait."

Of course he didn't. Though Mother might not appreciate having only a handful of hours to coordinate an engagement party. At least all the guests were already here. "Now if you'll excuse me." My legs surprisingly supported my effort to stand. "I need to see to our company." With swift steps, I exited the room. But I turned left instead of right. Yes, I intended to visit with our guests. Later. For now, I needed away.

● ● ●

I ran my thumb along a tulip petal as velvety as it was delicate. My gaze wandered my secret garden, slow and absorbing, as if the color filling my vision could expel the gray and lifeless spots from my thoughts. My legs tucked beneath me, I sat upon a slightly damp tuft of overgrown grass, inhaling the freshness that came with the morning.

The blush of pink, purple, and yellow flowers trembled in the gentle breeze. I took it in, knowing their blooms never lasted long. It was sad, really. To grow and stretch toward the sun, reaching for life but only being at full beauty for mere breaths.

A reminder of my own existence. My sphere to which I was born.

Those in my class strained, meticulously pored over fashion, and grappled to fatten their already gorged pockets. But it was all for nothing. They flashed in the sparkling light of people's praise, then as quickly as they bloomed, they faded.

Movement to my left jerked my head and gaze.

Warren.

How had he known I was here? It was impossible he'd followed me. I'd already spent at least fifteen minutes in this private sanctuary.

"I would've come sooner." He spoke as if aware of my thoughts. "But your father and I had a few things to discuss." His words lost warmth on the final two words, and his mouth twisted. He shoved his hands into his pockets, adopting a casual stance. "Is it okay to enter?"

I returned my gaze to the blooms. I'd be here for their day to shine, give them the audience they deserved. "There's no door."

"That's not what I meant."

My space. My solitude. He was asking if he was welcome. No one had ever come here since I made it my own. I lifted my gaze and found him watching me as if my answer meant everything to him. I dipped a nod, inviting him into my secluded spot. And in doing so, there was something freeing about it.

"I saw you venturing this way through the study window. I guessed you were coming here."

"Quite a guess." I didn't bother to hide my skepticism. This particular clearing was camouflaged to the world, hemmed in by length of woods and overgrown brush. "Have you been here before?"

He inclined his head toward the sky. "I saw it from up there."

Of course he had. Was it wrong to admit to a slice of jealousy? I'd been coming here for seventeen years, and Warren had glimpsed an angle of this place I hadn't yet enjoyed. How I wished to see what he saw. "Was it lovely?" My voice rose barely above a whisper.

His attention drifted over the blossoms. I wasn't sure he'd heard me. Finally his gaze settled on mine. "Breathtaking." His voice had a husky rasp to it. "You can see for yourself if you'd like."

Oh, that invitation to adventure. There wasn't a cell in my being that was immune to it. But this morning's conversation came dashing to the front of my mind. I was to be married. And soon. I doubt I'd have a single moment to myself from here to the altar. "There's much to be done."

His eyes searched mine, as if unsure whether to address the issue so loud between us. I'd been brash, accepting a proposal he hadn't even voiced yet. What if my forwardness insulted him? What if he'd decided not to marry me after all? He'd mentioned he had lingered in Father's study to discuss some things. But then, if he'd chosen to end it all, I suspect he wouldn't invite me for another tour of the skies. I grabbed hold of that sound logic and forced my gaze not to waver from his.

He crouched beside me, bringing with him the scents of sunshine, cedarwood, and comfort. "Tell me about this place."

He'd chosen a topic that seemed safe for both of us. "This was once a garden belonging to the caretaker. Long before my time." I broke away from his intensity and fixed my stare on a bee nestled in the folds of a flower. "Over there is what's left of it." I pointed beyond the cluster of rose bushes, where patches of grass overtook the remnants of a stone foundation.

He followed my gaze. "What happened to the cottage?"

"It burned down during my grandparents' time here. I came searching for the remains of the place when I was young. I broke away from our nanny when she'd thought I was in the library reading. I had to know. Had to see if the rumors were true." Oh the enthusiasm of youth. As the years progressed, that curiosity had dulled. It wasn't until this man beside me with his mystery and his biplane reawakened the parts of me I'd thought were gone forever. "I'm sure such adolescent adventures aren't entertaining to an adult, but a child's imagination is another thing."

"A precious thing."

The warmth in his tone was as comforting and pleasant as the sunlight caressing my face. "The garden was neglected, but I was drawn to it. Rose bushes and other flowers bloomed here and there. And I decided to take it as my own. I snatched some perennial seeds from the gardener and planted." How I'd had to scrub the dirt from the cracks in my knuckles and beneath my fingernails to hide my labor from my nanny and parents. But it'd felt good to work with my hands, rewarding. "I had no idea how to grow a garden. Only knew to bury the seeds in places of sunshine and water them." My lips tugged into a smile at the memory. "I came every day during my reading time to work."

I'd never shared this story with anyone. Not even Lilith. He listened without interrupting, his gaze so focused on me I found it difficult to concentrate.

"From the looks of things, it paid off."

"I came back the following spring, and there were blooms but no order. They grew wild. Tangled stems. Everything growing into each other." I motioned toward a cluster of plants to prove my point. "Any true gardener would be appalled. But I couldn't dream of anything better."

"For the flowers to be wild? Untamed?"

I nodded, the gentle wind stirring my hair against my face. "No manipulating their pretty faces. Just let them stretch toward life their own decided way."

"I like what you've done."

"You do?" I searched his eyes for any deception. Having once prided myself on being able to sort the phony from the true, my skill right now couldn't be relied on. I found myself hoping this man was different from all the others.

"I'm not an expert in this kind of thing, but I prefer your way of gardening."

"You wouldn't force them only to bloom in their tidy spots?" My voice broke. "Bend them to your own liking?"

"Are we still speaking of flowers?" He smoothed my hair from my cheek, his gaze the most tender thing I'd ever seen. "Or of you?"

I bit the inside of my cheek. Here I was. At my most vulnerable.

"What are you afraid of, Geneva?"

"Lots of things." My father. Failing my sister. Never being cherished for who I was. And most of all, love. Love terrified me. "But not you. I'm not afraid of you, Warren Hayes."

He cupped my face, his thumb stroking my cheek. "Geneva, above anything I want you . . . to be you. Not your parents' version. Not what society demands. But you. Show me the real Geneva Ashcroft."

"But she's nothing remarkable."

"She's everything I want." He withdrew a ring from his pocket and kneeled in front of me. "Would you, Geneva Maude Ashcroft, do me the honor of becoming my wife?"

I didn't have a choice, yet he respected me enough to ask. And he asked here of all places! My heart thumped against my chest as I nodded. "Yes."

Chapter 8 ———————————————————————

My PLANE WAS GONE.

The hired driver had dropped us off on the dusty lane leading to Farmer Ewing's field. Warren had been silent and broody the entire car ride here, setting my nerves on edge.

Now this?

My panicked gaze scurried over the bare fence posts bordering the rugged field. No biplane. No anything.

"I can't believe it." I tugged my hat lower, shading my eyes. As if reducing the morning sun's glare would magically make my Jenny appear. My heart bottomed out. This wasn't happening.

"Got to be an explanation," Warren muttered beside me. "Not like it's stolen. I can't imagine anyone else in this town knowing how to fly a Curtiss biplane."

But there was.

Tex.

My gut clenched. I had sorely disappointed a war pilot by not allowing him to work with me, and he'd filched my plane in devastating revenge. Oh why had I trusted him? I'd been careless. Foolish. So concerned with Brisbane's appointment that I'd let my guard down. And I'd lost my Jenny in the process. What were we going to do now? That plane had been my means of transportation, my disguise, but it was much more than that. Warren had given—

"Hullo there!" Farmer Ewing stood beside his barn, waving high with one hand and cupping his mouth with the other.

If I'd only had the presence of mind to attend to my plane yesterday. But my world had shifted. It wasn't every day one's husband came back from the dead and accused one of murder. But that suspicion seemed to be the growing trend concerning me.

I dashed toward Mr. Ewing. Maybe he could tell me about my missing plane. When Tex had left. Or if he knew where the thief had gone.

Warren, with his long strides, followed behind me across the field. The tall grass bowed heavy with morning dew, dampening my stockings, the hem of my dress.

"Where's my plane?" My tone was breathless. Did running cause brain swelling? Because my hatband seemed awfully tight against my scalp.

"A fine 'good morning' to you too." Garrison Ewing grinned, the crinkled lines fanning his eyes blending into the deep wrinkles on his face. "I thought I'd see you yesterday, Miss Starling."

My swift steps had earned me a cramp in my left leg, a squeezing set of lungs, and hopefully, that foul odor accosting my nose didn't mean I'd stepped in cow waste. "Please, Mr. Ewing." I drew a patchy breath. "Have you seen my plane?"

"Course I have." He nodded to Warren, who stepped beside me. "It's in my barn." He jerked a callused thumb toward the open door.

I peeked around his paunchy form and spotted the Jenny's tail. My relieved exhale proved noisy, lengthy, and the opposite of every manner drilled into me.

"Pretty sure folks three counties over heard that." Mr. Ewing gave a friendly wink. "Your gentleman friend came round yesterday. I'm surprised he didn't tell ya."

A low growl emitted next to me. There wasn't a rabid farm animal in sight. Which meant that rumbly snarl had come from my surly husband.

I hadn't yet mentioned Tex to Warren. Though my interactions with the pilot had been innocent, I could feel Warren's hot gaze searing into me. As if he needed another reason to distrust me.

Mr. Ewing prattled on, completely oblivious to the taut friction between Warren and me. "Young man said the wind was too strong out there in the open. Something about warping the wings. So we pushed the plane into the barn."

A tightness wormed across my forehead. This was not the time for a headache. "He's not exactly my friend, Mr. Ewing. But I'm glad he stowed the Jenny. Thank you for the use of your barn."

He reddened with my gratitude. "You're quite welcome, Miss Starling." His gaze shifted to Warren. "A different fellow today? This one a pilot too?"

Another growl.

"Yes. I mean no." I nudged Warren's shoe with my foot, only provoking his fierce glower. Fine. If he wanted to act ridiculous, then so could I. "This man's a hobo. Poor guy lost his voice. Some result of an internal parasite, I think. He can only grunt or growl." I held my gaze on the older man rather than peek at Warren and lose my composure. "I'm giving him a lift to the next town in the Jenny."

"How kind of you." The farmer gave Warren a wary look, then leaned closer to me, lowering his voice. "Just be careful, miss. A pretty thing like you is awfully tempting bait to a man down on his luck."

Warren stiffened, and I tamed my smile. "Thanks for the warning. But I'm safe with this fellow. You see, he's hopelessly devoted to his wife. He left her over some silly misunderstanding. Rather stupid of him." I shot a glance at my husband, who looked ready to throttle me. "But now he sees the error of his ways and how utterly wrong he was. That he needs his wife more than breath itself."

Mr. Ewing chuckled. "Sounds like something from the movies."

"More than that." I sighed dramatically. Nothing like absurd theatrics to go along with my point. "Poetry couldn't convey this man's affection. And I get a role in reuniting them." I leveled Warren with a look. "Here's hoping he's not too hardheaded to embrace the chance while he has it."

The farmer scratched his chin. "How you know all this if he don't talk?"

"He's gifted in pantomime."

A strangled sound caught in Warren's throat. Could've been a laugh or a scoff, but I thwacked his back as if it were a cough. Our gazes met. Was that a twinkle in his eye or a trick of the sunlight? Either way, it disappeared too quickly.

"Thank you for allowing me to use your field for the flight shows." Despite the dull ache still in my head, I gave the farmer my warmest smile. "I wish you'd allow me to compensate you. It would make me feel better about all the ruts I left in your field."

"No, Miss Starling. I couldn't take your money."

"So you've said." Which was why I'd paid his tab at the general store and left his account with a generous credit.

"Been pleasant chatting, but I got chores to tend to. Nice meeting you, Miss Starling." He tipped his hat to us. "You take care now. Hope to see you back someday." After a parting smile, he walked off, whistling.

I winced at the high-pitched melody, my temples throbbing against the satin liner of my hat. I peeled off my constraining cloche. My eyes slid closed as I rubbed my forehead, subduing the tightness. The emotional fatigue of the past day—who was I kidding? past *weeks*—had caught up with me. With the cool breeze kissing my face, I lifted my lashes. My vision cleared in time to catch Warren cutting me a strange look and storming away.

Was he upset about Tex? What else could go wrong between us?

I hated this.

Hated the sight of his retreating form. A band tightened around my heart, constricting more and more with each of his departing steps. I didn't want to see him leave any more than I wanted the sky to crash down on us. But it seemed the heavens had already split. Everything I'd dreamed, so lofty as the clouds, showered over me with piercing shards.

With a heavy sigh, I turned toward the barn.

Sunlight poured in one solid stream through the large doors. The vast space was filled with rusty tools, hay, and my favorite gateway into the skies. A water pump squeaked outside in the distance as I examined the Jenny. Tex had taken good care of her. Even topped the fuel.

At some point between my trek across the field and now, a pebble had lodged in my left shoe, rubbing against my instep. My stocking was probably torn as well. I leaned against the barn wall and bent awkwardly, digging out the troublesome stone.

Warren entered the barn, a handkerchief dangling from his fingers. At least he hadn't left. Was this all I had to look forward to? Being frightened at every turn that my husband would abandon me?

I straightened as he moved close. Touchably close. I opened my mouth to question him but froze as his free hand cupped my chin. With gentle lifting, he tilted my face toward his. My heart did a barrel roll in my chest.

"Poetry, huh?" Was he only whispering in case the farmer was close? Or another reason? "I remember you fancy that rubbish."

What? Oh, that. "I'm expecting a full pantomime of those sonnets you wrote me."

His lips twitched.

"Is that handkerchief my punishment?" I tried not to sound breathless. He was only touching my face. His hands had once explored more intimate parts of me, but his nearness made my pulse thud. "You intend to gag me for teasing you in front of Mr. Ewing?"

"This, Stella . . ." He lifted the cloth, which had been dampened. That explained the squeaky water pump. ". . . is to fix your face."

My mouth parted. "What's wrong with it?" I knew he hated all the cosmetics. He'd scowled at me the entire car ride while I'd been applying them. Darkening my blond brows with cake mascara in the back of a moving vehicle over bumpy roads hadn't been easy. But I'd had no choice. Same went with my crimson lips and heavily lined eyelids. I couldn't allow him to wash it all off. "It's part of my disguise."

"Are you planning a career onstage?"

I frowned. "If you even say as a burlesque dancer—"

"No, as Groucho Marx."

I sputtered. "What?"

"Your brows are a mess. They smeared when you rubbed your forehead." He tipped my head back some more. "Hold still." With gentle swipes, he cleaned the smudges from my face, his eyes intent, as if the task was of utmost importance. His scowl remained, but his mouth seemed pressed in concentration.

As for me, I couldn't think of anything but how close Warren's face was to mine. The warm billows of his breath against my skin. How all I had to do was lift on my toes and our lips would meet. And how that probably wasn't the best idea, considering the mountain of problems between us.

He lowered his hand, and I could almost see the mask of indifference slipping into place. No! I wasn't ready for him to shut me out again. Not when I had to explain.

"About the man Mr. Ewing mentioned—"

"Not now." He started to pull away, but I grabbed his lapels, stilling him.

"His name is Tex, and he's a pilot. He fought in the war."

A muscle leaped in his jaw.

"He approached me after my first flight show here and asked if he could take a turn in her. I let him. He taxied the locals around while I went to Brisbane's appointment."

His head dipped. Three months ago I'd have expected his kiss. But now he only lowered to look fully into my eyes. "That's all?" His voice was threaded with skepticism.

"Yes." I held his gaze so he could see my sincerity. Not like it would help any. It certainly hadn't worked so far. And by the tightness around his mouth and the cold glare in his eyes, it didn't work now.

Why did I even try?

I ducked beneath his arms and stepped away. "I know your opinion of me is low, but really, Warren, don't."

"Don't what?"

I spun around, my voice tight. "Don't add adultery to my growing list of faults."

"Do I have cause to?"

"You don't have cause to believe I'd purposely hurt you, yet here we are."

He fell quiet, then moved toward the right wing and examined the struts. Had he no intention of responding?

My temper flared. "Brisbane could be the killer, but you let him off the hook without so much as a thought. There must be a strong case against me for you to believe I could harm you."

"There is." Warren peered at me through the gap in the propeller blades. "This next town we're going to, Hanover, do you know anything about it?"

I almost stomped in frustration. Apparently my innocence wasn't something up for debate, considering how easily he switched topics. "I haven't heard of it before reading it on Brisbane's list. I don't even know if it's connected with anything. It's just a guess." My headache threatened to return. "It's all been one guess after another. But it did lead me to you." For better or worse, right?

He stepped around the wing, moving toward me. "Why do you think Brisbane is to blame for any of this?"

"Because it looks suspicious. He deceived me at your funeral, knowing full well you're alive. Then he disappears and breaks contact with you."

"What reason would he have to kill me? Other than having you all for himself?" His gaze roamed my person in a way that would be entirely indecent had he not been my husband. "Though that's a strong motive."

I rolled my eyes. "If he wanted me, which is complete nonsense, then why would he try to frame me for your murder by giving my letter to the authorities?" I countered my own argument. "It doesn't make sense."

"None of this does." He turned away, running a hand through his hair, his eyes narrowing in contemplation. He'd always had an impressive profile, but the scruff on his jaw framing his scowling mouth gave him a roguish appeal.

"In my heart I don't believe Brisbane's guilty. Even if he had a motive, as you say, he couldn't have written those terrible notes. Unless he—"

"Notes?" Warren's broad frame became rigid, like the Jenny beside him. "What notes?" He stood full height, gaze targeting me.

"I should've told you. I know that now, but I was warned not to say anything or else—"

"What are you talking about?"

"Someone was sending me threatening letters."

Chapter 9

Four and a half months earlier—April 14, 1922
Geneva

THERE WAS SUCH A THING as too much sparkle.

From the jeweled combs in my hair, to the sequined frock, to Warren's diamond ring on my finger, my entire person glittered. If someone catapulted me into the sky, I could easily guide my fiancé's plane at night. Though I would rather be in his Jenny than standing at the receiving line of yet another evening formal. Parties. Parties. Parties. It seemed like my debut all over again. But this particular rigmarole was in honor of Warren and me. Our engagement.

My fiancé stood beside me, discussing paper mill drivel with Mr. Delchester, one of Father's business associates. Warren was dashing in his formal evening wear, but I couldn't get past the image of him sitting next to me in my secret garden with dirt coating his trousers and a ladybug climbing his shoulder.

And those words he'd spoken. I'd played them in my mind again and again like a favorite Victrola record, the melody of his voice, the lyrics of his declarations.

As if hearing my heart's whispers, he glanced over. His perfect mouth lifted into a warm smile. With Mr. Delchester now gone and my parents commandeering the conversation with the Reinholts—the last family in the receiving line—we had a rare second of privacy. Well, as much privacy as one could get at a crushing event like this.

Warren leaned over, and the scent of cedarwood and some kind of pleasing spice stirred delightfully around me like a spring breeze. "How many compliments can a man give before he appears ridiculous?"

"It depends on the giver and the recipient."

He appeared amused by my answer. "Not the compliment itself?"

"No." I straightened my glove with a small smile. "Because the same words can be spoken by a handful of gentlemen, and all have a different effect."

"So if I said that you look beautiful tonight, my words would be judged alongside the scores of other fellows who remarked the same?"

"Not necessarily." Especially given the way he currently looked at me. "But it does lack creativity. You're a newspaperman. Shouldn't you be able to come up with something more sensational?"

"Like your hair's the shade of a dried corn husk? And your teeth are so straight and white they remind me of my grandmother's picket fence?"

He'd said those ridiculous words with such a neutral expression, I had to choke back my laughter.

"Sensational enough?" He smirked.

"Never mind. Your first remark is perfect."

"Are you certain? Because I was about to compare the slope of your nose to a hill I went sledding on as a kid. Almost broke my leg."

My lips sputtered a most unladylike laugh.

"My dear Geneva." Beatrice Reinholt approached, her parents close by. "Elegant as always, I see." Her words were so syrupy sweet, I was surprised she didn't gag on them.

"Beatrice, you made it to our engagement reception." I'd made it sound like she had traveled a long journey rather than several halls of our home, to which her family had been guests. I also hadn't tacked on that she was welcome or that I was pleased with her being here, something her narrowed eyes told me she'd caught.

I exchanged pleasantries with her parents, and they shook Warren's hand with a hearty congratulations before moving deeper in the room. Beatrice, unfortunately, lingered.

Of course, she was decked head to toe in the latest fashion. Her headpiece, glittering like the chandelier above us, nestled perfectly in her artfully bobbed hair. The more mature ladies in our class turned their noses up at the current hair trend, but no one would say such a thing to Beatrice. Not when her father's business handled most of these families' money. No matter how high the hem or low the neckline, Beatrice got a free pass.

Unlike me.

My long tresses were piled on my head. My gown was cut of the best cloth, stitched to perfection, and covered with shiny things, but next to Beatrice, I must've appeared decades older. And boring.

More so, Beatrice was pretty. Not the porcelain kind with delicate features and dainty mannerisms. No, with her wide-set eyes and sharp, angled cheekbones that slanted to pouty lips, she had an alluring way about her. If I was the angel in white, she was the one wearing red, holding out the forbidden fruit to the man of her choice. And right now she eased closer to Warren and blinked her mascara-laden lashes at him.

"I offer you my most heartfelt congratulations, Mr. Hayes." That low, sultry tone sounded more suggestive than celebratory.

Warren gave a slight bow at her words. "I'm the luckiest man alive." He slid his arm around my waist, drawing me to him. Then he leaned close, his warm breath puffing against my temple, followed by the light press of his lips.

I froze.

His kiss only lasted a second, maybe less. But my awareness jolted. His strong fingers—capable of finessing airplane controls, gliding winged beasts into the sky—now effortlessly curled into my side, slightly bunching my dress. Some would consider his hold territorial. But there was something else in his touch. That which I'd never experienced. Several things really. I couldn't delve deep into all the emotions pulsing through me. Not here under society's probing eye.

Though I couldn't miss the hints of protectiveness. And it shot straight to my heart. I'd always been the defender, for myself and Lilith. Sure, the Ashcroft name instilled fear in most, but there was a difference between being guarded as if a piece of property and being defended as a person with a beating heart. Warren's touch was the latter, and it made me want to tuck myself into the folds of his arms and hide there for the rest of the evening.

That was, until I spied Father out of the corner of my eye. There would be consequences for certain. The Ashcroft Angel would be labeled something far more slanderous.

Beatrice strutted away in a swish of scarlet satin, and I peered up at my fiancé.

Something in my expression caused his smile to fade, and my heart shrank. I never wanted to be the reason his warmth grew cold.

"Did I overstep?" He dropped his hand from my waist and placed a respectable distance between us.

I'd always loathed the confining societal boundaries that allowed no wiggle room. But never more so than now. Warren was my fiancé. He should be granted the right to kiss me whenever and in front of whomever.

"My opinion never matters." My gaze swept the onlookers. "But if the roasted duck waddles off the table, it startles the guests." I repeated what Cecily always poured into my ear.

His head tipped back with a curious bend to his brow. "Duck?"

I tacked on my practiced, demure smile for demonstration's sake. "We're standing in front of everyone. On display like a holiday duck with all the costly trimmings. There are rules we have to follow." Meanwhile across town, The Silver Fountain swarmed with people my age, dancing the foxtrot, drinking like it wasn't illegal, and wearing clothes that would make Mother's wrist ache from fanning herself. Only ten miles separated our estate from the local speakeasy, but the gin joint might as well be in another universe. "We must play the part. Smile. Nod. And definitely not kiss."

"That wasn't a kiss." His lips tugged into a smile. "It was a peck."

"Isn't that the same?" I was woefully unpracticed in this sort of thing.

His eyes smoldered, and my breath tripped in my throat. "When you give permission, I'll show you the difference."

Heat suffused my face. My mind scrambled for a response. For certain this man would one day kiss me. And more. Of course I'd have this startling realization in a place where all eyes were fastened on me. I was saved from answering by a gentleman's approach.

Warren noticed as well, and a friendly smile warmed his face. "Ah, Terrence." His voice heartened as a fellow strode toward us.

"Cousin." He extended his arm for a handshake, but Warren hauled the man into a masculine embrace complete with loud shoulder slaps.

I tried not to gawk at the display of open brotherly affection. Hugging another man as if it were Christmas morning in front of a fire rather than in a ballroom? My fiancé didn't have an ounce of ceremony in his address. And it was fabulous.

"Sorry I'm late." Terrence's gaze bounced around as if uncertain. His tone was so quiet that I leaned in to hear him. "My last appointment went considerably over. Then of course the drive here from the city."

"No harm. I appreciate you coming on such short notice." Warren still smiled, as if heartened to have a blood relative in attendance rather than an entire ballroom full of strangers. "Terr, I have the pleasure of introducing you to Miss Ashcroft." Warren regarded me with that tender look in his eyes. "Geneva, my cousin, Mr. Terrence Hayes."

The man's attention shifted to me. His mouth opened as if to greet me, then wobbled shut. Poor man was nervous.

"Mr. Hayes, thank you for joining us tonight." I offered a friendly smile. "It's such a delight to meet another member of Warren's family."

The tightness around his eyes relaxed. "Thank you for the invitation."

"Of course. Though I should warn you, I fully intend to pester you this evening for stories about my fiancé. The more embarrassing, the better."

Warren's low chuckle sifted into my ear even as his warm hand settled on my back. "There's plenty enough, I'm sure."

Terrence watched us with a curious expression. He was just as tall as Warren, with the same shade of brown hair. But that was where the resemblance ended. The man's face was much fuller, where Warren's was lean. Warren had been favored with a defined jaw, and it appeared one would have to dig around Terrence's fleshy chin to find some firmness.

Warren waved his cousin closer. "There's something I want you to look into for me. A new project that I'm leaning toward and need to know the legalities behind."

Terrence nodded as if they'd had this conversation a thousand times.

He and Warren exchanged a few more remarks, then Terrence wandered away, looking more like a lost puppy than a grown man.

"Think he'll be okay?" Goodness knew, this crowd was a tough one.

Warren nodded. "Terrence can fend for himself. He's more confident than he appears. Have the war to thank for that." His gaze tracked his cousin crossing the room. "Most men return broken, but it helped Terr become more self-assured."

"Was he a soldier?"

"No, the ordnance corps." His eyes flicked to mine. "Us Hayes men didn't enter combat. Just helped prepare others for it." A shadow crossed his face, tightening his features for a brief second—similar to his reaction when he'd last spoken of the war. There was a story hidden behind that handsome demeanor, but I didn't have time to explore it.

My parents glided past, finished with greeting our guests and obviously ready to start the evening. I received a brisk nod from Father, indicating he wanted us to follow. Heaven forbid we loitered and the evening started without us.

I slipped my gloved hand into the crook of the arm Warren offered. I leaned in, dropping my voice. "Perhaps we should sic Miss Reinholt on your cousin. She seems fond of Hayes blood."

He quirked a smile, but it was more contemplative than amused. "Won't work. Terrence doesn't have a fortune. He does do well for himself with his law firm."

Judging by their snippet of conversation, I suspected Terrence handled Warren's business accounts.

"But he's not wealthy by any stretch."

I'd thought it was a trick of the flickering candles, but I had noticed the fabric of Terrence's tuxedo was a smidge faded around the knees and elbows. "Oh." Beatrice wouldn't think twice about the man. I glanced toward the tinkling laugh belonging to the youngest Reinholt. She was flirting with Kent Brisbane.

"Though I could be wrong." Warren followed my gaze. "She seems enamored by Brisbane, and he's even worse off than Terrence."

We strolled by other couples while working our way toward the middle of the floor to start the dancing. "Sadly no. She'll tease. Preen under his attention, but she wouldn't consider him for anything more than a plaything. She did that our entire debut. It was nauseating."

Sure she'd spun around the dance floor with every handsome man, but she'd only wanted to sink her claws into the ones who graced the society pages.

The orchestra struck up a number, and I sighed at how boring it was. So slow I could almost fall asleep in the lull of the rhythm. Just once I wanted them to play something jazzy. Something I could lose my breath with and get lost in fast footwork.

Warren eased my hand into his, and I slid my other onto his shoulder. Never mind. I wouldn't fall asleep. Not with his warmth pressing through the fabric of his gloves or the way his dark-brown eyes burned into mine.

Lilith lingered on the fringe of the dance floor, fiddling with her gloves. I knew she'd appear once we'd finished greeting the guests. She dreaded being forced into conversation, having once compared it to facing a firing squad.

"She looks distressed." Warren noticed my sister as well.

"I believe she's nervous. Her beau, Lieutenant Cameron, is confirmed to arrive in the city within a few weeks. She's worried Father will—"

Warren froze. "Not Lieutenant Paul Cameron?"

"You know him?"

We resumed our sway, Warren shifting even closer to me. "I've known him for years. Haven't seen him since he went off to war. But . . . he died in combat."

Hmm. So it appeared the lieutenant not only allowed Lilith to believe he'd been killed, but also his former friends. My estimation of his character dropped significantly. Could such a man—one who deceived others into believing him dead when he was most certainly alive—be worthy of trust? Perhaps I was too cynical. "We thought so too. And he nearly did. He woke up in an infirmary in France, fevered and without his right arm. It took a while to recover and even a greater while to summon the courage to write Lilith again."

"Who'd have thought?" he said, almost to himself. Then his gaze latched on to mine. "He worked for my family. I wish he would've written. I would've given him a good job. I may still, if he's interested."

A million questions spun in my head, but one rolled to the very front. "What's he like?"

"You've never met him?"

I shook my head. "Neither has my sister. They fell in love over letters."

"What would you like to know? It's been a long time since I've been around him, but he's tall—"

"No." As if I cared one bit about his appearance. "Is he kind?" I knew from experience men acted differently around each other than in the presence of a lady. Lieutenant Cameron could say all the flowery words to my sister, but Warren would know his character.

He seemed taken aback by my question, and it touched a nerve. Did he truly think all that interested me was appearances? "He can have the looks of Adonis, but if he has the heart of Hades, I don't want him anywhere near my sister."

He smiled at my agitation. "You're different than all of them." He jerked his head toward the crowd. To the cream of the crop. To the wealthy of the wealthy. People who were envied for their status.

I felt it a compliment of the highest sort, but from a different perspective, it could also be viewed as an insult. Before I could question him, he leaned closer.

"Lieutenant Cameron is a hard worker with loyal qualities. Your sister couldn't choose anyone better."

My shoulders lowered in relief, and I squeezed Warren's hand in gratitude.

The next few hours flew by in a flurry, and soon I was back in the comfort of my room.

"Oh, do hold still." Lilith tugged at my corset with a laugh. After the maid Iris had fumbled her way through the door, I had taken one look at her flustered state and had given her the rest of the night off. Mother had overworked the staff, and tonight's party had been even more taxing.

Besides, I needed the time alone with Lilith to discuss what Warren had revealed about Lieutenant Cameron. Which had made her ten notches past giddy. While I still held reservations about the officer, I adored seeing Lilith this way. It was rare for her to break from her reserved shell, and I was grateful for these special moments.

"Did you know that dance halls have corset check-ins? Where ladies strip them off to be freer to dance?" Lilith eyed me as if she told a great secret. "Can you imagine? How scandalous."

"I wouldn't mind one bit. I'd love to be free of it," I said even as I stepped out of my own. The pale pink and lace seemed harmless, but that contraption was like a boa constrictor. I hadn't worn my corset over the past weeks, but tonight Mother had been present while I'd been dressing. It couldn't have been helped. "All this fuss for our engagement. Warren owns a million papers. We should've just announced it in them and avoided all this fanfare." My cheek muscles seemed filled with lead from smiling all evening.

"But think of what you would've missed. You danced with Warren several times." Lilith practically sang that last statement. She commenced to waltz across my bedroom. "How lovely you are, darling." She affected a terrible masculine voice. "What stunning lips you have. What beautiful children you'll give me."

Laughing, I chucked one balled stocking at her for a direct hit on the arm. "Warren wouldn't say such crass things."

"Calling you lovely is crass?" Lilith arched a brow.

"You know which part I meant. And your impersonation skills are awful." My scold held no weight alongside my growing smile.

She beamed as well, but quickly sobered. "Beatrice Reinholt is so green, I considered plucking her up and setting her into a pot beside the garden vines. Don't give that jealous woman any opportunity to think you two aren't madly in love. I couldn't bear for her to try to steal him away from you. He's too good of a catch."

I bit my lip. "She's beautiful."

"So are you." Her sisterly tone was endearing. "What's odd is, I caught her meandering the family halls when Mother sent me to fetch her shawl."

"Really? Wonder what she was up to." I pulled the pins from my hair, my scalp tingling with relief.

My gaze landed on a note next to my powder puff. That hadn't been here earlier.

Lilith noticed as well. "Another note from Warren?"

"I don't think so." I'd told Warren of my love for poetry, and he'd taken it upon himself to pen his favorites. This paper was different, and it wasn't folded like his notes had been.

I worked it open and read the short typed words. My fingers crinkled the edges, my heart thudding hard.

"What's the matter?" Lilith stepped behind me.

"It says, 'You don't deserve any of this. Prepare to have it all ripped from your hands.'"

Chapter 10 ————————————————————————————————

WITH ALL THE OPEN-MOUTHED STARES I now received, one would think Charlie Chaplin was strolling down this small-town sidewalk rather than a female pilot. Where the silent film icon wore a black derby, I was capped with a leather helmet. Instead of his baggy trousers, I donned snug coveralls. Yes, a rare sight for most, but just like ole Charlie, I had a part to play.

Though it was more than a costume, for my getup was more conducive to flying than the frock I'd worn earlier. When Warren had insisted I pilot us to Hanover, I'd studied the map, then ducked behind the massive barn door and changed.

The skies had been perfect for flying as the Jenny left one open field only to land an hour later in another. Though Mr. Glasgow, the farmer we'd just spoken to, had been far grumpier than Mr. Ewing.

Ugh, cranky men. Which reminded me. I glanced at Warren.

In our short trek from Mr. Glasgow's farm, my husband had glowered at every gentleman whose gaze had lingered on me longer than two seconds. He'd perfected the intimidating scowl to the degree that I questioned if he even had blinked.

If he offended most of the town, no one would attend our flight show. Then we would have no inlet to investigate. Not that I expected to find anything here. But we had to at least give an effort. And we couldn't siphon information from cows and roosters. No, we needed humans, and Warren was scaring them all off.

I gently pressed a hand to his elbow, staying him. He angled toward me, the sunlight touching his face, highlighting copper hues in his stubbled jaw and flecks of liquid gold in his eyes. He gave a literal form to the word breathtaking. Because I was pretty sure just looking at him sucked all the oxygen from my body.

His brow, also favored now with a bronze-ish tint, arched higher, and I realized he expected me to say something.

I scraped for my voice. "I should've told you earlier about the threats." Warren hadn't received my confession about the notes well. He'd only asked a few basic questions, then had turned mute, as if taking on a new profession as a mime, only without the miming. I'd taken his silence as his way of processing what I'd said, but his mood had only grown fouler.

"Since before we were even married." His ever-present scowl firmly marked his emotions. "You've been getting those notes all this time, and you never mentioned it. Not once, Geneva."

"Stella," I reminded, removing my hand from his sleeve. "I was wrong to keep it from you. But I wasn't sure who was behind them, and several notes warned dire consequences would come if I said anything. If I could go back and change things, I would." I'd change a lot of things. "I was scared."

His glower withered. "How could I have protected you if I never knew you were in danger?"

I hadn't been the one who'd ended up in fatal danger, though I didn't feel it wise to say such. My fingers curled tighter around the stack of handmade flyers I'd been carrying since we'd stowed the Jenny. "We're supposed to be looking for clues, not rehashing the past." My argument was weak, and he knew it.

"Those notes seem a pretty big clue to me." He jerked his head toward the drugstore. "Did all of them say the same thing?"

"Different words." We resumed walking. "But the general idea was that I was unworthy of everything, and all I hold dear would be taken from me. And looking back, that was . . ."

"What?"

"That was what happened." I fused my gaze to the ground, watching my booted steps until they slowed altogether. My eyes drifted to his. "You got taken from me." He still hadn't returned. He was here physically. I could reach out, run my fingers over his sturdy form, but his heart was far removed from mine. Warren had come back from the dead, but could our marriage?

His gaze scorched mine, eyes flashing with some unreadable emotion. We stayed in this heated silence for several seconds, until he released a frustrated breath. "All you hold dear?" His tone was low, husky. "I don't recall that being your view of me."

And there it was. The hurt. He could mask it as annoyance, anger even. But there was no mistaking the anguish in his handsome face. Pain I had brought by my own foolishness. But to revisit that evening before his crash would also mean touching a gaping wound of my own. And I couldn't. Not now, here in the middle of the sidewalk, surrounded by people gawking at us. "I didn't mean—"

"Are you sure this town means nothing to you?"

I pulled in a breath. "I never heard of Hanover before reading Brisbane's list." I hushed my tone as a woman with a baby buggy pushed past. "I told you that." Warren hadn't a forgetful nature. Quite the opposite. Being a mechanic, he possessed an intellect that was always processing, sorting. He'd no doubt sifted each of my words and pieced them together to his own fitting for some unknown purpose. "Why do you keep asking me?"

"You'll see," he muttered and cut a direct path to the drugstore.

What did *that* mean? I didn't think my heart could stand any more surprises. Hollywood and Broadway couldn't produce enough drama to compare with what filled my present life. With a sigh, I followed him inside.

"Well, what do we have here?" An older man in a white suit jacket stood behind a cluttered counter and inspected us as if we were outlaws.

"We're fliers." I forced a bright smile, though it felt shaky. "Here to put on an amazing show for the residents of Hanover." I held out the advertisement.

He inspected the flyer I'd sketched by hand. His aged blue eyes crimped with suspicion, then rounded. "An air circus? Here?"

"Of course." If I could stand before the wealthiest, most influential notables in the country, then I could keep my chin from sagging in front of the proprietor of Frank's Drug & Emporium. "Barrel rolls, loops, and if time permits, rides to those brave enough to try."

A few people edged close, and I stepped back to address them, all the while scanning for the familiar face of Kent Brisbane. Not that I really imagined finding him here, but it was rather disappointing not having much of a lead. "This event is for all ages. So bring your entire family. We're in Farmer Glasgow's acreage."

The proprietor's silver brows rose. "Now how did you convince that sharp-eyed geezer to let you do an air show there?"

Hadn't been easy. We'd landed on a good flat area, a smooth ending to an even smoother flight, but were met with the rocky shouts of Mr. Glasgow. He hadn't been pleased to have a flying machine on his farm. His veins had bulged in his wide forehead, as if I'd landed wheels on his best heifer.

I risked a glance at Warren, who appeared to be biting back a smile. Okay, maybe not a smile, but definitely not a frown. Relief surged through me. The tense emotions from a few moments ago had settled. For now at least.

From Warren's slight show of amusement, he no doubt recalled my toe-to-toe exchange with the gruff farmer. Though when I'd explained Mr. Glasgow could keep 50 percent of tonight's profits, his tune had changed from a tomcat's feral hiss to a kitten's purr. Warren had raised a brow at my generosity. But this wasn't about the money. It never was.

"He gave his hearty consent." I shot a smile at Warren. I couldn't help it. It'd taken a lot of charm to get that man's crusty edges to soften, and I was as proud of that success as my first time behind the Jenny's controls.

"Well, I'll be," the man muttered in wonder.

"You really have a flying machine, lady?" A squeaky voice rose from the nearby candy bins.

I smiled at the grubby face of a young boy, probably no older than eight. "We do. And you can see it for yourself later this afternoon." I handed him a flyer.

His face lit with excitement. He pored over the paper with bright eyes, but that hazel gaze soon dimmed. He must've registered the fee at the bottom.

A dollar per family wasn't an extravagant amount compared to the other flying circuses. Most charged two dollars per person. We asked fifty cents for a single and one dollar for an entire family. Anyone wanting to take a jaunt in the Jenny would pay an additional fee to cover fuel expense. But judging by the boy's sloped shoulders and sad frown, he must've considered the initial cost a king's ransom.

I eased closer. "But in each town we select one family that gets free admission. It's tradition." *Starting now.* "How about it?"

Rather than acting excited, the boy's rust-colored brow furrowed, and his freckles seemed like dots of fire in his grumpy expression. "Ma says never to take charity." He folded his gangly arms in front of him and adopted an air of offense.

"Well . . . what if . . ." I stammered, searching for a resolution.

Warren's solid frame sidled next to me. "What's your name, young man?"

Hazel eyes blinked up, up, up at Warren. "Neil Klavons, sir."

He nodded. "It's not charity, Neil. We honor hard work." Warren's gaze briefly met mine before turning back to the child. "The tradition my wife mentioned is about employing a town resident to hand out our flyers. We need someone to spread the word about the show." He spoke as if conducting business with a steel magnate rather than a four-foot-tall kid with holes in his trousers. "Payment is admittance to the show along with the family." His eyes narrowed in that professional manner I'd glimpsed many times. "Do you know anyone up to the task?"

Neil straightened and puffed out his scrawny chest.

I suppressed a smile.

"Yes, sir." He all but saluted. "I can work as hard as the best of them." He stuck out his hand, and Warren, with an executive nod, shook those small fingers.

"It's a deal," he said.

I swore I heard a feminine sigh behind us.

Warren peered at me, but I was too focused on not melting into a sappy puddle right next to the tubs of molasses. The man I'd pledged my life to had emerged from his hardened shell just now, and my tongue had fainted, soon to be joined by the rest of my person.

Warren cast me a questioning look, then relieved me of the brochures. Oh yes. The flyers. He handed them to Neil, and one would think those were hundred-dollar banknotes for how wide his eyes bulged.

His spindly legs dashed out of the drugstore. "Air circus tonight! Come witness the show!" Neil's voice was sweet, if not a tad ear splitting.

Warren grinned, the skin framing his eyes crinkling. Such a good sign when it came to Warren. It was also my weakness. I barely restrained my fingers from touching those alluring crinkles, which was for the best, considering I was a bit shaky and wouldn't want to poke his retina or do anything else that'd make him stop smiling at me.

"A man's got his pride, Stella. No matter the age." He leaned close. "Plus, spreading the word for us would help free some time so we can investigate."

The man was brilliant.

"That was a swell thing you did." A woman inserted herself between us, dabbing her eyes with a handkerchief. "Young Neil lost his pa two months back, and that was just . . ." She blew her nose into the lacy cloth, the sound resembling a honk of a dying goose.

"What she means is, you are very welcome to our little town." The drugstore owner gave an approving nod. "Now you're one of us." Hearty murmurs of affirmation surrounded us.

Gone were the suspicious glares and tentative looks. If only we could win over every town, this endeavor would be a lot easier.

I tugged Warren by the wrist and led him to a secluded corner between the backhoes and gardening gloves. "You realize you called me your wife in front of these people."

His head tilted. "That I did."

"Which spoils my plan of introducing you."

He groaned. "Not as a hobo again."

"No, as a traveling salesman."

"At least that's respectable."

"Selling kazoos for rabbits."

His lips quirked.

"You have to admit I can be creative when I choose to."

"You can be a lot of things."

I wasn't sure if his remark was good or bad, but my intentions of asking him were cut off by him easing closer and me getting that pesky brain fuzz again.

"I know this is all your show, but may I make a suggestion?"

First the crinkly eyes and now Warren spoke without the growl in his voice. We'd made definite strides in our relationship over the past fifteen minutes. Now to get past that minor obstacle of him thinking I was a murderer. "Of course."

"Let's visit Ruth Fields."

My brows scrunched. "Who?"

His gaze narrowed, as if weighing my every response. No, more like judging. Another test? Just when I'd thought things were improving.

"Who is Ruth Fields?" I demanded.

"She's the reason you wanted me dead."

————————————————————————————

Chapter 11

Four months earlier—April 21, 1922
Geneva

"THIS IS THE LAST OF them." My shoes sank into the soft ground of the shoreline, but my heart lifted as I took in the serene view of the lake nestling at the far edge of Ashcroft property. I dared not step any closer. I enjoyed the sight of the water, though always from a safe distance. "You know all my secret hideaways now."

Warren threaded his fingers through mine, and I savored the warm press of his palm. "You'll have to create new ones for me to intrude upon at our home."

His words wrapped around me. Our home. Our lives were to be united in less than two weeks. Married. And everything would be different. But would it be a good kind of different? A gentle breeze rustled the branches of surrounding maple trees, even as a stirring rippled the edges of my thoughts. What would my days be like at the Hayeses' town house? Would it be like my parents'? The Ashcroft estates were lofty structures, but every one carried a drafty chill of indifference.

"I'll have a lot of explaining to do when I get back," I said, forcing my mind away from questions I wasn't certain I wanted answers to. "No doubt Cecily is complaining to Mother that I crept away from under her watchful eye." Not like it'd been difficult to escape.

"More like you crept away from her closed eyelids. I've never seen a woman fall asleep so fast."

"She's exhausted." I sighed. "Along with the rest of the staff." Events and parties every day and night. Tending to us as well as the guests. Those poor souls deserved time off and a generous bonus. But Father would never grant it. The house staff ranked low on his list of consideration. Which was why we always had trouble keeping help. Cecily had been the only one who'd stayed over the years, and I supposed it'd been more out of love for Lilith than anything else. She had been more of a mother to my sister than our own. And though I hadn't the same bond with Cecily, I still felt for her as well as any unfortunate human working for John Ashcroft.

My gaze drifted to Warren. What kind of employer was he? I couldn't imagine him being as unfeeling as Father, but then I didn't exactly know him. "I'm wondering . . ."

His eyes met mine. "Yes?"

"Once we're married, would it be okay if I added Iris to your staff?" I knew Cecily would never leave while Lilith remained under my parents' roof, but Iris? She needed rescue the most. "The poor girl's awkward around my father, and I think she'll flourish away from this place." I was too nervous to gauge his reaction. This topic required money. His money. Warren would have to pay her wages and provide her lodging in his home. It was bold of me. But it was also too late to retract my words.

He withdrew his hand from mine, and I tried not to let my shoulders curl forward. Pinning my gaze to the patch of shoreline beneath my feet, my attention snagged on something I hadn't considered in over a decade. I stooped as low as modesty allowed and brushed my fingers over a childhood treasure. "A white pebble." I worked the tiny stone from its earthen home.

He crouched beside me, his expression curious.

"When I was younger, I believed all white pebbles were drops of heaven." I embraced the shift in conversation, giving Warren as much time as needed to think about my request. "At an Easter service, the minister preached about heaven, the nearness of God, and I thought I heard him say something about white stones. So every time I saw one, I dug it from the dirt and placed it in a satin pouch." I'd completely forgotten about that. Funny how memories returned. "If ever I felt sad or lonely, I'd go hunt for a stone from heaven."

His brow furrowed. "Were you sad often?"

"Let's just say I built up quite the collection." A collection I still owned to this day, kept safely stored in a bag in my dresser drawer. My upbringing wasn't wholly disappointing. I'd always had nice things and clothes. But my parents had often been gone or too busy with society to give any attention to their children. My nannies hadn't exactly cared for me. To them it was just a job. Lilith, at least, had Cecily. "Of course when I was older, I realized I'd misunderstood the minister, who really meant 'the Great White Throne.' Not stones. But by that time my stash of rocks meant something to me." I extended my hand, displaying the white pebble for his perusal.

His fingers made a slow sweep over my open palm, his touch awakening my skin. "A stone from heaven." His eyes held mine, his fingertips stroking a mesmeric path on the hollow spot of my hand.

This interaction was by no means scandalous, yet it felt intimate. He lifted the stone from my palm and inspected it as if I'd presented him with a priceless pearl rather than a dirt-crusted rock. I expected him to toss the stone back onto the shore, but with a bend of his handsome mouth, he stowed it in his pocket.

He reached for me, helping me stand. Instead of stepping back, he eased closer, and his hand cradled the curve of my jaw, lifting my chin ever so gently. I'd never seen his expression, or anyone else's for that matter, this tender. And just like the white pebbles, I tucked this moment in the memory pouch of my mind.

"You asked if I'd welcome Iris into my employ." His tone was warmly adamant. "Once we're married, everything I have belongs to you. It's not my house—it's ours. It's not my staff—it's ours. And as my wife, you'll have the run of it. Everything to your liking."

My lips parted in shock.

"Does that surprise you?"

He had no idea. The man spoke as if our marriage would be a partnership. Something completely other than I'd been raised to believe.

And there it was again. This awkward awakening that seemed to only happen around Warren. It was like I'd been sitting in a dim room for years and his presence brought a glow, exposing things around me that were always there, but I'd never been granted a clear glimpse. For instance, his kiss at the engagement reception. That moment exposed a thousand other absent ones.

I met his curious gaze. "Sorry. I . . . got lost in thought."

"About?" He picked up another rock and tossed it in his palm.

I shifted my weight from one foot to the other. Courage meant boldness to step out when everything within you screamed not to. Though the same could be said of stupidity. But this man was soon to be my husband, so I should probably warn him about my recent discovery of a longtime void. "I was thinking of the other night in the receiving line when you . . ."

"Ah, the peck, yes." He dipped his chin, as if taking all the blame. "I'm sorry about—"

"No." I flashed my palm. "Please don't apologize. It got me thinking." I breathed deep and willed myself not to blush. "About kissing."

His lips ticked up at the edges. "I see."

My hands fell to my sides. This wasn't coming out right. "I don't know how else to say it, but as far as experience goes with kissing, I have none."

He threw the stone into the lake, and that smile he held captive broke loose. "I can tutor you."

Goose bumps erupted, for which I'd blame the late spring breeze rather than Warren's offer. "Yes, well. I'm certain you have many pointers, but I don't think you understand what I mean. Apart from you, I've never been kissed. Not once. Not even so much as a motherly kiss to my cheek."

His face slacked. "Never? From anyone?"

I shook my head. My parents weren't affectionate. Not with each other and especially not with me. Even Lilith. I loved her dearly, but I'd never so much as kissed her brow. I'd never even thought to. Which was why the press of Warren's warm lips to my skin had stirred me to realize my own coldness. "It's strange, isn't it? And to think I've lived over two decades without noticing anything amiss. Perhaps I have no feelings."

"You have feelings, Geneva."

"What if I don't? What if I'm incapable of affection? That's why I'm warning you now. It's possible you'll marry a cold soul."

He shook his head. "I hate to bust your theory, but there's no such thing as cold."

"What?" Of course cold existed.

"Look it up, Geneva. Cold is simply the absence of heat." His lips bent in a roguish smile. "I've seen your spark. All we have to do is draw out that fire in you. I've got a feeling that will be time well spent."

I blinked, unsure how to respond. If anything, he was the fire. It was because of his warmth, his energy, that I was able to recognize how lifeless my family was.

He stepped toward me, his gaze melting into mine. "What is it you want?"

I took in my surroundings. The lake sparkled with thousands of beads of sunlight. Maples towered over us, their plush leaves offering shade. Three months ago the water had been frozen and the trees a lifeless gray, everything dead and cold. God revived the wintry earth, His breath alighting spring. Could He do the same to my icy heart? Just like those white stones, I hadn't thought much about my faith lately. Maybe it was time to change that.

"I can tell you what I don't want." I angled my chin, catching the sun fully upon my face. "I never want to be like my parents."

His eyes softened. "Is that what you're afraid of?"

I nodded. "That, and you'll be miserable married to me. Especially if I become like them."

His expression turned thoughtful. "Let me ask you this. Are you like them now?"

Was I? I hardly knew.

Warren sensed my hesitation and caught my hands in his. "You're concerned about your maid's welfare. You're attentive to your sister to the point you wring your hands if you feel she's overtaxed."

Did I? I glanced down at my fingers, but they were so comfortably enclosed in his. I hadn't known him long, but his touch was soothing, confident, and somehow exactly what I needed.

"Who else cared to find an extra room so my cousin didn't have to drive back to the city after our engagement party?"

Mother wouldn't spare the staff to accommodate Terrence, so I'd slipped away during the dessert course and seen to the preparations myself. But I hadn't realized Warren knew anything about it.

"I meant what I said the other day." He dipped his face closer so I could glimpse the sincerity of his eyes. "I want you." He dropped his hands from mine so I wouldn't confuse his meaning. "As in, I want you to be *you*."

He didn't step back, so I drew nearer. If he desired the real me, I should put effort into understanding my own needs. And right now I needed to practice touching, specifically touching him. During all our interactions, Warren had been the one who'd initiated any contact. Time for me to try. I tentatively reached toward him. He stood still, his heated gaze beckoning me to continue, sending a flash of fire down my spine. I rested my hands upon his chest, a good starting point since my palms only pressed against his suit coat.

He was right. I wasn't like my parents. Nor would I ever be. But I did need to be taught how to show my affection, and who else to learn from than my fiancé? "I'm ready."

He swallowed. "To go back to the estate?"

"No." I trailed my fingers along his lapel, wandering to his strong shoulders. "I'm ready for my first lesson." My heart pounded against my ribs, my breath pinching. "You promised to teach me the difference."

The gold flecks of his eyes sparked, though he didn't move. Hunger burned in his gaze, but I knew he remained still out of gentlemanly respect, allowing me plenty of time to change my mind. His thoughtfulness only stirred my determination. I reached up, and with a shaky breath I traced my finger along his lower lip, my own skin tingling at its soft fullness.

He watched me as I touched him. Savoring the moment, I continued my exploration of his handsome face.

There was something about his jaw that had fascinated me since the day we'd met. Maybe it was its sharp curve leading to a perfectly cut chin, or perhaps how he always had it firmly set, highlighting his air of confidence. I ran my hand against his cheek, feeling a muscle flex beneath my palm, then skimmed my fingers over his jawline.

His left arm curled around my waist, keeping his other at his side. A deliberate move. He could easily crush me in a full embrace, hemming me in completely, but he held back. I could easily break free if I wished. But the only desire I had was to feel his lips against mine.

So I braced my hands against his chest, lifted on my toes, and . . . had no idea what to do next. I shuddered. What did I do with my mouth? Were my lips to be sealed tight or parted?

I'd only witnessed this type of exchange three times in my life. The first when I'd sneaked into a silent movie, but the kiss was dramatic and fuzzy. The other on Fifth Avenue as I passed an amorous couple. The last at a society ball when I'd stumbled upon Beatrice Reinholt in a darkened alcove, working her charms on a local millionaire. I'd learned nothing from those instances. And now the momentum was lost.

I risked a glance at Warren. "I . . . I don't know . . . how . . ."

His hand spanned my lower back, pressing me closer, even as his other slid behind my neck. "Mirror me," he coached. The marked tenderness in his gaze erased my fears, my embarrassment.

Shivers rocked my body. My breath patchy, I studied his mouth. Those full lips were relaxed, opened slightly. I patterned mine the same.

His head dipped lower, a slow descent, and I lifted on my toes. A nervous excitement fluttered my lashes as my eyelids drifted shut. His lips brushed mine, feathering lightly, a mere sampling taste. He kissed me again, but this time with chaste pressure, lingering and exploring before pulling away. Like any good teacher, he was easing me into this.

But I wasn't a patient student. My fingers bunched his lapels, and I pulled him back to me, pressing my mouth to his, demanding more. I felt the curve of his surprised smile, then kept my lips pliably soft as he worked over them. After several enjoyable moments, I caught on enough to give back.

Like an intimate dance, this was a progression of movements, a delicious series of give and take. His hands sinking into my hair. My arms winding around his neck. But then, as if the tempo shifted, Warren broke free from the contours of my mouth and trailed kisses along my jaw, a fiery trail down the column of my throat. I clutched him feebly, never wanting this boiling pleasure to simmer.

But Warren eased back and rested his forehead on mine. "You, Geneva Ashcroft, are a quick study."

I smiled, the haze clearing. "Only if the topic interests me." I couldn't help it. I kissed him again.

He groaned. "Let's get you home." His gaze roamed my face with an intensity I felt to my toes, contradicting his docile words. He didn't want to return to the estate any more than I did. But Warren seemed to have more self-control than I, for he twined his fingers into mine and tugged me alongside him.

● ● ●

"You're needed on the telephone, sir." Our butler Kendrick discreetly approached Warren, who sat across from me at the dinner table. He excused himself from the room, each step marked with purpose. Like everything he did.

Miss Reinholt stared with interest as Warren walked out of the dining hall. She wasn't one for subtlety. Which didn't explain why she'd left that threatening note in my room. Lilith was convinced it was her, but I wasn't as persuaded. Though I knew she was jealous of me, I couldn't help but feel a slice of pity for her. Okay, maybe just a crumb. Her parents were as domineering as mine. The Reinholts might let her have free rein over her fashion and shorn hair, but they'd gripped her matrimonial leash without mercy. As I, she had no slack given.

Warren returned within minutes, deep brackets framing his mouth as he approached Father. "I apologize, but I must return to the city. Immediately."

My fork clattered to the plate, and everyone's gaze flew my direction. "Pardon me." I'd been almost in a euphoric state since our time beside the lake, and this announcement? I struggled to keep my mood from drowning.

Warren strode to my side and caught my hand in his. "I know our wedding's soon. I hate to leave. But this can't . . ." He sighed and raked a hand through his hair. "There's something that needs my attention that cannot wait." He gripped my hand tighter, as if willing me to understand.

"Of course." I responded with an air of indifference, but my heart plummeted.

Warren cupped my face, his expression earnest. "I promise nothing will keep me from standing before the minister in two weeks."

"Don't be late." I leaned into his touch. Too bad everyone's gaze was pinned upon us, or else I would've made the goodbye more memorable, recreating our time at the lake. Warren didn't seem to have that hesitancy. He leaned and swiftly gave me a parting kiss.

A few gasps erupted, but Warren only flashed me a wolfish grin. "That's so you remember to miss me."

I swatted at his arm, and he chuckled as he exited.

Dinner resumed as if there'd been no interruptions, and I rallied to keep my mood from sinking. I glanced around this familiar scene—one I'd viewed a thousand times, but right now it seemed as if I were seeing it for the first time. All the people gilded in real gems while foisting fake smiles upon their neighbors. The food was excellent, the delicate china without flaw or chip. The conversation was the pinnacle of refinement. Everything was perfect but hollow. Gutted out. My life seemed a crystal castle filled with every grand token, though truly it was a prison of broken things. A gilded facade.

And in two weeks I would be free from all of it.

Mother caught me in her narrowed gaze. Judging by her pale complexion, as waxy as the centerpiece candles, my exchange with Warren had embarrassed her. The Ashcroft Angel had fallen out of her regimented line. Had kissed a gentleman in front of all her guests. No doubt I'd be getting a propriety lecture later. But then again . . . I leaned to the side for a clearer view of her. What if her ghostly pallor had nothing to do with my behavior?

After dinner I made my way toward Mother's bedroom. She wouldn't appreciate my prying, but it was for her own good. I crossed the plush carpet into her suite. The faint scent of her rose perfume lingered. I opened her beauty cabinet and scanned the bottles, tins, and jars overwhelming the shelves. Mother was determined to fight aging and often tried every shiny thing that hit the market. But I'd come here solely in search of—

"What are you doing?"

I spun at Mother's voice, my hand skipping to my heart. "Don't sneak up on me like that."

A dainty scowl hovered beneath disapproving eyes. "You're the one doing the sneaking."

"It's not a secret." I turned back to the open cabinet, browsing the labels. "I noticed how pale you've been lately, and I'm making certain you aren't taking those awful complexion wafers."

She placed a hand over her hip and inclined her chin. "How can I when you dumped them all in the rubbish bin?"

I most certainly had. "But that was at the town house. I completely forgot to check if you hid any here." I swept my hand in front of the shelves, earning another scowl.

"You're being silly. It's just a beauty product."

"Mother, it's harmful." I'd read articles about the suspicious ingredients, but who considered such a risk when beautiful skin was on the line?

"You want to know what's truly harmful?" She locked me in her sights, her head tilting to the right like it always did at the onset of a lecture. "Follow me." She reached past, shut the cabinet door with a haughty click, then breezed into her bedroom with an air of grace. Because even if my mother was upset, her poise would be faultless.

Before I could fully enter the room, she spread her arms in a dramatic sweep. "You're falling for him, Geneva."

I blinked. "Warren?"

She nodded. "I could see the admiration in your eyes. Then with your cooing at dinner." She placed the back of her hand across her forehead. Where Father was empty of all emotion, Mother's piled higher than the Woolworth building.

"I didn't coo."

Now those fingers pressed against her chest. "Don't make that mistake. You're too much like me."

I forced myself to inwardly acknowledge I was nothing like her. She blossomed under having the world's attention and preened at every mention of her and her famous parties in the society pages. She also turned a blind eye to whatever Father did. While she disapproved of him forcing an arranged marriage, she hadn't uttered one word in my defense. I vowed never to do that to my own children. Though I doubted Warren would be anything like my father. Warren seemed good. Loyal. The kind of gentleman who would scrape out his own heart with a dull serving spoon before hurting mine.

"He's charming, to be sure." Mother descended onto the bench at the foot of her bed like a queen onto a throne. "But they're all alike."

"No. I won't allow you to lump my fiancé into the same repulsive bog as other suitors." They had all been after my money, my family's status. Not him.

"Heed my warning and detach yourself. Don't feel anything toward him." Her eyes widened in admonition. "You'll survive married life much better that way."

As far as relationship advice, that took the medal for most discouraging. "Warren's not like that."

"Did he tell you why he was called away most urgently?"

Her cold tone made me flinch. "No."

"Kendrick said it was a woman on the other line."

"That could've been anyone. A family member even." Terrence's face flashed. Was Warren's cousin married?

She inclined her chin, as if I were the one being obtuse. "The woman obnoxiously refused to give her name when Kendrick asked."

I bit my lip. That was peculiar. But still, nothing to lose my—

"Mark my words." She sniffed. "Your fiancé has a mistress."

September 3, 1922
Stella

I BARELY RECALLED STEPPING OUT of the drugstore. Warren followed, but I couldn't look at him. My emotions were already brittle from his bombarding accusations, now only to be dealt a severe blow by his betrayal. I'd never heard of Ruth Fields, but Warren brutishly remarked that she'd come between us. What else could I think? "Are we talking about . . . a mistress?"

"Yes." Warren's frosty tone bit into me with icy jaws. "But you already knew about her, didn't you?"

Instead of growing numb, a thousand pricks of fire burned through me. How could he? My mind scrambled back to Mother's warnings. I'd dismissed every one of them, but they'd proven true. "I never wanted to believe it."

He scoffed. "I shouldn't have held any hope you wouldn't know. You're a lot of things, *Stella*, but you're not naive."

I spun on my heel and almost stabbed him in the chest with my pointed finger. "So you're mocking me?"

His cold bearing was more than I could take. He dipped his head closer. "What do you want me to do? Applaud you on the discovery? Sorry to disappoint, but I refuse to celebrate the secret you tried to kill me over."

He accused me of horrible things, ridiculed me for what I was innocent of, yet all the while bore the blame of adultery? Shouldn't he be the one who begged for forgiveness? But I couldn't detect the slightest hint of guilt in his eyes. "You think . . ." This was madness. "I'd kill over a mistress?"

Warren watched me more intently, his gaze searching mine. But he said nothing. Which in itself was an answer.

My vision blurred, and a hot tear blazed down my cheek. I dashed it away. "If that's what you think"—I folded my arms, tucking away my shaking hands—"you're free to leave me." I'd thought I could salvage the wreckage between us. Scrape together the warped fragments, but the devastation was too great. "You can take the Jenny and go fly to the arms of your mistress."

"My . . ." He flinched, his eyes stark with something I didn't have strength to examine. "Wait. Do you—"

"I defended you to my mother again and again. She insisted you were unfaithful." Another tear, but this time I let it fall. Let him glimpse the hurt he caused. Though he only stood there stock-still, blinking in rapid succession, as if *he* were the one trying to process the madness. "Maybe I'm naive after all. Because I believed every word you said in our vows."

My last sentence seemed to snap him from whatever delusion his thoughts had traveled to. I could only wince to think what he'd accuse me of next.

He held up a hand, almost in . . . surrender? "No. That isn't what I mean." He drew near. His face, like granite only a moment ago, twisted in anguish.

My fingers curled into fists. Warren never had been cruel. But now it was as if he purposefully engaged me in some sort of mind game. Well, I refused to play. "You accuse me of the unthinkable, then rub my nose in your unfaithfulness, and you expect me to be sorry for heaven knows what? I was a fool for ever trusting you." For believing he could be different from the rest of them. "Just go to your Ruth Fields and leave me alone." I rushed down the dusty walkway, willing my eyes to stop clogging with tears, ignoring the stares of the townspeople and desperately hoping the slap of boots behind me didn't belong to a man who'd just dashed my heart into splinters.

"Wait." His deep tone held a strange sense of urgency. "You've misunderstood."

Oh, this was now my fault again? I skidded to a stop. Taking a deep breath, I faced him, priming to wage battle, but the look in his eyes made the words die on my lips.

"It's only been you." His voice broke, and his hands outstretched to . . . reach for me? Then as if realizing all the brokenness between us, he dropped his arms to his sides. Nodding to a man who looked on with concern, Warren leaned in and lowered his tone. "I never had an affair. Never broke our vows."

I blinked, his words cradling my heart with fragile hope. "Then what's all this about? You said Ruth Fields is a mistress." I followed suit and kept my voice down. This wasn't a conversation to have in the middle of a sidewalk.

"Yes. But not mine." His gaze softened. "Your father's."

I went still, staring blankly at his face. He slid an arm around my back and led me to the side, allowing an older couple to pass. Relief swept through me. Warren had stayed true. He was referencing Father. Father had a mistress. I wasn't surprised. But how had Warren discovered it, and why did it hold significance to the plane crash?

He kept me curled into his side, and I glimpsed a reemergence of the man I married. Though this only heightened my confusion. I moved away from his touch, putting much-needed distance between us. "What's going on?"

"Will you take a short walk with me?"

My eyes widened. "You're not taking me to see her, are you? I can't face my father's lover. Not like this."

"I'm taking you to see her, but not the way you think." His hands cupped my shoulders in a somberness I wasn't sure I was prepared for. "I'm taking you to her grave. Ruth Fields is dead."

• • •

Warren led me down a narrow lane to a country cemetery. He kept by my side, granting me time to sort through my emotions. But I could only watch one foot walk in front of the other, without feeling.

I met his eyes and was overpowered by the concern in them. He was different now. That much was obvious. His gait was more relaxed even while my joints seemed dipped in lead. Did he finally conclude I wasn't a cold-blooded killer? Though why would he assume I would kill him over my father's mistress?

My gaze stretched across a field of headstones. Did I really want to see proof of my father's neglect, the last thread of respect for him ripped to shreds? At least now I understood why Warren had barraged me with questions about this town. He'd been testing me, gauging my knowledge of my father's lover. "I shouldn't feel anything toward my father anymore."

"It still stings though."

"Everything does." My gaze tied to his, and he caught my meaning, for he nodded solemnly.

"She was buried here, you say?"

His eyes swept the rough-hewn markers. "I believe so."

We paced the uneven rows of the dead. Sunlight danced upon us, a bright contrast to the solemness of this place. Grass grew tall, some of the stones were leaning. One in particular had crumbled into several large chunks, as if these poor souls had been tossed here and forgotten. A piece of my heart wanted to tidy up these sites. To prove that someone cared, and while I didn't know them, I knew the harrowing journey of walking through life neglected, ignored.

My eyes sought the name Ruth Fields.

Questions piled on like the dirt on a fresh grave, burying any hope I had of my parents' marriage being anything but a show. What would I learn from coming here? Would seeing this grave really bring any healing? Or more bitterness?

"There." I pointed. "Ruth Fields. September 7, 1872, to July 22,

1921." Her resting place had been marked by a thin cross, her name roughly etched into the wood. The edges were darkened with rot from the damp elements. She'd passed only last . . . Wait. I squinted at the date. "Warren, look. She died on July twenty-second. That's the day of your plane crash, only a year before."

He rubbed a hand over his jaw. "Yeah, I noticed that too."

What a peculiar concurrence. "How did she die?" Did I even want to know? I should resent this woman. Scoff at the brazenness of having a cross for a marker. But I couldn't. Staring down at her humble grave, I somehow knew she'd been a victim of my father. Used for his own want, then discarded. I knelt in the tall, dewy grass and pulled the weeds choking the marker.

Maybe she'd thought partnering with a rich man would grant her freedom from trouble, only to discover it had bound her with heavy shackles. I balled the grass in my trembling fingers and threw it aside.

A warm hand settled on my shoulder.

"How did she die?" I repeated.

He stooped beside me, eyes on her grave. "From what Brisbane said, a stomach illness."

"So natural causes?"

"Supposedly."

But that one word told me he harbored the same sickening suspicion. The instance with Mr. Yater flew to my mind. Father's business associate had claimed he'd been swindled and had turned up dead after dining with Father. He'd also died of a stomach ailment.

I took in a shaky breath. "How did you know about her? How did you even think to turn Brisbane on her trail?"

Warren stood and held out his hand to me. "An anonymous letter sent to my office."

I dusted off my fingers and accepted his help. The letter couldn't have been from Ms. Fields. She'd passed on almost a year before I'd even met Warren. "Perhaps sent by a jealous husband? Was she married?"

"No."

Another thought crashed heavily into me. "Did she have children?"

Could John Ashcroft be the father? Did I have a sibling walking this earth that I had no clue about? My head swam, and I pressed a fingertip to my temple.

"No children." He brushed a piece of grass from my sleeve. "Brisbane checked thoroughly, and there aren't any records of births or marriage certificates."

I exhaled and cast one more look upon her grave before turning away. "Someone must've known about all this if you received a letter." And what of my mother? I couldn't shake the itch that Mother had been aware. Why else had she warned me before my wedding not to become attached to Warren, to not fall in love with him? No wonder she was so hard. To have known and been able to do nothing. I suddenly grew tired.

"It's a puzzle." Warren fell into step next to me. "Though I don't think it's coincidence that Brisbane wrote this town on the list you found."

I smoothed the hair from my face. Why had Brisbane jotted this place in his notes? Had it something to do with Ms. Fields, or another reason? "There are nine other towns logged. Do you think there's a connection?" Another thought crashed into me. "What if Brisbane's disappearance is linked to what he discovered about Ruth Fields?"

He squinted against the sun, his brows flattening like they always did when deep in thought. "It's possible."

We climbed the hill leading to the main road in silence. Warren moved differently than he had since our reunion. The tense lines of his body, the stern set of his brows, and his rigid gait were now relaxed. It appeared he no longer labeled me a murderess. While his defenses had lowered, mine had raised.

He cleared his throat. "I'm sorry for everything."

His general apology halted my steps. As if he could put one bandage over a hundred wounds. "You know that word—*everything*—can be interpreted many ways, and I still can misunderstand. Sorry for what? Stepping on my frock this morning when I was packing?" I sent him a look. I couldn't care less about his dusty footprint on my dress, but I did care about his overall depth of his regret. "Sorry for coming here? About insisting on continuing this search?" I'd crammed my hurt and confusion into a tight box of self-control, which now busted at the joints, spilling all my feelings into a messy heap between us. "Sorry I found out you were alive? Sorry for marrying me? Sorry you ever met me? That I was even born?"

"No," he said, too tame a response to my wildness. "I'm not apologizing for any of that. Except maybe your dress. My actions, my words, caused damage." His gaze met mine. "I'll try to make up for what was lost."

"What if it's ruined forever?" That was the dress I'd worn when he proposed to me in my secret garden, but we both knew this went beyond just cloth and thread. He was talking about the fabric of us, the strained stitching of our relationship. The trust. The bond. Everything that was the foundation of marriage. In tattered remnants of what was once a beautiful garment.

"I pray it's not." His knuckle trailed my arm, and I tried not to respond to his touch. "I'm sorry for believing you tried to kill me."

"How could you ever?" My voice hitched, and I hated it. I was supposed to be callous. I'd known how to pretend all my life. But Warren held captive all my masks, kept them locked away and out of my reach.

He shook his head. "One reason was that I thought you knew of Ruth Fields. Before she died, she contacted your father."

My brows lowered. Judging by our recent conversation, I'd guessed my father's affair held significance, but I'd assumed the main factor behind Warren's accusation would be the parachute. Or more specifically, the lack of parachute. And how its absence had been my fault. Though he hadn't once mentioned my terrible error.

I glanced over to find him watching me, awaiting my response. "Did Ms. Fields threaten to expose him?"

"Most likely. I don't know the content of the letter. Just that she sent him something. The details were vaguely jotted in the note I got."

"And if she exposed him, she'd crush the image he so carefully constructed of our family. It would've ruined his chances in government. Think she was blackmailing him?"

"That was my theory."

I began walking again. Standing still, the weight of it all pressed onto my shoulders until I felt I was sinking into a grave. "But Father announced his plan to run last November, months after she'd passed."

"There were hints in the papers before that, including mine, suspecting his interest in the senatorial seat. He no doubt had been planning it for a while."

True. He was calculated, and I never knew his schemes until he needed me to be a part of them. Marrying Warren the major one. "I still don't see how this includes you and me."

"Your father knew I knew."

Oh. Warren, the beloved son-in-law, the prized golden boy of the newspaper world, my father's gateway to great publicity, had slid into a threat. A threat to Father's reputation and more than that. "You had Brisbane digging up information about Ms. Fields."

He nodded. "And if he uncovered anything suspicious about her death . . ."

His voice trailed off, but I didn't need the finish. I knew it. And the finish would be my father. His reputation, his career, and maybe even his life if he indeed had Ms. Fields killed. How terrible was it for a daughter to believe her father capable of murder? About as evil as it was for a husband to think so of his wife. But Father and I were worlds apart. I'd thought Warren could see such differences. That he didn't ripped open my heart.

"What's got me baffled is that when I went to your father with my suspicions, he just sat there," Warren continued. "He didn't confess or deny it. He only implied that you were aware of it and wouldn't like it if I printed anything harmful."

Of course Father would use me to his advantage. Warren had confronted Father about the affair, and in turn Father used Warren's regard for me as a weapon against him. "And you believed him without offering me a chance to defend myself?"

"We argued that night, remember? I came to you right after I spoke with him, to gain your support. But when I told you I might print something unfavorable about him, you begged me not to. Then shut me out altogether." He removed his hat and ran a hand through his hair. "But even before that, you were closed off, and I had no idea why. It was like you all of a sudden turned cold, just like . . ."

My father. Warren was right, yet also wrong. I had withdrawn from him, but not for the reason he'd assumed.

"I thought his influence had finally won you. That you'd switched to his side. You've always been fiercely protective over your family."

No doubt he was thinking of Lilith. Even my complying to all of Father's rules so easily. I guessed to an outsider it'd appear I was devoted to them. Warren had thought I was a part of a cover-up to protect my family from scandal. "So you suspected I tried to kill you based off one argument and my pensive mood?"

His gaze knotted mine. "I heard you."

My head tilted in question.

"Talking to one of your parents on the phone after we fought." His voice dipped low. "You told them you'd do whatever it takes to comply. That you'd follow through with their plan. Then the next day you never appear, but my plane's sabotaged."

Oh.

I slid my eyes closed. How things had spiraled out of control. I could only imagine how I'd sounded that night. "I was upset. Distressed. Because no one crosses Father and gets away with it. I was trying to protect you, and so I told Mother I'd try to convince you not to print anything negative. I didn't know it was about an affair. I'd never even heard of Ruth Fields. You were the only one I wanted to keep safe from Father's consequences." I met his gaze. "The plan you overheard wasn't about me sabotaging the Jenny but persuading you from smearing his name. Yes, it was wrong. I'm sorry. I shouldn't have gone behind your back, but I was scared."

He was quiet for a moment. "Scared of your father?"

I nodded but wouldn't detail further. If I accused my father of killing Mr. Yater without a shred of proof, I'd be doing exactly what I'd faulted my husband for.

Warren took a step closer. "I should've confronted you right away about the phone call, but I was still angry. I figured I'd have a cooler head come morning. But there wasn't another chance to speak with you, because you weren't at the airfield."

The morning of his plane crash. I hadn't gone because I was suffering across town. It was all a series of unfortunate circumstances that resulted in a broken marriage. "Where do we go from here?"

He checked his pocket watch and expelled a sigh. "We need to talk more, but we have less than two hours to search this place for signs of Brisbane or anything else before our show starts."

My smile was delicate, as fragile as the bond between us. "Our show?"

"Yes, Stella Starling." He swept one of my curls between his fingers, caressing the dark strands that had once been golden as the sunshine beaming on us. "Let's venture into the skies together."

Chapter 13 ————————————————————————————————

THERE WERE ONLY TEN STOREFRONTS in the small town of Hanover, and our freckle-faced advertising agent had plastered them all in flyers. If the youngster lived in the city, my husband would give him an after-school job at one of his papers. But we were a long distance away from the lights of New York City.

My brow crumpled. "I don't see a lodging place." I turned a slow circle, eyeing the buildings as if a hotel would magically appear.

He nodded. "Maybe one of the proprietors has a room for rent above their shop."

"We can ask around in the market." And maybe grab something to eat. I strode into the charming building nestled between a barbershop and an attorney's office. Warren trailed close, but I hadn't realized exactly how near until I whirled around and almost knocked into his chest.

His hands went to my elbows, steadying. His simple hold ignited fire across my body.

"I forgot. What should your name be?" My tone was conspiratorial. "You can't use your real one." I browsed the stack of newspapers by the door. As usual I was on the front page. At least it was a smaller article this time.

Warren only had to come forward and reveal he was alive for me to be removed of suspicion. But that would only place us both in grave danger. We couldn't reveal anything. Not until we figured out what had happened. Who the real culprit was. I turned the newspaper over so my face wasn't in clear view. "Do you want me to come up with your new name? I'm very creative at this sort of thing."

His lips curved in that luring way that always stole my breath. "I'm well aware—"

"There's the people of the hour!" A loud voice boomed like the start of a Hisso engine. A man, stuffed under tight suspenders and taller than the bread bin beside him, strode toward us. "Heard you brought a flying machine to our modest town."

"Sure did." Warren stripped any trace of refinement from his tone. "Are you coming out to the show today? It's in Farmer Glasgow's field."

"You two must be miracle workers gettin' that old codger to let you use his spread." He outstretched his beefy fingers. "The name's James Tutler."

I stiffened beside Warren, worried of what would spill out of his mouth. We hadn't finished discussing his part of the ruse.

Warren shook the older man's hand. "Stan Starling." He nodded at me. "And this is my wife, Stella."

A smile tickled my lips. *Stan and Stella Starling?* How Warren had said that with a neutral face, I'd never know. Because in the history of stage names, ours would rank highest for most absurd.

"Glad to have you here." Mr. Tutler leaned against the wall, as if he had all day to stand in the entrance of the market. Though there wasn't exactly a huge crush storming the door. "We don't get much entertainment round here. Except if you count the time old lady Hadley mistook her husband's gin for her gout tonic." He laughed, the bulge of his gut jiggling in tandem with each chortle.

"We heard of this place from our good friend Kent Brisbane." I spoke up for the first time. "Said the locals here would be a welcoming crowd."

"Brisbane. Brisbane." Mr. Tutler slid his thumbs under his suspenders, and I feared the extra strain would snap the frayed things in two. "I don't recall anyone by that name."

My shoulders lowered. But truly I'd be surprised if the private detective would've used his real name while investigating. "We also came here to pay our respects to an old family acquaintance. Ruth Fields. We just visited the cemetery." I still had dirt lodged beneath my fingernails from the futile effort of clearing her grave.

"Ruth Fields?" A new voice entered the conversation.

A woman half my size and three times my age approached. I inched over to include the older lady in our little circle. Her large hat covered most of her face, but I didn't need to see her eyes to glimpse the woman's view of Ruth Fields. Her tone dripped with disapproval.

She steadied a veined hand on the newspaper rack. "Rumor is she was a fallen woman. Came here to live out what was left of her days."

My lips pressed together. Would my father's name be leaked? I'd never lived in a small town, but I'd heard gossip carried like the wind. "Funny thing about rumors—sometimes they're true, and other times they hinder us from getting the entire story."

"Rightly said, darlin'." Tutler rocked on his heels, his chins dipped in hearty appreciation. "Mrs. Gibbons is our town talebearer. Flashes the title like one would a best-in-show trophy at the county fair. Just last month she had the entire community convinced the new factory that's rumored to be built is going to turn our town into a metropolis."

"Oh hush, Jimmy." She looked as if she might snatch a newspaper and smack him upside the head with it. "And it's common knowledge about Ruth. She would've been the first to confirm it—that is, if she welcomed any visitors." Mrs. Gibbons faced me with a condescending smile. "The woman stayed in her cottage like a recluse. As if she was a decrepit old lady, but she wasn't. She was actually quite striking." Her tight voice held sparks of jealousy. "But Ruth wouldn't let anyone inside her cottage except that young nurse."

"Nurse? We heard Ms. Fields was awfully ill," I supplied, trying to pour a little compassion on the woman's judging tone. But it had the reaction of kerosene to a flame.

She snorted. "Ill?"

"Ivy?" Mr. Tutler warned with little subtlety.

If the woman sniffed one more time, I'd stuff a handkerchief in her twitchy fingers.

"Ruth Fields was no more ill than I am."

"But why employ a nurse?" Warren interjected.

"Same hair color and build as Ms. Fields herself." She fussed with the lace of her sleeve. "But then again, I wouldn't want my children bearing the shame if I was such a fallen creature."

My heartbeat stalled, only to pick back up with the fury of a thousand motors. I forced my mind to stay in the lane of reason. This didn't mean anything. And if Ruth Fields indeed had a daughter, it didn't mean the child was Father's.

"All rumors." Mr. Tutler moved past us and wrapped a burly arm around the not-so-frail Ivy Gibbons.

She shoved her shoulders back. "Then why'd the young lady return several weeks back and visit Ruth's grave on the anniversary of her death? A common nurse wouldn't spare the effort." Her chin lifted, as if she'd won the conversation.

"That's impressive you can recall the day." Warren had the presence of mind to remark.

Meanwhile my mind had sputtered for any coherent thought.

"Not too hard to remember. The young woman came by the druggist, and I knew her right away when I saw her left ear. The upper lobe is folded over." Mrs. Gibbons tapped the side of her hat where her own ear would be. "Usually she hides it, but I spotted it that day."

That was a lot of information to dissect. The nurse had visited Ruth's grave a year from her death, which also happened to be the same day as Warren's plane crash. That still struck me as bizarre. Were the two incidents related somehow? How could they be? New York City was three hours from here.

"C'mon now, ma'am." The heavyset man talked to Mrs. Gibbons as if she were his grandmother. "Let's get you back to your house so you can rest before the big show tonight."

Mr. Tutler winked at me and gave Warren a comradery nod, then steered the older woman out of the market. I stared at the empty door until Warren nudged my shoulder. He motioned down an empty aisle.

After ensuring we were alone, he leaned in. "That doesn't mean what you think."

"What? That I could have another sibling?" Even saying the words made my stomach dip.

"Many women are similar in build and hair color. That doesn't prove the nurse is Ms. Fields's child. There has to be more evidence than the word of a local busybody."

He was correct, of course. I knew better than to take rumors at face value. "Well then." The only thing we could do was rise to this new challenge. "Not only will we be looking for Kent Brisbane but also for more about this nurse."

• • •

I tugged my goggles from my eyes and raised a hand, waving to the crowd. It was one of my smoothest landings yet.

Warren shifted in front of me. "Well done, Stella." Admiration danced in the golden flecks of his eyes. He'd taught me these tricks, and it was a look of approval that shot more excitement through me than a series of barrel rolls. "Though you scared me on that final loop."

He climbed out of the cockpit and helped me down, his fingers gently squeezing my waist, the sweet burn of his touch firing through me.

"I thought for certain the engine would stall," he said. His hands lingered on my sides, and I wrestled back the rising emotion. The gesture was small, seemingly inconsequential, but this was his first show of any affection since our separation. I took it all in, the sweep of his thumbs, the light pressure of his palms, the way his gaze tracked my face. My body craved more, but my heart pushed for restraint. The bruises of his accusations were still fresh.

"I . . . I was very aware of the engine and how much strain I could put on her." I stepped out of his hold. After adjusting my leather helmet, I approached the cheering audience.

My gaze scanned the masses. I didn't expect to see Kent Brisbane's face among them. I didn't know exactly what I was looking for, but I knew I couldn't give up. And now I could add a possible missing sister into the mix. What if this nurse happened to be my father's daughter? Would I feel that connection like I did with Lilith? Would this person resemble me at all? So many questions.

"Thank you! We have one more air flight for the evening, and then we'll give rides to any brave souls for two dollars a passenger."

Warren coughed beside me. Yes, that was cheap. With the price of fuel alone, we'd barely break even. But from the enamored expression on these people's faces, I knew many had never seen a flying machine, let alone ridden in one. If I could give them a memory of a lifetime, I would.

"Okay, Stan." It took Warren a long second to realize I was addressing him. "You take controls on this flight. And keep it steady for me, okay?"

His brow lowered, but then he gave a quick nod and climbed into the rear seat. With a final grin to the crowd, I moved to the front of the Jenny and spun the propeller into motion. The engine growled in response. I launched into the seat in front of Warren and sent up a quick prayer as he accelerated the plane and began an incline. We peaked at around a thousand feet.

I angled back and mouthed the reminder, *Keep it steady.* Then I climbed out of the cockpit coaming, bracing a hand on a wooden strut and stepping onto the lower wing. I climbed through the maze of struts and wires between the two wings.

The Jenny and I shared a bond. She was loyal. Sturdy. But also underestimated. When given the chance, she was able to venture past the limits everyone had set upon her.

The day was calmer than most, but cutting through the sky at this speed didn't guarantee the smooth handful of seconds needed for my stunt. But I trusted Warren. I smacked my hands against my trousers to stir feeling in my limbs. Wind pushed against my frame with a bullying force. It was either fight to keep my muscles loose or be swept away like a stiff, dead branch.

After a steadying breath, it was time to defy the opposing elements. I clamped my hands on the upper wing, and using the intersecting wires as a foothold, I climbed atop. Gripping a strut, I rose to my feet.

With my stance widened for balance, I tugged the scarf from my neck and held it high. My smile unfurled, and I swept my gaze over the spectators below, my blood roaring loud in my ears.

It was like I stood on top of the world.

As if up here, at this altitude, I was closer to the God and farther from my problems. I knew the error of that logic. God was near at all times, but there was something about journeying the skies that made me feel alive, renewed.

I braved a glance at Warren. His alarmed eyes peered at me from beneath his goggles. I'd terrified him. Not wanting to frighten him further, I watched each step on the wing and returned to the cockpit. Though I couldn't help the jolt of excitement coursing through me, as if I'd cheated death again.

He landed even smoother than I had fifteen minutes prior. The wheels rolled to a stop and strong fingers tapped my shoulder. I twisted in my seat and met his glare.

"What?" I raised my hand, acknowledging the thundering applause, then turned back to Warren.

"Was that necessary?"

"Next time I'll hang by one hand from the wingtip."

His exhale was part exasperation and part . . . affection. "What am I going to do with you, Eva?"

I should correct him for not using my stage name, but I was too overcome. He was the only person who'd ever called me Eva. And since our reunion, he hadn't once. Until now. My heart stirred with familiar longings that had begun the morning of our wedding day.

Chapter 14 ————————————————————————————

Four months earlier—May 3, 1922
Geneva

TODAY WAS MY WEDDING.

I clutched the satin sheets to my chest, the morning light edging through the damask curtains of my room. This would be the last time I'd waken in this bed. Nerves made my skin tingle, yet my heart was light. I snatched my robe and looked at the clock. Six o'clock. At noon I'd no longer be an Ashcroft.

Since our arrival in New York City, Warren had dined with us every evening, erasing any misgivings I might have had when he'd left so suddenly from the country estate.

He'd explained his press foreman had suffered a terrible accident, and the local hospital refused him care. The foreman's wife had telephoned our estate by collect, begging for Warren's assistance. My fiancé had seen to the man's recovery even though the injury hadn't occurred on the job, and he'd reimbursed Father the charges for the call. I believed him. Mother's offhand comment about him keeping a mistress burned at the edges of my mind, but I refused to fan its embers. Why would Warren invent a story like that if not true?

All week had been a flurry of activity preparing for the ceremony. Mother had been in her glory, making all the decisions, ordering everyone about, determined to make my nuptials the grandest social event of the decade.

For the hundredth time, I wished Lilith were here. I'd hated leaving her behind with Cecily at the country house, but she'd insisted, claiming she needed to regain her strength before traveling. A part of me wondered if her delay could be blamed on her upcoming meeting with Lieutenant Cameron. He was due to arrive in the city next week, and Lilith, prone to nervous spells, might have needed the extra days of quiet to gather her courage. She'd promised to be here for the wedding. While my heart knew she'd keep her word, my jittery nerves needed more convincing. I hustled to the library, knowing no one would be in this part of the house at such an early hour. Father would no doubt be awake, but he'd be in his study until breakfast. I could make the call without fear of being overheard.

Moments stretched long as I waited for the connection to the Ashcroft country manor. The gravelly voice of our butler rumbled over the speaker, and my fingers squeezed tight around the candlestick phone.

"Good morning, Kendrick." My tone pitched high. "Please tell me Lilith and Cecily are on their way here."

My words were met with stone silence.

"Kendrick?" Had we been disconnected? "Hello?" A rustling noise followed, like someone placed a hand over the receiver. What was going on? I pressed the speaker harder against my straining ear, as if it'd help clear the muffled voices.

"Miss Geneva?"

I knew that shrill voice. I'd heard it most of my life, calling me in for lessons from the garden, scolding me for pecking my lunch. A voice I wanted desperately to hear in the foyer and not on the telephone. "Cecily, why aren't you on your way here?" Would Lilith even make it in time if they left now? I glanced at the grandfather clock by the window. It'd be close, but it was possible. "Have Kendrick use the roadster. It goes faster and—"

"Lilith can't make it to your wedding."

My gut seized so fiercely I thought I would retch. The horrible realization sank in. I'd thought mostly Lilith had remained behind to avoid the wedding chaos, to emotionally prepare for meeting her beau, using a weak constitution as an excuse. "She told me it was only a spring cold." But then . . . she'd had a cold the night of the ball a few weeks back. Was Lilith sicker than she'd let on? The thought of her suffering made me crumple into the wingback chair, stretching the telephone cord taut. "I need to know. How ill is she?" I could cancel the wedding. Warren would understand that Lilith needed me. Father? Well, he'd get his way. I'd still marry, but only when my sister had fully recovered.

Cecily's whimpered cry pierced my ear. "She's not sick."

Relief began trickling through me, only to revolt back into dread. If Lilith was better, then why the distraught tone? Cecily sounded almost as if she wished my sister were ill. Because if Lilith wasn't under the weather, why wasn't she on her way to me?

"Tell me everything, Cecily."

Another cry, followed by the sound of a blowing nose. "I'm so sorry, Miss Geneva." Her voice had been so snively, it'd taken me a second to understand, but her following words spilled through the speaker with agonizing clarity.

I dropped the phone.

Lilith lied to me.

• • •

I'd wanted the first glimpse of my new home to be when Warren escorted me across the threshold as my husband. My face was to be bright with anticipation, not soggy from tears. Everything was out of focus, whether from my blurred vision or fogged mind, but I barely recollected his butler leading me through the entryway to the study.

After the telephone call with Cecily, I needed Warren, so I'd secretly asked our butler, Gregory, to drive me here. I'd hated pulling him from his duties, but I couldn't summon the family chauffeur. Those requests had to be approved by Father first.

Now stationed in front of the picture window, I folded my arms to stave off the rampant chills. But the morning sunlight streaming through the large glass pane did nothing to warm my shivering body, thaw my frigid thoughts.

My gaze roamed the space. A desk, I assumed to be Warren's, stood on the wall opposite me. A sofa and two tufted chairs huddled around a coffee table. Everything seemed the typical office furnishings, except for the brass-plated birdcage hanging on a stand beside me.

"Geneva?"

I turned at the sound of Warren's voice. He stilled his approach, taking me in. My hand went instinctively to my hair. I hadn't brushed it. Warren had never seen my hair down, and now he was getting a full glimpse of it cascading everywhere in unruly waves. And what was I even wearing? I was afraid to glance down. I couldn't remember discarding my robe and changing. But thankfully, I had. I wore a simple frock, plain and unremarkable compared to the dress I was to don in only a few hours.

Warren's long legs quickly chipped away the distance between us. "You've been crying." He opened his arms, and I blinked, unsure what to do. Just like the kiss, this was also new for me. No one had ever offered me comfort, to share my heavy burden. And Warren outstretched his arms even wider as if determined to carry it all for me.

I fell into his welcoming embrace, burying my face into his shirt, savoring the warmth of his body wrapping mine. It seemed as though he'd dressed in a hurry. His tie was crooked, and a few spots on his waistcoat weren't fully buttoned.

"I'm sorry if I woke you." But I wasn't too remorseful, because his heartbeat thudded in my ear, as soothing as it was steady. "I had to come. I had no garden."

"No garden?" He stroked my hair, running his hand the full length to my lower back.

"A place to think." I feebly rested a hand on his chest, watching it rise and fall with his rhythmic breathing. "My place where I feel safe." After what Cecily had told me, I wasn't sure of anything.

"Safe?" He tightened his hold but shifted back to peer into my face. "Why do you need to feel safe? Has someone threatened you?"

Those horrible notes flashed into my mind. I'd received another two days ago. It'd been left on the doorstep, addressed to me. The sender couldn't have been Beatrice Reinholt. She and her family were currently aboard the SS *Leviathan*, sailing to England. I had no idea who or why someone would write such alarming things.

"How'd you know?"

He dropped his hold around my waist to frame my face, his expression comfortingly adamant. "Who is it? I'll deal with them."

"I don't know." I blinked and shook my head. "No. That's not why I'm here. I mean, it's about Lilith."

His brow lowered. "Someone's threatening Lilith?"

My lungs fought for breath, the dread returning. I slid my eyes closed, willing my mouth to form the words my heart refused to believe. "I just found out." My fingers bunched his shirt, needing to grab ahold of something since everything else spiraled out of control. "My sister ran off with Lieutenant Cameron."

His hands fell away. "No. Not Paul. He wouldn't act so rashly." His jaw tightened. "Are you certain?"

I nodded, my hair sliding against my face, sticking to my damp skin. He smoothed it back, and my breath shuddered. "I telephoned her this morning. Cecily told me there was a note in the foyer. Lilith left hours ago with the lieutenant. Said she was eloping." My watery gaze snapped from somewhere on his collar to his concerned eyes. "You know the man better than me. Is he . . . honorable? He . . . He wouldn't claim to marry my sister only to use her, would he?" I hadn't even known Lieutenant Cameron had arrived in New York, let alone been seeing Lilith. I'd been under the assumption the officer intended to meet her at our Manhattan town house. It seemed he'd had other plans.

Things clicked into place. Lilith must've known. She hadn't remained behind because she'd been sick, but for a rendezvous with Lieutenant Cameron without all of us there. I'd known she'd feared

Father's reaction, but I never dreamed she'd resort to marrying in haste. If they'd even married at all.

Warren gazed down at me. "When I knew him, he treated everyone with decency and respect."

That helped a little. Though Warren hadn't seen the lieutenant since he'd gone overseas to fight. War could change a man.

"You think they're married then?" I tried to fix his buttons, but my hands were too shaky. "Or if they aren't, do you think we could recover her before she does something she'll regret? But that would mean . . ."

"Postponing our wedding." He set his hand atop mine on his waist-coat, stilling my frantic movements, keeping his tone gentle. "We'll do whatever's necessary. Your sister's safety is most important."

My lips parted in surprise. He was willing to put his plans, his future, on hold for Lilith's sake. My heart swelled with a rush of affection. Even my own parents would need persuading to postpone the wedding. I could almost see Mother fainting at her ruined plans. And I didn't need to imagine Father's displeased reaction. But even if we delayed the ceremony, how would we find the runaway couple? They could've escaped to anywhere, even as far north as Canada, considering how close it was.

"We need to discuss the first course of action." Warren took on a calculating tone, as if trying to sort out each step. "Perhaps call back Cecily and get all the information."

That probably was the best place to start. "I may have panicked and dropped the telephone earlier." After our maid had said, "Lilith ran off to marry Lieutenant Cameron." Seven words that had caused a wide scope of emotions to spin through me. Though one stood out from the rest. I couldn't quite tug free the spike of betrayal. Lilith had lied to me.

"Sir?" Warren's butler hovered near the open door.

"Come in, Jenkins." He motioned the man into the room.

"A telegram arrived for Miss Ashcroft."

My brow crumpled. "How did anyone know to reach me here?"

Jenkins handed me the telegram. "I believe it was delivered to the Ashcroft residence, and Mr. Gregory sent it here."

Oh. Our butler at the town house had been behind this. I nodded and faced Warren to explain. "Gregory dropped me off."

Jenkins excused himself from the room, even as I tore open the telegram and hastily began reading.

"It's from Lilith." My eyes greedily took in the typed letters, but my brain couldn't get past the first two lines. "She *is* married. They eloped last night." My fingers bobbled the paper, and it fluttered to the rug. My glossy eyes met Warren's. "I talked to her yesterday afternoon. She didn't breathe a word. I didn't even know Lieutenant Cameron arrived."

"Was that all she said? Maybe there's more to offer some explanation." Warren scooped up the telegram, even as I sank onto the sofa.

"'Geneva,'" he read aloud. "'Married Paul Tuesday evening. I'm so happy. Did this for me and for you.'"

I jolted, my fingers splaying on my thighs.

"'We're both free,'" he continued. "'You don't have to go through with it.'" Warren's large body stiffened, and he turned wide eyes on me. "Through with it? Does she mean marrying me?"

Warren's pained expression brought me to my feet. I should have finished reading the telegram. I was just so in shock. How could Lilith have done this? I'd thought she confided in me about everything. Now she would miss my wedding. If there was even going to be one now. I hazarded a glance at Warren. His jaw was taut, and his gaze wary.

I owed him an explanation. "There's something you should know." I took a tentative step toward him. "My father wants an alliance between us."

"I don't care what he wants." He tossed the telegram onto a side table. "It only matters what *you* want. What aren't you telling me?"

I swallowed. "Father has a role in all this. You see . . ." I sank back onto the sofa, and this time Warren joined me, his closeness a comfort. I smoothed back a lock of hair. "When he decided to run for office, he factored in every possible way to gain an advantage. A specific facet of his strategy involved me. He wanted me to marry you for—"

Warren's palpable shock froze my words. "Wait. You mean *you* didn't request a match with me?"

Of course Father would spin it that way, placing the entire blame upon the elder Ashcroft child. "Was that what you were told? That it was my hope for a marriage with you?"

He gave a solemn nod. "In a letter from your father."

My heart panged at Warren's somber face. He had wanted to marry me solely based on thinking I had been the one who wanted him. Now it made sense why Warren had acted like I had a choice that day in Father's study, because he'd thought I had.

"So none of this was your idea, and you've been roped into everything." He exhaled slowly. "I knew it seemed too good to be true. You can have your choice of any man alive."

The way Warren spoke, he meant it. He looked at me like I was some kind of treasure rather than a pawn to be tossed here and there at Father's bidding.

"I never get a choice in anything." My parents decided my wardrobe, my publicity, everything. I hadn't even picked my own wedding gown. "Father wanted me to marry someone with influence. Either with newspaper or radio."

"Newspaper, huh?" He stroked the sharp turn of his jaw, not making eye contact with me. "So it wasn't the daughter who wanted an alliance with me. It was the father. Stemming from his political hopes."

"He thinks having you as a son-in-law would give him favorable publicity."

He released a derisive snort. "I see."

"No, you don't. Because he said if I didn't marry you, I'd leave him no choice in his match for Lilith." How calm Father's face had been, speaking of my and Lilith's future as one would a business arrangement. Detached. Unfeeling.

"Who would've been Lilith's intended?"

My eyes squeezed shut. "Ralph Bumont."

Warren launched to his feet. "You're joking." He paced the floor, as if unable to remain still. "That man's three times her age. And . . ." He ran his hand through his hair, further disheveling his dark locks. "He collects mistresses like one would cuff links. The man probably has several diseases by now." He stopped and muttered something under his breath. "Sorry. I shouldn't have been vulgar."

It was nothing I hadn't said myself. Though I couldn't help but savor a sliver of relief at Warren's stance on mistresses. Ralph Bumont was a disgusting old man who probably did have diseases from all his relations with women. Where Warren had influence in the newspaper world, Mr. Bumont was a former governor. The man wielded power in the political realm. I watched the realization dawn on Warren's face, and my heart tugged his direction.

His gaze hooked mine. "It was either you marry me, or he'd force Lilith to marry Bumont? That's why in the telegram she said you were free because she married Paul."

"Lilith didn't know the full consequences." I'd shielded her from the worst of it. "But she knew I was doing this for her."

He took a long second, as if processing. Then he regarded me with a mask of politeness. "There's nothing forcing you to marry me now. You don't have to go through with it."

I hated the pain in his voice. I didn't know what Father had said to persuade Warren to want to marry me, but I did know that Warren and I were similar. He'd now feel as if he'd been used, manipulated, just as I. How much more hurt for him to realize I'd been forced into this entire thing?

I rose and moved toward him. "Lilith was right. Her rash elopement set me free."

He gave a slow nod.

"But she's also wrong."

Shadowed eyes met mine.

"Because she set me free to choose. I now have the choice myself. It's solely my decision." Not my scheming parents. Not society.

My attention fixed on the birdcage I'd spotted earlier. But there was no feathered creature inside. "The cage door is open." I reflected more to myself.

Warren followed my gaze. "It's only for decoration now. It once belonged to my grandfather."

I ran my finger along one of the thin bars.

"Geneva." His voice was husky. "I won't hold you to this." He reached his hand out, then dropped it to his side. "I won't be the one who puts you back into the cage once you found freedom. I couldn't forgive myself if you viewed a future with me as confining as life with your parents."

My heart warmed. He hadn't known me long, yet he understood me more than anyone, including Lilith. "You're different, Warren." I took the hand he stretched toward me only seconds ago. "You never cage me. You bring me into the skies." I squeezed his fingers and tugged him closer. He obeyed willingly, advancing close enough where I had to tilt my face to peer into his. "I believe with you, I could learn to fly."

His intense gaze made my breath cinch in my throat. "I won't hold you back from anything you want, Eva. If you want the skies, I will teach you how to soar them."

I blinked. Had he realized what he'd just said? Ever since Mother's tirade against the nanny who'd nicknamed me Genny, no one had dared call me anything but my full given name. Though I didn't want to point it out, lest he never say it again.

"You'd teach me to fly?" Yes, he'd mentioned this before, but I hadn't been convinced he was serious.

"My job at the base was teaching recruits to fly. But"—he eased back, putting distance between us—"you don't have to marry me to learn. I'll willingly teach you."

"You forget, Mr. Hayes. That decision is mine now." I reached up with my other hand, framing his face like he had mine only moments ago—that precious gesture when he'd told me he'd put Lilith first, for my benefit. Then as one would murmur "sweetheart" or "darling," he'd called me "Eva." As if my name was an endearment. I eased closer, and he did the same.

His mouth hovered enticingly close to mine. "And what's your choice?"

"You." I closed the gap, and our lips met. There was something different about this kiss than the one at the lake. For it was more of a sealing of our hearts, our dreams, and soon our lives. He broke away first, then decided it a bad idea, for he pressed a kiss to the corner of my mouth, teasing the edges of my lips until claiming them fully.

"I choose you too," he murmured in that deep timbre, filling my body with heat. "Today and always."

I circled my hands around his neck and stretched on my tiptoes to be closer. "Warren Hayes, will you still marry me?"

Chapter 15

STANDING IN FRONT OF YET another crowd in another small town on Brisbane's list, I was thankful we'd found decent lodgings in Hanover. Of course *decent* was a generous term for a lean-to just off Farmer Glasgow's barn. Though it had been clean. For the most part. Of course, Warren had given me the rusty cot, opting for a pallet on the floor. Only two months ago he would've been nestled beside me, his arm draping my waist, tucking me close to his solid chest.

I longed for his touch, but I wasn't sure how to bridge the gap mistrust had opened between us. It was as if we'd partnered in a dance, both uncertain of the steps, our movements off rhythm to a familiar song.

We needed to get past this somehow, but now wasn't the time. We'd stayed an extra day in Hanover to gather more information about Ruth Fields and her nurse, but nothing new surfaced. I wondered, not for the first time, if we'd been going about this all wrong. What if this list of towns had nothing to do with Brisbane's disappearance or Warren's plane crash? We could be wasting valuable time for nothing.

Well, maybe not for nothing, since Warren and I enjoyed putting on an air circus. There was something about leaving our glittered lives behind and embracing our shared love of the skies.

After a successful first half of the performance, Warren stepped forward to address the spectators. He detailed the latter part of the show about giving rides in the Jenny. He went on to explain the fee and rules, freeing me to search the crowd. For what, I had no idea. So far we hadn't learned anything helpful, and I tried not to let the disappointment surge.

I wandered farther into the flock of Deepcreek residents, skimming the various faces, smiling at little ones who gawked at me as if I were some silent film star instead of a lady with a flying machine. Perhaps I could locate the resident busybody and strike up a conversation. Fresh with purpose, I quickened my pace, but a large hand bit into my shoulder.

I faltered, the hostile hold only tightening. Wincing, I glanced up at my captor.

The man's face hardened with recognition, and my mouth went dry.

Wild eyes narrowed beneath a stern brow. "I know who you are, missy."

Dread slithered across my body. It happened. I'd been discovered. The crowd hemmed me in, hiding me from Warren's view. But I didn't dare pull my gaze from this man's hateful stare.

How foolish of me to assume a silly disguise would prevent people from recognizing me. Would he call the police? Turn me in? I tried to shirk away, but his fingers clamped harder. I held in a yelp of pain. Or of fear. I hardly knew.

"I . . . I believe you're mistaken, sir."

"I'm not. You know I'm not. Think you could hide forever?" His laugh soured with disgust. "But then again, I shouldn't expect much more from you." The man stood directly in front of me, his hair long and unkempt, but there was a savagery about him that made me squirm.

He called me a vulgar word, snapping me from my daze. My knee twitched, ready to strike. I dropped my gaze to judge the distance, and my jaw slacked. The man was missing his left leg. Now that I was more alert, I noticed a crutch wedged beneath his other shoulder.

Some of my vehemence fled. "Please remove your hand."

"Leroy." A cautious voice sounded from behind, but I was too wary to peel my eyes off my attacker. An older gentleman slid beside me, his movements slow and wary, as if approaching a wild animal. "Leave her be."

His lips curled into a snarl. "Why should I?"

"Because she's my wife." Another voice joined the fray. Warren had come. "Let her go. Now." His jaw tightened like granite, his flinty eyes glaring with controlled rage.

Relief swept through me. I'd never seen Warren so fierce.

But Leroy didn't remove his hand, and my shoulder throbbed. He scowled at Warren, then aimed his scathing glower on me. "She was my wife first, mister."

"What?" I couldn't bite back my high-pitched squeak.

"Now, now." The older man stepped closer to Leroy. "This woman isn't Missy."

"Yes, she is." Leroy's chin quivered. "She has to be. It's been four years." A sob built in his words. "It has to be her." His gaze remained unfocused, clouded almost. He clearly was disoriented, prompting my compassion.

Warren, too, seemed to catch something was amiss. "Sir?" His hand cupped Leroy's on my shoulder, and the man flinched but otherwise didn't move. "I understand the tricks the mind can play, but this woman is my wife."

"No!" His yell caused an infant's cry. "She's just hiding under all that makeup. She's my girl."

"Leroy," I said. "There are some things that can't be covered up. Listen to my voice. I'm sure you can recognize your own wife's voice. Does it sound anything close to mine?"

His brow bent.

I inclined my chin. "Now look at my face. What color eyes does Missy have?"

He stared at me for a long while. "Brown," he said at last. "Brown eyes."

I eased closer so he could peer into my very blue ones. "Mine are different."

"She's shorter than Missy." The older man latched on to my reasoning. "It's easier to get taller, Leroy. But no disguise can make a woman shrink four to five inches."

The man stifled a cry, yanking his hand from me and pressing it to his matted hair. His eyes cleared. "I'm sorry. I'm really sorry."

I took a step back with a slow nod. "It's okay." At least it would be when my pulse returned to unalarming levels.

Warren tucked me under his arm, and I nestled into him. Leroy's shoulders curled forward on a heavy exhale, and he crept away, hanging his head.

After several seconds, Warren peered down at me. "Are you all right?"

I rested my head against his chest. The warmth of his body next to mine was a much-needed comfort. "I'll be fine. Just shook me up." The crowd dispersed, and I was thankful I didn't have a few hundred pairs of eyes on me so I could collect myself. Funny, I could stand on a narrow airplane wing yet struggled composing myself when I'd thought someone had discovered my true identity.

The older gentleman faced us. "Sorry about that, folks. Leroy came back from fighting the war and was a bit shell-shocked. He returned to the States with no leg and to a home with no wife. His woman ran off with 'nother while he was away."

I frowned. Poor man. "How awful."

The older fellow grimaced. "Tore him up, it did. Leroy's never gotten over it. Some of us think he may have been gassed while overseas. He never admitted, but his moods turn so quickly. It's just—"

"We understand," Warren interjected. "The war wasn't kind to many of our men."

I thought of Lilith's husband, Lieutenant Cameron, and how he'd also lost a limb during combat. Did he have emotional struggles like Leroy? I'd only heard from my sister once since she'd eloped, but what if she was unhappy?

Warren studied me closely, and I managed a smile for his sake. He knew my nervous habit of running my index finger over my thumbnail, so I stuffed my hands into my pockets.

He brushed my hair from my forehead, trailing his fingers along my jaw to frame my face. "Are you still up for flying folks, or do you want to call it a night?"

We'd planned to leave for the next town at first light, so this might be the only chance those here in Deepcreek might have to fly. Who was I to deny them? "You know being up there soothes me more than anything."

"I know." His eyes deepened with an affection I wasn't ready for, his touch a tender contrast to the man who'd roughly handled me only moments ago. "If I could, I'd build you a castle in the sky."

I leaned into him as a response. We first needed to rebuild our marriage, but this was an encouraging start. I subtly rolled my shoulder to rid it of the aching tingle.

Warren's eyes fell to my movement. "He hurt you, didn't he?" Soon his fingers were on my body, gently massaging the sore area.

"I'll be fine. Leroy's the one who's hurting." My gaze strayed to the direction the soldier had left. "I wish there was something we could do for him."

When Warren didn't respond, I glanced up at him. He studied me with undisguised admiration. So different than the frozen glare from three days ago. "Why are you looking at me like that?"

"Because some things never change." His hand slid down my arm in a slow sweep. "You haven't changed."

I'd changed plenty. I was completely unrecognizable from the poised and polished socialite, but I understood what he meant. He was thinking of the specific instance of when he'd first heard of me, the story he'd shared with me on our wedding night. "I'm a lot different than the young girl who'd written that letter." I summoned a smile, endeavoring to lighten the mood. "Plus, the old Geneva would never have worn pants." I rubbed a hand over my thigh, pulling Warren's attention, his gaze inching slowly down my trouser-clad legs. This morning, I'd gotten an oil stain on the ones I owned and had borrowed Warren's extra pair, tacking the sides and rolling up the hems for a better fit.

"It's no secret I approve." His mouth flickered like an edge of a flame, fascinating to watch and hot to the touch.

I rolled my lips inward to keep from smiling. Because we'd had this conversation before, to which Warren had been extremely in favor of the back view. "I remember *exactly* what you approve."

"I won't deny it." His chuckle was low and husky. "Those trousers look far better on you than me."

We were easing into our old ways, and a part of me clung to the hope it brought. After the startling encounter with Leroy, it was like navigating the Jenny into an equilibrium flight, where the aircraft was linear and steady. This familiar banter was my very own equilibrium moment, reclaiming my calm. "I suppose after staring at cowhides for the past several minutes, mine's a tad better to look at."

Surprised laughter rumbled from his lips. On his last flight, Warren had no doubt used the rear flanks of cattle to judge the direction of the wind by the way their tails had swished. And with the unpredictable breeze, he'd had to employ nature's weathervanes to scrape a smooth landing. "It's a trick of the trade, Stella dear." He bent close enough to cause a shiver to race through me. "And give yourself more credit. You have one of the finest back—"

"Stan!" A blush crept up my neck, and he seemed pleased his words could still affect me. "Behave." My scold had no force behind it, which he knew given his wicked grin.

The following hours, we flew the locals around, and they loved the experience. Those precious moments in the air had bolstered my heart, lightening my spirits. We ended the show, and the crowd dispersed toward their homes. While I counted the air performance a success, we failed in finding lodging for the night. Warren had asked around and most recently stumbled into conversation with the town doctor.

"I bet if you bring your flight shows around next year," the older man said, "there'd be plenty of space for you."

This tidbit piqued our interest. "Why's that?" I asked.

"Rumor has it, a large factory plans to build just outside county line.

Folks are preparing to welcome the host of builders needed for construction. The town committee is devising plans to get funding for a modest hotel. The factory should bring a lot of jobs to our small community. We need it."

Warren and I exchanged a look before my husband nodded. "Sounds promising."

The doctor adjusted the brim of his boater. "Nothing's set in stone, mind you. But most of the residents are hopin' and a prayin' it happens. Until then, though, we don't have a place with extra rooms."

"We'll manage." Warren hooked his arm around my waist, like he'd done a hundred times over the first months of our marriage.

We bid the doctor good night and saw to securing the Jenny.

"A factory, huh?" Warren said once we were alone.

"Just like the other towns." I grabbed the rope from inside the cockpit and tossed it at him. "Think it's a coincidence?"

He tied a knot around the fencepost and cut me a quick glance. "Could be. You know how hard it is to get real estate in cities nowadays. Smart move, branching out into rural America. There's an abundance of land as well as a good supply of eager workers."

I tossed him the other rope, my own mind a webbing of tangled thoughts. I was glad these small towns would flourish, but it seemed our search shriveled dry. We'd learned nothing today and now faced an evening with no shelter, except for lying on the hard ground beneath the Jenny's wings. With a sigh I rounded the plane to help Warren secure the tail. My foot caught in a deep divot. I jutted out my hands, but nothing could prevent me from falling.

Something squishy cushioned my hit, and I curled onto my side, willing this to be a bad dream.

Warren yelled my name. My real one. I heard the swish of his long legs coming toward me and knew I should throw out a warning.

"Don't come closer," I cried, wrinkling my nose at the invading stench. I rolled onto my back, away from the fresh pile of manure, which had softened my fall but now caked my person.

He took me in, his eyes filling with concern. "Are you hurt?"

"I don't think so." I draped an arm over my forehead and accidentally flung feces at Warren. I peeked from beneath my elbow at my husband eyeing the brown glob on his white shirt with horrified curiosity. "Sorry," I offered, but my shoulders shook, then my lips quivered, until finally my laugh broke free. My head tipped away from the cow waste as my laughter emptied out of my chest, leaving my side achy and my heart lighter.

I finally glanced at Warren, who remained stone-still with an arrested look on his face. "I can't believe I've gone this long without hearing it." He crouched close, his gaze unusually soft for such an absurd moment. "I didn't realize how much I missed your laugh."

I could be catty and remind him that his awful behavior had been the reason for my lack of humor. That grief had stolen my laugh. But how could I rob either of us of the moment? His expression was that of fascination, his smile of wondrous contentment, as though he'd lost something of great worth only to find it again.

After several weighted seconds, he seemed to remember his wife was sprawled on the manure-covered ground and extended his hand. "Here, let me help you."

"Oh no," I protested. "I'm covered."

"I don't mind." He widened his stance and reached for me again.

I allowed him to pull me to my feet. My word, I stank to high heaven.

He gave me a once-over, his eyes dancing with amusement. "Let's go get you cleaned up." He retrieved our small traveling bag from the back cockpit. Due to space, we had condensed our belongings to the barest minimum.

"Last time I checked, we don't have a room. No room, no utilities."

His flash of smile made my insides melt. "I was thinking more on the lines of that pond. I'm sure you saw it when we were flying earlier."

"No." I tensed. "I can't."

His brow furrowed. "Why not?"

I shot a hesitant glance in the pond's direction. "I . . . I don't know how to swim." I'd never gotten the chance. Growing up I hadn't been allowed to swim in our lake, and I was too scared to try on my own.

"Then tonight will be your first lesson." He nodded with determination even as his eyes crinkled with . . . something a bit more mischievous. "I'll make sure you enjoy it."

Chapter 16 ———————————————————————

Four months earlier—May 3, 1922
Geneva

ON WEDNESDAY AT NOON ON the third day of May, I pledged my heart, my future, my entire life to Warren's care. He'd said his vows in a solemn, reverent tone, which proved to me in no uncertain terms that he took his commitment seriously.

He looked resplendent in his suit. Of course, most brides believed her groom to be the most handsome, but I struggled to pull my gaze from him. As per the fashion of the day, my Juliet headdress was an enormous lace contraption that I nearly yanked from my head—once on accident and twice on purpose. Unfortunately, my gown wasn't much better. If I had my choice, I would've selected a simple white frock, elegant and timeless. But Mother had insisted I wear a gown with several layers of intricate lace, making me feel like a walking doily.

But I didn't care. I'd wear a dress made of potato sacks as long as by the end of the day, I became Mrs. Hayes.

The guests were the cream of society, but with all the illustrious names in the guestbook, my favorite one was missing—Lilith's. Once Mother's initial shock over my sister's hasty marriage subsided, worry took its place. Though I suspected her anxiety was more about the nasty rumors that would no doubt arise than any concern about Lilith. Father had no reaction whatsoever. Unsurprising. He probably already had a plan to bribe the press to squash any hints of a scandal. Despite my parents' opposite responses to Lilith's elopement, they both proceeded as if my sister never existed. I could not. With the flurry of the ceremony, the feelings of betrayal remained like a bruise that only stung when my thoughts pressed upon it. And Warren was sensitive to it all. He hadn't questioned me when I fell quiet at luncheon. He merely gripped my hand when my smile faded at the empty seat beside Mother's. It was as if he'd been attuned to my every thought and feeling.

After all the fluff and fanfare finished, Warren and I returned to his town house.

His . . . empty town house.

I gave Warren a curious look. "Where's the staff?" No butler opened the door. No housekeeper, maid, or any of the help lined in the foyer to greet the newest member of the Hayes family.

"As to that." He shut the door behind us. "I gave everyone the day off and paid for them to stay at other lodgings."

No doubt the Hayeses' household employees were cozy at the Ritz-Carlton. Because that was how Warren operated. His generous heart and his thoughtful mind blended to make a wonderful man. My man.

He took my hand. "I hope that's okay? I know it's unconventional. But I wanted our first moments as husband and wife to be only us."

My smile bloomed, putting him instantly at ease. "I think it's a lovely idea. I don't suppose you're up to giving me a tour of my new home?"

He gave me his arm, and we walked up the grand staircase.

My free hand slid along the waxed banister. It was much the same layout as the Ashcroft one, but the furnishings, while nice, were somewhat outdated. I bet Warren hadn't changed a thing since his parents had passed.

He led me down the halls, showing me various rooms and tying each space to a story from his childhood. He pointed out the window nook where his mother had read to him when he was a child. The collection of old newspapers he and his father had amassed over the years. There was a spot on the hallway where Warren had once knocked a hole through while trying to help move furniture. I enjoyed listening to his warm memories, his words making this house seem more alive. I'd known he was an only child, but I hadn't realized his close relationship with his parents. From what I gathered, they'd doted on him, poured their wisdom into him, and instilled in him values. Faith had been the motivating influence in their family.

He led me to an ornately carved wooden door. "Allow me." His arm brushed mine as he leaned to turn the brass-plated knob. "This is yours, Mrs. Hayes." Pride shone in his voice as he addressed me with my new last name. Even his smile was different. Not a formal, stiff one. Nor a wolfish smirk one would expect from a man on his wedding night. But a soft, personal smile meant only for me.

We stood side by side in the corridor as I took in the space I now called my own. Just like the rest of the house, it was woefully outdated.

Warren scratched the back of his head. "I know this isn't what you're used to. But like I said beside the lake, you can change whatever you like."

"It's inviting." And it was. I couldn't have picked the colors any better. Buttery yellow paired with cream molding lent a tranquil warmness. Mother's bedroom had been bold crimson and gold, filled with lofty furniture that never felt welcoming.

I stepped inside, drawn by the ambiance of the early evening light filtering through the landscape window. My trunks, sent over earlier, stood beside a tall wardrobe. My gaze drifted to the four-poster bed. There was a canopy of cream satin with delicate stitched flowers.

"The bed's new." Warren's voice was threaded with uncertainty, as if he sifted his words before speaking. "There hasn't been one in here for as long as I could remember."

My brows lifted. "Your mother didn't sleep in this . . ." My voice faded as realization budded within me. "She stayed with your father, I take it." Warren's mother had passed more than eight years ago. I wagered this room hadn't been lived in since. My gaze drifted to a door on the opposite wall, which I suspected led to the connecting room. That must've been Warren's father's room. With the senior Hayes's passing right after the end of the Great War, that room now belonged to his son. My husband.

149

Warren's parents were considered high society, and it wasn't the norm for couples to share a room in our sphere. The upper crust were stuffed into their traditions, like I was currently crammed into my corset. Mother was adamant about having her own space, and Father his.

Warren nodded, his eyes slightly dimming. He no doubt missed his family. "My parents were inseparable."

I offered a small smile. "Sounds like they had a beautiful life." A fulfilled one. What was the point of having wealth if you sacrificed happiness? Warren's parents managed to have both and had raised an excellent son.

His hand rested on my lower back, pulling my attention to his handsome face. "There's no rush between us, Eva." His gaze flickered to the bed, then back to me. "Only this morning we considered delaying our wedding. For now, we can keep things . . . formal between us, if you'd like." His neck reddened above his collar, but his gaze pierced mine, reflecting the sincerity of his words.

I opened my mouth to respond, but something on the vanity behind him caught my eye.

I froze.

A note had been propped against the mirror. Just like the first threatening letter I'd found in my room the night of my engagement. My heart seized. "How did that get here?" My voice shaky, I pointed at the paper.

Warren followed my gaze, unaware of my struggle. "I put it there. I thought I should return it to its owner."

Its owner? My initial panic had been due to its location on the vanity. But now that I'd given the letter a thorough look, the paper was different than the others. It appeared older and had creases from being folded several times. I inhaled a calming breath. I was safe here.

"Remember during one of our early conversations, I told you I've known about you for a long while?"

I nodded, recalling that peculiar discussion with perfect clarity. He'd been teasing me about my nickname, the Ashcroft Angel, and had said he had proof I was *saintlike.*

He motioned. "This is how."

I tossed him a skeptical look, my mind trying to decipher the hints he tossed me. "You wrote a letter?"

"No." He fetched the note from the vanity. "You did."

"What?"

His smile built, pride shining in his eyes. "Your penmanship no doubt improved, but this was inked by your hand." He held it out for me. "Written thirteen years ago."

I unfolded the paper, and my eyes rounded in wonder. I knew exactly what this was but didn't understand how Warren came in ownership of it. "'Dear Publisher,'" I read aloud. "'My name is Geneva Maude Ashcroft, and I'm writing to you because I am very concerned.'" I lifted my lashes, my gaze meeting his over the edge of the letter. "I wrote this when I was ten."

"Yes."

"It's about the treatment of children on the city streets." Which Warren no doubt knew, since he was the one who gave me back the letter.

Over the years I might not have had this paper in my possession, but I'd never forgotten its contents. Or the circumstance that had prompted me to pen it to begin with. It'd been winter, and there'd been a boy, no older than eleven or twelve, manning a shoeshine station outside a barber shop. He'd been polishing a gentleman's expensive leather shoes, all the while being practically barefoot. His feet had been wrapped in parcel paper, but his toes had turned blue. I recalled he'd slipped on a patch of ice and had spilled the polish on the man's coat. The man had beaten him on the side of the head, making his ear bleed.

"A child was mistreated, and I remember people just walked right past like he had no worth. I wanted to defend him."

Warren stepped closer, his attention solely on me.

"Mother always bragged, saying when an Ashcroft spoke, people listened. So I went straight home and reported it to the paper." In the letter, I'd begged for society to uplift instead of cast down the neglected and poor, especially the children. I ended the missive with a heartfelt apology on behalf of those of my station.

I shook my head. "I thought it got lost in the mail. Or whoever read it chucked it in the rubbish bin since I was only a child."

"Your letter went straight to my father's desk." Warren stood so close, the warmth from his side pressed into me. "He had every intention of printing it but made the mistake of checking with your father first."

I groaned. "You don't have to tell me. Father forbade it."

He nodded.

A sardonic smile formed. "I remember being so filled with purpose when I wrote this." I waved the paper. "Thinking I could change the world. It shows how juvenile my thinking was. I couldn't even persuade my own father to the cause."

"You changed someone's world. Mine." Warren peered down at me, his eyes lit with an admiration that made my heart squeeze. "I was twelve at the time. I read your letter and felt convicted. You were so specific about the young boy and his shoeshine stand that I was able to locate him."

I blinked. "You did?"

"Made Father give him a job inside the mailroom so he could stay warm. Dad even paid the kid an advance so he could buy shoes." His thumb traced the curve of my jaw. "You did make a difference with your words, Geneva." He leaned in, the spice of his cologne enveloping me. "I think so. And so does Brisbane."

"Brisbane?" My brow furrowed as I tried to make the connection. "Your friend from the garden party? You let him read the letter?"

"He was the shoeshine kid."

I sucked in a breath. Brisbane? Warren's friend was once the young kid on the street that day? "His scar," I whispered to myself, then met Warren's eyes. "I knew I'd seen him before. Now I feel bad about being pert with him."

Warren laughed. "In Brisbane's eyes you truly are an angel." He slid his hand behind my neck and pressed his lips to my brow. "And in mine too. My angel." Another kiss. This time to my temple. "My Eva."

I eased back and peered up at him, my fingers tingling to touch him. So I gently cupped his perfect face. "You kept my letter all this time."

"I did." He turned into my hand and kissed the edge of my palm. "It helped me see. See people for who they really are. That everyone has value. Your four paragraphs did more for me than a hundred humanitarian books my mother shoved at me."

I set the letter down on the vanity and rested my hands against his chest.

"That's why, when I received the note from your father about your interest in me, I didn't hesitate." He nuzzled my hair even as I melted against him.

"You could have told me about this sooner."

"I wanted it to be the right time." He pressed another soft kiss to my forehead. "Speaking of timing, I promised you I wouldn't rush things between us." He took a dutiful step back, but his gaze remained hot on mine.

"Warren." I erased the distance between us. "I appreciate your noble idea, but . . ." I slid a hand down my dress. "I don't intend to live in this gaudy thing until my maid returns. No fewer than twenty buttons line my spine, all out of reach." The lace around my neck itched, and my corset was cinching my diaphragm. "Can you help me? Now, if you don't mind."

He swallowed and gave a tight nod.

I turned around and almost sighed as his warm fingers brushed the base of my neck, unclasping the several hook and eyes on my collar. While he unbuttoned me, I tugged the pins from my hair, my scalp tingling with relief as my locks skimmed my shoulders and arms.

His hands paused.

"Is there a problem?" I knew he had several more buttons to go on my waist, though I also understood how easily the lace snagged. "I don't care if it rips. Not as though I'll wear this again."

"There's no problem. I was just . . . admiring your hair." His voice was deeper than usual. He lingered for a long second, then I felt his hands on my back, finishing the unbuttoning and freeing me completely.

I turned to thank him, but my sleeves slipped down my arms, my dress lowering before I could catch it. I was still covered by my chemise, corset, and bloomers, but Warren's jaw clenched, a vein throbbing in his throat, as if he employed every fiber of his strength in gallant resistance.

"Is that all you need?" He kept his gaze molded to mine.

I nodded, but then a thought struck me. "Wait. Do you need help undressing?" As soon as that was out of my mouth, I wished it unsaid. I wasn't sure if men had assistance disrobing like us women. "I mean, I don't know anything at all about men's underthings. Or if men even wear underthings." Leave it to me to make an awkward moment even more uncomfortable. A blush climbed my neck, but Warren didn't seem to notice, because he was fascinated by a spot on the rug.

"I guarantee mine aren't half as tempting as yours." He took another step back. "Which is why I should leave you to . . . whatever you need to do."

"Oh, wait." I rushed to him, pressing my dress to my chest. "Can you unclasp my necklace? That's the last thing, I promise." I didn't realize how needy I was. Maybe it was good for me not to currently have a maid so I could understand and appreciate how much she did for me. Perhaps I could be more independent and, in the future, purchase a wardrobe I could easily slip on and off myself.

I turned and lifted my hair, giving him easier access. Within seconds I felt the brush of his fingers on my throat. Only this time there was a tremor in his hands. He undid my necklace and pressed it into my palm.

"Thank you." I set it on the vanity and returned to where he stood. Driven by gratitude and impulse, I kissed him sweetly.

His large body remained rigid, his arms pinned to his sides. I frowned. I understood he wanted to keep things formal, but he could at least kiss me back. Hadn't we already established that aspect of our relationship? When he didn't move, I kissed him again thoroughly, daring him to remain unresponsive to the pressure of my mouth against his, the feel of my fingers sinking into his hair. His head tilted so I wouldn't have to strain on my toes to reach him, but that was all the movement he seemed to allow himself.

I tipped my chin back to peer into his face. The flecks in his eyes seemed like flashes of molten gold. Their smoldering depths revealed he wanted me. But he fought against it, forcing his tightly leashed passion into the confines of gentlemanly restraint.

I marveled at this man I'd married. Warren Hayes was a powerful newspaper tycoon, yet he preserved a decade-old letter as if it were priceless. He could wrangle an aircraft into the heavens, manipulating levers and pedals, subduing the winged beast to his will. Yet he refused to place any demands upon me.

Now I understood.

I'd told him this morning I'd never been given a choice in anything. That others had determined the boundaries of my life. Since then, Warren had deferred to me. In his study he'd gifted me the freedom of choosing to marry him. And now he gave me entire control over our initial intimacy. My heart surged with affection, and my body flushed with want.

Coaxing his mouth again with mine, I tugged at his bottom lip, teasing it to open. But the man was impenetrable. "Warren."

His eyes slid shut. "I promised you."

I kissed his jaw, feeling it tighten beneath my touch. "Yes, but you're forgetting." I bunched the fabric of his shirt and pulled him flush against me. "I never agreed to that promise."

He stiffened for an excruciating second, then the tight leash of his emotions snapped. His arms crashed around me, his mouth hot on mine. He feverishly kissed me, as if his first husbandly duty was to render me dizzy with his touch. We fell into a delicious rhythm until our chests heaved for air.

I tugged at him weakly. "I have another complaint."

"And that is?" he murmured as his lips explored the soft flesh around my collarbone.

I sucked in a sharp breath in pleasure. "You didn't carry me across the threshold."

He straightened, his hands still tangled in my hair.

My gaze fused to his, even as my fingers worked his shirt buttons. "You think that one will do?" I nodded toward the connecting door to his room.

His alluring grin sent my heart pounding. "I aim to please." He scooped me up, hauling me against his chest, and carried me to his bed.

MY COURAGE DWINDLED AS I stood at the pond's edge. The whole of it wasn't exactly large. I could easily skip a stone across its surface from bank to bank. But it wasn't the length that made my heart shiver, but the depth. Also, the murky water made me question if I'd truly emerge cleaner than when I'd gone in. Which was saying something, considering I reeked like the backside of a bovine.

Warren set our bag beneath a tall maple and shrugged off his shirt. Then his undershirt. A sight I'd glimpsed many times, but still, my pulse pounded. How many times had I wakened lying across his chest, with his steady heartbeat beneath me, my fingers splayed upon his muscled abdomen? At that moment his suspenders had fallen to his sides, making his trousers sling low. Heat pooled in my stomach even as Warren caught me gawking.

His mouth hitched. "Should I?" His fingers dangerously tugged the waistband.

I shook my head, hiding my smile. "Don't come to me if leeches nestle in certain spots."

He winced. "Better leave them on." His gaze swept my fully clothed frame. "Do you need help?"

Warmth suffused my face. Since our wedding night, Warren had become quite skilled at undressing me, which had often led to other things. "No, thank you. I'm going to remain safe on the shore. But if you don't mind wetting our extra washcloth." There was thick brush to my left, which I could duck behind and give myself a sponge bath so I wouldn't be exposed to all the world. Out here in the open, anyone could happen upon us.

"What about your hair?" he challenged. "It's clumpy."

I wrinkled my nose.

"Swimming isn't hard." He folded his arms distractingly across his chest. "I've never seen you fail at anything you've set your mind to. This won't be any different."

It'd taken me all of two minutes to work up the courage to ask Warren to fly me into the skies the first day we'd met, which most would consider more dangerous than wading in a pond. "I'm scared of water," I blurted.

Warren grew quiet, his gaze on the rocky ground. "You never mentioned that before."

"I never told anyone." And I wouldn't have said anything to him but for this awkward circumstance.

His eyes lifted to mine, a curious blend of hope and tenderness in his expression. "I pray one day you'll be able to trust me again to tell me all your secrets." His gentle emphasis on the word *all* told me he referred to much more than my anxiety over swimming. "Let me jump in and test the depth."

Before I could respond, he plunged into the water. Within seconds he resurfaced, his hair in dark lines over his eyes. He tossed his head back with a grin, the weighted mood from a moment ago sinking to the bottom of the pond. "Feels good in here. Grab the soap flakes from our bag and come in."

"Too deep," I surmised. The water reached the line of his shoulders. If I jumped in, it would be over my head.

His gaze caught mine. "I'll hold you."

I took in his handsome face, rivulets of water twisting along the slopes and planes, catching on the stubble on his jaw.

"I promise not to let go."

But in a way, he'd already let go. He'd disregarded our initial encounters and every following gesture of my affection, choosing to believe I'd destroy the very life I adored. I might not have said, "I love you," but I'd never spoken those words aloud to anyone. Ever. And for good reason. Besides, I'd proven my devotion. Shown him. I'd not withheld any part of me during those first months of our marriage. I'd emptied my heart into our bond. Those quiet spaces of my soul, which no one had glimpsed but the Almighty, I'd revealed to Warren, excepting that final week before the crash. And he'd let go of all those truths to grip a devastating lie.

Though what could I say? He'd apologized and seemed repentant. I glanced at the water with a sigh of surrender. "I'll come in. But I'm keeping my underclothes on."

I made quick work peeling off my outer layers. This was by no means romantic. I was covered in cow dung and sweat, but I could feel my husband's gaze on me, most likely to ensure I wouldn't run away. Though I was tempted to.

When down to my pale-pink bloomers and lacy chemise, I rolled off my stockings and balled them up. The evening breeze traipsed over my legs, but for the most part, the September air was warm. I grabbed my vanity case from the bag and retrieved some fresh soap flakes.

The shore was dotted with rocks, so I treaded carefully so as not to slice my instep on sharp stones. Warren moved to the water's edge, reaching for me, beckoning.

My toes curled against the silty ground. "Is it cold?"

His lopsided grin would forever be my undoing. "Depends on how you define cold."

I scrunched my nose. "That's not reassuring." His arms stretched for me, and my gaze fell to his callused hands. Hands that, a few days ago, had searched my body for weapons. I forced the jarring thought from my mind, only to have others swarm at me.

I needed to get past this. "Give me a moment." I shifted my attention from my husband and lifted my eyes to the heavens, focusing on the surrounding beauty.

We had taken full advantage of the last remaining daylight hours for our air circus, and now twilight descended upon us. I took in the calming blues and purples artfully brushing the horizon in vivid strokes. We might have already concluded a show in the skies, but the Creator seemed to paint the heavens in a grander display. If God's fingerprints pressed upon the dusk, which lasted mere minutes, how much more could His touch beautify the human heart? I prayed He'd cradle mine, for it felt broken and withered. To the point I struggled trusting my husband, trusting myself.

My gaze sank to the pond. Perhaps this could be a good starting point to build from. I could rely on Warren to hold me through my fear of water, and cling to God to help me through the rest.

I inhaled a cleansing breath and crouched so Warren could reach me. Our eyes met, and I nodded. His hands slid under my arms, tugging me to him, into the water.

My yelp silenced the crickets. I gasped for breath, feeling my body temperature plunge to arctic levels. My mouth opened but couldn't form words. I hooked my arms around Warren's neck and wrapped my legs around his waist. It was all I could do not to drop the soap flakes.

"I got you." His voice was strong in my ear, but then he chuckled. "Well, it seems more that you got me."

I squeezed him tighter.

"I know it's a bit cold—"

"A bit?" I squeaked. The water's icy jaws had sunk through my undergarments, making the air in my lungs burn. His arms shifted, and I clung. As much as the pond was glacial, I was terrified of being dropped.

"Relax, darling. I was just adjusting my grip." Awareness registered in his eyes the same second it lit inside me.

This was the closest we'd been since our separation. Our faces only inches apart, the line of my body pressing into him. We might be in icy water, but his burning gaze swept over my face, a surging want darkening his eyes. Then as quickly as the fire blazed between us, he blinked and it all turned to ash, carried away by the evening breeze.

His throat worked on a swallow. "You have crud everywhere, even in your hair." He kept his focus somewhere over my shoulder, as if purposefully keeping from looking at me. "Lather up, then we can get out of here."

I opened my fist, staring at the soap flakes as if they were something foreign. My foggy brain caught up, and I attempted washing my one arm while keeping a death grip on my husband.

"Your legs are anchoring you to me," he said in a somewhat strangled tone. "You can use your upper body to scrub."

I tested his theory, barely lifting my arms from their post around his neck. When I didn't float away, I eased back slowly. He gave me an encouraging smile. I quickly ran the flakes along my skin, the soap leaving a filmy residue.

Not wanting Warren to release his hold, I washed his neck and shoulders. He lifted his arms one at a time so I could wash them as well, while keeping a firm grasp on my waist.

"Very good." Warren gave a satisfied nod. "Now you need to hold your breath."

My heart clenched. "Why?"

"Because I'm going to dip us under so you can clean your hair."

I knew it had to be done, but every part of me balked at being submerged.

"I won't let you go," he murmured against my temple. "Trust me."

My voice was a reedy whisper. "I don't know if I can." Which was the crux of it all. This wasn't about the water and his strength. This was about us. "I'm scared to trust again." And I knew he could say the same of me. I still hadn't told him where I was the morning of the accident and wasn't sure I could ever do so. "I thought you were dead. You let me grieve you for six weeks." I'd suffered nightmares that hadn't evaporated even though I'd wakened. "You could've returned to me. Ended my pain. Because not only was I . . ." My mouth slammed shut. I couldn't go there, but I could offer something else. "I had guilt on top of everything else."

His hair curled around his ears, flopping onto his forehead. A bead of water dripped from one of his locks onto my collarbone, cutting a cold path over the swell of my chest. But Warren's gaze didn't stray from my face, his voice thick with emotion. "Guilt?"

"The letter the authorities have. I told you I wrote it to Brisbane, and my words got twisted." My lower lip quivered, and it had nothing to do with the cold water. "That I was upset about our argument, but there's more."

His expression softened. "Tell me."

"The parachute." My eyes squeezed shut, and a tear leaked out. "The last time we flew together, I'd taken them from the cockpits to check the shroud lines. I read in one of your flight books they should be inspected often, and I didn't recall even checking them once." How I'd pored over those manuals, wanting to know everything I could about aviation, applying all the valuable insights within, only to commit a major mistake. "Warren, I forgot. I forgot to return the chutes."

He gathered me closer. "It's okay, love. I saw they were gone before I even took off."

"You did?" I blinked. "Why didn't you put yours back? I saw the chutes when I went to the hangar after . . . the crash."

"Because I got a new one. I finally found that Type A brand I'd wanted for the past year. Though I didn't realize I'd be testing it so quickly."

So that was how he'd survived the crash. I wrapped my arms tighter around him and buried my face in his neck. "I thought it was my fault. I couldn't bear it. I wrote that in the letter to Brisbane. Not about the parachute, but about my shame of having your blood on my hands. I was a mess. I couldn't even think straight."

He made soothing noises and whispered a kiss against my brow.

I swallowed back the lump in my throat. "I'm just glad you had that spare chute. That you're still here with me."

"I'm sorry I hurt you. That I let you grieve me when I could've come to you." A shadow swept across the ridge of his brow. "I wasn't in a good state either. My mind was poisoned against you."

I remembered our harsh words to each other the evening before his crash. I thought of the other pain I'd been experiencing that Warren knew nothing about.

"If I could go back and change things, I would, but we can only go forward from here." He rested his forehead on mine. "I'm committed to earn your trust. To be able to deserve you."

I shivered. Unsure from the water's chill or the intensity in my husband's eyes.

"As for now . . ." His lips feathered against my cheek, the stubble framing his mouth sending chills along my skin. "Let's go under water and then get out of this ice block. Wrap your legs around me tighter and hold your breath, okay?"

I nodded.

Warren counted to three. His sure grip clutching me close, he dipped us beneath the surface. My eyes pinched shut at the shock of cold, like pricks of icy needles all over my skin. I managed to vigorously scratch my scalp, freeing the debris from my hair.

He brought us up, and I scraped in a patchy breath. Both of us dripping, he gently eased to the bank and hoisted me onto land.

He climbed up beside me, his gaze stalling on my wet form. My chemise was practically transparent and clinging to me like a second skin.

His throat bobbed. "Eva, I want—"

"Hullo there!" A loud voice made me jump. "Starlings, you around? Farmer Jay thought you wandered over here."

Warren muttered something under his breath and launched to his feet. He helped me stand as well.

"No one can see me like this." I glanced down at my drenched body.

"I'll go see who it is and what they want." He grabbed his shirt, hanging over a branch, and in a fluid motion, tugged it on. His wet trousers were no doubt uncomfortable, but he didn't take the time to change them.

I snatched fresh clothes from the bag and skittered behind the tall brush. Confident Warren would keep any strangers from coming near me, I hurried to dress. I trembled all over. Was it lingering shock from the icy water or the residual awareness from my husband's scorching gaze at the pond's edge? How his dark eyes had lit with desire?

By the time I walked into the clearing, I found Warren with the older gentleman who'd intervened earlier during my confrontation with the soldier.

"Mr. Harrison has an extra room for us," Warren explained as I approached.

"Has a separate shower and everything." The man's mouth quivered at the edges. "Though it looks like you two already took care of that."

Warren cast me a quick look, then addressed Mr. Harrison. "We'd like to pay you for the hospitality."

"No need." He waved us off. "After your generous understanding with Leroy, the missus and I refuse to accept anything."

"That's very kind of you." I smiled. The country was beginning to grow on me. "Is Leroy a relation of yours?"

"No, ma'am." He removed his straw hat and turned it in his knobby hands. "Leroy's family was once our neighbors. Known him since he was a youngster. We're such a close-knit community. We take care of our own around here."

"That's a beautiful thought." So unlike the glittering sphere we'd left.

We followed Mr. Harrison to a separate lodging behind his ranch. According to the older man, they'd built it for his parents to move into, but his father had refused to leave his homestead in Wyoming. The place was a charming one-bedroom cabin. Modestly furnished but lacking no comfort. Well, except for electricity.

The older man left us. Warren trimmed the wick and lit the lantern, giving the room a cozy glow. There was a sofa, two armchairs in the main space, and a wrought iron bed through the doorway by the kitchen.

With a gentle smile, Warren kissed my forehead. "Sweet dreams, dear Stella."

"Actually, Stan"—I bit my lip—"I was thinking the bed is large enough for both of us."

He froze.

"That is . . ." I was flustered by his response. "I mean, you don't have to. It's just the bed seems more comfortable."

Warren moved closer, my heart quickening with his every step toward me.

I wasn't just inviting him to sleep beside me. We both knew that. Would intimacy only confuse things between us or bring us together? In all my years of reading etiquette books, I'd learned how to properly hold a spoon, pour tea, and officiate a societal function. But nowhere within all those pages had it discussed how to repair relationships.

He took my hand and brushed his lips over the inside of my wrist. "I can't."

My heart curled in on itself. After how his thirsty gaze had drunk me in at the pond, I hadn't expected a rejection. As much as his refusal stung, a part of me softened with relief. My emotions had been thin these past few hours, and I wasn't certain if I could truly surrender . . . everything yet. But I'd been willing to try.

Keeping his eyes on mine, he gave my arm an affectionate squeeze, then turned to check the door. I watched him close the windows and latch them.

He glanced over his shoulder at me. "Sorry if this makes the room stuffy. But I'm more comfortable with everything locked." His eyes darkened with a grimace. "Just in case our friend Leroy decides you're his runaway wife again."

My shoulder tingled, as if to remind me of the incident. "I feel bad for him. He'd lost so much. Even his own faculties."

Warren nodded. "The war stole a lot from our men."

"I can't help but think of Lieutenant Cameron." Just as Leroy had forfeited a leg in battle, my sister's husband had lost an arm. But so much more had been taken. "What he must've seen and all he's lost."

"Paul faced hardship growing up. But still smiled through it."

I trimmed an oil lamp to take with me into the bedroom. "I think that smile is what Lilith fell for. She was always a fool for dimples."

Warren stiffened.

I lit the wick and shook out the match, barely refraining from rolling my eyes. "I wasn't saying *I* preferred men with dimples, only that Lilith—"

"Paul doesn't have dimples."

My brow furrowed. "Of course he does. Two deep ones." Something I remembered clearly from his photograph.

Warren shook his head. "A man just doesn't grow dimples."

I lowered onto the sofa, afraid to ask but more afraid not to. "What are you saying?"

"Describe him to me." He claimed the seat beside me, setting a hand on my jiggling knee.

I closed my eyes, imagining the sepia-toned picture. "Well, he has light-colored hair and dark-brown eyes."

Warren nodded. "Anything else stand out to you?"

"No. Why?"

"You didn't mention his freckles."

"Because he doesn't have any." I eyed my husband. "What's going on?"

Warren peered at me, his jaw tight. "Your sister didn't marry Lieutenant Paul Cameron."

Chapter 18

I WOKE WITH A SCREAM choked in my throat, my heart pounding even as I was pinned to the mattress. My eyes popped open, my rapid gasps easing as I took in the tiny bedroom.

"You're safe, darling." Warren's deep drawl soothed into my ear. His arm anchored over my waist. His warm chest pressed into my back, his rhythmic breathing a steady metronome to my racing pulse.

My eyes slid shut.

My husband wasn't consumed by death. He was with me. I had no idea how he'd come to be beside me in the bed, but I was grateful. I'd foolishly thought since Warren was alive, the nightmares would end. That I'd no longer be tormented in the dark, but the shadows had returned last night, thrashing my peace.

"You're here." I rolled over, facing him.

He withdrew his arm, his hooded gaze moving over me. "I am."

"But . . . I thought you didn't want to join me."

"You thought I didn't *want* to?" His chest rumbled with a groan, and he flopped onto his back, blinking at the ceiling. "Eva, it's not a matter of me not wanting you. Believe me, I want to be with you more than anything." His head lolled my direction, and he peered at me from beneath his dark lashes. "But I broke your trust. Last night in the pond, I saw the pain in your eyes."

I bit my quivering lip. His gaze dropped to my mouth.

"Man alive. This isn't easy." He stacked his hands behind his head, as if trapping them would prevent him from reaching for me. "But it's right. We get a second chance to rebuild our marriage, and I don't want to mess things up. I want you to trust me again." His fierce stare aimed at the ceiling. "Trust me to be the husband you need. Trust me with your heart. Trust me with your body." His own body was rigid, as if his control was so tightly coiled my touch might snap it. "Trust me with your secrets."

Oh.

"But I won't pressure you." He swallowed. "I'll be here when you're ready to talk."

"What if I'm never ready?" Shame sank into me with deep fangs. I couldn't even face it myself.

"The Geneva Hayes I love never cowered from anyone, including herself."

My breath thinned. He'd said *love*. I didn't even know if he realized it. My heart begged me to spill everything, but my mind knew better. "How is it that you came to be here?" I patted the space between us.

"You screamed my name. I thought you were in danger." His voice gentled. "Thankfully, you left the door unlocked. But I was ready to rip it off the hinges to get to you. You were—"

"Having a nightmare."

"Yeah."

"I dreamed you were dying again," I said softly.

Concern marred his brow. "Do you get them often?"

"At first it was every night. But now only here and there."

"Maybe your distress about Lilith caused it."

That was possible. Warren had suggested we discuss the situation about Lieutenant Cameron after a good night's rest, but it'd taken me a while to fall asleep. If Warren was persuaded that Lilith's husband was an imposter, how could I simply doze in blissful slumber?

"What should we do?"

He leaned on his side, propping on his bent elbow. "Confront him as soon as we can."

What if Warren was mistaken? As a publisher of several newspapers, he'd encountered numerous people over the years. One face could easily blend into another. "Are you certain he's not the same man?" My foot brushed his, and I kept it against him, needing the comfort of a simple touch.

His gaze dipped to our tangled feet and then to me. "One look at him and I'll know."

But by addressing this matter, another one would arise. "If we go to Lilith, then our cover's blown. My family will know about us. About you, I mean, being alive. We haven't solved anything about the plane crash." And I wasn't sure we ever would. These past two towns had been disappointing as far as gaining any information. We had uncovered that bit about Ruth Fields potentially having a daughter. But nothing regarding Brisbane's disappearance or any clue pertaining to Warren's plane crash. Or the person who'd caused it.

"Maybe this is the lead we've been looking for?"

I furrowed my brows.

"When you learned I knew Lieutenant Cameron, you told Lilith, right?"

"Of course."

"Did she write to this man about it?"

Had she? I closed my eyes, searching my memory. I imagined she would mention that in her letters, considering how happy she'd been to discover Warren had known Lieutenant Cameron. Though I couldn't recall her ever saying so. "I'm not certain."

Warren scratched his stubble. I'd never seen him go this long without shaving, but I wouldn't dare complain. The bristle along his jaw was a great facet of his disguise. And while a beard was considered unfashionable, I found it immensely attractive.

He caught me watching and dropped his hand. "Suppose Lilith told this man I knew Lieutenant Cameron. He'd have no choice than to convince her to run off with him."

"Because if Lilith introduced him to us, you'd know he wasn't the real lieutenant."

Warren sat up. "This guy would *also* realize he can't keep his wife from her family forever, so what does he do?"

I grabbed on to his logic. "He tries to get rid of the only person who can expose him." It all made sense. "But if this man doesn't think twice about killing . . ." My heart squeezed. "Lilith could be in danger."

Warren nodded gravely. "That's why I suggest we go as soon as possible. Do you know where she's staying?"

"I kept her letter in my Bible." I moved to our bag, which needed tidying up. Two people living out of one canvas sack wasn't easy. I dug my hand to the bottom, searching for my travel Bible, which was only the New Testament. Warren's waistcoat spilled out.

I was about to offer an apology, but something seized my focus.

The bedframe squeaked, followed by Warren's footsteps. But I couldn't peel my gaze from the floor. Because right beside his rumpled waistcoat lay a white pebble.

I scooped it up. "Is this . . ." I turned to show it to Warren, who was now very close.

"Your stone from heaven." His face softened. "I pocketed it that day by your family's lake when we shared—"

"Our first kiss." I squeezed it, wishing I could return to that day. "You kept it all this time?"

He nodded.

"You thought I tried to harm you. Yet you still held on to it?" My husband was a walking contradiction. He'd assumed the worst of me yet carried my token.

His hands came to my shoulders. "I was angry. Hurt. For a while there wasn't a reasonable thought in my head." His voice was hoarse with emotion. "But love isn't like a faucet. I can't shut it off at will."

My heart soared, giving me a high that not even a turn in the Jenny could rival.

"I never stopped loving you. Doubt I ever could."

My eyes slammed shut, damming the flood of tears. I laid my head on his chest, his heart pounding a love song just for me.

He pulled back and cupped my face. "I didn't confess my feelings to rush yours." There was a sheen over those beautiful eyes. "I realize now what I couldn't understand then. You have a difficult time expressing what's in there." He tapped my heart. "But until you do say those words, I fully intend to carry out our agreement." His head bent close to mine. "I'm a man of my word, Mrs. Hayes."

Warmth spreading to my toes, I recalled the first time Warren had declared his love for me. At the time it'd thrown me because I hadn't been prepared, but he'd only sweetened the moment by drawing up an unofficial agreement between us. Warren vowed that the moment I'd say aloud "I love you," he'd seal my declaration with a passionate kiss. And no doubt more.

Speaking of kisses, Warren lightly pressed his lips to my forehead and then drew back. "Now about Lilith's letter."

Oh, right. We hadn't the time to dally when my sister could be in serious trouble. I retrieved my Bible and slid the folded envelope from its pages. "This is the only one I have."

Since the telegram on my wedding day, Lilith hadn't contacted me until she saw in the papers about Warren's accident. I withdrew the letter from the envelope and scanned her feminine script. "There's not much here." Almost nothing about her and the could-be-imposter husband. It was mostly her condolences and her heartfelt wish to be near me. Was this a plea that I'd missed? I'd been so consumed in grief I hadn't pored over her letter like I should've.

"What if this is a cry for help?" I handed the page and envelope to Warren.

He read over her words. "It's hard to tell from only a few sentences."

This was my fault. I hadn't even written her back. I could hardly breathe during those days.

"This return address." The envelope crinkled in his hand. "I recognize the town." He stooped to get our map from the bag, along with Brisbane's list.

He motioned me to the bed and spread everything onto the mattress. "Look." His index finger tapped a spot on mid-upper New York. "Glenfield. And it's close to here." He pointed at a name I recognized—Turnberry. It was the last town on Brisbane's list. "We could rearrange our itinerary. Hit Turnberry next and stop at Glenfield beforehand."

Doubt crept in. "Lilith might not still be there."

"It's worth a shot, though, don't you think?" He eyed the map again. "Especially considering how close your sister was to one of Brisbane's towns."

"Do you really think this man was behind your crash?" I tried to think of a connection between Brisbane's list and Lieutenant Cameron, but all that dominated my mind was dread. My sister was at the mercy of a man who might have lied to her and who knew what else.

"We'll find out soon enough." He gave my shoulders an affectionate squeeze.

Two things bothered me excessively—one, the fact that my dear sister could be in danger. The other, if this man was an imposter, then what happened to the real Lieutenant Cameron?

Three months earlier—May 24, 1922
Geneva

WARREN SURPRISED ME WITH A kiss on my cheek as I sat at the table for breakfast. I thought he'd still be at his office. In fact, that was where he'd been when I'd awoken. I'd learned rather quickly that publishers worked all different sets of hours, and the job was quite demanding. We hadn't taken a wedding trip because Warren had spent so much time away for my family's house party in the country.

"Hot off the press." He set the morning edition of today's newspaper in front of me.

An enormous picture of my father's face looking uncharacteristically friendly was enough to ruin my breakfast. My hand went limp, the toast I held suspending dangerously above my coffee.

Warren noticed and slid my mug to the left. "He insisted on being featured today. And as a dutiful son-in-law, I obliged."

Were there traces of disdain in his voice? Or was it bleeding into my ears from my own thoughts? I had heard Father's plan for running for office over the past year. Yet seeing it in black and white caused a burn in my chest.

"As always, he got what he wanted." What he'd been willing to trade his daughter for. But I hated that he was using my husband for his own political advancement. I realized a candidate must get their name out while campaigning, and Father's was in big, bold letters.

Ashcroft Hopeful of Party Nomination

My gaze drifted to Warren. He watched me intently. Over the past three weeks of our marriage, I'd wondered what that specific look meant. It seemed he had somewhat of a mechanic's brain that examined things from every angle, as if configuring how the object of their focus worked. When he looked at me that way, I felt like he was peering into my being and trying to figure me out.

"Are you up for another flying lesson?" He claimed the seat beside me and reached for a piece of toast.

My mood lifted. Warren had kept his promise and had been teaching me how to fly the Jenny. He'd covered takeoff to landing and everything in between. He'd even taught me how to manipulate a parachute in case of an emergency. "You know I'm always in favor of that, but aren't you going back to work?"

"My meeting got canceled. And I finished up early." He slathered butter on his toast and sent a smile my way. "I've been enjoying our lessons. It's just the two of us and the sky."

I beamed at him in return. "I've enjoyed them too." I also had learned a great deal. Warren believed I'd be able to fly solo at the controls soon.

Jenkins appeared in the doorway. "Mr. Ashcroft is here, sir."

My jaw slacked. Father? Here? "Why?" I blurted, as if our butler would know the reason.

"An audience with Mr. Hayes, madam," he responded.

I turned to Warren. "Was this planned?"

He shook his head and took a long swig of his coffee. "I'm as surprised as you are."

But I was more than surprised. My insides twisted. These beginning days of our marriage, I'd purposed to make this new house my home. Warren had supported everything from my menu changes to granting me access to redecorate rooms. But more than that, I'd felt safe. We'd been growing closer, and I'd been trying my best to be the wife he needed. Not a rich socialite stuck in her ways. I didn't want to give him any reason to return me to my parents.

"He's in the parlor, sir."

"Thank you, Jenkins." Warren set his mug down and pushed back his chair. "You don't have to join me." He must've read the apprehension on my face.

I hadn't seen Father since the wedding. Nor any other Ashcroft. I hadn't even heard from Lilith since the telegram on my wedding day. And Mother seemed occupied soaking in all the attention my marriage had brought her, while simultaneously striving to quiet any rumors about my sister's hasty elopement.

Warren waited patiently for my response.

"I'll join you. Father's not one to visit. He makes people come to him. You must've impressed him." I smiled at him, though I couldn't quite get my heart behind it. Winning Father's approval always came at a price. Yet Warren was also a businessman. Maybe he knew how to handle Father without losing too much of himself.

He extended his hand to help me out of my chair. "The only person I want to impress is you."

"I'm not nearly as hard to please as my father."

"But you're the one I love."

I stilled, hunching halfway between sitting and standing. And I just stayed there, as if my body had locked. Everything in me petrified stiff at his casual declaration. But there was nothing casual about it. He'd said he loved me.

A warm hand settled on my back as I straightened, and Warren drew close. "I didn't mean to scare you." His words were tender, soft, and encompassing, like a summer breeze. So then why was there an icy draft whipping through my soul? Had my parents' coldness ruined me forever?

Our eyes met, and there was no harshness in his brown depths, only affection.

"I . . . I just need some more time."

"Understandable." He nodded. "But now that I've said it, I won't take it back. I love you, Eva."

Why did this hurt? My heart shouldn't be gripped with fear at hearing my husband's beautiful remarks. But the fault wasn't his. It was mine. I'd been terrified of love my entire life, dreading I was incapable of it.

"Every moment with you has been a gift." His hand soothed along my back. In the hushed dark hours, he'd mapped out my body with those fingers, but this simple caress was just as intimate.

I nodded along dumbly.

"Touching you, holding you each night is something I'll never lose the wonder of. But it's more than that. I want our hearts to be just as tangled as our bodies. To be one, as the Scriptures say."

I'd teased him once that he could be a poet, so skilled he was with expressing his thoughts. But this anxiety had lived with me longer than he had. It would take more than a flick of my will to dislodge it.

His hands sank into my hair, which tugged my small smile. My parents had never allowed me to wear my hair down as I'd always wanted, but Warren more than encouraged me to do so.

He nuzzled my cheek. "I'll wait as long as you need. I won't rush you to say 'I love you.' Just know this, Eva Hayes." His lips were like fire on the soft flesh beneath my ear. "When you say those words, I'm going to show you exactly how welcome they are."

All my skin ignited with his promise. "With a kiss?"

His grin grew slow. "Yes, and much more." He then took his time convincing me of the benefits of this new agreement between us. "Is it a deal?" He spoke against my lips.

"Yes." My voice was so breathy, it hardly sounded like me.

"Good." He took my hand and shook it like it was a genuine business transaction. "I'm thinking this is the best set of terms I've ever negotiated."

I feebly slapped his arm, but I secretly agreed. He assured me of his patience, and in time I believed God could help me learn to love. To say the words that'd never escaped my mouth.

"Let's go see what Mr. Ashcroft has to say, then we'll go fly."

Father. Right. I could endure his coldness for a few minutes if it meant climbing into the cockpit for a longer while.

We entered the parlor, which had been the first project I'd tackled. Since this was where we received most guests, I'd thought this space should be paid attention to above the others. Sunlight streamed in the large picture window, bringing out the elegant designs on the cream tufted sofa. The newly papered walls were also cream with sage-green paisley, giving the room a warm, welcoming sense.

"Mr. Ashcroft," Warren said upon entering the room. "To what do we owe the pleasure?"

"Hello, Father," I said, my voice slinking back to the reserved tone I hated.

"Warren. Geneva." He abandoned his spot at the large window. "It's a fine day," he said, with no emotion whatsoever.

"Indeed." Warren clasped his hands behind his back with a nod.

Father moved to the sofa and sat directly in the center, forcing Warren and me to sit separately on the wingback chairs. I mentally noted to purchase a settee, considering there was plenty of space for one.

"How's Lilith?" I asked. "Have you heard anything?"

"Why should I?" was all Father responded. "She's made her choice." He spoke every word evenly, his face neutral, but there was a chilly undertone. Lilith had embarrassed Father. Society columns had bred lies that Lilith was carrying the officer's child, hence the elopement. Such words made my temper rise, but they couldn't be avoided. Even Warren, with all his pull in the newspaper world, couldn't control what other editions printed about her. Maybe that was the reason behind Father's visit.

"I saw the article this morning." Father dismissed me and set his gaze upon Warren. "I thought now would be an opportune time to discuss our plan."

"Plan, sir?" Warren leaned forward in his seat.

"Yes, publicity plan. I need to be mentioned in your papers at least three times a week. I understand they can't all be front page or above the fold. But good placement nonetheless. I'll have my secretary give you what I want to be printed."

Warren took his time responding. "As your son-in-law, I'll support your efforts and help with your campaign. But as a publisher, I can't guarantee prime coverage."

"Of course you can."

"Then let me rephrase. I will not guarantee prime coverage."

I blinked. What was Warren saying? Was he refusing Father's plan?

"The article spaces in my paper," Warren continued, as if the room's air hadn't thinned to suffocating levels, "are not for your personal advertisements. I'll run the ads you've purchased. But as far as articles are concerned, I can't give you more than other candidates."

Warren was so different here. He wasn't harsh. His words weren't clipped. But he most certainly had a tone that offered no rebuttal. Only this tone was directed at Father, who never had his way challenged. Not like this.

"I advise you to reconsider." Father never threatened. That wasn't his way. But I knew danger lurked beneath his mask of indifference. He stood and gave a brisk nod. "I'm due to a conference soon." His determined steps took him out of the room.

Warren abandoned his chair and strode toward me, whisking up my hands in his. "I hope I didn't make you angry. Your father expects me to give him privileges that go beyond familial courtesy."

Unease snaked through me. Warren was right to confront Father, but I dreaded the consequence. "I thought that was in the contract."

"What contract?"

"Our marriage one."

Warren looked confused. "There wasn't a marriage contract."

Wait. What? "I thought it was understood that if we married, Father would give you a discount on paper or some kind of funding. And you'd give him free rein of coverage in your papers."

Warren's brows lifted when I'd said free rein. "There was no such thing."

Had Father just assumed that would happen? Why had he pushed this wedding if there was no formal agreement between them? Father wouldn't bank everything on a hunch, would he? A more alarming thought rose to the front of my mind. Was there something else Father was scheming? I thought of Mr. Yater—the man who'd crossed father in business a few months ago.

The man who'd turned up dead.

• • •

Warren had taken me flying, which had been precisely what I needed to clear my thoughts after Father's visit. By the time we returned to the town house, Jenkins informed us we had yet another guest.

Kent Brisbane waited in Warren's study. I rushed upstairs to change into something more acceptable than my husband's dusty trousers. Iris was in my room, hanging some freshly laundered gowns in my armoire. I held no guilt about swiping the young woman from my parents' employ. It'd had an immediate positive effect on her.

"Hello, Iris," I said upon entering and striding straight toward my vanity.

The maid lurched back, pressing a hand over her heart, the white ribbon on her mobcap waving with the movement, as if a flag of surrender. Apparently, poor Iris hadn't quite overcome her jumpiness. "Sorry, madam."

I smiled gently. "No apology needed." I lowered onto the bench and reached for my hairbrush. "And I know my mother was emphatic about the maids wearing mobcaps, but you don't have to wear one here."

She gawked at me as if I'd told her a salacious secret. "It's not a problem, Mrs. Hayes. I prefer wearing one."

Her answer surprised me. Most young women resented the old-fashioned headwear. "I'm glad you're here, Iris. I need to change rather quickly. Do you mind fetching me a frock? Any will do."

She scurried into my large closet and retrieved a dress. I smelled of the fresh outdoors, and truth be told, like Warren's shaving soap. He'd enjoyed showing me how pleased he was with my progress. I dabbed some fragrance on my neck and frowned at my hair. The wind had whipped whatever wasn't crammed beneath the leather helmet. Wincing, I pulled the brush through the knots while Iris gathered my underthings and stockings.

Within minutes I stood before Warren's study. Masculine voices sounded from within, but something in their tones stopped me from crossing the threshold. By their hushed voices, it was evident the conversation was serious.

"Are you certain it was her?" Warren.

"I saw her grave marker. She passed just under a year ago from a stomach illness. But the rumors are true nonetheless. It was her." The smooth voice no doubt belonged to Kent Brisbane.

Rumors? I knew from Warren that his friend was a detective. He sounded businesslike. Almost as if giving Warren a report. Perhaps he was. With Warren in the newspaper business, I was certain he had to fact-check stories before printing them. But wouldn't that be a journalist's job? An editor's? I had no idea about the inner workings of the industry. But I knew better than to eavesdrop on my own husband.

I stepped inside the study, and both men glanced over, standing on ceremony.

Warren's smile flashed, and he strode across the room. "I thought you'd be longer, considering how dusty the airfield was today." He brushed a kiss on my cheek.

Mr. Brisbane shook his head. "You make it seem like your wife needs ages to be presentable. Unkind of you, old man." His eyes twinkled in jest. "Good afternoon." He nodded at me with a smile.

I hadn't spoken to Kent Brisbane since the garden party. He'd attended our wedding, but with all the chaos with Lilith and busy moments of the day, I hardly remembered who I'd spoken to. This was the first time I'd set eyes on Warren's friend since discovering he'd been the shoe shiner who'd inspired my heartfelt letter to the newspaper.

"You mistake me, Brisbane." Had Warren's eyes narrowed? "I was simply telling Mrs. Hayes how pleased I am to see her so soon." His hand slipping around my waist, he led me to the sofa.

"As am I," he inserted smoothly. "How are you today?"

"Very well." The gentlemen waited for me to claim a seat on the sofa, then they were seated, Warren beside me and Mr. Brisbane across from us in a tufted chair. "What brings you by today, Mr. Brisbane?"

He smiled. "Please call me Kent."

It may be my suspicious nature, but it seemed he'd just poured on the charm, requesting me to address him by his given name to maneuver around my question about his visit. The man had an easy friendliness about him, and with his dark hair and smoky gray eyes, I was sure he had an ample share of admirers. Though all my admiration was directed at my husband. In my newly married bliss, I struggled finding any male even half as handsome as the man I called mine.

"Warren tells me you went flying today."

"We did." I smoothed a wrinkle on my lap. "I learned about the importance of wheel chocks and the safety of cranking." This morning had been the first time Warren had allowed me to crank the propeller. The speed at which those blades moved was terrifying yet awe-inspiring.

Warren chuckled beside me. "Mrs. Hayes is a fast learner. She'll be behind the controls in no time."

His words warmed me.

"I don't doubt it." Kent relaxed against the cushions. "Though I could only imagine the headline." He made an exaggerated sweep of his hand. "Ashcroft Angel Soars the Heavens."

That ridiculous name. Which wasn't even mine anymore. Perhaps over time it would fade away.

"Are you hungry?" Warren turned to me. "A tray should be here soon, along with something for us to drink."

My smile bloomed. I was once again impressed by Warren's thoughtfulness. I was in need of a drink. The dusty air had coated my throat and mouth, and I'd been in a rush since the moment we'd returned, which only intensified my thirst. I shifted to face Kent. "I remember from before that you are a private investigator?"

"I am." He shot a look to Warren and then back to me. "Started my own agency two years ago."

I nodded. "Perhaps you could solve a bit of mystery for me?"

His brows lifted slightly. "I'll do what I can to help. What sort of mystery?"

Of course, I could bring up the threatening letters, but I hadn't yet told Warren. I hadn't received a note in just over three weeks, since before relocating to my new residence. Perhaps now that I'd left the Ashcroft household, that was all behind me now. Why cause unnecessary attention to something as silly as a foolish prank? "I was wondering if you could tell me why my husband is calling me Mrs. Hayes every other breath."

The corners of his lips bounced like a flapper's heels on Saturday night. "I suppose Warren is trying to not so subtly remind me that you are indeed his wife."

"Correct deduction, Brisbane." Warren settled beside me again. "It's no secret the admiration you hold for the ladies."

Kent nodded, accepting rather than debating Warren's words. "And he also knows I have a special regard for you." Then his face softened. "Thank you for all you did for me, Mrs. Hayes." Of all the things he'd said, this was the sincerest. "I don't know where I'd be without your kindness."

"I was just a child," I reminded him, before he painted me a saint.

"One that had more sense than those who claim to have it." He gave a smile of approval. "I considered you an angel long before society called you such."

I sat there, unsure how to remark. Kent appeared genuine in his gratitude, though he also seemed forward in his admiration.

Warren tucked his arm around me. "And that's why I must remind him you're my wife. Brisbane can get forgetful when he turns sentimental." Warren wasn't annoyed or surprised by his friend's behavior. It was almost as if he expected him to act as such. "But for all his charms, I trust the man. Even if he's a scoundrel of the worst sort."

Kent laughed. "Likewise, though I suppose you'll calm your waywardness now that you found yourself a devoted wife."

Warren had been wayward? Or was his friend ribbing him back? I didn't have time to inquire, for the housekeeper came with a tray of sandwiches and lemonade. We concluded our visit, and Warren went to his study to field work calls before dinner.

I busied myself with getting to know the routine of the house. I wanted to run it to the best of my ability. I was conversing with the cook when Jenkins approached and handed me the mail.

I hoped for a letter from Lilith. I hadn't heard from her since the day of my wedding and was anxious to hear how she was faring. Even to just know she was okay. Did she regret running off and getting married?

But as I hustled up the stairs, I noticed the handwriting wasn't my sister's. No, it only had my name on it, as if it had been placed on the doorstep. I scratched open the envelope and read the sole line, my heart pounding hard in my chest.

Another threat.

You won't get away with this.

Chapter 20 ————————————————————————

September 6, 1922
Stella

"DO YOU THINK THE JENNY will be safe?" I threw a look over my shoulder, as if my airplane remained in view rather than stowed in a clearing about three miles back. Warren had smoothly piloted us here and landed on a flat stretch of land hedged by pines just outside the town of Glenfield. We'd usually seek out the property owner to gain permission to leave our plane, but time was of the essence. We didn't plan on staying long, just enough time to get Lilith away from her imposter husband.

"No one will mess with your plane," Warren reassured, tucking my arm closer to his as we walked down the wooded lane supposedly leading to my sister's cabin.

"That was nice of that milkman to give us a ride." Almost as soon as we'd entered the town, we'd met an older gentleman with a horse-drawn cart who'd not only given us directions but had dropped us off not too far back. According to the man, we still had another half-mile trek to reach our destination, but his kindness saved us time and energy. Unfortunately, he hadn't heard of my sister or her husband, only knew the location based on the return address on the envelope. What if Lilith wasn't here? How would I ever find her?

"That poor milkman never stood a chance," Warren said from beside me, breaking into my anxious thoughts. His gaze darted about, staying aware of our surroundings. "I've yet to see a man refuse you when you act like that."

I blinked. "Like what?" I hadn't been flirty or brazen. I'd just asked the man if he knew the way to Lilith's house.

"I don't think you realize it." He kept his focus ahead. "But when you ask a question about something important to you, your teeth sink into your bottom lip, and your head tilts to the side. It's quite striking."

"What? I don't do that." Did I? My mind traveled back to the conversation with the nice man. I couldn't recall tilting my head or biting my lip.

"You do." He nudged me. "I noticed the first day we met when you asked for a ride in the Jenny. Here I thought you were being coy with me. That I caused the reaction in you."

He did cause a stirring in me. His nearness. The sound of his voice. And right now the warm press of his side to mine made my thoughts trip over themselves. But by the lightness of this conversation, I realized what he was doing. "You're distracting me, aren't you? Trying to keep my mind from going mad with worry over Lilith."

"It's my attempt." His gaze flickered to mine. "But now I think you should remain behind and let me handle this."

My brow lowered. "We're in this together."

He led me off the side of the dirt road, tugging me behind a row of tall bushes. "I don't know what we're walking into. This might be dangerous. I'm only thinking of your safety."

"Yet you let me walk on airplane wings."

He sent me a look. "*Let* is a rather loose interpretation. You crawled out there without bringing me in on the decision."

I hadn't realized until this moment how tan his face had become from all our hours spent outside. He even had a faint line on his forehead from his flight helmet. His hair had grown over his collar, curling at the tips, highlighted by the sun. He wore ruggedness better than a tailored suit. But it was the concern in his eyes that stole my breath.

"I'm sorry. I still forget." I chewed the inside of my cheek. "When you go as long as I have thinking no one cares, it's easy to slip back into that mindset. I didn't mean to scare you with my wingwalking."

"I understand." He dragged his fingers along my arm. "I can't expect a few months of marriage to cure a lifetime of hurt. And then I piled more on."

Warren had apologized repeatedly for the pain he'd caused. Which was more than I could say for my family. "Please let me stay with you." I motioned toward the lane. "I need to see for myself the people I love are all right."

"Wouldn't my word be enough that Lilith's okay?"

Our gazes locked. "Not only Lilith."

Comprehension flashed in his eyes. This was the closest I'd come to saying I loved him. Something had happened inside me. Not the dull stab that usually cut through, but more of a gentle shifting. Like the kind when one was restless, unable to claim sleep, only to realize all that was needed was a slight adjustment, settling into that perfect spot. I'd feared I was incapable of love, as if it were beyond my reach. But what if it had been with me all along? Waiting for me to quit fighting against it and let my heart gently fall into place? And that place seemed to be wherever Warren was. I opened my mouth to say as much, but a twig snapped behind me.

"Not sure what you two are about, but this is private property."

I spun as Warren tried to step in front of me. Our shoulders collided, and Warren steadied me, subtly positioning himself between the stranger and me. But the man wasn't entirely a stranger, for his face matched the one from Lilith's photograph.

"It's him." My voice came out a strangled whisper.

Instead of being in an army uniform, the man wore a stained button-down shirt. One sleeve had been tied off where his right arm was missing, while his left hand clutched a rifle.

Warren gave a slight shake of head, indicating this stranger was *not* Paul Cameron, then he widened his stance, his neck muscles taut. The other man straightened, notching his chin higher, as if making himself taller. But I hadn't time for a masculine posturing match.

I lifted on my toes and glared over Warren's shoulder. "Are you Lilith Ashcroft's husband?"

The man didn't raise his gun but locked it closer to his side, his suspicious gaze still on Warren. "Who wants to know?"

His possessive tone poked my anger. "I do. Lilith's sister. If you don't believe me, I've her letter to prove it." I tugged the envelope from my pocket and waved it in the air.

"Geneva?" The man's brow softened as he tried to look around Warren. "Is that my sister-in-law behind you, mister?"

Mister. Well, that confirmed it. This guy did not know my husband. If the two were longtime chums, he would've recognized Warren. Did that also mean this person hadn't been the one who'd sabotaged the airplane? I would think if someone intended to kill, they'd know what their victim looked like. Though this man might have hired someone to take care of everything.

A surge of protectiveness rose within me. If this guy had been behind the plane crash, I didn't want him to know Warren was alive until absolutely necessary. Which was why I kept talking before my husband could get a word in. "Yes, I'm Geneva. Please take me to Lilith."

"She's up at the cabin." He motioned toward the road. "She'll be happy you came." He hazarded a glance toward Warren. "Who's your friend?"

"Oh him?" I linked my arm through Warren's. "He's a train hopper. I met him on my way here. I don't know his real name. So I've been calling him Jeffy."

Warren's eyes widened.

Surprise registered on my brother-in-law's face. "You don't know him?"

I waved him off. "I think he's foreign, since he can't speak any English. But he's cute. So I let him follow me around." I turned to Warren, whose eyes gleamed with . . . something. He was either silently applauding my intuitiveness or planning to throttle me.

But I continued in a high-pitched voice. "Isn't that right, Jeffy?"

Warren nudged my foot, but I only smiled brightly at him and patted his cheek. I now understood what he'd tried to express moments ago about fearing for my safety. Because I currently feared for his. This stranger, standing a couple yards away clutching a weapon, could well be my husband's killer.

I took in a calming breath. "Enough about me and my friend. Where's my lovely sister?"

He eyed me as if I'd lost my mind and then flicked a glance to Warren. "Right this way." He walked ahead of us toward the small cabin.

I bent to adjust the buckle on my shoe, hoping the extra time would put some distance between us and the gun. Plus, I wanted to chat freely without the man overhearing.

"A train hopper. Very creative, darling," Warren muttered. "Let's just hope he takes us to Lilith and not somewhere more out of the way." His gaze swept the woods beside us.

I straightened. "What do you mean?" I couldn't keep the alarm from my voice. "I purposely threw him off your scent so he wouldn't know you're alive." Though he'd discover soon enough the moment we saw Lilith again. She knew Warren and believed him dead. "Maybe *you* should stay behind. Then when my sister joins us—"

"Not going to happen." His tone was firm. "I'm not leaving your side. There's more to this than just me. Think about it." He leaned closer, keeping his voice low. "I'm sure this man knows about the five thousand dollars your family's offering and that you're wanted for questioning. I don't think he'll go to the police, considering he's posing as someone else, but he might call your father." His eyes narrowed. "Could be just the thing to get on their good side."

My parents had said they'd wanted nothing to do with Lilith now that she'd run off and eloped without their approval. I hadn't even considered Warren's theory, and now I second-guessed everything. Should we not have come? What about Lilith?

Warren kept a hand on my lower back, his gaze darting, as if every sense was on high alert.

My gaze searched too, but only for a petite redhead too young to face what was coming. We approached a modest house, not unlike Brisbane's hunting cabin. The porch sagged in the center, and the roof had been thatched several times. Lilith's husband waved us to follow him inside.

Warren touched my elbow, stilling me. "Let me go first. Make sure it's okay."

I nodded, my breath sharp in my lungs. He paused in the entryway, his profile remaining in view. His arms fell to his sides, and a peculiar expression darkened his face. He turned fully to me and held out his hand.

I crossed the threshold, and Warren's fingers wrapped mine. My lips parted at the sight, which had no doubt been the reason for his initial reaction. Clothes were rumpled and draped over rickety furniture. Not just a piece or two, but it appeared as if someone had taken a large trunk and strewn the contents about the room. Tin cans littered the floor, the lids opened and bent back, exposing decaying crud. Filthy dishes were stacked upon two end tables. A putrid odor hung in the same air as hundreds of dust motes, swirling about in the light from a large window. And perched on the sill was Lilith.

Her hair was tidy, her creamy complexion glowing with youth and radiance. She sat prim and poised, as though she were taking tea in one of the Ashcrofts' formal parlors instead of loafing in a ramshackle, dirty cabin.

Lilith's husband leaned his gun against the wall, and he shut the door behind us. "Sorry." He slid a palm over his neck and cast his gaze to the floor. "We weren't expecting visitors."

Lilith startled, as if plucked from a daydream.

Her husband motioned to me. "Look who I found while out hunting."

Her wide blue eyes snapped to mine, her dainty face puckering in confusion. "Geneva, is that you?" She blinked. "What happened to your hair?" But before I could respond, she noticed Warren. Her face drained of color. "Is that . . ."

I rushed to her, stepping over discarded shoes and empty bottles. "It is, Lilith," I said quickly. "Everything's okay." Well, somewhat. There were several situations that were *not* okay, including the one we'd just stepped into. Thankfully, she hadn't mentioned Warren's name, or his cover would've been blown.

I tugged her to her feet and inspected her more closely. There were no bruises that I could see. Her eyes, while shocked, were bright, with no redness or strain. I hugged her, pressing my hands along her back, relieved her slim frame wasn't emaciated. She seemed healthy, and despite the strong odors in the room, she still smelled like rose water. Her frock was mildly rumpled but clean looking. I clutched her close and whispered in her ear, "I needed to make sure you were safe."

She pulled back, her mouth crimping at the sides, looking far too much like Mother. "Why wouldn't I be?"

I cast a glance at the gentlemen. Lilith's husband was more uncomfortable than earlier. Warren stepped between the gun and the imposter, his gaze steadily on him. I'd forgotten how dangerous Warren could appear.

With my arm wrapped securely around Lilith, I leveled my glare at the imposter. "Care to explain why you took on Lieutenant Cameron's identity?"

Lilith's shoulders spiked beneath my fingertips. "What do you mean, Geneva?" Her blue eyes flashed with . . . anger? "How dare you come here and accuse my husband of outlandish things."

Warren folded his arms across his chest. "Geneva's speaking the truth."

The man's gaze narrowed. "I thought you didn't speak English."

"Never mind that." Warren's voice carried a dangerous edge. "I know you're not who you claim to be. Explain now, or I'm informing the authorities." Those were bold declarations, considering I was wanted for murder and Warren was still legally dead.

But his threat made the man shuffle backward, his throat bobbing with several hard swallows.

"Nonsense." Lilith shook off my arm and scurried toward her husband. With a defiant lift of her chin, she tucked her hand in his. "I have no idea why you've come—"

"They're right." The liar's voice sank low with defeat. "I've been trying to find a way to tell you, Lil. I'm not who you think I am."

Lilith's eyes rounded, and she yanked her hand away. Her mouth gaped open, but no words spouted forth.

"I will ask you one more time to explain." Warren's tone burned with intensity, making me hope he knew what he was doing. "Where's the real Lieutenant Cameron?"

All emotion left the imposter's face, and his voice turned stone-cold. "He's dead."

Chapter 21

WARREN GRABBED THE GUN, ALL the while keeping his glare on the imposter. "Geneva and Lilith, stand by me while this man tells us what happened to Paul." His tone allowed no refusal.

I edged toward Warren, collecting a shaking Lilith on the way. Her husband didn't try to stop her. Though he didn't have much choice since Warren held a rifle.

Lilith grasped my arm, her panicked gaze making her look younger. "What does he mean, Geneva?" Her eyes settled on my husband. "Warren, do you know what he means?"

The gentleman in question jolted. Lilith had said Warren's name, and now the proverbial cat was out of the bag—and hopefully it wasn't feral.

Warren maneuvered around us, placing himself between us and a possible killer. "We're waiting, sir. What do you have to say for yourself?"

"Lieutenant Cameron was my best friend. We fought side by side." He swallowed hard. "We were fighting in Meuse-Argonne when a grenade landed close. Paul pushed me aside and dove on top of it. I lost my arm, but he lost his life. He saved me."

Lilith's hand slapped over her shocked mouth. "You . . . lied."

He gave a solemn nod. "I did. I'm sorry, Lil. So very sorry." His voice broke. "All Paul talked about was this sweet girl who wrote him. He read me your letters. Told me how your words gave him courage." He took a step to the side to see her better, but she shrank against me.

"Let me guess." My tone dripped with anger. I hated the look of hurt in Lilith's eyes. "The lieutenant asked you to take care of my sister. And you decided a deathbed wish made it okay to deceive her?" The past year I'd done everything to protect her from a terrible marriage to the wrong man. Yet it had happened anyway.

"No," he answered. "There wasn't any deathbed plea. Just a broken man wanting to make amends in his own warped way."

"I don't understand." Lilith's brow crinkled.

"The guilt. There was so much guilt." His eyes tightened, and a cloudiness overtook his gaze, as if reliving those moments on the battlefield. "Guilt about all that was taken from Paul. All he wanted was a life with the woman he loved. I thought time would lessen my remorse, but after a while, it got worse. I wrote to you in Paul's name. It was wrong. I was hoping the delay would've seen you already married." He stared at her, unblinking. "But you wrote back with such heartfelt words, reaffirming your love for Paul. I thought the best way to honor him would be to take care of you. Then we kept writing, and I got to know you myself."

Lilith was softening. Her petite frame wasn't as rigid, and she released her grip on my arm. But I wasn't buying this.

From Warren's scowl, he wasn't either. "Lying to her was honoring the dead? You could've told her the truth. That Paul loved her and she was on his mind up to his final moments. What I think is that you wanted a rich young socialite to give you a life of comfort."

"Does it look like we live in comfort?" the man asked, not rudely but matter-of-factly.

"You couldn't have known the Ashcrofts would refuse Lilith's inheritance."

Most parents wouldn't want to see their children impoverished, but John Ashcroft had no regard for anyone but himself. Lilith's rash behavior brought scandal to their name, and he'd punished her for it.

Warren continued, "The only person able to foil your scheme was me. Lilith wrote that I knew Paul. You knew I could expose you, so you encouraged her to elope."

"Yes," he admitted.

"Only you realized you couldn't run from me forever, then you sabotaged my plane. You wanted me dead and out of the way."

"No," he denied even as Lilith whimpered. "I was nowhere near your plane that day."

"Easy to say. I need proof."

He held up his hand in surrender. "I didn't want Lilith to find out, but I would never kill someone for it. I've seen enough death." His frantic gaze jumped to each of us. "You have to believe me."

"We owe you nothing, especially our trust." I slid my arm around Lilith. "Everything about you has been a lie, from your name to your love for Lilith to—"

"I love Lilith." His words stumbled over each other. "At first I wrote only to appease my conscience, but I got to know you, Lil, through our letters. I fell in love with you." His pleading gaze met his wife's. "I'm sorry. You have every reason to doubt me, but don't doubt my love. Haven't I proved it?"

Lilith stood taller and nodded.

I gave my sister's shoulder a little shake. "Lilith, you can't seriously be thinking about staying with him. You don't even know his real name."

"Is it Michael?" she asked him quietly.

His chin dipped so low that one would think his jaw was filled with lead.

"That name on our wedding certificate?" Lilith looked as if she was piecing things together. "You said that was the name you were given at birth, but when your parents died, you took your grandmother's surname. And she changed your given one to Paul."

"My name's Michael Jamison."

"Quite the story. Never trust a man who invokes his own grandmother in his lies."

"You lied too." Lilith's gaze swung to me. "You said your husband died, and yet here he is." Detached and looking small, she took a few steps from me.

I shook my head, unwilling to mention she was the one who'd deceived me on my wedding day and the entire week prior. I hadn't even spoken or written to my sister since Warren's plane crash, so her accusation didn't hold any weight. But Lilith wasn't always the most reasonable when flustered.

"I thought Warren was gone," I answered softly. "I didn't know he was alive until a few days ago."

Warren scowled, probably not pleased with the turn of conversation. "I laid low because I wanted to find out who sabotaged my plane. I wasn't sure who was behind the accident, though now I think I have a good idea." He glared at Michael.

His eyes widened. "I told you I wasn't near the airfield."

"You can tell that to the police, then." Warren's tone was low and lethal. "I'm sure they would love to hear the entire story. Make sure you don't leave off impersonating a war hero."

Michael flinched but didn't cower. "I'll answer any questions they want." His courage must've returned because he took a commanding step toward Warren. "I don't have anything to hide anymore."

Warren matched his stride. "Good, because I'll tell your story—"

"Oh, please don't go." Lilith ran to her husband and linked her arm in his. "I forgive you. I forgive you for lying and . . ." She shook her other hand wildly. "And for everything else."

"Everything else?" Warren looked incredulous. "Meaning his attempt on my life?"

"He didn't," Lilith insisted. "He was with me that day you died. Well, you didn't die. But the day of the plane crash, we were together all that night before . . . and . . . and all that day." Her eyes met her husband's, and something passed between them. "So it's impossible for it to be him."

Head spinning, I moved slowly toward Warren, eyeing Lilith with disbelief. "You truly forgive this man? A total stranger?"

She rested her hand on Michael's chest. "He's not a stranger. He's my husband. And yes, I don't approve of his lies, but I approve of him." She pressed herself closer to him. "I may not have known his name, but he wrote me all these months. I know him. Just as well as I know you, Geneva."

That hit like a brick to the gut. "You won't go with us?" I was at a loss. "You want this kind of life?" I motioned to the disarray.

"There was a mix-up with his pension. It will be corrected soon." Her chin lifted, the frail shell she'd hid behind a moment ago now gone entirely. "I won't return to Father's control. I married the one I love. My place is with Michael."

The man's face crumpled. "I like hearing you say my name." He pulled her to him for a kiss that made my stomach revolt.

"This isn't going how I thought," I whispered to Warren. "How can we just leave her here?"

He shook his head, eyeing their spectacle with a frown. "Your sister makes her own choices. She chose to elope with him."

"But she thought he was Paul."

"Now she knows the truth, and look." He motioned to the embracing couple. "She doesn't seem bothered by it. There's nothing more we can do."

My shoulders curled forward with a sigh. "Then let's say our goodbyes."

Another dead end.

• • •

The stars were chunky and everywhere. It wasn't at all like this in New York City, where the evenings were hazy and dull. No, the sight above me almost demanded my attention. The stars were more than just slits of light, for they studded the expanse with incandescent energy, making it appear like a sky of a thousand moons.

"It's not like this in the city," Warren murmured beside me, echoing my thoughts. "But at least there we have a warm bed."

One I knew Warren missed just as much as me. Because the town of Turnberry, where we'd hosted an air show, hadn't any rooms to rent. With piles of straw from the nearby haystack tucked beneath us and a coarse blanket we'd purchased from the general store draped over us, we nestled beside each other on the very field we'd hosted a barnstorming event earlier. The temperature had plummeted after the sun went down, a cool breeze now teasing my face. There was so much absurdity about our current situation, but I couldn't find it in me to complain. Because Warren was close.

"What can I do to make this easier for you?" His voice was gentle, soft.

While I relished his intimate tone, I couldn't help but feel guilty. "I'm sorry about all this." I rolled onto my side, not realizing until I faced him that he was watching me. He was mostly shadowed in darkness, but having spent so many dark nights beside him, I could tell his eyes were intent upon me.

"Do you think these air shows are pointless?" Again, we'd discovered nothing—nothing about Brisbane, the crash, and I'd had to leave Lilith behind in a hovel with a liar. Warren had tried to snap me out of my foggy thoughts, but it hadn't been until I'd taken the Jenny's controls that my mind had become clear again.

I felt more than heard his laughter. "You can't convince me you're not enjoying this."

"What do you mean?" I huffed, even as I smacked my neck, squashing a mosquito. "As lovely as this view is, I prefer to sleep far away from bugs."

"No, I'm talking about the flight shows. I see it when you lift your goggles after you land. Your eyes are a brighter blue. It's like every time you venture into the skies, you steal a piece of it." His low voice rumbled with intensity. "It's maddening not to lose myself in them."

I swallowed. Many men had complimented my eyes, but none like Warren. He was the only one who knew how much flying meant to me. The skies were my safe place, which most would deem absurd. "But we haven't discovered anything helpful."

"Not true." Even in the darkness, I could see his smile flash. "We learned that the Wonder Tonic at the Turnberry general store is really moonshine. The barber's son is having a fling with the new schoolteacher. And that if I ever wanted to open a factory, rural America is the place to be."

I couldn't help but laugh. For all our investigating today, those gossip morsels had been all we'd uncovered. The only link between the towns had been the rumors of factories branching out. For the locals' sakes, I hoped those whispers proved true. More jobs for those folks would increase their quality of living. "I like the country."

"I know." His tone fell flat.

I realized I'd blurted my opinion too freely. I'd learned not to tell others about my preference for the country. My peers hadn't understood. Scores of women in our sphere loved the city. They thrived on living frivolously, flaunting their wealth, outdoing others in throwing the most elaborate parties. But while Warren cared for none of those things, his job was still in the city. There wasn't any way around that. If I was frustrated about our unfruitful search, Warren had to be even more so. He had no idea about the current state of his papers. He had an efficient publishing team that would run his empire in his absence, but I could tell the time away made him nervous. Plus we both suspected my Father was most likely pushing for control, which didn't offer any solace.

Not wanting to cause my husband any further discomfort, I added, "Though I'm content to be wherever you are."

"You mean that?" He levered up on his elbow. "When our ruse is over, when we stop the flight shows . . . you still want this?"

I didn't have to ask what *this* meant. It meant us. Did I still want to be together. His early belief that I'd attempted to murder him hadn't boosted our marriage any. And was it wrong that I still grappled with the hurt from him allowing me to suffer when he'd been alive the entire time? I knew he was sorry, and I'd forgiven him, but my heart seemed weak from everything.

Though despite the ups and downs, one thing remained true. "Marrying you was one of the best decisions of my life."

Yet in a way, I felt just like Lilith's husband. I withheld a secret from Warren. I hadn't told him where I was the morning of his crash. I couldn't bring myself to confess what I'd caused, or else the fragile bond we shared could be severed. I couldn't lose him again. My heart wouldn't survive the devastation. "So my answer is yes. That is, if you want to stay with me."

He wrapped his arms around me and drew me close to his chest, the corner of his collar scraping the edge of my left eye. The coarse fabric wasn't at fault for the rush of tears I held at bay by force of feeble will.

"I do." His tone was solemn, as if speaking a vow.

I wanted to revisit the conversation we'd shared before Michael interrupted us. I'd almost rallied the courage to tell Warren how I felt. But tonight it was as if my thoughts closed in on themselves. I couldn't draw a single word from them. This was how it had always been. Growing up in a family that never showed emotion, it was a struggle. I wanted to pull the cork from my heart and let it gush freely, yet there was a blockage. Something I couldn't quite tug free no matter how much I wished to. Instead, I nodded and clung to him harder. Could he feel the desperation in my touch?

We stayed like this, my hands bunching his shirt while his fingers combed through my short hair. Our lips were tight, as if we were both afraid to speak too soon.

Warren ended the silence. "Are you okay with going to the next town on the list tomorrow?"

I hesitated, and he caught it.

"You're worried about Lilith?"

"I'm struggling with leaving her." This morning I'd held every belief she'd be traveling with us. Warren and I had devised the plan to take Lilith back to Brisbane's hunting cabin. My sister and I would take the afternoon train to the area, and Warren would fly the Jenny there. "Maybe I should've tried harder." With her living in the next township over, I could easily return and plead with her.

"She still would stay." He trailed a knuckle across my arm, tracing the path of moonlight. "Lilith's determined. A trait you both share."

"But she's delicate." I sighed. "Did you see the state of the cabin?"

"It was hard not to."

I had no doubt Warren had been surprised at the chaos we'd stepped into. "Lilith hasn't been taught how to keep house. I know it's common sense to clean up after oneself, but she easily gets overwhelmed. When that happens, she shuts down."

"She didn't seem overwhelmed when she found out the man she married was someone else altogether."

"I know," I said quietly. "That's why I'm so bothered. Do you really think he sabotaged your plane? To keep you from exposing him?" Could my sister be living with a murderer? The idea made me shiver.

"You cold?" Warren gathered me against him again, his hands rubbing the bare skin of my arms back and forth, as if he'd made it his sole job to force away the chill. "He could be to blame. I knew the real Lieutenant Cameron. Michael confessed that was why they'd eloped in the first place. He could deny it all he wanted, but I'm certain money probably was the motivating factor. At least at the beginning."

"But after they were married, my parents cut Lilith's funding." I looked into his eyes. "If money's the motive, the man didn't get any. So why hurt you?"

"Maybe it didn't have anything to do with money by that point." His fingertips now ran along my back. "Perhaps he didn't want Lilith to know his wrongs, so he tried to eliminate the only person who could spoil that."

"Lilith said she was with him that day."

Warren exhaled. "She was quick to defend him. I found her excuse thin, to say the least. How many people remember what they were doing that exact day and time?"

I went rigid in his embrace. He'd referred to Lilith, but I suspected he aimed that jab at me, at where I was that day. I knew I should tell him. But not tonight. Not when I was in his arms. When he was so close. Because as soon as that truth left my lips, he'd be distant again.

● ● ●

We traveled to three more towns with no results. But despite our lack of success in the case, my marriage was improving. Warren and I fell into our familiar rhythm. Flirty teasing. Light touches. We hadn't reached the state of intimacy as before the crash, but it seemed we were on our way.

While Warren prepped the Jenny for takeoff, I visited the local drugstore, browsing the shelves for aspirin to subdue a lingering headache. I located what I needed and moved to the counter.

"Having another show tonight?" The owner stopped dusting the shelves and slid behind the register, his grin brighter than his white apron.

"No, sir. We're heading out of town. We're hoping to meet up with our friend Kent Brisbane. He's a private detective from the city." Warren and I had bandied about Brisbane's name so much these past few days to no avail. But what harm could it do to sneak in one more investigative question?

"Brisbane?" He scratched his head. "Now why does that sound familiar?"

I almost dropped the aspirin. "Are you acquainted with the family, perhaps?" Brisbane didn't have any family. None that I was aware of anyway. But I had to ask something to keep this conversation alive.

"You speak far too ladylike to be wearing men's trousers." He chuckled. "As for your question . . ." The proprietor's squinted gaze fell to the floor, as if the answer would rise from the cracks in the linoleum. "A gentleman in fancy duds and a shiny tiepin came in about a month or so back. He introduced himself as Sam Hendricks."

I perked. Brisbane always wore a diamond tiepin. Though many men wore gaudy pieces as such. It wouldn't be wise to get my hopes up.

He looked down at the tin in my hand. "That will be ten cents."

Oh right. I fished a dime from my pocket and handed it to him. "You must get a lot of people in here since it's the only drugstore in town."

He nodded. "Yeah, but I can spot an out-of-towner."

The bell jangled above the entrance, alerting us to the door. Warren strode in, his gaze searching until it landed on me. His growing smile made my blood rush.

"Stella, darling." He spoke my false name as if he'd said it all his life. "We've hit our first snag with the weather. It's starting to rain."

Rain would delay our leaving, but thankfully our rented room was paid through tomorrow. "I've been talking with this kind druggist. He believes he met our friend Kent Brisbane." I watched Warren's gaze flood with interest. "Though he hasn't said how."

The owner chuckled. "Haven't I? Guess not. Well, the man bumps into a corner table and knocks all my furniture wax onto the floor. Then under his breath, he said, 'Nice going, Brisbane.' He surely thought he was alone. But I was crouched behind the counter restocking the charge slips."

"And you remember him saying that?"

He gave me a funny look. "Course. It's not every day a man introduces himself with one name then calls himself another."

I refused to look at Warren. Because that was exactly what we were doing.

"I should've confronted him, but he didn't seem dangerous. If he wanted everyone to call him Sam Hendricks, then why should I complain about the matter?"

"Sam Hendricks," Warren mumbled under his breath.

"Sound familiar?" I leaned closer to him.

He nodded. "Did this gentleman say anything else?"

"Not that I can recall." He moved down the counter, and we followed him, the chatter from the radio news hour slightly louder. "He didn't stay long after he destroyed my display." The man's dry tone indicated he hadn't quite forgiven Brisbane for the blunder.

"Thank you for your time." Warren shook the owner's hand, who then promptly grabbed a few sacks of flour and hauled them to the back room.

"Okay," I said when the man was out of sight. "Who's Sam Hendricks?"

"He once worked at my paper. He was Brisbane's boss for a while."

"Where is Mr. Hendricks now?"

"He died five years ago."

I blinked. "What?"

"It's safe to assume that Brisbane had adopted Sam's name as an alias while scoping out these towns."

This was the lead we needed. "So now that we know the name Brisbane's been using, should we travel back to the previous towns and ask around?"

"We could." He grimaced. "But what reason would we have for stopping? We already held air shows in those places. Besides, I doubt Brisbane used the same false name twice."

Speaking of names, I heard a familiar one floating through the radio speakers. Warren sidled beside me as the broadcaster rattled away.

Straight from the New York City wire. Matriarch of the lumber mill empire, Helena Ashcroft, has been seized with a sudden illness. Doctors are not optimistic about her recovery.

Chapter 22 ——————————————————————————

"I DON'T THINK THIS IS a good idea." I lightly pressed my fingertips to the blindfold over my eyes. Everything was dark as Warren led me through the airfield hangar. The warmth of his hands on my waist pressed through my clothes.

He steered me to the left. "Trust me on this. The surprise will be worth it."

Saturday mornings had become our flying time. It was the bright spot of my week I always looked forward to, but what I hadn't planned on? Warren's sudden scheme of blindfolding me. The excitement in his eyes had been enough to persuade me to follow along.

But now I wasn't so sure. "I'm entirely at your mercy."

His lips brushed my ear. "I promise to be on my best behavior."

I took another hesitant step under his guidance. "What you judge best behavior varies with my interpretation."

He laughed, and I feigned a scowl only to realize he probably couldn't see my expression, since he directed me from behind. Soon his warm lips trailed along the curve of my neck. If we weren't at a public hangar, I'd probably let him continue his coaxing attentions, but as it was, I tilted my head away. "You're proving my point."

"Nothing wrong with a man kissing his wife." His hands skimmed my sides, settling lower on my hips. "Besides, no one's about, Eva. We have this entire hangar to ourselves. I couldn't have planned it any better." He sounded so pleased with himself that it made me laugh.

"And your plan involves me wearing this ridiculous blindfold?" The last time I'd allowed myself to get blindfolded had been at a garden party at the country house when we'd played blind man's bluff. I'd fallen twice during that short stint and had gotten grass stains on my frock. Hopefully, this time around would result in happier memories. "I don't know how you convinced me to do this."

His body pressed against my back. "I hope it's because you're enamored with me, darling."

I was. Very much. But once again my mouth wouldn't join in with my heart. Warren had no problem expressing his feelings. He said he loved me often. From when he'd kiss me goodbye before leaving for work to the rumbling murmur in my ear when he'd hold me during the night, and several times in between. He'd noticed my reluctance in speaking my emotions, but as of yet he hadn't pushed me to confess them.

He led me along, our footfalls loud on the concrete floor. "A few more steps." His hands bracketed my shoulders, and he turned me to the right. "There." His fingers lifted my blindfold.

My gaze widened. I stood before a biplane identical to Warren's beside it. "Did you buy another one?"

He aimed that beautifully crooked grin at me. "She's yours."

I had to have heard him wrong. "Surely you didn't . . ."

"Buy you an airplane? Of course I did." He stepped toward the propeller and casually ran his fingers along a blade. "Happy one-month anniversary, Eva."

I pressed my hand to my cheek, words falling short.

"Jewelry wouldn't impress you, considering the overflowing treasure box on your vanity." He expelled an exaggerated sigh. "You're a tough lady to buy for, Mrs. Hayes."

He couldn't have bought me a better gift, and he knew it. I launched into his arms. "Thank you!" I kissed him soundly. Warren had to have made use of his army connections. The Jennys had sold for only a fraction of the production cost since the government had a surplus of them, but they'd been snapped up quickly. "Though don't you think this is a bit extravagant? Us having two planes?"

"Husbands buy their wives automobiles. Why can't I buy mine her own airplane?" He winked. "I can paint it another color so it's not the same as mine. Most of the army planes have an SC number painted on her body so pilots can tell them apart." He stopped at my blank look and flashed a grin. "But our planes were built after being bought from the army, so there's no number. They look the same."

"And what's wrong with that?" I pressed against him. "We're a pair."

He smiled at that. "Always, love. Now that that's settled . . ." His gaze drifted to my plane. "I thought she'd be perfect for taking your test in."

My fingers clenched the collar of his leather flight jacket. "My test?"

"Only if you want to." He wrapped his arms around me. "It's not exactly necessary to fly an airplane."

I understood what he meant. As of now the government didn't require a license for aviation. Though I didn't expect that to last long. No doubt they'd soon regulate the skies as they did the roadways.

"You've logged more hours than army training for my cadets. Speaking of which"—he released me and slid his hand inside his pocket. "I wasn't going to show you this until after your examination, but this might help motivate you." He withdrew my flight logbook. "Take a look inside."

He handed it to me, and I lifted my brows in curiosity. I thumbed it open, and my gaze landed on a new signature. My mouth dropped. "Orville Wright signed this." The father of aviation penned his name on my humble logbook.

"That right there is as good as any license you'll ever get." He beamed at me. "If anyone ever questions your stock as a pilot, one look at that name will shut them up."

"But . . . how?" I had so many questions. "I always thought Mr. Wright disapproved of women fliers." It'd been widespread that he'd refused to teach Ruth Law Oliver, a trailblazing aviatrix. Mr. Wright held the belief women weren't mechanically minded. Yet he'd signed off on my training hours?

Warren gave an easy shrug. "I have my ways."

"You don't know how much this means to me." I kissed him.

"I'm getting a good idea." He tugged at my waist and drew me close.

I smiled up at him. "I feel thoroughly spoiled."

"Good. That's my intention." He grinned. "Just wait until your birthday."

He was already thinking about my birthday? I didn't turn twenty-four for another few months. "I don't need another gift." I patted his chest. "Besides, I doubt you could outdo this one."

He chuckled low. "You'll have to judge for yourself. At any rate, Terrence told me it's already in motion. Too late to back out now."

"What's your cousin have to do with anything?" Terrence Hayes was the family lawyer. Warren met with him often, but I couldn't understand how that would tie in to my birthday.

"Ah, ah. No more hinting." He took a step back. "You already got enough information out of me." He glanced at my new plane. "So what do you think? Are you ready to prove yourself as an aviator?"

A swell of nervous energy gathered in my chest. Could I do this? To pass the test meant I had to fly solo. Every other time Warren had been with me, an extra set of controls within his reach. I stared up at my husband. He had confidence in me. And for some reason that brought tears to my eyes. "My Father wouldn't even allow me to get my driver's license."

"What?" Warren blinked. "You're not serious."

"I am. He didn't allow it for several reasons. One, a woman had no place driving." I rolled my eyes even as I recited that rubbish. "Two, why put forth the effort when a servant could drive me everywhere. And three, he didn't want me to have any independence."

He released a strangled laugh. "All those cars your father has, and not one of them was yours?"

"It's not something I'm proud of."

He caught my hand in his. "I should've realized sooner. I thought, since we lived in the city, you preferred not to have a car."

Four weeks into marriage and there was still so much we were learning about each other.

"Is this why you wanted to learn to fly?"

I smiled warmly. "Before you came along, I was forced to comply with everyone's rules. When I saw your airplane in the field that day, I wanted to go against it all. And defying gravity seemed a good place to start."

"While we're on the topic of rules," Warren caught a lock of my hair and idly toyed with it between his fingers, "is your father a stickler when it comes to them, or does he think he's the exception?"

My brow lowered. "What do you mean?" Was he talking about Father's campaign, which he aggressively worked on? Or something else?

"It's nothing. Never mind." He shook his head and released my hair. "So do you feel like defying gravity today?"

Questions swirled in my mind, but I didn't want to ruin this time with Warren by talking about my father. A conversation about John Ashcroft was enough to lower even the highest mood. And today was our one-month anniversary. "I'd love to try to test today. To get my license to the skies, even unofficially, seems more appealing than one for dusty roads."

Warren laughed. "Yes, well, we'll get you that too, my love. A driver's license is next on the agenda."

A rush of warmth gathered in my chest. "Are you sure? You don't want me to be too independent. People will talk, you know."

"Let 'em." He kissed me and drew back with a smile. "Now let's make you an aviator."

• • •

Mother had never been so attentive. I wasn't sure what to think as I stared at her bowed head while she poured me a cup of tea in my front parlor. My hands had been unusually shaky, or else I would've done so. The month after I'd passed my flight test had been blissfully uneventful, but this past week I must've contracted something. Because I was now on my fourth day of a terrible rotation of chills and sweats. Presently I thankfully had neither. Perhaps the worst was behind me.

Maybe after Mother left I'd be able to catch up on rest. I'd been having difficulty falling and staying asleep, which probably hadn't helped my recovery.

"Here you go." She handed me the cup and saucer.

I had no appetite for tea or anything else, but I thanked her. She'd never visited this early before. I hadn't quite finished the morning paper, the society section still resting on my lap.

Mother stirred in sugar, the spoon clinking against the cup the only sound for several long seconds. "I've heard your husband hasn't been home lately."

"The rumor mill is churning, I see." Warren's work had been so demanding that I'd hardly seen him in the last few days. He called and checked in often, but he'd get home late, then would leave early the following morning. How Mother knew this, I had no idea, but I wasn't surprised.

"Your father told me. He went to your husband's office yesterday, only to be told he was meeting with top advertisers. The secretary recommended that your father make an appointment. I'm sure it was an oversight."

I clenched my teacup a bit tighter. Mother's call was out of duty to Father and nothing else. I should've known. Father wasn't one to be told such awful things like make an appointment. The world stopped for John Ashcroft and not the other way around. "Warren's been busy."

"I see." She took an elegant sip of her tea. "I suppose he wouldn't be home for dinner then?"

Ah, it was beginning to make sense. Mother came to secure an invitation for dinner tonight. That way Warren would be forced to talk to Father. "Warren hasn't been here for dinner all week. But you're welcome to come." If I could keep a meal down was yet to be determined.

Another sip. "That's all right, dear. We wouldn't want to impose on you. I'm sure you're relishing these moments of alone time. Goodness knows I always do."

I didn't know how to respond. Mother had always been alone. She'd spurned Lilith and me, leaving us to nannies and then boarding school.

My gaze fell to my lap, and a certain article caught my eye. Ruth Law Oliver, the aviator Orville Wright had refused to teach to fly, was featured. Only instead of highlighting her latest flight antics, it was an announcement of her retirement. "How odd. I was just thinking about her."

Mother sniffed. "About who, dear?"

"Ruth." I glanced down at the article. "She's in the paper this morning."

A sharp clink of the teacup on the saucer pulled my gaze. Mother stared at me with almost disbelief. "What did you say?"

That tone. I hadn't heard that chilly inflection for years, but I knew what it meant. I'd broken etiquette just as easily as she'd almost chipped my teacup. I bit the inside of my cheek to keep from saying something I'd regret later. "Fine, Mother." I folded the paper and set it on the coffee table. "I'm aware that you detest speaking of current events. I was only referring to Mrs. Ruth Law Oliver. She's retiring from being a pilot."

The line of her shoulders eased from their spiked position. She seemed more relieved than upset. Perhaps she still held hope I retained some semblance of propriety. "Well, women have no business in airplanes."

Now was not the time to tell her of my aviation pursuits.

"It's been nice visiting with you. I have some errands to run." She set the cup on the tray and dabbed her face with her napkin. "Perhaps you should take this time to catch up on your rest. You're looking rather pale and thin."

I hadn't told her about my recent bout with sickness. "I'll be fine, Mother. Thank you for the visit." Even though she'd only come to fish for information.

When she left, I did in fact return to my room, pausing briefly to browse the library. By the time I reached my bed, my muscles were achy. Perhaps I should nap instead of leafing through a Brontë novel. I set the book on the nightstand and stilled.

A note was on my pillow.

I recognized the envelope. It was another threatening letter. I was too tired to read it, to even feel afraid. I tossed it in the wastebasket and grabbed my swirling stomach. I needed to talk to Warren about this. About all of it. The notes. My parents' manipulation. I'd held back, not wanting to trouble him. He'd been busy, and honestly, I didn't want him to equate my presence with problems. I'd learned long ago that it was easier to sort out my own issues than rely on others who wouldn't come through for me.

Of course Warren was different. Wasn't he? I resolved to tell him. I pressed a hand to my forehead, dizziness setting in. But first I'd call the doctor.

Chapter 23 ———————————————————————————

September 12, 1922
Stella

SHEETS OF RAIN SURGED OVER the striped awning. It would be foolish to leave the safety of the drugstore. But I needed away. Because the radio broadcaster's words had wedged inside me, twisting against my ribs. If that wasn't horrible enough, a startling thought spiked from a dark space within me. I squeezed my eyes shut, trying to silence it all, but the rending chatter slowly flooded me. There was no quiet.

I had no choice. I ran into the downpour.

Warren called after me, but I knew myself. This was what I did. I rushed into chaos until all went numb. After Warren's accident, I raced into the skies. I walked on wings. I pushed every limit, wanting to quiet the storm that raged within.

But it hadn't worked. Because out here in the stinging rain, I felt my every broken piece.

Warren appeared at my side. He stripped off his jacket and draped it over my head. I met his eyes, unsure of what I'd find there. Rain beat against him, cutting paths along his face, but his gaze fixed on me. And in it was a fierce protectiveness, as if he'd fight all the elements, wrestle any force, to shield me from pain.

His hand gripped mine. With his other arm wrapped tightly around my waist, he led me through the din. Everything was gray. A misty blur. But Warren navigated us through the storm as easily as he did the skies. By the time we reached our rented room above the barber shop, we were thoroughly soaked.

My body shook. I could see my fingers tremble. But I couldn't feel it. Couldn't feel anything.

Mother was dying. Supposedly. There was a possibility I'd never see her again.

"Eva?" Warren's voice seemed distant. "You should change out of your wet clothes."

The broadcaster's words rippled through. *Sudden illness. Not optimistic about her recovery.* She was probably receiving the best care, but she was, no doubt, facing it all alone. Father showed her as much concern as he had Lilith and me. Sure, he probably stood dutifully by her sickbed while the doctors were there, but knowing him, he'd leave after they did.

"Eva?"

And what about that disturbing thought I had? The one that shattered me in the drugstore? That somehow this was all another ploy to control me. To get me back within their clutches? I wasn't sure what bothered me more—the fact that the dark voice had belonged to me or that the thought could possibly be true.

Large hands deftly worked the buttons of my frock. The fabric clung to my body, but he peeled it free. My skin chilled, but no more than the ice filling my blood. Within seconds a blanket wrapped around me. Warren, still dripping, sifted through our bag.

I sank onto the bed, my stare unfocused.

"Here, love." He approached, fresh clothes in hand.

I shrugged out of the blanket and worked to shed my damp underclothes. But my camisole bunched and twisted. I let out a growl of frustration, which sounded pathetic through my chattering teeth. I sank onto the bed, resolved to stay trapped in my wet things. It was my own stupid fault anyway. I shouldn't have bolted into the rain. What had it proven? When would I learn my rash decisions would always leave me worse off?

Warren moved beside me. His fingers skimmed my stomach and

worked the mangled hem, unraveling the mess I'd made. I lifted my arms so he could free me completely. There was nothing sensual about him undressing me. If anything it was impossibly tender. As if I could feel his love through the tips of his fingers, the warmth of his hands on my skin. He held up the dry set of my chemise and bloomers, and I shook my head. He seemed to read my thoughts as he reached for my nightgown. I was feeling better. I could easily clothe myself, but letting Warren take care of me was somehow healing. How often had he wanted to help share the burden, but I wouldn't let him? I'd stubbornly tried to handle everything myself.

I raised my arms as Warren slipped the nightgown over my head. He tucked a fresh blanket around me and pressed a kiss to my temple.

Then he finally changed out of his wet clothes. There was no awkwardness as I watched him. We'd stepped back into the familiarity as if we'd never strayed from it. Like even now, he climbed onto the bed and gathered me in his arms. His solid presence soothed the yawning ache.

His hands rubbed smooth circles on my arms. We rested for several minutes. As always, Warren waited until I was ready to talk. Usually, this was the part where I'd clam up or lightly touch the issue without diving in deeply. So I surprised myself by what flowed from my mouth next. "When the radio said Mother was sick, my first thought was born of panic. Like what if I never saw her again."

Warren hauled me closer. "That's perfectly normal."

"But my next thought isn't." My eyes drifted shut. "Because I then wondered if this was another stunt. What if my mother is faking an illness just to bring me home? A nice little scheme devised by Father, since none other has worked. He could easily pay doctors to lie. Submit a heart-wrenching radio bulletin." I rolled over and peered up at him. "My mother could be drawing her last breath, and here I'm suspecting it's all a ploy. What kind of person thinks that way?"

"One that's been hurt by others' manipulation." He pushed a wet strand of hair from my face but didn't pull his hand away. His fingers traced the curve of my jaw, his gaze following the movement. "Your father used your love for Lilith to try to force you to marry. Your mother went along with it. And that's just one instance I know of. I'm sure you have an entire lifetime of that treatment. They should feel ashamed of their actions. Not you."

I could only stare at him. I'd thought for certain he'd judge me a horrible person. Instead, he defended me. My mind traveled to my episode in the rain. I'd felt helpless, weak against the conflicting emotions. Warren had understood and shared the care of it. Seemed to *want* to lighten my burden. I'd so often refused help, thinking strength came from bearing the weight. But maybe that wasn't strength at all. It took more courage to lean. Not only on Warren but also on God.

"It's your call, Eva." He interrupted my thoughts. "Do you want to go see your mother?"

His question jolted me, snapping my gaze to his. "That would mean we'd have to return to the city."

He nodded.

"We can't." I blinked. "The world thinks you're dead. And that I killed you."

My body sank even more into him, and his grip tightened. "We'll go straight to the authorities and release a statement."

"What are we going to say? How are we going to explain ourselves?" We'd been romping all over New York the past ten days—me, even longer—posing as different people. What would we do? Just stroll into the police station and say it was all a big joke? But it hadn't been a joke. Someone had tried to murder my husband, and most of the nation thought it was me. Could I get arrested for not presenting myself for questioning?

"One thing the public loves is a sensation story." Warren shrugged. "So we give it to them."

"The truth *is* a sensation story."

"Exactly. That's what we're going to tell them." He dropped a kiss on the edge of my nose, as though the world wouldn't tip on its axis with such an announcement.

Oh, this couldn't end well. The spotlight would shine heavily upon us. I was used to attention, but this was altogether different. All my life I'd been groomed to never cause a scandal, never cause ripples in the sea of society. Warren and I would cause much more than ripples—we'd provoke a tsunami.

"Eva." His voice was gentle. "This is the only way we'll get to see your mother. Do you want to try to see her?"

"Yes," I whispered.

"Then we'll do what we must to make that happen. Tomorrow we'll release our statement, then go see her. Hopefully, there's still time."

With the storm still raging and nighttime encroaching, we were stranded here until morning. I prayed the rain would subside by then. "But what about our investigation? The world will know you're alive and . . ." What if the murderer tried again? The very thought had me tangling my fingers into his shirt with a desperate grip. I had my husband back. I wasn't about to let him go again.

He brushed my nose with his. "We'll face it together." Then he threaded his hand into my hair, combing through it with his fingers. He'd learned early on that relaxed me, but I was far from calm.

Warren was willing to reveal his secret—that he was alive—to any and all. He didn't even hesitate. He would do this for me. I could be brave for him. For me. I'd always prided myself on my courage. I could pilot the Jenny in choppy weather and jump off airplane wings with a parachute, but I hadn't been brave where I needed to be. In telling my husband I loved him. In telling him all my story. Our story.

"Warren, I don't want any secrets between us. Not anymore. I need to tell you why I was so withdrawn the week of your plane crash."

His hand stilled. "As much as I want to know, it can wait. You're exhausted. And I don't think you realize, but you haven't stopped shivering." His voice was gentle. "Let me keep you warm."

I leaned into his hand and cupped it with my own. "It's important to me that I do this. To also explain where I was the morning of your accident."

————————————————————————

Chapter 24

WARREN LEANED AGAINST OUR ADJOINING bedroom doorframe, a fierce scowl cemented on his face. "Is there something you're not telling me, Geneva?"

The hairbrush stopped mid-swipe through my hair. I stared blankly at my husband. The shadowed ridge of his brow gave him a dark look. But whatever he was upset about, it had nothing to do with my appointment today. He hadn't known I'd gone.

"Good evening to you too," I scolded. "And what are you talking about?"

He loosened his tie knot with a sharp jerk. "About your father" was all he said, which explained his foul mood. Father had that effect on people. "He's saying you know—do you?"

I sighed. "Know what?" I hadn't realized Warren had met with Father at any point today. Though I'd hardly been aware of anything lately. These past weeks I'd struggled with the flu, which had drained me. The doctor had given me something to help me sleep, and while the fever had subsided, nausea had remained. "What did Father do now?"

"A lot of things." He strode toward me, and I shifted on the bench, peering up at him. "If I know what's going on, I guarantee the other papers have been alerted. I warned him the news would get out. Scandals

217

always get prime coverage." He released a humorless scoff. "But he just wants me to continue painting him like he's a gift to humanity."

A scandal? My mind went back to the speculation over Mr. Yater's death. Had someone discovered proof of Father's involvement? Could my father be a killer? Nausea stormed through me, and I pressed a hand to my mouth.

"Eva?" Warren softened. "Are you okay? I thought you were feeling better." His gaze strayed to the pillbox on my vanity. "Maybe stop taking the medicine. I think it's been making you more withdrawn lately." His eyes lifted to mine. "Or is there another reason for your silence?"

I inhaled several slow breaths and sat perfectly still until my stomach settled. Warren was right. I'd been quiet lately. After I recovered from my bout of sickness, the persistent nausea had concerned me. I'd been scared I'd contracted something awful, but when I'd realized I'd missed my cycle—perhaps two—I'd gotten nervous for an entirely different reason. The doctor had confirmed this morning—I was going to be a mother. "I actually wanted to talk to you about something." I knew Warren would be happy about being a parent, but what did I know about raising a child? It wasn't that I didn't want to have a baby. No, I was concerned I'd fail at the endeavor. I hadn't had the best examples.

Warren nodded. "I'm willing to hear everything you have to say, but I'd like to finish this conversation first." He knelt beside me. "Eva, I may have to print something about your father that won't be well received by your parents. Though I did try to warn him."

I clutched the sides of the vanity bench, digging my fingers into the cushion. "What is it?" I said so weakly that Warren hadn't caught it.

"And do you know what he told me? He said if I respected you at all, I wouldn't dare act rashly. As if this was my fault. He was threatening me. I have no doubt."

Threatening. My thoughts shot to those wicked letters. Could Father be behind them? What advantage would he have in frightening his own daughter? Unless he'd been trying to keep me in a state of fear. Those notes had warned me not to tell anyone about them or consequences would arise—I'd lose everything. Warren was my everything. I couldn't lose him.

"Must you print it? Do you have evidence of whatever you claim my father did?"

Warren's head reared back. "I can't believe you said that."

My husband hadn't had to suffer a lifetime of being under Father's thumb. He didn't know what he was capable of. "It's a logical question."

"You think I'd slander your family without any proof?"

The blood drained from my face. If Warren ruined Father's campaign, I didn't even want to think of the repercussions. "Warren, please don't—"

"Maybe I should run a front-page spread about his little scandal. That will teach your father not to threaten me."

Warren wasn't thinking clearly. I'd never seen him this way. Though I'd experienced firsthand how Father could push a person beyond their limit.

But Warren didn't know whom he was dealing with. I gripped his hand. "I beg you. Don't print it."

Warren shot me a confused look. "Why?"

"Because." My stomach rolled, and another wave of dizziness coursed through me. I could hardly speak, let alone explain my thoughts. This was not how I wanted this evening to unfold. Warren had been busy with work these past weeks, and this was the first night we'd had together. This moment should be celebratory, not filled with strife. But I didn't know how to fix it. I wouldn't cheapen my announcement by blurting it out to stop Warren from arguing with me.

"I need more than *because*, Geneva." He hardly called me by my full name anymore. And in the past few minutes, he'd said it twice.

Though in his current mood, I wasn't about to point it out. I also didn't want to detail that I'd suspected my father could be a murderer. Because I would be doing the exact thing I'd asked Warren not to do—plowing forward without proof. Could I really say I believed Father capable of murder? That was a horrible accusation. And right now, with my emotions everywhere, with my body being in tumult, I didn't know which way was up or down.

"Aren't my wishes good enough? Can't you just believe me without having to know the full extent of it?"

Warren gave me the strangest look. "I'm beginning to believe you are more Ashcroft than Hayes."

I gripped my stomach, though his words hit far deeper. "How could you say that?"

He expelled a frustrated breath. "Because you're defending them."

"I'm defending you!"

"How?"

Was *I* under interrogation? Because it most certainly felt like it. "There's been rumors. And . . . and it's just my father isn't one to be trifled with."

He scoffed. "Neither am I."

This was escalating beyond control. Worse yet, he kept eyeing me as if unsure I told him the truth. Had he really thought I was privy to Father's illicit business? "Warren, let's talk this out. Tell me what you learned about Father, and we'll go from there."

He turned, his hard stare aiming at some spot on the wall. After several pounding heartbeats, he finally nodded. This time when he looked at me, I saw more than frustration in his eyes. The gold flecks were dulled, as if he was losing hope. "First, I need to know—do you trust me?"

"Of course I do."

"Do you love me?" He grabbed both my hands and clung, his voice unusually shaky. "Because what I'm about to say could change things. I need to know you're on my side."

"I'm always on your side." My tone was adamant. "I'm your wife."

"I asked if you loved me, Eva. Things could get intense, and I want to be convinced our love can stand against whatever's going to happen."

Love. My entire being reacted strongly to that word. Warren didn't understand the ugly spin to it. I couldn't bear to say the word aloud. "I care very much for you. More than I've ever cared for anyone."

Hurt deepened the lines of his face, and he dropped my hands. "Care?"

"This isn't easy for me."

"Loving me isn't easy for you?"

"That's not what I meant." How could I explain that dark void within me? "I struggle with confessing my feelings—you know that. It's vulnerable. Dangerous."

"It isn't hard, Eva. I've been patient, but I need more from you if we're going to face this together. It's either you love me, or you don't."

"That's unfair." I knew Warren was exhausted from working non-stop these past weeks. His emotions were stretched, like mine. Then having to deal with Father on top of everything hadn't helped. "Perhaps we should discuss this tomorrow when our heads are clear."

Without another word, he left the room. When he shut the door, the loud click seemed to indicate more than a wall had separated us.

Sleep refused to claim me, my mind a torrent of chaos. One article smearing Father's name would shatter years of his calculated planning. Destroy his senatorial hopes. He would retaliate. A shudder rocked my body, and my hand instinctively went to my abdomen. I couldn't allow him to harm Warren.

Something must be done.

I swung my legs over the side of the bed, and before I could talk myself out of it, I fled my room and moved through the darkness to Warren's study. My hands curled around the telephone. I'd once risked everything for Lilith. I'd do even more so for Warren, for our child. Determination marking my movements, I lifted the receiver and communicated the exchange to the operator.

I readied to wage an argument should the butler refuse to waken Father, but to my surprise, Mother answered the line.

"Geneva, it's late. You have better manners than to wake a household."

I tightened my grip on the speaker. I could be bleeding and gulping my last breath and Mother would delay my dying with a lecture. "I need to talk to Father. It's urgent."

"He's already turned in. It can wait until tomorrow."

"Warren's aware of a scandal involving Father. He may print it in his paper."

Her sharp gasp almost made me wince. "He can't. It will ruin everything."

She no doubt spoke of Father's campaign, while I worried over the harm he'd inflict on my marriage, my husband.

"Geneva, you must convince Warren not to print any slander. It would be best for everyone involved."

Though what if Father was truly responsible for Mr. Yater's death? Warren hadn't specifically said as much, but I'd assumed that was the scandal he referred to. He'd also implied he had proof. Could I in good conscience coax Warren to keep silent about such a thing? My gaze drifted to the birdcage. Even in the darkness I could distinguish its outline. Warren had rescued me from a confined life, freeing me from Father's clutches. I'd do the same for him.

"I'll go along with your plan."

Warren would be furious, but I had to persuade him. If not for his sake, then for our baby's. I hated to use our child as leverage, but he needed to understand the severity of what could happen if he crossed Father.

A shuffling noise sounded from the hall, making me lower the receiver.

"Geneva, are you there?" Mother's voice was shrill. "You need to make him see reason. Too much is at stake."

Yes, too much. I swept a hand over my stomach. "I promise to follow through with this."

I woke the following day, my entire body aching. After my conversation with Mother, sleep had been hard to grasp. Though I was tempted, I hadn't taken any medicine to help me rest.

Last evening hadn't gone as planned. Warren and I had to talk. I prayed he still wasn't in a foul mood. So much needed to be sorted out, and I'd promised him I'd be ready this morning. Hopefully, I could persuade him to leave things be where Father was concerned.

Still in my nightclothes, I knocked on his bedroom door. This was the first night I had slept in my room. We'd shared his bed since our wedding. A part of me hoped we'd be together again this evening.

I knocked again. Nothing.

Hesitant, I opened the door.

He was gone. His bed had been neatly made. His spicy scent hung in the air. Perhaps he was in the breakfast room waiting for me. I shuffled back, and my foot hit something.

I looked down, catching sight of a note he must've slipped beneath my door. I scooped it up and read.

We need to talk. I had to run to the office for something, but I'll meet you at the hangar for our weekly date. See you soon.

Today was Saturday. I couldn't fly this morning. But I would meet him and explain. Explain everything. My usual flying clothes—a pair of trousers and a loose-fitting blouse—were folded on the stool beside my armoire. Iris had laid them out early yesterday, since she had today off. I walked to that side of the room, wanting to get ready as soon as possible, but a warm sensation trickled down the inside of my thigh. My hand went to the back of my nightgown. Something didn't feel right. The fabric was stiff. I turned and shot a look over my shoulder at the cheval glass. My heart seized in my chest. My nightgown was stained red.

I was covered in my own blood.

September 12, 1922
Stella

WARREN'S ARMS TIGHTENED AROUND ME as we both reclined on the bed in our rented room. He'd lit a kerosene lantern, which emanated a warm glow around us. I closed my eyes against it. I deserved no light. Only cold shadows.

I pressed my fingers to my abdomen, the flat area of my stomach that should be rounded. A fresh wave of pain crashed through me, and I clung to it. It probably wasn't healthy to grasp hold of the grief, but it was my only reminder. I had no stretch marks. Nothing to show that I'd once carried a child within me. The pain was the only keepsake.

"I . . . I . . ." I couldn't utter it. Four words. It was only four words, yet they burned into the cracks of my lips like embers waiting to die unsaid.

He soothed a hand down my body, a gentle caress. "You don't have to tell me tonight. Just rest." He pulled me closer, the rise and fall of his chest steady against me.

I remained still, taking in the soft lull of his breathing, the very sign of life. Warren deserved to know. I tucked my chin and pulled my knees up, curling inward, as if protecting myself against a familiar foe—regret.

"I lost our baby." I couldn't keep the sob from climbing my throat, pushing out of me with a forceful shudder.

He went rigid, his arm heavy on my waist. "Our . . . baby?"

Tears squeezed from my clenched eyes. "I'm sorry, Warren. So very sorry." I buried my face into my hands, wrenching my body away from him so I could tighten into a ball.

But Warren wouldn't let grief ravage me alone. He scooped me into his arms, folding me against him, my side against his chest, most of my weight on his lap.

I cried harder. Because this was how we'd started our wedding night. Warren had carried me into his bed and held me this way for a time, kissing my body with unforgettable passion and tenderness. Our child might have been conceived that very night.

Now those same lips pressed against my forehead as he let me weep against him. His soft touch opened valves within me, the pressure escaping with each fallen tear. Tears Warren faithfully thumbed away as he kissed my temple and murmured soothing words.

After several minutes I fell quiet. Usually I'd weep until a headache ensued, but this time there wasn't any throbbing tightness.

Warren cupped my face, his eyes glossy. "You never mentioned it."

"I was going to." I sniffled. "I planned to tell you the night we argued."

Understanding dawned. "The night before the accident."

I nodded. "I found out that morning, but, Warren, that's not all of it." I pressed my cheek against his solid shoulder. "It was my fault. I killed our child."

He shifted. I could feel his gaze, but I couldn't face it. "Sweetheart, you miscarried. There wasn't anything you could do."

"No, there's more." I refused to allow him to believe I'd been faultless. "Remember those weeks that I was sick? The doctor gave me medicine to help me sleep through the fever aches and nausea. It was an opioid." I had no idea there was a connection between opioids and miscarriages, but the doctor had said he'd seen it often with women in early stages of pregnancy.

"You didn't know you were expecting." He spoke in my defense with such tenderness I could hardly bear it.

I hadn't realized I was pregnant when I'd taken the medicine, but that hadn't stopped the guilt from piling upon the pain, the physical and emotional anguish from the passing of our child. "I woke up bleeding that Saturday morning and rushed to the doctor. By that time I'd already lost the baby."

"You bore all that pain alone." He shook his head. "And then you thought I died that same day."

"I lost my entire world." I'd never experienced such loss, hadn't known it was possible to hurt so deeply. I splayed my hand over his heart, savoring its strong pounding. "At least I was able to get a part of it back. In a speakeasy, of all places." I meant it as a way to lighten the tone, but Warren's brow crumpled.

"We were finally reunited, and I hurt you more by accusing you of something horrible. Can you forgive me?"

"Can you forgive me? I should've told you. I wanted our moment to be perfect, but I shouldn't have waited." I shook my head. "Shouldn't have argued with you. Shouldn't have taken that medicine." My vision blurred. "I have so many regrets, Warren. So many."

"None of that was your fault."

I opened my mouth to protest, but Warren continued.

"Eva, listen. You hold no blame for losing our child. Nor the blame for the argument. I was hotheaded. I jumped to conclusions. You were unusually demanding about me not printing the story, but—"

"That's because I wanted to protect you. Which was the reason I telephoned Mother that night. I didn't want you to cross Father and get hurt."

We locked eyes. Might as well spill everything. "I'd heard rumors that anyone who betrayed him turned up dead. There was speculation over the death of one of his former business associates."

"Howard Yater?"

I nodded. "That's why I didn't want you to print anything. At the time I had no clue about Ruth Fields. I guessed you were going to question Father's involvement in that man's death. I was scared for you."

He shifted, still cradling me in his embrace. "Why didn't you say so?"

"I wasn't sure if it was true. I didn't want to blame Father based on gossip. Murder is a serious charge to throw around."

He blew out a breath. "And here I was accusing you of it." His tone weighed heavy with remorse.

I snuggled into him, needing his warmth. "Mr. Yater and Ms. Fields each went against Father." One betrayed him in business, the other supposedly blackmailed him. "And then they died of a stomach illness. That's too much of a coincidence, isn't it?"

"I'm uncertain about Howard Yater's passing. I haven't looked into it. But Brisbane couldn't find anything to connect your father to Ms. Fields's death."

Well, that was something. Though, it didn't exactly reveal his innocence. "If the truth comes out about their affair and her possible blackmail, people will no doubt theorize about her sudden death." I pulled all the pieces together aloud. "That alone could cost him the election."

"Which he knows."

"And you thought I knew." I hated bringing it up again, but we couldn't allow any more misunderstandings. "When we argued that night, you thought I was siding with him. You believed I was aware of his relationship with Ruth Fields." Which also went along with how he'd acted when we'd first visited the place where she'd died. He'd kept asking me if the town held any significance to me. "Then overhearing my conversation with Mother after we argued only encouraged you to think I could harm you." I patted the space beside him, and he opened his arms, letting me slide down next to him.

"I thought you didn't want your father's name to be soiled." He tucked me against him. "That you were shielding him. And because . . ." His hand absently stroked my arm. "I didn't think you loved me. When I asked you to say it, you couldn't."

My eyes burned again. "I struggle with saying those words. Not because of you." I twisted to face him. "Because of my upbringing. Mother cheapened that phrase to justify Father's schemes. 'We're sending you away to boarding school because we love you. Father bought you this publicity out of love. He wants to keep your reputation spotless for your future.'" But it was for his future. "'Father acts that way because he loves you so much.'" I sighed heavily. "After I turned eighteen, she stopped saying it. But the word was already twisted in my head."

"None of that was love, Eva. That's a self-serving imitation of it." His eyes steadied on mine. "Love gives, not takes. It never forces another person to sacrifice but sacrifices itself for the other person."

Another tear escaped, and he thumbed it away. He was right. My view of love had been warped by those around me.

Love gives. I peered at my husband. From our earliest moments together, he'd given. He hadn't even known me, and he'd gifted me a ride in the Jenny. He'd given me the choice to marry him when my parents hadn't. He'd taught me to fly. Bought me an airplane. He'd given me wings when my parents had only tried to clip them. Warren had shown me the true version of love.

I was reminded of a portion of a favorite Scripture from childhood before the world jaded my thinking. God so *loved* the world, that He *gave* His only begotten Son . . .

I understood now—it was reciprocal. One always followed the other.

"I should've never doubted you." Warren kissed my temple. "Or argued with you that night. It seems I can't say sorry enough."

"We've both made mistakes. I should've told you about our baby. Should've talked to you about the threatening notes. Should've told you how I felt." I reached for him. "How I feel."

He watched me with an affection that made my heart race. My fingers bunched the open collar of his shirt, and I tugged him to me. Being twice my size, he could easily resist, and while I did sense some restraint on his part, his body swayed toward mine. I slid my hands up his chest, gripping his solid shoulders. Such a familiar move, but it seemed new. Everything did. Open and bright. As if the hazy cloud looming over our marriage had finally cleared.

Nothing stood between us anymore. Well, except for one thing. I eased toward him until our faces were a kiss away. I wanted to be certain he could catch the sincerity in my eyes, hear the depths of my heart. "When I thought I'd lost you, it felt like the best parts of me died." I framed his face with both hands. My fingertips took in the hard ridge of the muscle along his jaw. He was bracing himself. The tentative hope in his eyes broke me. "I never want to be apart from you. I love you with everything in me."

His arms crushed me close, and his mouth claimed mine, working over the contours of my lips in a fevered measure. Everything pulsed heat. The press of his kiss, the span of his hands against my back, our quick sips of breaths.

This was the first time we'd kissed since our separation. Over the past days, Warren had pressed light touches to my forehead or cheek, but not my lips. He'd been chaste. Though that didn't mean I hadn't caught his gaze tracking me with banked hunger. Or the flexing of his fingers at his sides at moments he'd usually reach for me.

But now the lock he'd so determinedly placed on his passion crumbled as he levered over me, his bent elbows on either side of my shoulders, hemming me in.

His mouth moved over my body, as if making up for every part he hadn't had access to for so long. He lingered on my neck, dipping to my bare shoulder from where my nightgown strap had slipped, and explored the hollow spot near my collarbone.

A pulse of breath against my skin. A graze of his lips. The scratch of his stubbled jaw brushed slightly above my curves.

Then . . . he paused. Lifted his head.

He adjusted the strap of my nightclothes and rolled off me, only to gather me against him. "I love you, Eva." The glassy sheen of his eyes brightened those beautiful golden flecks. "I've never stopped."

I went in for a lingering kiss, my fingers climbing to the open space on his collar. "Now we need to fulfill the terms of our deal."

Warren's mouth stilled on mine. Having the mind of a businessman, he wouldn't forget our agreement. The one we'd made that first day he'd told me he loved me. "Eva, you're dealing with a lot of emotions right now. Between the situation with your mother and what we just talked about, I don't want this decision rushed. I'm okay waiting."

"But I'm not." In my eyes, our relationship had elevated to a better place than even before the plane crash. I withheld nothing from him. I would do so with my body too. I ached for him to share every part of me. To become one again in the entire sense of the word. "Please be with me tonight."

That simple plea was all it took. For he kissed me as if he could never deny me anything. There was something deeper to our uniting, a sealing of our renewed devotion to each other. Tomorrow would be a new challenge as we'd step out from hiding, but tonight, as I lost myself in Warren's tender attention, we only strengthened our bond.

— PART 2 —

Chapter 26 ────────────────────────────────

No more Stella Starling.

For today I would return fully to Geneva Hayes. It was time to live in the present. These past weeks I'd been wallowing in the past, trying to find answers. I'd been terrified I'd missed a clue to something important. But flashbacks wouldn't serve me any longer. I needed every ounce of strength to face the *now*.

I wasn't sure how the next several hours would unfold. It could end with me wearing a prison gray uniform, or worse, selecting a casket for my mother. Nothing seemed promising. Well, besides Warren's fingers steadily locked with mine. But that was more than a promise. It finally felt like a sure thing.

Last night had been memorable for many reasons. Yet what I savored most was the rekindling of our relationship. Yes, I was still in awe of the intimate moments. Through it all Warren had murmured his love for me, the deep rasp against my skin banding the broken parts of my soul. Because more than the physical, our hearts had knotted. My secrets weren't caged within me anymore.

And today we'd release more. Warren truly believed coming out of hiding was the best course of action, and so the second the skies had lit pink, we'd taken off.

The return trip home proved our rockiest flight to date. The engine hiccupped for an alarming minute, causing us to make an emergency landing. Warren, ever the mechanic, located the problem, but then the wheel had needed tending. It was as if the Jenny was as hesitant to re-turn as we were.

We finally reached the airfield just outside the city limits. The fa-miliar strip of earth was where I'd first learned to fly and later had my heart shattered into a thousand pieces upon learning of Warren's crash.

After landing we hurriedly stowed the plane in our section of the hangar, knowing it wouldn't be long before someone noticed and alerted the authorities. There weren't many fliers about, and for that Warren and I were grateful. He kept guard as I changed out of my trou-sers and slipped on a wrinkled frock. Mother would have a fit if she saw me. But then my heart squeezed. Mother was currently fighting for her life. I just hoped it wasn't too late.

Warren suggested we walk the extra mile to the automobile repair shop and telephone a hired cab. It'd be less suspicious having a driver pick us up from an automotive place than the airfield. We needed to remain undetected as long as possible.

So here I stood just off the side of the road, waiting for my husband to finish a call the car-repair shop owners had graciously allowed him to make. The sun glared upon me as a bead of sweat crawled down my spine. I could blame the heat, but my jittery nerves knew the truth. I was uneasy about going to the authorities. Was it the right move?

Warren exited the small garage and strode toward me. "All set. The cab company said they'll send someone here shortly." His gaze roamed over me. "You okay?"

"Yes." I wiped my forehead, careful not to smear my darkened brows. "Are we going straight to the station from here?"

Warren glanced about, as if making sure no prying ears were within hearing distance. Once satisfied, he shook his head. "Yes. After I called for a cab, I telephoned Terrence's office."

"Oh." My brows rose. "What prompted that?" He hadn't informed me about this part of his plan. I hardly knew Warren's cousin. From all War-ren's interactions with him, I'd gathered the man was decent, but my suspicious nature trusted no one. I could think of a million things that could go wrong if our story was leaked before we reached the police.

He led me by the elbow farther from the station. "I think it's best to have our lawyer with us when we speak to the authorities. Just in case."

"In case of what?" Would they arrest me? Arrest us both?

"It's always good to have someone who knows the law on our side." Warren blew out a breath. "But I didn't get to speak with him. Only his secretary. It's noon, which is Terrence's lunch hour. I forgot the man was as predictable as clockwork." He caught my wary reaction and interpreted correctly. The edges of his lips tipped up. "No, I didn't leave my name. Well, not my real one, anyway. Just the alias I always use when contacting my cousin."

That was new. "You give a fake name?"

His brows lifted. "I never told you why?"

It was my turn to let out a sigh. There were so many things I'd go back and fix those first few weeks of our marriage if I could. Communication would be one of them. Not that I was currently a master at the concept, but I was seeing how much harm could come by holding things in.

"You worked a lot before the crash. And when we were together, we were either flying, eating, or . . . being newlyweds."

His grin sparked, carefree and on the roguish side, as if we weren't about to capsize our world by the day's end. "That's one way to phrase it." He winked. "As for Terrence, I don't go to his office anymore because he once caught his research clerk eavesdropping on our conversation about issues I had with a rival paper. He intended to sell that information to my competitor."

"That's awful."

"Sadly, it happens a lot." He released me. "So when I need to meet with Terrence, I leave the code name—Thomas Hawkins—and he comes to my office, or we meet at a neutral place. Though this time I requested a meeting at the station."

It seemed Warren had been using a different name long before Stella and Stan Starling had been created. "Will your cousin come? I'm sure he'll be relieved knowing you're alive, but he might be hurt you didn't tell him." Then my brow lowered. "Or maybe . . . he might *not* be happy knowing you survived." I'd been so focused on my family as the possible culprits, I hadn't thought much about Warren's side. "Who inherits the Hayes fortune if you're gone?"

His gaze returned to mine. "You get all of it."

I hadn't worded my question correctly. I knew all of Warren's estate would go to me. But I didn't marry him for his wealth or his influence. I'd rather have him than all the money in the world. And on that score I had a good deal of my own. As much as my parents were controlling, they had honored the terms of my inheritance. I had a tidy sum in my name that Warren refused to touch.

"But if I got convicted of your murder—as someone has been so diligent to frame me for—I wouldn't inherit."

He nodded. "Then everything would go to my uncle, my father's brother. The line would continue through his family. He's been living overseas for years. I doubt he had any part with this."

"And Terrence?"

He stared at the empty road, keeping an eye out for our hired cab. "If anything, my death harms him financially."

I remembered Warren had said his cousin wasn't wealthy, but I had no idea who would stand to receive the bulk of Warren's assets. "What do you mean?"

"He's a distant cousin. So he'd be at least fifteenth to inherit. That would be a lot of people to kill." He shrugged. "And like I said, my death would harm his practice because he handles most of my business affairs. There's no guarantee whoever owns the papers after me would use his services."

That made sense. "Is there anyone you can think of who might want you dead? Besides my family, that is." Which would include John Ashcroft and my current brother-in-law, Michael. They both had strong motives for harming my husband.

"I've always tried to be a fair man, but I'm not self-deluded enough to believe I haven't made enemies over the years." He took my hand in his, his thumb stroking my knuckles. "But whoever it was knew we went flying on Saturdays. And had access to our house, since you've been getting those threatening notes."

My chin snapped. "You think they're related?"

"You think they're not?"

"I guessed they must be linked someway, but I can't see how. I've been getting those letters since the night of our engagement reception. Which would rule out Lilith's husband. He wasn't in town yet."

"Not that you knew of." He pointed out. "Who's to say he wasn't in the area prior to Lilith's knowledge? It's not like the man's a pillar of honesty."

Very true. "He could've been setting the scene to pull attention away from him." But it didn't add up. "Though I still received letters after he and Lilith ran off together. He couldn't have sent them, because there weren't any postal marks."

Warren rubbed his jaw. "He could've hired someone to deliver the letters."

It was possible. "Which reminds me of another letter. I will have to explain what I wrote to Brisbane." Something I wasn't looking forward to. What if the police didn't believe me? "Could I get arrested even though you're all right?"

Warren reached for me. "Nothing's going to happen to you. I promise." He nuzzled my cheek. "I tried to call Brisbane. Thought maybe he might've returned while we were gone."

I pulled back. "And?"

"No one answered. Not at his office or his flat."

So Kent Brisbane was still missing? Everything was so muddled in my mind. I jerked my head toward the automobile shop. "That was kind of them to allow you to make so many calls."

Warren shrugged. "I placed a twenty-dollar bill on the counter the second I walked in the door. They wouldn't have minded if I tried to call the moon."

It seemed every man had a price. The question was, did Kent Brisbane? Could he have been paid to disappear? Or even worse, frame me for a murder he'd tried to commit? I never imagined he'd harm Warren, a man who'd been like a brother. But what if I was wrong? Warren had contacted Brisbane after the crash, hiring him to investigate me. Then subsequently the police had wanted me brought in for questioning. Besides me, Brisbane was the only one who knew Warren was alive, and instead of helping his longtime friend, he'd vanished into thin air. Though that could also mean someone could've silenced him . . . for good. The attempt on Warren's life hadn't succeeded, but could the same be said for Kent Brisbane?

Chapter 27 ———————————————————————————————

OUR CAB LET US OFF a block from the police station, and we spotted Terrence waiting on the park bench. At our approach, his brown eyes widened, the newspaper falling onto his lap.

"Warren?" He scrambled to his feet, the abandoned paper fluttering to the ground. He braced a hand on the bench's armrest, never pulling his stunned gaze from my husband. "You're . . . alive."

Warren nodded solemnly. "I am." He tugged me to his side, his fingers curling protectively around my waist. "I want to apologize for letting you believe I was dead. It felt like my only option at the time."

Terrence stood there, face blanched. His gaze shifted to me, and he startled. "Geneva? Is that you?"

I knew my appearance had drastically changed, but I couldn't help but feel proud at how I'd managed to look completely different to the point Terrence was eyeing me closely, as if uncertain of my identity.

I gave a small smile. "Yes."

The lawyer's gaze teetered between Warren and me until finally settling on Warren. He gave a small shake of his head, his fleshy chin wobbling. "You're okay," he said in almost a whisper, then again slightly louder. As quick as a blink, his thick arms came around Warren, pulling him in for a brotherly hug. "I have a lot of questions, but I'm just . . . just glad you're here."

After several seconds, Warren clapped Terrence's back and stepped away. "We've come to make a statement to the police."

Then he'd intended to give the exclusive of our story to his paper.

But my husband was a strategic man who focused on one part of the plan at a time.

Terrence shook his head. "When my secretary gave me the message, I didn't know what to expect." He nodded at me. "My only guess was Geneva returned and possibly needed some counsel, so she used your contact name."

Warren flicked a glance at the police station not far from us, then regarded his cousin. "I want to get this done as soon as possible."

He sent a concerned look my way, and I knew he was thinking of my needing to see Mother.

"But first, let me brief you on what's happened these past few weeks." Being concise, Warren relayed Brisbane's disappearance and my role in searching for him using the clues left behind. He detailed about hiding out at Brisbane's remote cabin and our encounter at the speakeasy. Without pause he continued on about the threatening notes and how I'd feared for my life, which resulted in my hiding away.

Though that wasn't the exact cause, I didn't dare interrupt. Terrence nodded along, as if to tell Warren he was following the crazy turns in conversation.

Warren recapped the situation about Ms. Fields and also our discovery about Lilith's husband. "Then with the news about Mrs. Ashcroft"—he took my hand—"we decided it's best to return."

"That's quite a story." Terrence's brows perched high on his wide forehead. "You visited all those towns on Mr. Brisbane's list?"

Warren nodded. "I caught up with Eva for the last six, but she stopped at them all."

Terrence's gaze turned to me. "Did you find anything helpful?"

"Nothing that connected them all together. Or linked to Warren's crash." I had discovered the grave of my father's mistress and the true identity of my sister's husband. While we considered Michael Jamison a definite suspect, the towns hadn't seemed to have anything to do with Warren's crash.

"What about here?" Warren retook command of the conversation. "Has it been chaos?"

"Well." Terrence shifted his bulk from one foot to the other. "John Ashcroft has offered his influence in helping run the Hayes estate while his daughter was away." He sent a knowing look to Warren. No doubt Father would want to get his itchy fingers on Warren's papers. That was unsurprising. "The police have also been demanding. They wanted to go through all your affairs. Business and personal. They wanted to . . ."

"Find any motive on my part," I supplied, knowing the man was tiptoeing around the sensitive issue. I knew how guilty I looked. The letter to Brisbane had only reinforced it.

He gave a reluctant nod. "I was instructed to hand over all the files."

I fought to keep my brows from lifting but eyed Terrence for any suspicious signs. If he'd been chiseling money from Warren or tampering with his accounts, those discrepancies would certainly turn up. Though the man only darted glances at me as if wary about my reaction regarding the police's interest in me.

"Anything else?" Warren's tone tightened with what I could only perceive as impatience. I knew he didn't want to dawdle out here any longer than necessary.

"Nothing that can't wait until later." Terrence retrieved his newspaper from the ground and tossed it into the garbage bin. "I suggest we speak with Captain Severs. He's contacted me several times and seems the most open-minded of the lot."

"Very good." Warren dipped his chin in approval at his cousin, then regarded me. "Shall we?" He squeezed my hand and tucked it into the crook of his arm as if we were about to stroll into a ballroom rather than the New York City Police Department.

"I'm ready." But my twisting gut said otherwise.

● ● ●

"You expect me to believe that tale?" Captain Severs stacked his hands behind his head and observed Warren and me.

He'd specifically asked me to recount everything from Warren's

241

plane crash until this morning, and so I had. Before that, Warren had detailed how he'd survived the crash and why he'd remained in the shadows until now. The captain's face had remained curious throughout our spiel, but I'd detected ample amounts of suspicion in his dull blue eyes.

"It sounds fanciful. A socialite moonlighting as a barnstormer? Seems something that should be featured over there at the matinee."

Holding his gaze, I took a folded flyer I'd drawn for the shows from my clutch and handed it to him. "It's the truth. And simple to verify. All you have to do is take Warren and me to all the places we held performances. Hundreds came to our shows. I'm sure one of them could easily identify us." I offered this breezily, as if the captain of the New York City Police Department had the extra time to cart us around to country towns. Out the corner of my eye, I caught Warren's lips twitch.

The four of us—Warren and I, along with Terrence and the captain—were stuffed in a windowless room, three of us huddled around a table as nicked as it was wobbly. Terrence had opted to stand, leaning against the wall by the door. A choice I was now envious of. The tendons in my legs tightened even as a current of restlessness sluiced through me. Sitting poised and composed on this hard wooden chair only increased my urge to fidget.

I could catch the shuffling of feet and low voices from the hall. This entire place buzzed with activity, and though we'd asked for a private conversation with Captain Severs, no doubt every person in this building now knew of our presence.

The captain, a man I guessed to be in his early fifties, browsed the flyer. "Since we're exchanging paperwork . . ." He opened a file in front of him and placed the poster beneath a stack of papers. He thumbed through the pile and withdrew . . . my letter to Kent Brisbane. "Care to explain this? It sounds very nearly like a confession to your husband's accident." His thick index finger tapped twice on the paper, then slid it my way.

I picked it up, scanning the words I hardly remembered writing.

Kent,
The police were just here. They told me Warren's plane had been purposefully sabotaged. That his death wasn't accidental at all. They believe it was murder. I can hardly write for all the guilt pressing in me.
I carry all the blame for this. I should've told him my secret, but it's too late. But I need to speak to you. As soon as possible. I think you can help.

I glanced up to find the officer studying me. "I know how this appears, but I wrote this because Kent's a private detective, and I had hoped he could investigate Warren's crash. The guilt I wrote about had to do with . . . several things. By mistake I'd forgotten to return the parachute to my husband's plane, and so I blamed my carelessness for him not having the chute. And as for the other part of the note where I talk about telling Warren my secret . . ." I felt Warren's hand on my thigh, offering support. "I hadn't told Warren about our baby." The captain's gaze fell to my abdomen, and I folded my arms. I heard Terrence shift behind me. "I miscarried the morning of the crash. Dr. Phelps on Highbury Street will confirm it. I couldn't have tampered with Warren's plane that morning because I was . . . hemorrhaging." I closed my eyes, pushing away the rush of sadness.

"I'm sorry." The officer's tone softened, but I didn't miss that he jotted something on his notepad.

I was confident the doctor would attest to my account, and maybe I wouldn't have to delve into this again. I rasped in a thin breath, forcing my attention on the letter, words that had caused more trouble than they were worth. "May I ask how you got ahold of that? I don't recall mailing it."

His eyebrows, two black slashes over his hooded gaze, raised slightly at my inquiry. At first it seemed he wouldn't answer, but then his pinched lips broke open with an exhale. "Someone sent it here anonymously. We weren't sure what to think until we matched your handwriting to some samples collected from the Hayes household."

So the police were just as baffled about the sender's identity as I was.

"There's something else, Captain." Warren sat forward. "The man addressed in my wife's letter, Kent Brisbane, is the same private detective I hired to investigate the plane crash. I was supposed to meet with him eleven days ago, but he never showed. We're concerned he may have gone missing."

The captain tapped his jowls, regarding Warren with a tilt of his head. "I can assign some men to look into his disappearance."

Warren nodded. "Thank you, sir."

The older man grew quiet for several long seconds, his gaze shrewdly swinging from me to Warren. Finally he relaxed against his seat with a sigh. "My investigators have sorted through all your accounts and assets, Mr. Hayes. Your cousin has done a fine job of managing them. Everything's in order. We couldn't find a single error, and believe me, we searched." He scratched a tuft of hair. "I can't even accuse you of faking your own death for fraud or other suspicious activity. That's how clean your records are. You're to be commended. It's hard to find an honest man—in the newspaper industry especially."

Warren accepted his praise with a gracious nod. "Does this mean we can go?"

Captain Severs closed the file and looked at me, not unlike a disapproving parent. "Mrs. Hayes, there are aspects in which you didn't act accordingly. Did you know we were looking for you? That you were a person of interest in this case?"

My heart pounded. "Yes, sir. I knew."

"What do you have to say for yourself?"

Warren leaned forward as if to defend me, but I squeezed his hand, staying him. "You wanted me for questioning, but I didn't have any answers. Not then, at least. I knew something wasn't right." I went on to tell him about the threatening notes. "I can easily say I was scared for my life. While that was part of the reason I ran away, it wasn't the whole of it. I had a nudge in my gut to follow Mr. Brisbane's list. And it led me to Warren."

The man steepled his hands, and he stared at the apex of his fingertips. After skewering me in his narrowed gaze, he dropped his arms and pushed back his chair. "I can't say I entirely believe your far-fetched story. I'll be making calls to those towns and to your doctor, Mrs. Hayes." He pulled a severe face. "If I discover you've lied, I'll be knocking down your door, bringing you back in. For now, you're free to go."

He shook Warren's hand and scooped up the file. After a nod to Terrence, he opened the door and paused. "Mrs. Hayes, please relay to your father we're doing everything we can regarding your mother." He exited, leaving me blinking at his words.

Why would the police help with Mother? One glance at Warren told me he was as confused as I was. The only one who seemed unsurprised was Terrence.

Thankfully, he took pity on me. "You don't know, do you?"

I felt Warren's hand on my back as I met Terrence's sympathetic eyes. "Know what?"

"The news came out this morning. They suspect your mother was poisoned."

————————————————————————————

Chapter 28

AT THE POLICE STATION, WARREN called Jenkins to bring us our car. The butler had taken the overwhelming news with surprising mildness. While waiting, my husband also telephoned his paper, giving them our statement to go to press as soon as possible. Upon our arrival at my parents' Manhattan town house, I rushed to Mother's room— mostly dim, except for a stripe of daylight from between the thick curtains through the corner window. Growing up, this space had never been warm or inviting, but today it held heavy notes of somberness. As if death had invaded the air, pushing to make itself a resident.

My head spun, my chest aching from the continual press of my heart against my sternum. It seemed it would be a long while before Warren and I could rest and catch our breath. Though none of that currently mattered, because I could clearly feel the strong thud of my pulse, while my mother's remained a weak flutter.

The nurse Father had hired to take care of Mother sat quietly beside the head of the bed opposite me, her mannerisms sharp as she diligently watched her patient. I'd never seen Mother this frail. Lying in her large four-poster bed, her frame seemed all but swallowed by the quilt pulled high to her sunken chin. She lay alarmingly still, her skin so pale it appeared translucent. I moved closer to Mother and gently lifted her limp hand.

"Where is my father?" Any other man would be by his wife's side at such a critical time.

When the woman didn't answer, Warren laid a steadying hand at my waist.

"I'm right here." My father stood in the doorway.

He didn't look any worse for wear. No dark circles hung beneath red-rimmed eyes. No rumpled suit indicating a sleepless night by Mother's bedside. The man wore a crisp pin-striped jacket, his face freshly shaven, his overall appearance of one well rested. Nothing to imply that his bride of twenty-six years currently fought for her life.

That she'd been poisoned.

I still grappled with the horror that someone had tried to kill her. It could've been an accident. But with all the weird turns of events lately, it was more likely Mother had been targeted. Just like Warren. I pressed closer to my husband, clinging to his arm. That now made two people close to me who'd had their lives threatened. Though looking at Mother, I wasn't certain if she'd pull through.

Terrence had only told us what he'd heard from the radio news bulletin. The doctors had initially thought she had a severe case of the stomach flu but this morning confirmed she'd been poisoned. How they'd determined that remained unknown, but I intended to find out.

I could feel Father's eyes on me. I hadn't the chance to explain anything to him.

The last time I'd seen Father was at Warren's memorial service. So this was the first I'd been in the same room as him since learning about Ruth Fields. My lips tightened on their own volition. My lashes refused to lift to his persistent gaze. Everything in me rebelled against speaking to him. But I needed information only he seemed to possess.

I counted to ten, gathering courage with each slow intake of breath. My eyes focused on my father, who casually clasped his hands behind his back. "How did this happen?"

He flicked a glance at Mother. "No one knows."

Well, that was unhelpful. My gaze strayed to the nurse, who'd taken a sudden interest in picking at her thumbnail. The woman was young, striking, and harboring a secret behind those dark lashes and ocean-blue eyes.

I put a hand to Warren's elbow. He lowered his head to mine. Lifting on my tiptoes, my lips brushed his ear. "I want to talk to the nurse." I waited for him to nod. "Without my father here."

He gave me a look that said he'd rather gnaw off his fingers one by one than entertain John Ashcroft. "I'll get him out of the room. Under protest, but I'll do it. For you." He gave me a warm smile before kissing my cheek.

"Try to get him to talk," I whispered, knowing I'd given my husband an insurmountable task.

He released me with a double squeeze of my hand. "Mr. Ashcroft." His tone turned identical to the one he'd used at the speakeasy. No emotion and utterly cold. So much for Warren getting any information out of Father. No chance he'd be induced to talk when addressed in such a way. "A word with you in private, if you can spare it."

Father nodded, and the men exited. The nurse seemed to sense my intentions, for she nervously tugged on her apron, refusing to look at me.

I smoothed Mother's hair back on her forehead, my brow furrowing at her stillness. I could barely spy the rise and fall of her chest. Who did this to her? My gaze drifted toward the door where my father had just left. Could he have? I shivered at the thought.

With a deep inhale, I faced the nurse. "Thank you for taking good care of her." My warm tone pulled her from her fussing. "My father isn't one to elaborate, and I have several questions." I knew he was paying for her services, so I needed to tread carefully. "Do you mind if I ask you? Nurse . . ."

"Nurse Redman," she supplied with a genuine expression of surprise. "I'll answer what I can, Mrs. Hayes."

"I know the bare minimum. I heard on the radio yesterday the doctors thought she was seized with a sudden illness, then only recently deduced she was poisoned." My voice quivered.

She gave a barely perceptible shake of her head. "The maid called the doctor after finding Mrs. Ashcroft collapsed on the floor in her own vomit yesterday morning, struggling with stomach pain. Since then Mrs. Ashcroft has suffered violent bouts of retching lasting several hours. She's been slipping in and out of consciousness." The nurse spoke as if reading a clinical report, but now she looked at me with a curious bend to her dark brows. "Your mother regained clarity for a few minutes. And told me . . . she was poisoned."

My heart raced. The words *stomach pain* and *poison* bit into my mind with jagged fangs. If Mother had died without ever mentioning the poisoning, I was convinced the doctors would've ruled it natural causes. Just like Howard Yater and Ruth Fields. My father's face flashed before my eyes, and I pushed it back. I couldn't accuse him until I knew more details.

"Why isn't she at the hospital?" I figured I knew the answer but wanted to hear it from somewhere other than my screaming thoughts.

"The doctor called the hospital and instructed for a room to be reserved for her, but Mr. Ashcroft refused. He feared her condition would worsen if we moved her."

I knew it. Fire ripped through me in angry bursts. What if Father had only insisted she remain here so she'd be limited in medical help? As if he wanted her to die.

She continued, "We couldn't be certain at first because poison symptoms often match that of a virus. But because of her confession, the doctor had to inform the police."

Ah, now it made sense. I couldn't imagine Father contacting the authorities, attracting any more attention than necessary. Major newspapers, my husband's included, had scouts lingering at police stations and hospitals, ready to snatch a story of interest. Which probably also accounted for the news leak on the radio yesterday.

I took a calming breath. It wasn't as if my fury against Father would help anything. "What are her chances?"

The nurse's eyes flitted to the closed door, then back to me. "Until we know the poison, we can't give her an antidote. Though the major concern is dehydration. We need to get more fluids in her. When she stirs, I try to give her a sip or two." She nodded at the pitcher on the bedside table. "But she drifts back asleep before getting much in her."

"Will she live?"

"It looks like the worst is over. She hasn't retched in two hours, which is a good sign. Though I can't promise anything. We don't know what's in her system."

Her jerky glances and tight mouth were at odds with her graceful movements of tending to Mother. She adjusted Mother's pillows, glided a hand over her forehead to check her temperature, and poured a glass of water.

I took a delicate step toward the nurse. "Did she say anything else to you?"

She brushed a hand down her apron, avoiding my eyes. "She said the word *headache* a few times."

I didn't see that as something extraordinary besides the fact that the nurse had said Mother experienced severe stomach pain. When I'd had the flu just prior to my miscarriage, all the retching had made my head throb fiercely. But somehow I didn't think I'd yet unearthed the secret the nurse obviously hid. "There's more, isn't there?"

Nurse Redman's shoulders spiked with a clipped inhale.

"You can tell me," I said softly. "My only aim is to help her." I gestured to Mother, sleeping only a few feet away.

She bit her lip, white slashes denting the pinks of her mouth. "Before you came in here with Mr. Hayes, I was alone with her."

"Yes?"

"And she said someone's name. Her eyes briefly opened too. It was like she wanted me to know something important." As if sensing she was relaying too much, she retreated a step. "But I'm not wholly certain of anything. It could just be her muttering under delirium. Patients in distress are known to do that."

"I understand. Will you tell me what she said?"

She locked eyes with me, then movement to our right caused us both to jolt.

Mother. She writhed, her face twisting as her hands clutched her stomach. I moved to her side, while the nurse scrambled to get the glass of water.

"I'm here." I gripped her balled fist. "I'm here, Mother."

Her dry lips broke open on a painful moan. "Gen . . ." Dark lashes barely fluttering open, she lolled her head toward me. "Clark."

My heart pounded. I knew exactly who poisoned her.

Chapter 29 ————————————————————————————————

"I KNOW WHAT HAPPENED." I barged into Father's study, surprising both him and Warren. Growing up, I'd never stormed into this room uninvited, but at the moment I couldn't bring myself to care. Not when there was a more pressing matter—Mother's health.

From Warren's tight expression, the two of them must've been in a heated discussion, but I'd have to explore that later. "I need to confirm a few things first." I crossed the plush carpet to the bellpull and gave a determined tug.

"What did you discover?" The tense line of Warren's shoulders lowered as he moved toward me.

"After you two left, Mother woke up."

Father rose from his desk and started toward the door.

It took me a second to believe what I was seeing. "Wait." I held up my palm. "She's already back to sleep."

His face fell, making my own slack with wonder. He seemed almost disappointed at losing the opportunity to see Mother. But it was difficult to ever determine what was genuine concerning my father. A sigh slipping from my lips, I glanced over just in time to catch Cecily waiting in the doorway.

"Did you need something, sir?" The maid turned a hesitant gaze on Father.

"Geneva does." He reclaimed his seat behind the desk.

I stole a glance at Warren, drawing courage from his solid presence, something he'd seemed to catch on, for he pressed a reassuring hand to my lower back. I faced the aged woman who'd tended all my scrapes as a child, brushed my hair, taught me manners I later defied. "Cecily, I need to ask you about yesterday morning. Can you recount everything from when Mother woke until you found her on the floor?" I knew Mother always rang for Cecily within moments of rising.

She frowned, the creases deepening in her pale face. "Mrs. Ashcroft asked me to run errands for her, so I left young Iris to tend to her dressing and styling for the day."

Wait. Did she say . . . I darted a look at Warren, whose gaze squinted in confusion. "Iris? My maid?"

Cecily blew out a long breath, ruffling the white lace on her uniform's collar. "With you both gone, the girl was frightened she'd get let go because of no work. Two weeks ago she came here asking if I'd take her on again."

Iris had willingly crawled back to the house I'd tried to save her from. Though I suppose I couldn't fault her. She'd been nervous she'd have no place of employment. No roof over her head.

Cecily's plump hand trembled. Warren had also noticed, stepping to her side and leading her to an armchair.

Her eyes widened. "No, sir. I can't sit while the rest of you stand. It's not proper."

Warren offered a compassionate smile. "I insist."

She reluctantly lowered onto the chair, keeping her gaze from straying Father's direction. I stepped between her and Father, as if to show that I'd battle for her if he so much as uttered an objection. I wasn't sure what had happened to me while I'd been conducting air shows, but somewhere along the way, boldness had bloomed within me. I no longer feared John Ashcroft.

"Cecily, I'll go find Iris in a moment, but I want to hear from you first. Did you know if my mother was fighting head pain at all yesterday morning?"

She gave a rapid nod. "Iris told me when I returned that the mistress was having a migraine."

"I see." I kept my hand behind my back so she wouldn't glimpse what I held. "And Iris gave her headache wafers?"

Cecily blinked. "Yes. She said Mrs. Ashcroft demanded a triple dose since they're mild."

A triple dose? My eyes squeezed shut. "Did she get it from Mother's cabinet rather than the general medicine one beneath the stairs?"

Another nod. "I scolded her for invading the mistress's shelves, but Iris said Mrs. Ashcroft was in so much pain, she felt it quicker to get the wafers from there."

I released a sigh. "That's what I thought." I opened my palm, which held the incriminating tin. "This is what Iris used. Look." The label said *Fenwick's Headache Cure*, but I knew better. I opened the lid and glanced around. "Fenwick's wafers are circular. These are square. Mother changed them out."

"Then what is it?" Warren leaned over, examining the so-called medicine.

I met his gaze. "It's arsenic."

Cecily gasped and flapped her hand in front of her face.

I held it out so Father could see. "These are Clark Complexion Wafers. Mother always used them until I begged her to stop because they're harmful." She'd loved the product, saying it made her skin glow, but after reports of women falling dead from "the safe dose of arsenic"—as it'd once been printed on the label—I'd taken them from her medicine cabinet.

I thought I'd gotten rid of all of them, but it seemed Mother had tricked me by hiding a stash in an old headache wafer tin. "Iris gave her a triple dose of poison. Though I doubt she's aware of it." I'd only known because the nurse had said mother had mumbled the word *headache*. Then when her pain-filled voice sputtered *Clark*, I'd instantly put the two together.

"So the poisoning wasn't intentional at all." Warren surmised my thoughts. "It was an accident?"

"It appears so." I nodded. "I'll give these to the police and let them know."

Father opened his mouth, but I sharply inclined my chin. He blinked and said nothing. If anything, he should be grateful. It removed any suspicion from him.

I held his gaze. "When Mother recovers, I'm sure she'll tell the whole story. But for now I think it's safe to say it was all an accident." Thank the Lord. I was already fidgety being back in the public eye while Warren's assailant was still on the loose. It was a relief Mother's ailment wasn't in any way linked. "I should probably speak to Iris before this gets out. I don't want her to feel guilty for something that wasn't her fault."

Cecily shifted in her chair. "Um, Mrs. Hayes?"

I tilted my head. Having been so used to Cecily calling me *Miss Geneva* for almost a decade, it sounded different coming from her nasally voice. But maybe it wasn't what she said but rather how she said it. The nervous lilt reminded me of our telephone conversation on the morning of my wedding, when she'd told me about Lilith running away. "What's the matter?"

"Iris is gone." She wrung her apron in her lap. "I haven't seen her since this morning after word got out that the missus was poisoned."

Ah, so she was scared my father would pin it on her. Very reasonable. "When did you last see her?" Poor thing. No doubt she was terrified.

"I've never seen her so jittery. She darted out of the house right after breakfast. She didn't even have her mobcap on." One thing with Cecily, when she was nervous, her mouth ran like a sieve. "I should've known something was wrong then. She always wears her mobcap because it hides her misshaped ear."

I jolted. Misshaped ear? I'd only heard that in connection with one other person recently. Warren pressed a hand to my elbow, a knowing nudge telling me he'd caught it as well. "Which ear, Cecily?"

She blinked at the turn in conversation. "The . . . the left one."

Warren tapped his own ear. "Is the top part of her lobe folded over?"

Cecily's soft brown eyes glanced back and forth between Warren and me. "Yes. She's very shy about it."

My breath shallowed. I'd always wondered why Iris had insisted on wearing a mobcap when I'd told her it wasn't necessary, and this explained it. This description exactly matched the one we had of Ruth Fields's nurse. Could the woman who'd been living in my home have been the mysterious nurse? Or . . . possibly my sibling? "Thank you, Cecily. Would you mind tending to Mother to give Miss Redman a break?"

"Not at all." She all but jumped from her seat.

Once she was out the door, Father folded his arms. "What's all this fuss about a maid's ear?"

"Would you really like to know?" I took a confident step toward him. Ever since that day we'd heard about Ruth Fields and her nurse, I'd questioned if I had another sister. Now was my chance to pry the answer from the only person who knew the truth. "While we were gone, we met an older woman in Hanover who prattled on about a nurse with a folded ear. This nurse had taken care of Ruth Fields during her final days."

Father flinched, but I continued. "This woman gave us a description of the nurse and implied she was Ms. Fields's daughter because they resembled each other. Being aware of your relationship with Ruth Fields, I'm now left with the question—is this nurse my sister?"

He rose to his feet, the only noise the squeak of his chair.

I braved another step. Now I was standing opposite him, the desk between us. "I have every right to know."

Color flooded his face, and I almost blinked to be certain. I wondered if Mother's situation had tossed him off-kilter, because I'd not glimpsed so many reactions from him in a long time. If ever.

His arms fell to his sides. "You weren't supposed to know about her." He shot an accusing look at Warren, as if blaming him for my knowledge of his mistress rather than Father's own actions. "Though I should've guessed he'd tell you."

"You may choose to keep secrets from Geneva, but I won't," Warren inserted, coming to stand beside me. "She's your daughter, but she's also my wife." His tone surged with a protective edge, and his locked jaw and fierce eyes said he wouldn't put up with my father's nonsense. "Now answer her question. Is this young woman—the one who tended your former mistress and possibly was under your employ—your child?"

Father's face remained stoic, but there was something in his eyes I couldn't quite decipher. He stood quiet for several awkward seconds, as if deliberating what he would reveal. Finally he looked at me. "This young woman may be Ms. Fields's daughter, but she isn't mine."

My breath whooshed out of me. But then how could I be certain he spoke truth? "Please don't lie to me, Father."

A shadow swept across his face, and it almost seemed like . . . hurt? Though it happened so quickly I could've imagined it. He pushed his chair in and moved to leave the room. His steps weren't rushed, nor his gait rigid. Other than the previous slips of mild emotion, there was nothing now that would convey this conversation had rattled him.

"Geneva." He paused at the door but didn't bother to look back at me. "You and Lilith are my only children."

Then he left the room.

• • •

As expected, the news of Warren's return from the grave surged throughout New York City. A large crowd had gathered outside our home by the time we'd returned that evening. We'd remained at my parents' town house for several more hours, monitoring Mother's condition. She still had a stretch of recovery before her, but she had roused for several minutes and even nibbled on a piece of toast. She confirmed my supposition about how she'd been poisoned with a dismal nod of regret.

If only she would've disposed of those wafers like I'd begged her to, this wouldn't have happened. She wouldn't have been so dangerously close to death's door. Speaking of a door, I wasn't certain how we'd reach our own, so thick was the mob before us.

Warren's paper was the first to cover our story, but with the expediency of radio, the word had spread rapidly. My heart pumped fast in my chest.

"It will be okay." Warren's hand clasped mine. "They're all just curious."

I shivered. "I don't care if all the world knows you're alive. I just don't want your attacker informed." It unnerved me. I'd been overly cautious, even at my parents' home. My father might not have been to blame for Mother's poisoning, but I remained suspicious about his involvement in Warren's accident. Which was why I hadn't allowed Warren to eat or drink anything while we were there.

"I promise to be careful. But right now my main concern is you."

I blinked. Why me? I was about to ask, but someone walked by our idling car. Warren leaned over and kissed me. His hands cupped my cheeks, a clever maneuver to shield my face, while his hat obstructed any clear glimpse of his. Whoever it was had passed, but Warren was slow to end the interlude.

When he finally eased back, his eyes were hazed before blinking it away. "We'll continue that later." His mouth tipped at the edges. "But first we need to get inside the house."

I peered out the window. "Do we make a run for it?"

"I'm going to turn around and park a block down. We'll walk the side street and go through the staff entrance." He cut a glance at me. "Though maybe no one would recognize you." He motioned toward my hair. "Your back was turned when your father first caught sight of you earlier. You should've seen his face."

I laughed with a shake of my head. Cecily had reacted strangely when she'd opened the door at our arrival. I'd grown accustomed to my dark locks, but it'd been a shock to those familiar with me. But Father's behavior had been the oddest. "I've witnessed more emotions in him in a span of hours than I've seen in years. But at least it seems Mother will be okay." Now to find Iris. We'd waited around after Mother had fallen asleep to see if the runaway maid would return.

She hadn't.

Warren parked the car away from the traffic, and we walked briskly toward home. We cut through the small garden and weren't surprised to find the staff entrance locked. After Warren gave several light taps, Jenkins opened the door.

He'd seen us earlier today when dropping off the car, and it still seemed he resumed his casual stance. The moon could fall from the sky, and Jenkins wouldn't flick an eyelash. I smiled, and he responded with a perfunctory nod.

Warren set a hand on my arm. "I need to see to some things. I'm concerned about Brisbane. I know the captain said he'd assign men to the search, but I'm going to reach out to other detectives I've hired in the past, see if they know anything." He exhaled, the lines framing his mouth deepening. "But first I'll call the police and inform them of our large homecoming party out front."

"Do you think you should ask for a guard?" There was a quiver in my voice, but I didn't care.

His gaze softened. "I doubt they'll spare an officer, but maybe I can ask for extra patrols. Especially given the fact that the street is currently stuffed with busybodies."

I nodded. It seemed we had the same amount of people out front as we had attending our flight shows. "I'm going to get cleaned up."

He brushed a kiss to my lips before exiting the room with Jenkins. I exchanged light conversation with the cook, who hadn't recognized me at first but now smothered me in a tight embrace. Jenkins, the cook, and the head housekeeper were the only current staff in residence, the others having left to find more secure work.

I headed upstairs and reached my bedroom. The last time I'd been within these walls, my heart had been weighted with grief. I glanced around, taking in the armoire and vanity. The large bed situated beneath a high ceiling. It was familiar yet somehow different. Or perhaps I was the one who'd changed. Everything seemed bigger, more stately. Though we'd been cramped in tight spaces over the past weeks, so anything with more square footage than a hatbox would seem grand.

A part of me already missed the simpleness we'd just left behind. Of things being only Warren, me, and the Jenny. Because after being absent for so long, Warren and I had a lot of work to catch up on. Him infinitely more than me. Which was why I'd already taken a long bath, unpacked our meager bag, and was lying across my bed in deep thought by the time Warren entered my room. He appeared as tired as I felt. It was a little after 10:00 p.m., but it seemed much later.

I breathed relief as he sat beside me, his weight dipping the mattress. Inching toward him, I turned my hand over, wiggling my fingers, beckoning his to join mine. "I've been waiting forever to get you alone."

His lips flicked into an easy smile. "Words every husband wants to hear."

I'd meant I wanted to talk, but Warren interpreted my words another way, for he eased down and kissed me. Apparently he hadn't been teasing when he'd promised in the car to continue our tryst. I slid my hands up his chest, locking my fingers behind his neck, clinging to him because his touch rendered me breathless. What I expected to last only a handful of seconds eased into long pleasurable minutes, one kiss melting into another, strengthening in intensity.

His hand slid up my leg, and I feebly tapped him on the shoulder. He released my bottom lip and pulled back, his hooded gaze on mine.

"It was such a strange day."

"Yes." He nuzzled my hair. "But we made it through together."

Together. I would never tire of that word. After Warren's accident, I'd never felt more alone. But thank God we had each other and could face the obstacles side by side.

I leaned into Warren's touch, and he took it as permission to kiss me again. This time on my neck.

"Did the crowd leave?"

"For now." His fingers worked a slow trail down my arm. "I'm sure they'll be back. But let's not focus on tomorrow's problems." He moved to my bare shoulder.

I smiled. Warren was acting like . . . well, Warren again. During our first weeks of marriage, this sliver of the evening had been our intimate time. And at present he seemed interested in renewing the habit.

"I was thinking about Father."

Warren groaned and rolled me on my back. "I suggest a new rule. No mention of our odious relatives on this bed."

I smiled at his teasing. But I couldn't help but think of a similar rule, the one Lilith and I had come up with about no talking about our parents in the Ashcroft breakfast nook. My heart saddened. Was Lilith happy with her choice to remain with Michael? Or was she regretting it?

"Suggestion accepted, husband." I adopted a light tone, pushing thoughts of Lilith far away. "Shall I move to the chair so we can continue the discussion?" With a teasing shove to his chest, I rolled away.

He growled playfully and scooped me up before I reached the edge. "Not a chance, Mrs. Hayes. Forget what I said. I don't care what we talk about as long as you're in my arms."

I rested my cheek against his shoulder. "Do you think Father told the truth? You know, about Lilith and me being his only children?"

He hauled me closer. "It's hard to tell with him. He seems very reluctant to discuss his former mistress."

It was easy to get sidetracked with Warren staring at me with such admiration while his hand ran along the line of my body in aching tenderness. But something was bothering me, and I couldn't put my finger on it. "Don't you think it's strange that Ms. Fields waited so long to contact my father? From what you said in that letter you got, the affair happened years ago. Why blackmail him now?"

His full lips pressed together, his fingers now toying with mine. It seemed he couldn't stop touching me. Not that I minded. "We're not entirely certain that was the intention of her letter. But why else would she contact him? Maybe she needed money, and that was her only option."

"But Father has always been wealthy. Why not ask sooner?"

"Maybe she didn't need the money until then. Something desperate may have turned up. Maybe her health issues also drained her accounts."

I was quiet for a long moment, and Warren peered down at me.

"What's going on in that head of yours?" His voice was a soft rumble in my ear.

"Why do you think Iris—if that's really her name—sought employment with my parents? If she's the person we believe her to be, then her profession is nursing. She's not a maid. I think she must've known about Father's affair with Ms. Fields."

"Most likely."

"Do you still have that letter? The one sent anonymously to you about Ruth?"

His brow lowered. "It's in my study, I think." He ran a knuckle down my cheek, bringing my gaze to his. "You want to see it, don't you?"

"I just don't think I'll be able to sleep until I know one thing."

He was already sliding off the bed. "That's enough motivation for me." He tugged open the door. "Then I'll personally help you to sleep." His grin was part determination, part amusement, and entirely full of mischief.

Within minutes he returned, letter in hand. He held it out to me. "I couldn't find the envelope. Brisbane might have it."

"That's okay." I gently took the single page from him. "This is what I wanted to see anyway." I scanned the letter. It was typed and . . . My head tilted. "I think it matches."

"Matches what?"

I moved swiftly to my vanity and retrieved the folded paper beneath the tray. "Look." I pressed it into his palm. "This is one of those awful notes I've been getting."

A shadow fell upon his brow as he read the threatening words. His jaw tightened, his gaze narrowing into slits of fire. That particular note was from a few days after Warren's crash. "It says"—he glanced up—"that you deserve to have everything taken from you." This version of Warren reminded me of a hero from a romance novel. He radiated lethal energy, ready to battle anything that could harm me.

"Yes, all of them held a similar theme like that. But the message isn't what I want you to see."

He scowled. "It's hard not to."

"Maybe this will help." I placed the papers beside each other on the bed. "Look at the typeset." I pointed to the word *Ashcroft* on the first note, then *deserve* on the second.

Warren leaned close. "The *r*'s are dropped on both."

"Precisely. It appears they were typed on the same typewriter. Which means it's possible whoever tipped you about Father's affair is the same that's been writing these awful notes."

He nodded. "How long have you been getting them?"

"Since the night of our engagement. This one here"—I tapped the edge—"I received a few days after your crash."

Understanding darkened his expression. "Besides your family, only one person has been at both the Ashcroft country house and our town house. Your maid. Ms. Fields's nurse."

Chapter 30 ———————————————————————————————

A DISTURBING RATTLE OF GLASS woke me with a jolt. My vision clouded along with my mind. Where was I? What town were we in? After traveling nonstop for weeks, those thoughts were always present when first opening my eyes. But the familiar skim of quality sheets against my arms and a canopy bed surrounded by buttery-yellow walls proved a beautiful reminder—I was home.

Sunshine filled my bedroom, and my husband filled the doorway. In his hands was a breakfast tray. Surprise expanded in my chest. I'd thought he'd left for the day, considering the workload that sat heavy upon those broad shoulders.

"Sorry." Warren gave a sheepish grin. "This was much more romantic in my head." He looked curiously at the carafe of orange juice that seemed in danger of teetering over. That must've been the sound I'd heard.

I hopped off the bed, coming to his aid. Plucking the pitcher from the tray, I intended to smile at Warren, but my mouth pulled into a yawn instead.

"Good morning, my beauty." He leaned to kiss the side of my head, then crossed the room, setting the tray on my bed. "I didn't mean to wake you."

I followed behind, placing the carafe on the bedside table. "What's all this?" I smiled at my breakfast spread. Bacon stacked next to a couple pieces of toast with burned edges. The pile of scrambled eggs leaned slightly on the runny side. This was not our chef's work but rather from my sweet husband. Though . . . now my suspicions heightened.

"You've never cooked for me before." I studied his face, trying to judge his expression. "How come you aren't at the office?"

"Would you rather I be there, love?" His fingers toyed with the lace of my nightgown, tracing the low neckline.

"Of course I want you with me." Any hazy residue I had from a good night's rest vanished at his burning touch. "But I know how much work you have. I didn't expect to see you until late."

He drew me near, his lips brushing my hair. "I couldn't leave you. Not today."

Something in his tone made my heart dip. "Is there something you're trying to prepare me for?" Yesterday's events flashed through my mind, one fiercely taking hold, pulling a gasp from somewhere deep inside me.

I lowered onto the bed beside the tray. "Is it Mother? Oh no. Is it worse than we thought?"

"Eva." He set a hand on my shoulder, lowering his face so our gazes were level. "Your mother's better today. I already checked with Cecily. I've spoken to a few detectives and hired them to search for Brisbane. I'm not leaving my friend's welfare up to the police." He kept his tone casual, but I could tell Kent's disappearance really bothered him. "The crowds returned like we expected. Our story has been sensationalized in the other papers. Speculation abounds. But other than a juicy scant of gossip about us, there's nothing drastically wrong."

I exhaled. "Good." After the world had thought me a killer, fleeting rumors didn't bother me as much anymore.

His head tilted. "You seriously don't know why I stayed home." He swept a hand toward the tray. "Why I made you breakfast?"

I smoothed the napkin over my lap and picked up my fork. Might as well grab a few bites. I hate cold eggs. "Is it because you're trying to persuade me into—how do you phrase it?—pleasant pastimes?" I sent him a suggestive smile and patted the bed beside me.

He laughed outright. "Will that work? If so, I'm making you break-fast every morning from now on," he teased and settled beside me. "No, my little minx. Since you apparently forgot, today's your birthday."

I fumbled the fork. "It is? It's the fourteenth already?"

"Indeed." He pressed a kiss to my temple, then picked up the carafe, pouring me a cup of juice.

With all that had been going on, I'd completely lost track of dates. I took a forkful of eggs and bit into something crunchy. A piece of shell. My husband was brilliant at many things. Cooking wasn't one of them. I took a sip of juice to wash it down.

"So tell me, wife, would you like your present now or after dinner with your cake?"

My first thought? Hopefully, he wasn't making the cake. But that got pushed aside by a pressing question. "When did you get me a gift?" He couldn't have purchased anything while we hosted air shows. We'd shared the same bag, and the Jenny hadn't much space for storage. If he had bought me something, I would've found it.

"As to that." He kicked out his legs alongside mine. He was dressed for the day, formal except for his bare feet, which prompted my smile. The man hated putting on socks until necessary. "I've been working on your present for a while now. Even before we were married."

This caught my attention. I vaguely remembered him mentioning my birthday present the morning he'd given me the Jenny, but back then he hadn't delved into much detail. "Truly?"

He nodded.

"In that case"—I beamed at him—"I don't think I can wait until din-ner." These past weeks had been heavy. Warren's surprise meal and mystery gift brought an unexpected lightness to my heart. We still had so much to unravel concerning who was behind the accident, monitoring Mother's health, finding Brisbane, and now the addition of trying to locate Iris, but I relished this moment. Alone time with Warren was a gift in itself. "You're not going to blindfold me again like you did with my Jenny?"

He smiled. "Not this time. I couldn't hide the Jenny like I can this gift."

"You have your present with you?" I looked him over, then eyed the eggs warily. "It's not hidden somewhere in my food, is it?" If so, I needed to chew carefully.

"No." He chuckled. "I wouldn't want you to break a tooth. Now, no more hinting. Close your eyes and stick out your hand, please."

"Okay, but I'm trusting you." My lashes lowered at his amused grin. I held out my palm, and within seconds something coarse dropped onto it.

"You can open them."

I did, and found . . . a rock? The jagged stone was light gray and about the size of a golf ball. "Is this to match my white pebble?" Was I to carry it around on my person like he did mine? Did he want to start a rock collection? I truly had no idea.

"Do you remember our talk in your parents' garden when you asked if I'd marry you if you had nothing to your name but a hundred acres of swampland?"

I smiled. "Vividly. I was testing you. Trying to see if you truly wanted me for . . . well, me. You said you'd still marry me—"

"To which you called me a liar." He wagged a finger at me.

"I did." I laughed. "You also said you would prove it."

"And that is how." He pointed at the rock in my hand. "Because do you know where I got that?"

I shuddered. "Please don't tell me you bought a hundred acres of swampland."

"It's not swamp, but it is land." He wrapped his arm around me. "I know how much the country means to you. So I bought you a lot of space to build your dream home. Terrence worked it all out for us. The land's under your name. It's roughly a hundred acres."

Oh my heart. I pressed a hand to my chest as if physically keeping the pounding organ from bursting through. "Warren!" I threw my arms around his neck, my knees knocking the tray, some food sliding onto the quilt, but I didn't care. "I can't believe . . . this is . . . I'm completely at a loss for what to say." Eyes welling with happy tears, I grasped his sneaky face with my free hand and kissed him. "Thank you."

"I'll do anything to make you smile." He rested his forehead on mine. "It's a favorite hobby of mine."

If words could melt, I'd be a puddle of swooning female beside the crumbs of bacon that'd fallen from my tray. "So where's our future country house going to be?"

"Upstate. The property backs into the Adirondacks. But there's a nice flat stretch for your gardens and maybe a landing strip for the Jenny."

This was too much. Mountains, forests, gardens, *and* a house on top of it all. With that much land, maybe we could build a flight training school for those who couldn't afford to learn. I was nearly overcome. "You planned this even before we were married?"

"I had the idea. The sale finalized a few weeks after the wedding." He pushed a lock of my hair from my temple and brushed his nose along the spot. "You happy?"

"Deliriously." Not for the reason of the extravagance but because Warren had given me something more tangible—hope. For so long, I couldn't climb my way out of the shadowy rut. I'd grappled, clawing through the devastation, the pain, all the broken things in my life. Warren gifted me something to look forward to. A place of new beginnings. Yet not just a place. A home. Where we'd share a part of our lives. Hopefully, raise children. Setting a hand on my stomach, I whispered a prayer of thankfulness, taking this moment to savor the flooding joy. I lifted my gaze and found Warren watching me with such love in his eyes that my own glossed over.

His thumb traced the curve of my face, settling under my jaw. He gently lifted my chin, tipping my face toward his. His fingers slid over my palm, still holding the rock. The stone nestling between our joined hands, he claimed my lips with heated depth. The scrape of his beard against my skin flushed like fire. I knew he'd shave soon, and that thought alone had my fingers running along his jaw, relishing the strength beneath as he kissed me.

Too soon he pulled back. "Happy birthday, my darling."

I grinned up at him, wound my arms around his neck, and—

A knock sounded.

My gaze swiveled to the door. Who would interrupt us so early? I exchanged a look with Warren. He grabbed my robe from the foot of the bed and handed it to me. I slipped it on as he moved toward the door.

He glanced back, ensuring I was covered, then opened the door. Jenkins.

"Sorry, sir," he said in a monotone voice. "But you told me to inform you if there was any development regarding our former maid."

I straightened.

"Of course. Anything turn up?" Warren leaned on the doorjamb all casual, but I was already rising out of bed.

"As a matter of speaking, yes." Jenkins nodded. "She's waiting for you both in your study, sir."

• • •

I had never gotten dressed so fast in my life. In less than ten minutes, Warren and I stood before the study door, pausing so I could claim a steadying breath. I was convinced Iris had been the author of those terrible notes, and it wouldn't do to enter the room flustered. Because in all honesty, it stung. I'd done nothing but look after her welfare, while she'd threatened mine.

Another breath.

"Ready?" Warren asked.

That gorgeous jaw I'd skimmed my fingers across only moments ago now hardened like granite. Perhaps I shouldn't be as concerned about my temper as I should be about Warren's. Of course, he would never hurt a woman. But I couldn't imagine him being overly polite to Iris after her cruel treatment.

I nodded, and he opened the door.

Our former maid sat in the armchair by the fireless hearth. Upon noticing us, she jumped to her feet. Her gaze fell on me, and her head reared back. I really needed to return to my natural hair color soon. But she also looked different now without her uniform. Her slim frame donned a simple frock of light green, similar to the shade of her eyes. Her left ear, the feature that'd first jolted our suspicions, was concealed beneath her cloche hat. But what raised my brow was her mannerism. It seemed unchanged. Upon every encounter, she'd behaved jumpy, flinching at every noise. Now judging by her wringing hands and darting glances, that hadn't all been an act. Which only confused me more. How could someone so skittish pen such forceful words?

"Hello, Iris." Warren took a commanding step into the room. "We have some questions for you."

I moved beside him, aiming to address the letters, but she spoke first.

"I . . . I came here to tell you I didn't poison Mrs. Ashcroft." Desperation clung to her tone. "I know it was wrong of me to run away. But I panicked. I didn't want to be accused."

"Why did you come here and not to my father?" I could guess the answer to this but wanted to gauge her response.

Twin spots of color dotted her cheeks. "Because I'm more comfortable with you. You don't have reason to believe me, but—"

"I know you didn't poison her." I dropped onto a chair as a mixture of emotions played across her face.

"You do?" Her head tilted, as if unsure she heard correctly. "I was certain your father was going to have me arrested." Her shaky voice revealed she still seemed uncertain.

"There's no concern about that." I smoothed out my skirt, trying to tame the rising aggravation. She had come to *me* for help, the woman she'd been tormenting. "Mother is on the mend and has confirmed it wasn't your fault."

She placed a hand over her heart in relief. "Thank you, Mrs. Hayes."

I stole a glance at Warren, who seemed content to let me navigate the conversation. "Though I do wonder why you didn't recognize the wafers were different, considering you're a nurse."

Her thin lips quivered. "No, I'm not."

"That's interesting." There wasn't any reason to expect honesty from a woman who'd deceived me from the beginning, but I fought a scowl nonetheless. "Because Ivy Gibbons from Hanover says otherwise." If it wasn't for the gossiping grandmother we'd met in the grocery mart, we would've never become aware of this young lady.

Her face crumpled. "You know?"

"We know a lot of things," Warren said crisply. "Like you've been writing my wife threatening notes."

Her startled eyes met mine as I withdrew her last letter from my pocket. "Perhaps you should start from the beginning. Who are you really? How are you associated with Ruth Fields? And why you thought it a good idea to taunt me."

"My real name is Pauline Cartwright." She swallowed, her skin so pale the webbing of blue veins stretched visible across her forehead. "This . . . this past July I asked for the day off to visit a relative. I don't expect you to remember, Mrs. Hayes, since it was the week of the plane crash. But I went to Hanover to visit Ruth Fields's grave. She was my aunt."

Things shifted and fell into place in my mind. This woman wasn't Ruth's daughter but her niece. That explained why Ivy had detected a resemblance. It also ruled out Ms. Cartwright as a possible suspect in Warren's accident because Ivy Gibbons had mentioned seeing her that very day.

"Go on."

"I moved to Hanover to be with her when she fell sick. She told me about your father."

Warren came to stand beside my chair, silently offering support while keeping his probing eyes on Ms. Cartwright. "What did she say?"

Her gaze bounced to the door, and her feet shifted. She was debating whether to make a run for it, that much was certain. But finally her arms collapsed against her sides. "She fell in love with Mr. Ashcroft when she was younger. And I'm sure you're aware of the rest."

"Unfortunately, we're not." I could tell by her closed stance she didn't intend to easily surrender information. "Please tell us what you know."

Her lips broke open with a sigh, but she said nothing.

Warren folded his arms across his chest. "You can tell us here, or I can contact Captain Severs at the police station, and you can explain to him why you wrote those letters to my wife. It's your choice."

"It's his fault," she sputtered. "Mr. Ashcroft, I mean. He's the reason why my aunt is dead."

I gripped the armrest, my nails digging into the upholstery. She'd confirmed my fear. "How?"

"My aunt hadn't spoken to him in years. She left him alone like he ordered. But then she got sick and needed his help. She begged him in a letter. He never responded."

"Yet you say he killed her?" Warren voiced my very question.

"Don't you see?" The pleading in her tone surprised me. "He ignored her. Which is the same as a refusal. His dismissal made her health decline even more."

I inhaled deeply. It wasn't as I'd assumed. Father didn't murder her in cold blood. He'd only treated her like he did every other human being. Ruth Fields had asked him for money to get well, but Father had refused, and she'd gotten worse. "And you tended to her until she passed?"

She nodded. "Yes."

I shifted in my seat. "And how did you come to work for my father? I'm guessing you knew who he was. You must've sought the position for a specific reason."

"I know it sounds awful, but after my aunt passed, I grew angry. He denied her the only thing she wanted. It destroyed her." Her shoulders lowered on a sigh. "After seeing to her burial and taking time to mourn and settle all her accounts, I came to the Ashcroft home—"

"For revenge?" I arched a brow.

"In a way." She didn't meet my gaze. "I also wanted proof. I searched the country estate, then Mr. Ashcroft's town house. But I couldn't find what I needed."

It was all starting to make sense. She wanted to find proof of the scandal so she could blackmail my Father. Or ruin him like he had her aunt. "Is that why you tipped off my husband in an anonymous letter hinting about the affair?"

Her head reared back, as if surprised I made the connection. "I thought maybe he could find the evidence. I didn't care how the word came out. I just wanted it known."

Never mind. This made no sense at all. "If Warren discovered the truth, you couldn't blackmail my father." Why would he pay her to keep quiet if the news broke out all over the papers?

Her brow lowered. "I never wanted money."

"No?" Warren's jaw tightened. "You just wanted to scare my wife."

"It just isn't right. You sit in the lap of luxury, enjoying everything she should've had." Her eyes narrowed, her hands flapping with her words. "Do you think it's fair to carouse around with all your wealth and happiness, while my poor aunt died with a broken heart? She was denied the only love she ever wanted."

So that justified everything? "It wouldn't have worked." I scoffed. "I lived with my father for over twenty years, and he never showed any love. It was useless for Ms. Fields to hope for it."

"It's not him I'm talking about." Her gaze held mine. "When she wrote your father, she didn't ask for money. She begged to see you. Her only daughter."

Chapter 31 ───

I STARED AT MS. CARTWRIGHT, her words staggering through me, tripping over my every defense. Whatever I'd imagined her reason for taunting me, that particular one had never entered my mind. Nor should I let it. It was utterly absurd. "You're lying." That was all she'd been capable of since her first day under Father's employment. She'd worn deceit as easily as she'd donned her mobcap.

Her chin tucked, as if I had been the one who'd launched a verbal punch.

"Ms. Cartwright." Warren's voice throttled deep with warning. "You haven't given us any reason to believe you. In fact, your behavior encourages the opposite. You've lived under my roof, receiving wages from me, all because my wife wanted a better position for you. And this is how you respond? First, trying to scare her with letters, and now throwing unfounded claims? What has she done to you but show kindness?"

Her gaze met mine, but I couldn't detect much regret in her eyes. "I thought you knew all along. That you purposefully shunned your mother because she was a farmer's daughter."

"My mother's a daughter of a railroad owner," I said calmly. I didn't understand how this woman had fallen under such delusion, but she wasn't about to convince me anything otherwise. I knew her sort. "I think you've made all this up." Yes, my father might've had an affair with Ruth Fields, but it seemed this young woman grasped it as a means of extortion. "I've seen my share of con artists. You've invented something to blackmail me with, and I refuse to join your little game. Unless you have any proof, go swindle someone else." I looked pointedly at the door.

Tension hung in the air while she stood quiet, pinning her stare to a spot on the floor, her hands switching from clasping in front of her to fussing with her sleeves. Finally, she lifted her head. "I told you it's not about money." She moved toward me, renewed determination marking her delicate features, but stopped as her gaze hit Warren's protective stance. Her bluster withered, and her posture slouched slightly. "I don't have proof. That's why I sought employment with your father."

"Because you wanted to find evidence?" My fingers tapped a restless rhythm on the scrolled armrest. "Did you purposefully apply for the position so you'd have freedom to search the houses?"

She seemed to consider my words carefully before tucking her arms into a tight fold across her chest. "I thought I would easily find what I needed to expose everything. Your father's affair, your illegitimacy. Then the life you lived would be ripped away, and you could see how it felt to have nothing. Just like my aunt." Her soft voice practically rattled off the very words from those letters—*have nothing, ripped away from you*—but her tone was oddly without malice. As if she felt she was serving some twisted form of justice. "But I couldn't find anything."

"You're telling us you don't have anything to back up what you've said." Warren rolled his lips inward, and I knew he was forcing down a cutting remark.

"No, but I heard my aunt, Mr. Hayes." Her voice pitched high with strained desperation. "I watched her weep as she recounted the story about giving up her daughter to Mr. and Mrs. Ashcroft because she couldn't afford to take care of her." Her wide eyes settled on me, causing an uneasy twisting in my gut. "She couldn't afford to support you anymore, so she pleaded with your father. Mrs. Ashcroft took you in but dismissed my aunt, saying she'd toss you into the streets if my aunt ever tried to contact you. Aunt Ruth stayed away all those years to protect you."

Warren glanced over at me, and I could only blink. Ms. Cartwright could clearly secure a role on the stage with that performance. Though was there any truth to it? She'd admitted she planned on finding evidence and then exposing me as a fraud. But what if she was the fraud? How would I even know how to sort the real from the fake?

"Ms. Cartwright, did your aunt say anything that would be considered proof?"

She shook her head. "She only told me her story."

"I see." I stood on shaky limbs. "Then if there's nothing else, please excuse us. We need to go check on how my mother's faring."

She opened her mouth, most likely to protest my claiming Helena Ashcroft as my true parent, but then seemed to think better of it and crimped her lips tightly.

"As of now, Ms. Cartwright, we go our separate ways." Warren walked her toward the door. "I'll give you a month's wages to tide you over until you secure a position elsewhere. You are not to contact my wife or slander her name. Being in the publishing business has made me an expert on libel suits."

That struck a healthy dose of fear in her eyes, but she quickly recovered. After a tight nod, she strode from the room with her chin tipped so high that I was surprised she didn't scrape her nose on the ceiling. Warren saw her out, no doubt to get her final wages and ensure she left without snooping any further in our rooms. Though I knew she wouldn't find anything. I certainly didn't have anything that would confirm her ridiculous tales. Which was probably why she'd returned to my parents' town house. Cecily had claimed it was because the maid had feared for her employment while we'd been away, but now I knew otherwise. She'd gone back to hunt.

A slight niggle wormed through my chest. What if . . . this woman was right? Could my upbringing have all been a lie? Everything I'd regarded as fact be false? I'd never flaunted my high social standing, but my parents assuredly had. As well as the press. Only to turn up I'd been born on the wrong side of the blanket? Was it possible?

Funny I should question the truths surrounding my birth on the anniversary of its very day. Twenty-four years ago, I'd entered this crazy world, but which woman had welcomed me into it?

• • •

"I need to see the letter Ruth Fields sent you." I stood in the open doorway to the dining room, where Father was eating breakfast alone. Warren was close behind. I could feel the warmth of his body, the brush of his fingers against mine.

With not even a glance my direction, Father continued chewing his food, followed by an unhurried sip of coffee. "You're more demanding than I remember. I don't think it's a becoming habit for you, Geneva." He folded the newspaper he'd been skimming and finally met my gaze.

I straightened, unperturbed by his usual dismissal. I'd come for answers, and I would get them. He hadn't extended an invitation, and I didn't wait for one as I entered the dining room, forcing confidence into each step. "I don't particularly care what you feel is becoming or not. All I want is to see the letter." I could come right out and ask him the truth as I'd done yesterday, but he had never been forthcoming about anything. Perhaps there was something in the letter that would help. If she'd pleaded with my father to see me, then wouldn't she state her case, providing why she had the right?

After hearing Ms. Cartwright's accusations, a cloudy veil had fallen upon my thoughts. Little by little I strove to regain clarity, picking through the tangling confusion, dusting off old memories. Had my parents let anything slip over the years? Had I missed something important? But now as I held the issue up to the light, I caught a glaring flaw. I understood if Ms. Fields had stayed away while I was a child, but I'd been an adult for several years. Even when she'd died, I was almost twenty-three. If she was as desperate as Ms. Cartwright had adamantly professed, why hadn't she written to me directly?

Though perhaps reading what she'd penned to Father would answer that as well. I folded my arms at my father's impassive expression. "I can wait as long as it takes for you to fetch it."

"I don't have it."

Those words set my strategy into a tailspin. "What?" The question ripped from my lips with a forceful tone I'd never unleashed in his presence. Warren stepped beside me, claiming my hand. I knew I was a tight ball of agitation, and if my father sensed my vehemence, he'd become even more indifferent. My lungs pulled in a long, calming breath. "Do you know where it is?"

"I don't keep nonsense lying around. I burned it the second after I read it." He tucked the newspaper, which wasn't from Warren's presses, under his arm and stood. "Now if you'll excuse me." He turned on his heel and moved toward the door.

"Is Ruth Fields my mother?"

His steps slowed, though not a dramatic freeze one would expect after such an alarming question. He pivoted, the usual mask of complacency firmly tucked in place, shielding any and all emotion.

I met his unflinching gaze. "You said yesterday that Lilith and I were your only children, but you never specified who exactly my mother was."

"I'm surprised at you." He cut a narrowed glance at the open door. "You shouldn't rattle off absurdities in open spaces. Your name's been bandied about enough already." His long fingers tapped the newspaper, where I was certain my husband and I had headlined.

Warren turned so only I could glimpse the flash of annoyance rolling over his features, then shut the door to prevent the servants from eavesdropping.

"No one can hear now." I approached Father, and his gaze tracked my movement, as if uncertain of what his unruly daughter would do. "Father, tell me the truth."

"I did yesterday."

"Expound, please. I heard an accusation that I was Ruth Fields's daughter."

His blue eyes flicked to the ceiling, then to me. "Don't entertain falsehoods."

"Are you saying it's a lie? There's no truth in any of it?" I searched his face for any tic, a twitch of the lashes, a flare of a nostril, but nothing. "Because if I think you're holding back, I'll find out one way or another."

"This person, the one who put this notion in your head, I'm assuming it's the maid you were determined to find last evening."

I didn't dare tell him. While I wasn't fond of Pauline Cartwright, I refused to push her into my father's line of sight. "Does it matter who said it? All I want to know is who my true mother is."

"She's upstairs resting. If you care for her health, you won't bring up this nonsense with her."

I bit my tongue. Of all people to scold me about caring. Though this was another form of manipulation. Warren had said Father pulled this same trick the day before the plane crash when trying to convince my husband not to print anything about the scandal. He'd twisted Warren's love for me as a weapon. Just as he now did with mine for Mother.

"How is she today?"

He shrugged. "Better."

I caged the rising sigh. His shuttered expression signaled he was through with this discussion. "We'll go check on her."

I didn't quite make it to the door when Father said my name. I turned and found him watching me.

"This person who claimed Ruth Fields was your mother. Did they have any proof?" He cut a hard glance at Warren, and I could swear I glimpsed a spark of . . . something. Bitterness? Anger?

"No." I stepped between him and my husband. "There's no proof."

He executed a tight nod and exited the room.

Warren glared at the door. Father hadn't acknowledged him except for that disdainful look near the end. No doubt Warren had caught it.

I linked my hand in his. "I'm sorry he's like that." What if Father was annoyed at Warren being alive? Hadn't Terrence said Father had pressed the issue about the line of command with the newspapers while I'd been gone? That question fueled more. Was Father behind the plane crash? All to get his hands on the newspaper Warren had intended to expose him in?

"I couldn't care less." Warren's voice broke into my thoughts. "I'm angry he didn't mention your birthday. That man has no consideration for anyone but himself."

I quietly agreed. And that was what concerned me. How far would Father go to get his way? To quiet everyone who could ruin him? I squeezed Warren's hand. "Let's check on Mother, then we can be on our way."

He nodded, and we climbed the stairs. Her bedroom door had been wedged ajar. One sweeping glance inside and my mouth dropped. Mother scuttled into bed, working to climb upon the tall mattress. She succeeded but not without a weary groan.

"Mother."

Her head whipped my way. She tugged the blankets over her, as if I hadn't just caught her out of bed.

I stepped into the room. "Where's Nurse Redman?"

Her hand lifted in a feeble wave of dismissal, but sweat beaded her brow, and her chest rose with heaving breaths. "Gone until noon," she wheezed. "She said . . . said it was good for me to stretch my legs."

"Though I doubt she meant when you're alone." I cut the distance, Warren behind me. He helped support her steady while I propped more pillows behind her back.

"I'm fine. Hello, Warren. I'm glad to see you're back among the land of the living." She tugged her blanket higher while offering a dignified nod to my husband. Sharp eyes framed by too-pale skin landed on me. "How's my daughter on her twenty-fourth birthday?"

I couldn't say I was doing well. Not when I hovered in a current state of unease. But I smiled at her gesture. "I'm glad to see you're doing better." Better than yesterday, that was. She still appeared a mite frail for my liking.

Her gaze drifted to the side window. The curtain had been pulled, leaving a slice of sunshine on the thick carpet. Her cracked lips expelled a wistful sigh. "This weather reminds me of the day you were born. The entire week it had rained and stormed. I was miserable from all the dreariness. Then the morning of the fourteenth the sun finally came out, and you were born a few hours later. I remarked to your father it was as if the heavens opened and dropped you."

Mother was never sentimental. Perhaps her health scare had softened her. Or maybe there was another reason. "You haven't talked much about the day I was born." I sat on the side of her mattress. "Was I born here or at the country house?"

"The country house." Her fingers stroked the tassels on the pillow cradling her arm, her face taking on an unfamiliar touch of nostalgia. "I couldn't bear the smells of the city. I was ill the entire time I carried you. The country air was kinder. Your father remained here until the night before your birth. I worried he'd miss your entrance entirely."

I doubted my father had been overly concerned, but something made me feel . . . strange. "Mother, are you okay?" I rested a hand on hers. "I just—"

Cecily swept into the room, her face pinching tight. "Ma'am, if you're hungry, please ring the bell. Don't venture to the dining room."

Mother sniffed. "I don't know what you're talking about."

Cecily seemed to let the matter drop but angled to Warren and me, lowering her voice to a whisper. "Gregory spotted her near the dining hall door."

And now it all added up. I waited for Cecily to place the tray by Mother's bedside. Once everything was in order and to Cecily's liking, she left, and I gently pounced on my newfound knowledge. "You overheard my conversation with Father about Ruth Fields." Several emotions splayed across her face, but she wrangled them all under a mask of composure. "That's why you went through that spiel about the day I was born. Because you heard me questioning about Ruth Fields being my mother."

Her eyes flashed. "I'm your mother." The sharp edge to her voice made me flinch, something she realized as well, for her mouth leaked a lengthy sigh. "I'm your mother," she repeated much more softly. Her gaze flicked to Warren, who stood devotedly by my side. "I did overhear. I caught what you asked your father before the door was shut."

"And?"

"I don't want her to ruin your life like she did mine." Her fingers clutched the blanket tightly, her knuckles draining white. "She destroyed my marriage before it even started."

"Father wouldn't tell me anything."

Her lips pressed together. "He wouldn't, dear. Because to him, there isn't much to tell."

"But you just said—"

"Your father had a . . . relationship with the woman. He ended things so he could marry me. But Ruth wouldn't accept it." She exhaled, disturbing the tendrils of hair framing her lean face. "After you were born, she visited me, claiming the most outlandish things. That you were the daughter she was supposed to have and that I didn't deserve any happiness with your father." She shook her head. "Then she started turning up at places we were. Finally, I—" Her mouth clamped shut.

"You what?"

"Nothing."

"Mother, please."

Her gaze snapped to mine. "You don't know what you're demanding. It's humbling for a woman of my standing to admit I wasn't enough." Her polished veneer crumpled, like a hammer to porcelain. "Ruth may have come from a farming family, but she was beautiful and alluring. And when she was around, it reminded your father of what he gave up to . . . achieve his goals."

He hadn't married Mother for love but for advancement. It shouldn't surprise me. I'd never witnessed any affection between them, but it seemed my mother had once wished for it.

"The more she came around, the further into his shell he went. I think he may have loved her. Or maybe he felt guilty for pushing her into madness. I don't know. But then she did the unthinkable."

"What happened?"

"She tried to kidnap you."

Warren's head reared back as a gasp parted my lips.

Mother didn't seem to notice our shocked responses, her gaze drifting out the window. "One day I'd gone to run errands, and that woman snuck in and grabbed you when your nurse had stepped away. The butler stopped her. Your father refused to press charges. Just pretended it never happened. The woman was obsessed with becoming your mother. That if she couldn't have John, she should at least have you."

"She sounds unstable."

Mother nodded. "It made no sense, but in her heartbroken state, she couldn't be reasoned with. I was scared she might try again, so I paid her to leave us alone. I spent a large sum on that woman, not fully trusting she'd stay away. But by that time there was a wedge between your father and me." Her voice thinned to a hollow drone. "He didn't want much to do with me, only the influence behind my father's name to help grow his lumber mills."

There was a sadness in her tone I hadn't been prepared for. All this time I'd believed it was a mutual disregard for each other. She slumped against her pillows, her energy depleting by the second.

We should let her rest, but I had a few final questions. "She wrote Father last year."

Mother blinked. "I hadn't heard. Though he doesn't share things with me."

"Did you know she passed away?"

Her mouth tugged down at the edges, pulling at the deep lines in her face. I hadn't realized how much she'd aged these past months. Had I caused extra stress by my disappearance? Or perhaps it was Lilith. I hadn't yet divulged what we'd discovered. Mother still believed Lilith had married Lieutenant Cameron. But that was a discussion for another day.

"No, I didn't know," she said softly. "Though I can't feel any sympathy. Ruth Fields destroyed what I wanted."

Love.

Chapter 32

WARREN REGARDED ME, HIS MOUTH pressed in a solemn line. "This isn't the birthday celebration I had in mind." He nodded at my barely touched meal. "I promise I didn't cook any of it," he teased, but a shadow flickered over his concerned eyes.

"I'm sure it's wonderful." I'd only been able to manage a bite of potatoes before my stomach had declared a strike. "I don't have much of an appetite."

He pushed his own plate aside and took my hand. "I know it's been a . . . different sort of day."

I expelled a humorless laugh, which nearly extinguished the candle. Warren had taken extra care to prepare a candlelit dinner. He'd even brought in the gramophone, now sitting on the far end of the table, so we could dance afterward. But my mood had only sunk lower with each troubling thought.

"What's bothering me most is that I don't know who to believe. We've heard two contrasting versions of the same woman. Ms. Cartwright said Ruth Fields gave me up because she couldn't take care of me. But Mother said this lady was senile and tried to kidnap me."

I stared at the candle, the pulsing flame, the bead of wax rolling down the side, musing over the weird truth of its purpose. The more it gave off light, the more it died. It was consuming itself. Something I feared would happen to me if I obsessed over finding out who really had birthed me. "I want to trust my mother, but what if she made it up? She could've easily paid off servants and doctors to confirm her story."

His fingers encased mine. "For what it's worth, I've never seen your mother that vulnerable."

True. In all my years, she hadn't revealed any of her feelings about her relationship with Father. She'd always played the role of detached yet dutiful wife. Today she'd all but spilled her heart about her loveless marriage. "It saddened me to hear about their early days. All those times she pushed me to do my father's bidding, I wonder if it was her way of winning his approval. Or . . ."

He gently squeezed my hand. "What?"

"She said she paid Ruth to leave us alone, but what if it was hush money? If word ever got out that Helena Ashcroft paid my father's mistress to keep quiet about me, that would devastate her. Mother cares too much of what society thinks of her. Just like Father."

"You think she lied?"

"There's a chance of it. But how would I know? It happened long ago. I doubt any proof exists. Another thing. Mother acted as if she was distraught about Ruth attempting to kidnap me again. If that was the case, why was she gone so much when I was younger? I saw more of my nannies than my parents during those days. Also, why ship me to boarding school? If Ruth was as raving mad as Mother suggested, the woman could've easily found me." Glenwood Academy had been celebrated for its stellar educational program, but its security measures had been lacking at best. "That doesn't exactly say concerned parent to me."

"Maybe by that time your mother thought the threat had passed."

Possibly. "Her story was persuasive. Which it should be, considering she had twenty-four years to perfect it. She was convincing, but so was Ms. Cartwright." I released a weighty sigh. "What if I never find out? Can I live with never knowing?"

Warren hooked his foot around my chair leg and hauled it toward him. Then as if deciding I wasn't close enough, he scooped me onto his lap. "You know I trained cadets how to fly during the war."

I nodded, unsure where this was leading.

"I also taught them how to fix their planes in a scrape." He occupied himself with running his fingers through my hair. "I couldn't shake the feeling that I should do more. I felt like a coward. Here I was, safe on American soil, while the men I trained risked their neck overseas. I wanted to be there with them."

My heart squeezed. I knew that was a normal response. Every man wanted to do their share in protecting their friends and destroying the enemy until the threat was annihilated. I shuddered at the thought of the Germans shooting at my husband's plane. The mortality rate of pilots had been higher than other branches of soldiers.

He continued toying with my hair, warm knuckles brushing the soft flesh behind my ear. His touch was soothingly distracting, but I wondered if he needed this diversion more than me. "I appealed to my superiors but got rejected. I found out later my father played poker with high-ranking officers. He was behind the constant refusal." Warren shook his head. "I was more than disappointed—I felt betrayed."

"I'm sorry." I offered a consoling smile. "I'm sure he had his reasons."

The gold flecks of his eyes dulled. "He did." His touch fell away. "When the war ended, I came home wishing I could've done more. Of course, I confronted him about it. Asked him if he pulled strings because I was the heir to the Hayes empire." His voice took on an emptiness. "But he said that wasn't the case. There was another reason."

"Which was?"

"I don't know. He suggested we talk the following morning because it was late, and I was in no state to have a logical conversation. But then . . . he got called away for an urgent business trip and never made it home."

My hand flew to my open mouth. I'd known Peter Hayes had died of a stroke in Chicago, but I didn't know the full story. "I'm so sorry, Warren." I grasped his hand. "You didn't get to say goodbye."

He shook his head. "No. At least I had the good sense to resolve things before I went to sleep that night. It would've been worse if my last conversation with him was an argument."

"Like how it almost was with us." My chin lowered before I could fight against it. We'd fought about my father, and then Warren had been gone.

"We got a second chance." He smoothed my hair back. "This time I won't ruin it." He whispered the words against my temple like a promise, searing it into my skin with a kiss. "I didn't tell you that story to stir sad memories about us, but I never found out the reason why he needed me to remain here. I had to come to peace with it. With everything." He laced his fingers through mine. "I think everyone wants to look back on their days and see something like a stuffed parcel wrapped up nicely and tied with a bow. No loose ends. But it doesn't work that way. We don't always get the final pieces to the puzzle. Though that doesn't mean our lives are incomplete."

"Thank you for sharing with me." I offered a fragile smile. "I understand what you're saying, and in a way I'd rather *not* know. Because if it does turn out that I'm Ruth's daughter, then . . ."

"Go on, love."

"That would mean I was born out of wedlock. Would that make a difference . . . I mean, would that change how you . . ." I didn't know how to phrase it, because I cared too much about the answer. He'd married me in good faith, believing he'd united with someone from a respectable family. I was aware of many men who prided on "good breeding," and while I loathed that term, I knew it could be an issue.

He swept up my fingers and gently kissed the tips. "I love you." Not breaking eye contact, he pressed our joined hands to his chest. "If you want, we'll search for answers. This would normally be something I'd hire Brisbane for. If he doesn't resurface soon, I'll hire someone else. Whatever you choose, I support you fully."

I nodded.

"But know this—your parentage changes nothing. It doesn't alter who you are. Or my love for you." A protectiveness hovered within the borders of his tender smile. "It doesn't matter what your last name was or should've been, because now you have mine. We are family. You and me. And that's all I care about."

His words infused a strength that held up my sagging heart. He was right. Knowing who had birthed me didn't change who I was, or anything else. Of course there would always be doubt until I knew for certain. But one thing I did know. Warren was my family now. And once again I was reminded of his beautiful gift. The house in the country. "Warren, instead of booking an appointment with an investigator, can we make one with the house builder?"

He kissed me, which was my favorite way of him saying yes.

After several seconds, he eased back. "Since you're not hungry, how about a dance?" He gestured toward the gramophone. "I had Jenkins search high and low for the recent love songs."

"Jenkins?" My gaze landed on a stack of records. A laugh ripped from my lips as I scooted off Warren's lap. I could hardly picture the formal butler postponing his duties to gather ballads and sonnets. "I'm certain he welcomed that task."

Warren stood, his easy grin lighting my own. "I know he was secretly appreciative. Beneath that prim exterior, he's a true romantic at heart."

"Oh, he's good at romance, you say?" A tease skipped over my lips, and I launched it at him. "Then perhaps he can give you some pointers."

With a playful growl, he darted after me, and I jumped back with a yelp. Skirting around the table, I laughed at the mischief in his eyes.

"Come here, Mrs. Hayes." Standing opposite, he moved with me lengthwise of the table. "I'll show you how romantic I can be."

I lunged toward the door for an escape to continue the chase throughout the house, but before I reached the threshold, his arms darted out, catching me by the waist. He swung me around, my feet lifting from the floor as his mouth executed delicious "punishment" kisses along my neck. I expelled a blissful sigh. Getting caught had been my aim.

Setting me down, his hands took a slow path over the swell of my hips, settling low on my back. Then he started swaying with me in his arms, the contour of my body pressing against his.

I smiled at him, linking my arms around his neck, joining the soft rhythm. We didn't need the gramophone after all. "What kind of dancing is this?"

"I have no idea, but I like it."

"It's scandalous."

"Surely a man can be scandalous with his wife." He dropped a kiss on my lips.

"You know, today's the first birthday I've ever been kissed on."

"Why stop there?" He twirled me under his arm, only to draw me in closer. "I can love on you more than that." More time spent with me. Time he sacrificed so I could have a pleasant day.

I knew he had a mountain of work awaiting him. I wouldn't be surprised if he headed to his office the minute I fell asleep. "You made my birthday special. Thank you."

"It wasn't wholly pleasant for you." The smile slid from his face. "I'm sorry about the issue with your mother and Ms. Cartwright."

"It's okay." I snuggled against his chest, breathing in the scent of his soap mixed with the starch of his collar. "Well, actually, it isn't okay, but I'm hoping in time it will be. That I'll accept a loose end."

He tightened his grip. "You're one amazing woman."

I peered at him. "I may be tolerant of letting that issue go, but there's one loose end I want resolved. I don't think I can rest easy until I know who's behind your accident."

Warren stopped swaying. "Not tonight, love."

"I can't help it. Whenever I think about it, something pricks at me."

Warren dipped me, as if a last-ditch effort to get my mind back on our dance. He guided me back to him in a smooth, slow lift until our faces were nearly touching. We locked eyes, his breath grazing my cheek.

"Whoever tried to kill you depended a lot on chance."

He tipped his head back and groaned. "And you implied *I* was unromantic."

"I'm trying to be serious." How easy it would be to get lost in him. This man, whose soul twined with mine. I could forget about our troubles for one night and yield to his beckoning touch. But the twist in my gut had only grown stronger. This needed talking out. An apologetic smile rolled over my lips. "Don't you think it's strange that the killer was so inept?"

His brows rose slightly. "Would you rather they succeeded, darling?"

"Of course not." I feebly swatted his chest. "It's just . . . whoever it was only sabotaged your plane. What if you had taken my Jenny? Mine looks identical to yours, but is newer and . . ." I stopped at Warren's arrested expression. "What?"

"Eva." A shaft of air parted his mouth, and his arms dropped from my waist. "There's something I don't think you realize. I waited for you to mention it, but when you didn't, it made me rethink—"

"Mention what exactly?" Dread tripped down my spine.

"I should've talked to you about this earlier." Another heavy exhale. "I don't even want to say it. Because the possibility of what this means terrifies me." He ran a hand through his hair, mussing the curls. "Remember yesterday when I said *you* were my main concern?"

I nodded dumbly.

"That's why I've hardly left your side." He gripped my shoulders, concern etched into every line in his face. "I'm not certain who was the intended target. The killer could've been after you."

My throat thickened. "Me?"

"I didn't take my plane that day. I flew yours. But it hardly mattered because they both were sabotaged."

"WHAT DO YOU MEAN YOU took my plane?" My fingers wrapped around the back of a chair for support. "And they were both sabotaged?" I think I would've known if the airplane I'd been flying for the past weeks had been tampered with. Since Warren's accident, I'd been diligent, ensuring the bolts were tight, oiling all the exposed parts, and keeping a sharp eye on the motor.

Warren jerked his tie knot, loosening it. "When I checked my plane that morning, the right tire was flat. I assumed a rock tore through but didn't think much more about it."

A gasp sputtered my lips. "No, that was *my* plane. Mine had a flat tire. And I thought because . . . oh." I slammed my eyes shut, pressing a fingertip to my temple, as if it would help recall a twenty-second conversation on the worst day of my life. "Al apologized for something." The hangar manager, Al Donaldson, had hovered over me like a mother hen when I'd arrived at the hangar the afternoon of the crash. My heart had been shattered, my body twisted in cramping pain, and my mind had been a blob of incoherence, but those anguished moments were slowly coming back to me.

I lifted my lashes, my gaze latching on to my husband. "Al told me . . . about the tire. He said he replaced it just before I arrived because he was ordered to move the Jenny. The police wanted the space cleared so they could search." I shook my head. "I just assumed the remaining plane was mine since it was stowed in my spot." Looking back, I doubted Al had mentioned the flat tire to the police. At that point Warren's crash had been ruled an accident. It wasn't until later that the authorities had claimed foul play. "You don't think the sliced tire was accidental?" We'd had to change tires a few times over the past months. Landing a seventeen-hundred-pound airplane on two thin circles produced a lot of deflated wheels.

"No. I don't. Because it forced me to take your plane."

"So we're back to you being the target."

"It was your plane, so you still could've been the intended victim. *Or* both of us." He pulled out a chair, motioning for me to sit, then claimed the space beside me. "I feel like an idiot for not catching the slit in the fuel line. I was in a foul mood and rushed through preflight check."

The line hadn't been completely severed, only slightly cut to allow for a slow leak. One that wouldn't have been noticeable until *after* Warren turned the propeller for the engine to take in the gas. By that time he would've been done with his checks and ready for takeoff. The fuel had seeped a slow drip, providing enough gas to make it into the air and fly a stretch before the tank emptied.

"Once in the sky, you were too far from the field to glide it in."

"Yeah." He rubbed his brow, a frown pulling his mouth. "The lake was the only place."

"Then you parachuted out."

"The point I'm making is the cut on the wheel *and* the slice in the fuel line were no doubt done by the same person."

I sighed. "Now we only need to find their identity."

"Whoever it is knew we flied together on Saturdays."

True. "But really, I can't tell our planes apart." There was a serial number on a small plate in the cockpit. No one paid attention to those. Well, besides my mechanic husband. "I'm guessing the killer couldn't either. If they didn't know which was which, they had to damage the tire on one plane to get us into the other."

He nodded at my logic. "But you always stowed yours in the same spot. If the killer watched us, they'd discover that. That's why I'm concerned they were after you specifically."

A chill raced over me. The thought of someone watching us for the sole purpose of murder froze my blood. Warren slipped an arm around me as I sat processing. "I had no idea I was flying yours."

His mouth arced in a small smile. "I suspected as much. That day you found me at the speakeasy, you told me you'd flown your plane. Remember how I reacted?"

"I was in a weird state of shock. All I remember is your scowl." I imitated the fierce glower he'd worn like a favorite hat those first few days.

He chuckled low. "I'll never forget your snappy remark. 'Well, of course I flew my plane. Yours is at the bottom of the lake.'" He squeezed my hand and pressed a kiss to my forehead. "You were blissfully ignorant that you were piloting my plane, and that alone set me on the course to realizing you weren't guilty. Then when you didn't know about Ruth Fields, I knew I was entirely mistaken."

"But someone is guilty." That thought made me want to tuck Warren inside the Jenny's cockpit and attempt a transatlantic flight. Crossing an ocean by plane seemed less scary than walking around New York with a bull's-eye on our backs. "Question is, who would benefit from us both gone?"

Warren shrugged. "My uncle's in France. He has his own fortune. There's no need for our money."

"Okay." I tapped my chin. "Who would benefit from *me* gone?"

He swept up my hands in his and kissed them. "I hate this line of thinking."

"But we need to examine from every angle."

"I love to examine your angles, but not like this." He lowered our hands but kept them joined on my lap. "Maybe we're thinking of the wrong motive here. Not everyone kills for money. What if there's another reason?"

"Like what?"

"Jealousy, hatred, revenge." He rattled them off as if reciting a grocery list. "Taking justice in one's own hands. Can you think of anyone who might feel that way?"

"Pauline Cartwright wrote that she wanted to take everything from me, but she had an alibi for the day of your accident. That Ivy woman saw her in Hanover on the anniversary of Ruth's death."

"Ivy also said Ms. Cartwright was a nurse. She obviously doesn't have all her facts straight. We already know the maid was off the day of the plane crash, *and* she knows we go flying on Saturdays."

My nose scrunched. "It's possible, but . . . I don't know." My gut reaction said no, though I wasn't about to completely blot her name off the suspect column. "What about Terrence? He could be jealous of you. You're the Hayes with all the wealth, power, and dashing good looks." I threw in that last part in jest, though it was no less true. Warren possessed everything Terrence didn't.

He offered a small smile at my tease, but soon sobered. "I can't see Terr doing anything like that. Besides, if he wanted to get rid of me, he would've done so by now. The man had plenty of opportunities over the years." He shirked out of his jacket and draped it on the chair beside him. "It could be Lilith's husband. I don't trust him or that flimsy story he told us."

My chest squeezed. How I longed for my sister. I knew she'd made her choice, yet I couldn't help but feel her decisions would cause her unhappiness in the long run. "We're overlooking a key suspect here."

"Your father."

"Brisbane."

We spoke simultaneously, but I was the first to recover after a beat of silence. "You're right. My father has several motives. Though I can't get past Brisbane's strange disappearance. Why hasn't he shown up? Why did he vanish days after your accident? And furthermore, why didn't he meet you at the speakeasy or his cabin afterward? Maybe we haven't been able to find him . . . because he doesn't want to be found."

• • •

The following morning, I reentered the dining room. The table had been cleared, of course. The gramophone gone, as well as the records. And Warren's chair was empty. Since my husband was nowhere else in the house, he'd probably gone to the office. He'd planned on making a brief trip to grab some paperwork to go over at home, since he wasn't comfortable leaving me alone yet.

I hated adding extra pressure on him, knowing how behind he was on everything, but he'd insisted. I was surprised when he hadn't returned by lunch. I waited another couple of hours, tending to tasks around the house and speaking to the cook about teaching me the basics of meal preparation. During the weeks-long escapade, it would've been helpful to know how to cook, since some of the rented rooms had small kitchenettes. Not that I expected to be on the run again, but a girl should always be prepared.

I spoke with the maid about returning my hair to its natural color, to which she recommended ammonia. My mouth twitched in horror. There was no chance I'd pour that foul stuff on my head. We decided a wig might be the best option while my roots grew out. I'd have to drag Warren to a wigmaker's shop, considering he'd asked me not to leave the house without him.

At 2:00 p.m. I reclined on the sofa in the parlor, an open book perched on my lap. I still hadn't heard from him. Had he lost track of time? Had an emergency arisen at work? Perhaps I should check in with him. At that moment the telephone rang, followed by measured steps in the hall.

Jenkins appeared in the parlor doorway, everything about him formal, from his pressed suit to his stiff posture. "There's a call for you, madam."

"Warren?"

"No, Mr. Brisbane."

What? Heart pounding, I jumped to my feet, the book falling to the floor. "Kent?" I rushed past Jenkins, whose brow didn't even budge at my scurried movements. I dashed for the telephone and spoke breathlessly into the mouthpiece. "Brisbane? Is that you?"

"Geneva. It's a relief to hear your voice." The connection was awful. He sounded like he was shouting in a tin can.

"Where are you? We've been searching everywhere for you."

"We're near my cabin." The crackling static almost overpowered his voice. "I'm with Warren."

My gut soured. "Why?" Why would Warren leave without telling me? The cabin was two and a half hours north of here. What could have possibly been so important that he didn't have time to inform me? Plus, I didn't like that Warren was alone with Brisbane. He might have been a longtime friend, but I didn't trust him after his mysterious disappearance. And now his sudden reemergence. Something was off.

"Sorry, Geneva. We had to hurry, or we would've missed the lead."

Wait. What? "You have a lead? You know who's behind Warren's accident?" That would be the only thing that would've lured Warren. Annoyance flared, but I swatted it down. His desire to keep me safe would've prevented him from informing me of his plans. He'd have known I would've wanted to come along, and he would've been right. I hated being stuck here, but even I could see it was for the best.

"I can't go into all that now."

Of course not. "Then put my husband on the phone."

"I can't. I had to come to town to make the call." His voice drifted. I pressed the speaker firmer against my ear to make out the words. "He's back at the cabin with . . ."

"With who?"

"Look, Geneva, just come. Warren said to drive the roadster. When you get here, we'll explain everything."

My weight bounced from toe to toe. I knew better than to accept this. I didn't fully trust Brisbane as it was, and the crackling connection only heightened my frustration. "Tell me now."

"We caught the person. But there's more to it. Now please hurry."

No wonder they had to rush. Warren wouldn't let the culprit slip away. Though I didn't like the idea he was alone at the hunting cabin with a murderer. "I'll alert the police."

"No." His voice was adamant, but something else in his tone hit me strangely. "You won't want to do that. Get here as fast as you can. She's insisting on speaking with you first."

She? "Brisbane, who are you talking about?"

"Lilith."

THE LINE DISCONNECTED.

So had my heart. I could no longer detect a sturdy beat. Everything dulled. Blurred.

They'd caught Lilith?

Of all people. My dear sister? Her lovely face flashed through my mind. It was a mistake. It had to be. She couldn't have been behind Warren's crash. Her tender heart wasn't capable of that sort of evil. Or deceit. But then . . . I'd never guessed her to deceive me on my wedding day either. Or flippantly shed every layer of caution and remain with the man who'd tricked her for over a year.

But that didn't make her a killer.

Why would she want to harm Warren? It couldn't have been to shield her husband. Because at that point, she hadn't known Michael was an imposter. My thoughts tangling, I hung the speaker on the hook and sank onto the chair beside the narrow table.

If Lilith had no motive for hurting my husband, what other purpose had she for sabotaging the plane? Warren's words from last evening resurfaced. *The killer could've been after you.*

I clutched my stomach. A vain attempt to quell rising nausea. I refused to believe it. My sister and I had a good relationship. At least, we had. There was absolutely no reason for her to—

My breath thinned.

"*Sense and Sensibility,*" I whispered, as realization clawed me with terrifying intensity. I'd gifted Lilith a novel of Jane Austen's about a pair of siblings. But that hadn't been all. On a youthful whim to show my sisterly devotion, I'd willed her my jewelry and my entire inheritance should something happen to me. A flowery scribble on the inside cover.

Though it'd been years ago. Kid's stuff. Only I hadn't been a child at that time. I'd just turned eighteen, buoyant with frivolity and stupidity.

By marrying Michael, my sister had been cut from our parents' funding. Would she resort to something drastic to get money? Every part of me flooded with uncertainty and dizziness.

The inscription probably wasn't legal. A proper will required witnesses and other lawful aspects to be official, right? One simple call to Terrence would clear it up. But I hadn't time. If Lilith had tried to kill me, then—

No, this was foolish. It hadn't been Lilith. Could I truly believe Brisbane—someone I'd met only a few times—over a sister whose bond went beyond blood? Besides that, he'd said another questionable remark that tipped my suspicions, making me reach for the telephone. Determined to verify at least part of Brisbane's claims, I gave the operator the exchange for Warren's office.

My husband's secretary answered.

"Hello, Edmond. This is Mrs. Hayes." Thankfully, this connection was clear, unlike the previous one. "Is Warren available? I'd like to speak with him."

A metal thunk, like the closing of a filing cabinet, clashed through the speaker. "I'm sorry, ma'am." His tenor voice held kindness. "Mr. Hayes left the office this morning."

My throat tightened. "Was anyone with him?"

"Yes, Mr. Brisbane stopped by. I figured he had an appointment with Mr. Hayes, considering they left together."

"Thank you, Edmond." Brisbane *had* been at the office. The efficient secretary had worked with Warren long enough that he would have recognized the private investigator. A sliver of relief unfurled within me, but not enough to calm my riotous mind. "Can you recall what time they left?" It would take at least a couple of hours to reach the cabin, and that estimate didn't include traffic. If Edmond had seen the men leave any later than eleven, there wasn't a chance of them being in that region of the state.

"I would say around nine o'clock. I'm sorry, but Mr. Hayes didn't specify where he was going. By this time of day, I suspect you'll see him before I do."

You better believe I would. At least Brisbane's story checked out. He was with Warren. Judging by Edmond's casual response, my husband hadn't been dragged out of his office against his will. That was something, at least.

Brisbane's instructions niggled in my mind, but that wouldn't do.

I glanced outside. Looked like a perfect day for flying to the country.

I gathered my compass and spread the map of New York over Warren's desk. My gaze landed on my destination. I marked it with a pencil, then planned my route. I'd never flown directly to Brisbane's cabin. Still, if I followed the Hudson River north until it branched into Roundout Creek, I could continue west, using the smattering of ponds and other landmarks as my guide.

Now to change into coveralls, grab a few more necessities, and devise a sound plan for when my wheels touched ground. Because similar to my stance on cooking, a girl should always be prepared.

• • •

My thoughts whirled louder than the roaring wind coiling my sprawled body.

The vague call from Brisbane still had me baffled. Accusations of Lilith aside, there'd been a definite point in the conversation that didn't make sense. If only I could've spoken to Warren. He would've known the news about Lilith would devastate me. Yet he'd tasked Brisbane to deliver it, then demanded that I leave the city for the middle of nowhere? They could've easily brought her to me.

What if it was a trap? A cleverly planned setup to lure me? Perhaps I could blame my consumption of mystery novels for my suspicious theories. Too often those fictional heroines ignored the strong pinch in their guts and ran headlong into danger.

Which was why I'd chosen a danger of a different sort. Currently the Jenny, piloted by another, buzzed in the distance, no doubt circling back, and I was suspended from a twenty-eight-foot silk parachute. Seconds ago I'd leaped from my Jenny's wing at two thousand feet, grateful my gear had successfully opened. Now floating downward, my gloved hands worked the shroud lines. I prayed no crosswind tipped my chute. If too much air entered the ivory canopy too quickly, I'd be whipped around like a paper kite.

I didn't have time for snapping limbs on the encroaching pine trees, so I twisted and pulled, teaming with the gentle breeze, positioning to land on a clearing half the size of a football field.

I focused on loosening my joints, freeing all stiffness. Last thing I needed was an ankle fracture. Or worse. I tucked my chin to my chest and made certain my toes remained behind my bent knees.

Three . . . two . . . one.

I contacted the soft ground, skidding on the balls of my feet, distributing my weight for proper support. The bulk of the collapsing chute tugged my shoulders, knocking me off-balance. I fell onto my backside. It didn't matter, as long as there weren't any broken body parts.

Blood pounding in my skull, I lay on a tuft of grass, catching my breath.

I snapped alert and shed the chute. Time to execute the rest of the plan. One thing I'd realized over these past months. I didn't have to face everything alone. It was crucial to rely on a faithful God and learn to seek aid from others.

In this instance, Tex.

Earlier at the hangar, a sharp twist in my gut had startled me. I'd paused my dizzying pace for the first time since Brisbane's bizarre call. My initial hope had been to approach the cabin undetected and survey the situation before making my presence known. Flying forfeited the element of surprise. The Jenny's loud engine hadn't been designed for stealth. But I could use its powerful growl to my advantage. It could serve as a decoy. For that I needed another pilot, and the former combat flier lived in the township next to my destination. Thankfully, I had been able to locate Tex through the small-town operator, and he'd jumped at the opportunity to get behind the controls, despite my detailing the possibility of danger.

I glanced eastward into the afternoon sky, the plane appearing nothing more than a silver pin tucked into folds of blue satin.

By now he would've spotted my massive deflated chute pooling beside me on the ground, signaling I'd landed safely and to ready for the next stage of this hasty operation.

I had five minutes to get to the cabin.

I turned a swift rotation, memorizing this narrow scrap of field so I could return later to collect my gear. The engine grew louder. I needed to move. I had to be there precisely when the Jenny soared over the house. My joints tingled, a chaotic residue of adrenaline from my dive through the air mixed with nerves about what was to come.

The cabin stood a half mile from here, nestled between rolling hills. Great for concealing my jump from the Jenny, but not so great for my wind-battered body. I had to traverse over a steep incline and partway down it.

I forced my legs into motion, cutting through the patch of flat land, then up, up, up. Rocks shifted beneath my boots, felled trees blocked my path, and swarming gnats stuck to my dewy skin, as if this forest opposed my trespassing. Despite it all, I kept a decent pace. Determination sparred with my cramping muscles until I crested the hill. Ducking behind a tree trunk, I doubled over, bracing my hands on my knees, panting for breath.

Only a small stretch remained. I pressed on.

Ferns grew high, and pine branches skimmed low. Finally the apex of Brisbane's A-framed lodge came into view.

The Jenny dipped in altitude, aligning with the small structure. All Tex had to do was a single buzz—a very low yet harmless flyby over the cabin. One fast pass should be enough to startle whoever was inside, flushing them out to investigate.

Spasms burning the backs of my legs, I stooped behind tall brush about fifteen yards from where I hoped my husband was. No question everyone within the cabin could hear the approaching aircraft. I leaned over, fixing my stare on the tiny A-frame. My bones hummed as the airplane swept over. Dangerously lower than I expected, as if Tex intended to brush a wingtip on the chimney.

Show-off.

I waited for activity from the cabin, but . . . nothing. My heart sank. This was my entire scheme. I didn't have a plan B. What if no one was inside? Or what if this was to draw me out here only for something to occur back home?

With a huff, I craned my neck to check on Tex, only to spot him circling back for another swipe.

What? No. I'd only told him to buzz once. I didn't like the strain the altitude dive put on the engine. And there was always the risk of stalling. Something Tex should know since—

Movement yanked my eyes from the sky. A figure had darted out of the cabin. The porch beam blocked their profile, but I could make out the jutting barrel of a rifle.

And it was aimed at the approaching Jenny.

Chapter 35 ——————————————————————————

A SHOT FIRED.

The Jenny cried in agony.

Smoke billowed from the gurgling engine. The plane—Tex!—disappeared behind the tree-lined hills.

It all happened fast yet chillingly slow. I froze, helpless. The rifle lowered, and the gunman emerged from behind the porch pillar, allowing me a clear glimpse of the killer.

I gasped.

Terrence Hayes.

The man who'd shared the same blood as my husband. Had attended our wedding. Had seemed grief stricken at Warren's memorial. Who now sprinted in the direction where the Jenny had vanished.

His bulky form tore uphill, opposite where I stood. He must've thought I'd been in that plane. Why else had he shot at it? And by his fevered pace, he intended to finish what he'd started. I checked the skyline in vain, praying that somehow Tex had scraped through. A farming spread lay beyond the tree line. Perhaps the young pilot had managed a safe landing. But what would happen should Terrence discover him?

I glanced at the cabin. Torn. Should I go warn Tex? Or try to find Warren?

An anguished groan broke through the dead silence. It had come from the cabin. Warren, and he sounded in pain. Had Terrence harmed him? Fear jolted my body into motion. I ran toward the noise, praying I'd made the right choice. Tending to Warren meant leaving a possibly injured Tex at the mercy of a madman. I couldn't fight off Terrence myself. I needed help. I needed my husband.

Please don't let me be too late.

I dashed across the open space. I had no way of knowing how deep into the woods Terrence was. I was exposed like a doe in a field. Could easily get picked off by a bullet should he return. And more armed men could be inside watching me from the very window I ran toward.

Sweat dripping down my spine, I reached the side of the timber building. My breath whittled to thin spurts. I ducked beneath the smudged pane and listened for any sort of commotion. But all fell silent. If Terrence had henchmen, surely they would've already made their move. I lifted on my toes, my calves protesting, and stole a glimpse.

Two dark-haired men were bound, their backs toward me. Warren and Brisbane. I pressed closer to the grimy glass, searching for fiery red locks. The rest of the cabin appeared empty. No Lilith. I wasn't sure if that was a relief or a concern.

Warren's head bowed, shoulders shaking.

I rounded the front, up those stairs I'd once tumbled down, and eased inside. Brisbane caught sight of me first, his eyes widening. I nodded at him but pinned my gaze on my husband. "Warren?"

He jerked against his bindings, and his red-rimmed eyes locked on me in shock. "Eva . . ." His voice was raw. "Eva, I thought . . ." He glanced toward the front window, which had afforded a view of the hills Tex had vanished behind. He'd no doubt thought I'd been in the downed plane. That must've been that sorrowful bellow I'd heard. His grief. I'd choked on that very pain two months back.

I grasped his face, letting him drink me in, then kissed him, unsure if the tear squeezing between us was his or mine. "I'm here," I whispered against his lips. But we weren't out of danger yet. Terrence could happen upon us any second. With renewed determination, I knelt to untie the ropes around his legs. "We need to hurry. We have to get to—"

"Eva, listen." Warren shook his head, as if snapping from his daze. "You need to get out. Run. Get far away from here." His urgent tone sent chills across my dewy skin. "Now."

"What?" I tugged at the bonds. Wouldn't budge. "I'm not leaving you. Where's Lilith?"

"Not here. She never was. It was a ploy to get you here." His gaze flicked to the door, then to me. "But you don't understand. It's Terrence."

"I know."

"No, you don't. If he suspects you're in here, he'll detonate it."

My fingers froze. "Detonate what?" But Warren didn't have to explain, for I spotted it. A box sat in front of him and Brisbane. One peek inside and horror twitched my fingers to my parted mouth. It was loaded with wire-wrapped explosives.

A bomb.

Just two feet from me. The connections were complex. Antennas jutted every which way. A skill Terrence must've picked up from the war. Warren had said during the war Terrence had worked in the ordnance corps—the division that crafted weapons.

Panic surged. But then . . . fury exploded. How dared he. "I'm leaving. But you're coming with me."

"I hope I'm invited," Brisbane chimed in, all casual, as if requesting an invitation to a luncheon. "Look behind you, Geneva. The floorboard to your left. Loosen it and grab the knife. Get this party moving quicker."

I pried the wood from the floor, unsurprised Brisbane had a secret hideaway. The narrow gap beneath held quite the arsenal. I snatched the knife, and it sliced through the ropes with little effort, freeing my husband. Brisbane's bindings were more knotted, as if Terrence had suspected the private detective would know how to escape the confines.

Not even a potential bomb blast could make the man sweat. His gaze latched on something over my head, then skimmed over my face. "I didn't call you."

The blade cut through the bonds at his legs. "I gathered." Of course, I hadn't at the time of the conversation. I hadn't known Kent Brisbane long enough to identify his voice. But I'd detected something was off. "I don't drive."

Brisbane raised a brow. "Pardon?"

"Terrence made a mistake. He told me on the telephone Warren said I should take the roadster." I shifted and worked at the ropes binding his torso. "Warren wouldn't tell me such a thing because I've never driven a car before." I shook my head. "But I don't understand. Why Terrence?"

He eyed the knife near his ribs. "The man found a dirty way to claim a fortune."

How was that possible? According to Warren, his cousin was too far down the family line to inherit.

"I'm relieved you found us." Brisbane's deep voice broke into my flustered thoughts.

"And I'm relieved you finally surfaced. We searched everywhere for you, Kent." I concentrated on the next cut even as Warren shifted behind me, probably hands deep in Brisbane's weapon box.

"I wasn't gone nearly as long as you two." He spoke conversationally, as if we had all day to shoot the breeze. "I came here two days late, and Warren was already gone. I had no way of contacting either of you, since you were gallivanting around as circus performers."

I yanked the last rope free. "Yes, well. If we make it out alive, you have some explaining to do."

He grabbed a pistol from the hole in the floor. "We'll make it out alive. Hayes." He handed the gun to my husband, who snatched it. Then Kent pressed a pistol into my fingers. "Here."

I had no idea how to use a firearm, but I'd rather have a weapon than not.

Warren helped me stand. His gaze held fire and love and just enough banked fury to almost feel sorry for Terrence when my husband got ahold of him. Almost. Then we fled the cabin as fast as our feet could carry us.

But it wasn't fast enough.

"Going somewhere?" Terrence emerged from the row of trees, his chest heaving. Clearly he was out of breath, but that didn't stop him from advancing toward us, his rifle aimed directly at me.

Warren and Brisbane raised their weapons, so I did as well. It appeared we were in a standoff, but Terrence didn't seem the least affected.

"Hello, Geneva." His tone was deeper than I remembered, but that hardly mattered, because a boxy mechanism suspended from a braided cord around his neck. In the center, a circular dial, like one would find on a . . . radio. The bomb. It was detonated through a radio frequency. "I don't know how you managed to get from the mangled plane to where you're standing without a scratch, but bravo."

The Jenny had been wrecked. What about Tex? My heart tore as I shot up a silent prayer.

"Drop your gun." Warren's hardened glare and lethal tone flared solely on his cousin. "It's three against one. You don't stand a chance."

Terrence grasped that Warren wouldn't dare advance as long as Terrence pointed his rifle at me. He continued as if not hearing the threat, his gaze darkening mine. "Your husband and his crony made a noble effort this morning, but I knew the second I spotted them outside my office that they were on to me. I surprised them before they got me." He spared my husband a glance. "The raging husband bit. Too predictable."

I could almost feel the seething waves rolling off Warren.

Terrence tilted his head, studying me. "But you . . . I underestimated you. I didn't see this"—he jerked his head at the sky—"this charade coming or how you pulled it off." His eyes narrowed. "What made you suspicious?"

My breath scraped along my dry throat. He peered at me as if truly wanting a response. Incredulous. But then again, if he had that mechanical mind like Warren, he'd want to know where the squeaky cog was in his well-oiled plan.

Out of my peripheral, Warren subtly nodded, and I understood the signal. He wanted me to keep Terrence chatting. No doubt to allow more time to devise an escape plan. Perhaps I could use this to my advantage. "Hardly any deductions involved." Fancy words always flew off my tongue when my nerves were frayed. "Warren told me everything before he went to your office."

Doubt flashed in Terrence's eyes, but he schooled his features. "He said you didn't know."

I shrugged. "He'd say anything to protect me." Just as I was now doing. It seemed air shows weren't my only performing skill. As of two seconds ago, I'd become an actress. "Don't think you'll get away with this. I've told the police. Spoke directly with Captain Severs." I threw out the name Terrence would recognize—the officer we'd all met with a few days ago.

"Captain Severs?" He shook his head. "Now I know you're lying. That man doesn't move for anything. He let you off the hook so easily, even with that incriminating letter."

My breath burned in my chest. My letter to Brisbane. The one that had the world believing I'd killed my husband. Terrence had fed it to the authorities.

"Yes, my dear." His mouth quirked at my glare. "I had to retrieve some files from Warren's study and decided to search your room. Imagine my surprise when I came across your little note. With Warren dead, might as well let you take the fall for it." He cut a derisive look at my husband. "What a wasted effort that was. But all is not lost. We're all here now, aren't we?"

I bit back dread and shoved confidence into my tone. "Yes, and Captain Severs knows I'm here. I told him where I was headed."

"Of course you did." The man wasn't speaking maniacally. His voice even toned, his gaze sparking interest, like he was discussing a case. Not at all like a villain from the nickelodeon who swirled about in a velvet cape and stroked his mustache. "If you told the cops, where are they?"

"Not here. He didn't believe me. I had no proof." I leveled my gaze on him. "But know this—if Warren, Brisbane, and I all turn up dead, that man will come after you."

Terrence swallowed, his feet shifting. "You're bluffing."

"Am I?" I notched my chin higher.

Gaze darting between the three of us, his mouth sputtered. "Th-Then perhaps we all die. There are enough explosives in there to take out half this hill." He tucked his chin, gesturing to the transmitter around his neck. "All I have to do is turn this dial, and we'll go."

"Now who's bluffing?" Steel threaded Warren's voice. "You wouldn't blow yourself to bits."

Dizziness threatened, and I could see my gun shaking. "Surely we can figure this out."

But Terrence seemed no longer interested in chatting. Sweat dotted his hairline, rolling into the folds of his forehead. "Don't make me do this."

Warren shrugged, keeping his pistol aimed at Terrence. "Go ahead and try," he drawled out. "I doubt it'll explode. You were never any good at tinkering."

I pulled in a sharp gasp. Why would Warren goad him? Was that smart?

Brisbane cocked his head. "You have a point, Hayes. Your cousin never could measure up to anything you do. His bomb won't work. Just a pile of wires and crumbly powder."

"Is that what you think?" A wildness entered Terrence's eyes. "That you're better than me? Of course it is." Terrence's voice held traces of what I could only label as hurt. "You've always felt that way. I was your charity case. The poor cousin."

Movement from the woods made me jump. Something flew through the air, striking Terrence in the back. A rock? He stumbled forward, his rifle dipping.

Shots went off. Terrence yelled, crimson darkening his chest. He teetered forward, but his finger curled around the trigger. Warren lunged. The gun fired.

My side burned, scorching. I'd been hit. The dizziness that had tickled the edges of my mind earlier now invaded with overwhelming force. My breath bled from me and sounds drained.

Warren's gaze skimmed over me in alarm, his mouth moving, but I couldn't understand. A lanky shadow stretched across the dirt.

I fell onto it.

Chapter 36 ―――――――――――――――――――――――――――――

"WAKE UP, LOVE." THAT BEAUTIFUL timbre floated into my soul, nestling. "Everything's okay now." Something warm yet callused—a palm?—framed my jaw, and I leaned into it. "That's my girl."

My lashes fluttered. Wooden beams, uneven and ugly colored, striped the ceiling above.

I knew this place. Brisbane's cabin. Then it all flooded back, and my eyes shot wide. "There's a bomb in here." I lurched to sit, but a firm hand kept me against the cot, a burning sensation throbbing in my side.

"You can't make jerky movements." Warren guided my head back onto the pillow.

"But the bomb." Did he not care we lingered in a room stuffed with explosives? I started to roll off the cot, but again he held me fast to the lumpy cushion.

"You're safe." He lowered his face, his gaze level with mine. "I removed it. Besides, the bomb's disabled. There's no chance of it going off."

I blinked against the encroaching daze. "Disabled?"

"Saw to it myself."

My husband tinkered with a bomb? And he acted relatively calm about it? I scowled, angry that my mind wasn't processing fast enough. I was forgetting things. Important things. But I couldn't yank the thoughts from the jumbled haze. Though I *did* know I wasn't thrilled about Warren handling explosives. "You could've blown yourself up."

That should've sounded more forceful, but my weak voice gave out toward the end.

"Lie still." He made a shushing noise I didn't find at all soothing. "It wasn't difficult, Eva. It was done in seconds, and you didn't even realize." He lifted a hand to silence any protest.

I couldn't formulate a coherent response. Why was I so sluggish?

"Please don't get worked up. I disabled it right after you cut my ropes, when you were talking to Brisbane."

That particular moment popped into my mind. My cutting Brisbane's bindings, Warren shuffling behind. At the time, I'd thought Warren had been rummaging Brisbane's secret arsenal, but apparently I'd been wrong. My husband had been disarming a bomb. I also guessed his friend had purposefully kept me in conversation, distracted, so I wouldn't catch Warren in the act and panic. A wave of tiredness rolled over me, my thoughts coloring gray again. And why did my side throb, as if having its own pulse?

"Quit shifting. You need to lie still. I just got the bleeding to stop."

"What?" I glanced down. I was in my camisole. Well, for the most part. It had been rolled up, exposing my middle. Strips of bandages adhered to my left side. What had been dull and distant only a moment ago now rushed with sudden clarity. The bullet. Warren had shot Terrence, then Terrence pulled the trigger before hitting the ground.

"I was shot," I said, barely a whisper.

"Yes. I think you collapsed from shock. Mostly." His eyes were gentle. "Thankfully, the bullet only grazed you. If we keep the bleeding down, you won't need stitches. Terrence wasn't as lucky. Both my shot and Brisbane's made contact. Brisbane took his body to town, where he'll contact the authorities and see what they want to do with him. They'll no doubt want to speak to us. I'd rather you get in as much rest now as possible."

He was dead. "I'm sorry about Terrence." There was more to the story, but I couldn't imagine how awful Warren felt. Terrence had been his cousin, after all.

"You're my only concern." Warren's voice held a tremor.

He spoke nothing else for several seconds, but the tender brush of his knuckles along my jaw said more than words. There was something different in how he touched me, looked at me.

"I never knew such pain until the moment I thought I'd lost you. First with the Jenny, and again with the gun."

I gasped. The Jenny. Tex! Warren had no idea that I'd recruited his help. The poor man was out there somewhere, probably in excruciating agony. Or worse. "Warren, the man who flew the plane, you need to go find him. He could be injured." My words spilled into each other, but Warren remained utterly calm. "Please go find him. I'd never forgive myself if he died."

Nodding, Warren reached for the blanket at my feet and covered me. Then he stood and was out the door.

Guilt burned more than my wound. I was a terrible person. If I would've told Warren earlier about Tex, then he would've been able to get to him sooner. The young pilot had only wanted to help, and now he—

He . . . stood in the doorway.

"You're alive!" I moved, but Warren scowled over Tex's shoulder. "How?"

"A little banged up but right as rain." Tex gave an easy grin, though on closer inspection I could see he hadn't walked away unscathed. Upon approaching, he favored his left leg, and several scrapes lined his grubby face. Strands of . . . hay? . . . covered him from head to toe. I couldn't even begin to guess what had happened.

He pulled over the chair my husband was once bound to and sat. "I'm hurt that you have no faith in my aviation skills." The twinkle in his eyes looked far from pained. "Once the engine was hit, I knew I was in for a crash landing. If it weren't for the hills, I would've been in trouble. But it was steep enough on the other side to give me something to work with."

I exhaled. "So you were able to glide in?"

He scratched the side of his head. "In a manner of speaking, but it wasn't smooth. The land was bumpy, and there were fences."

Fences? As in plural? That explained the scrapes, and the rocky landing probably inflicted a lot of bruising. "And also haystacks?"

He grinned. "I didn't crash into them. Instinct took over, and as soon as she stopped, I climbed out of the cockpit and searched for cover until I knew what was going on. A pile of hay was the nearest thing."

Which was why Terrence had thought I had escaped. He hadn't spotted Tex.

"But I'm sorry for wrecking your plane."

"It wasn't your fault," I said warmly. "Besides, people are what matter. I'm thankful you're still with us."

"And that he saved our lives." Warren clapped Tex on the shoulder. "If it wasn't for this man, I don't want to know how things would've unfolded."

I sent a questioning look at Tex's bashful dip of the chin.

Warren continued, "Tex is not only a good pilot, but his throwing arm is top notch."

My mind reeled to that moment outside. We'd all been at a standstill until something hit Terrence from behind. Ah. The haze cleared. "You threw the rock at Terrence."

"I couldn't get near enough to tackle." He shrugged. "I did the next best thing."

"Saved us all." Gratefulness laced Warren's voice. "The closest thing I had to a plan was to provoke Terrence to reach for the transmitter. I knew the bomb was dead, so I spurred him on." He grabbed a pitcher off the table. "The second he'd lower his gun to grab the dial, I was going to strike." He poured a glass of water and approached. "But Tex helped speed things up. And good thinking on your part, Eva. Asking for help in the first place."

Only Warren would understand how much growth had taken place for me to reach that point. Ignoring my aching body, I smiled at him in appreciation.

"Here." He lifted the glass of water. "Your side might feel like fire for a bit, but you should probably get some liquids in." He pressed the cup to my lips.

As soon as I swallowed, a question leaped off my tongue. "But why did Terrence target me? What did I ever do to him?" Earlier Brisbane had said Terrence was after a fortune. I didn't understand how that would involve me.

Warren adjusted the blanket. "Can't it wait until after you've rested awhile?"

I arched a brow, trying to keep my face from twisting in pain. My side hurt and my temples pounded, but I couldn't relax until I knew why a madman had been after me.

He scrubbed his hand over his face with a resigned exhale. "Right." He grabbed the other chair and straddled it, much like he'd done a couple of weeks back when we'd first arrived at this cabin. So much had transpired since that day I'd found him at the speakeasy.

Tex groaned as he stood. "I'm just gonna . . . keep a lookout for Brisbane." He tipped his fingers in a salute and made his exit.

Warren downed the rest of the water in the glass. "Did you know that garnets are used for more than just jewelry?"

Um. Whatever I'd expected, this wasn't it. "I . . . uh, didn't."

"The lower quality ones are crushed and used for industrial purposes. Garnets are used in abrasive paints, concrete, sandpaper, and the list goes on." He rubbed the back of his neck. "Each individual product requires its own factory for manufacturing."

I drew my brows, trying to find the significance. "You said factory, as in all those rural towns? They kept mentioning factories springing up and creating more jobs." My head tilted. "That was the only link between the places on Brisbane's list."

He nodded. "Yes, that was the connection. The factories. Brisbane discovered that a corporation intended to utilize the small towns for its garnet production."

"That's great for them, but how does that tie to us?"

"Your land is the garnet mine."

"What?" I jolted and instantly regretted it. My torso screamed, and I clenched my teeth against the searing ache. "Our future home? There's . . . a mine on it?" My birthday present from Warren.

He abandoned the chair and knelt beside me, covering my hand with his. "The corporation must've scouted the land and discovered it. By the time they approached the owner, he'd already sold it to me. I had no idea. Terrence handled everything."

A sickening sensation hollowed my gut. "So the corporation approached Terrence."

Warren grimaced. "They offered five times what I paid for it." His thumb ran along my palm. "Brisbane came to me this morning with his suspicions. He was upstate at our land, trying to get proof. Came back late last night."

"And that's where he's been all this time?"

"Yes, though he said he tried to find us—he had no idea where we were."

Which made sense since we'd been posing as Stan and Stella Starling.

"Brisbane was suspicious about Terrence for a while." He scowled. "Wish he would've told me, but he wanted proof first. Because every paper he came across was legal."

"How did Brisbane get the list of towns?"

"Stole it from Terrence's office. He searched for the deed, but all he found was the purchase agreement. Since I specifically asked Terrence that the ownership be in your name, Brisbane guessed that Terrence later weaseled his own on the title deed somewhere along with yours."

Being a lawyer, he no doubt knew the proper channels to get it changed. Either that, or he paid someone off to add his name to the title.

Warren continued, "If I caught it, he could simply say it was a slip-up in the paperwork."

"But he didn't intend for you to catch it."

He squeezed my hand. "No, he wanted us both dead, but mainly you. Then the land would go to him, and he could sell it for a lot of money."

My chest tightened. Terrence could no longer hurt us. We were safe. I dwelled on those two thoughts until my heart calmed. "So if Brisbane took the list in search of answers, how did it get in the cigarette case?"

"Brisbane always keeps a backup of his notes and important leads. You found the extra copy in a duplicate cigarette case. He held on to the original list."

"Ah, go on."

"We had to get to Terrence's office to look for the deed. He never opened before ten, but this morning he was there early." He blew out a breath. "Got the drop on us right when we entered the door. He held Brisbane at gunpoint and forced me to drive us here. Then he lured you. Apparently it was a plan he'd been working on since we both resurfaced. He already had everything he needed for the bomb."

And we all but fed him the idea about Brisbane's cabin that day we'd shared the story of how we'd stayed at his friend's secluded cabin in the woods. "So this entire time he intended to blow us all up."

"But you outsmarted him." He lifted the blanket and checked my side. Satisfied, he covered me again.

Sadness sifted through me at the lengths people would go to for wealth. "He pretended to be Brisbane and said Lilith was behind the crash."

Warren frowned. "He targeted your weakness—your love for others."

"Yes, though in the end . . ." I gazed into his brown eyes, those warm pools I could forever dip my soul into and let it soak. "Love conquered hate."

Conscious of my bandages, he braced his hands on either side of me and lowered his head until his lips slanted over mine. "Amen, Mrs. Hayes." He kissed me. "Amen."

Chapter 37 ————————————————————————

Seven months later—April 1923

A SMALL CROPPING OF PINE trees separated me from my future. I launched out of Warren's car, the spry grass cushioning my oxfords. Nature had shed its winter garment of sluggish grays and heavy browns and was now arrayed in that vividness that only blushed with spring. A newness. Oh, the wonder of fresh beginnings. I could feel the glories of it down to my bones. Today we'd finally view our new land.

"Wait, Eva," Warren called. He unfolded himself from the car, the noonday sun highlighting his masculine form. "You're a tough girl to keep still. Like this morning, when you darted out of the house the instant I suggested this trip." He raised a knowing brow. "Though I'm sure missing your father's luncheon had nothing to do with it."

It certainly was motivation. "We visited them before coming here." I felt the need to point this out. My relationship with my parents was what it had always been. I had hoped after Mother's health scare and our own scrape with danger they'd be more welcoming. But Father remained aloof. And Mother? It seemed those moments she'd shared about Ruth Fields would serve as the only glimpse of softness beneath her hard shell. Nothing new had surfaced about Ruth Fields and the possibility of her being my parent. But I was content with who I was and Whose I was.

My gaze fell on my husband. "As for the luncheon, I'd rather skip the governor's prattle about how Father's lumber mills and paper plants are an asset to industrial New York." To me, it sounded like our state's leaders were trying to appease him. A consolation prize of sorts.

September 28—nearly two weeks after our frightening event at Brisbane's cabin—John Ashcroft had secured the senatorial nomination for his party. Though on November 7, he'd lost the election. My father hadn't encountered a setback in his entire life. He'd always pushed forward, shoving whatever and whomever from his way. I'd never known another person who'd risk the welfare of those around him to grasp what he desired most.

Until Terrence.

Warren's cousin had been just like my father in that respect. He destroyed in order to create his own happiness. Though in the end, his sinister pursuit of wealth had become his own ruin. Which reminded me. "There isn't some hidden garnet mine on *this* land, is there?"

The authorities had confiscated the deed from Terrence's safe, which in fact had his name on it. A brief investigation had taken place, but Warren and Kent Brisbane had been cleared of any blame in his death, thanks to the overwhelming evidence against Terrence and Tex's testimony. Warren had rewarded Tex handsomely, as well as featured his heroic flying skills in his newspaper. The exposition had helped Tex land a position as a pilot for the United States Airmail Service.

"No, my darling." Warren took my hand in his. "This land is garnet free."

"Good." Though I felt his hesitancy in each skim of his thumb over my fingers. "What's wrong?"

A soft exhale escaped his lips. "I'm hoping you won't be disappointed at what's beyond those trees." He tipped his head at the row of pines. "There's no mountain range. Or lake view. I don't want you to regret selling what we had."

"Listen, Mr. Hayes." I framed his face with the hand not holding my purse and lifted on my tiptoes, closing the gap. "It was *my* idea to sell that property. I wasn't concerned about losing a pretty view but helping those communities. You saw how thrilled they all were about more jobs pouring in. How hopeful. Without that land, there'd be no production. No factories to bring in work for those families." I couldn't help it. Hosting those air shows had opened my eyes. We'd not only left wheel ruts in those farmlands but also pieces of my heart. We'd met the owners of the mining corporation, and they had the locals' best interest in mind. Besides, with the extra money from our sale, we intended to pour back into those towns. After we purchased new planes, of course, to then give flying veterans a chance to create their own aerial circuses. "It was the right thing to do."

"There you go again, Mrs. Hayes. You just can't help being brilliant." His eyes held mine, a heat building between us that had nothing to do with the warm sunlight. His lips grazed my forehead. "I'm still in awe I get to call you mine." His gaze drifted over my face, my hair, taking an intense interest in how the breeze stirred golden tendrils against my temple. He lifted the rogue lock, his fingers toying with the edges. "I'm beginning to like it styled this way."

Not that I had any choice. For the first couple of months, I'd faithfully worn a wig, waiting for my hair to grow. Once the blond reached the edge of my crown, our maid had snipped off the black. So now my bob was all natural and only long enough to tuck behind my ears.

"I have easier access to your neck." To prove his point, he dropped a lingering kiss there. Then another.

"You're stalling." I backed away, a smile tugging my lips. "Take me to the spot of my future home, husband." Before I could utter another demand, Warren scooped me up in his arms, as if carrying me over the threshold of a brick-and-mortar house rather than stepping through a line of trees.

I laughed. "This isn't exactly necessary."

"You're not fooling me." His spicy scent mingled with the fresh pines, making me inhale deeper. "I know you secretly love this."

I did. At least once a week I'd purposefully fall asleep in the library just so Warren would carry me to bed.

The canopy of emerald limbs disappeared. Our land was just over my shoulder. I shifted to catch my first glimpse, but Warren's face slacked. Then his steps slowed.

I stared at his parted mouth. "Is it worse than you remembered?"

He shook his head. "See for yourself, love." In one fluid motion he set me on my feet.

I sucked in a breath. This wasn't what I'd expected. Warren had me believing our land was nothing but weeds and burs. "Those are flowers." Lots of them. As if God rolled out a blanket of bluebells and daffodils dotted with snowdrops. It was a field of blooms, and my eyes couldn't get enough.

"I wondered why the previous owner said you'd enjoy this place." His mouth tipped in a warm smile. "I assure you, Eva, this wasn't how it looked in January."

Then the ground had been frozen and dead. But now it was alive with color.

A curving stream glistened in the sunlight, sparking my smile. Could this be any more perfect? Clutching my bag in one hand, I grabbed hold of Warren's fingers with the other. "Come on." I pulled him with me, and we broke into a run at the same time, as if our minds were as joined as our hands.

Ferns skimmed my legs and dew seeped through my stockings, but it didn't slow me. We reached the brook's edge, our chests heaving but hearts lighter.

Still grappling for breath, I leaned into Warren's side. "I grabbed something from my parents' house earlier. Well, really, from my old bedroom."

"Ah, so that's where you escaped to while your father insisted I introduce him to William Hearst." He rolled his eyes. "One publisher under his influence apparently isn't enough."

I playfully tsked. "No more talking about him." I dug in my purse, withdrew the suede pouch, and handed it to my husband.

"What's this?" He untied the leather strip and opened the mouth of the bag. "It's your . . . stones from heaven." He poured some of the white pebbles into his hand, but not nearly the entire contents. The pouch had been stuffed full, each stone representing a lonely moment during my childhood. Something my husband was aware of. "Oh, Eva." He returned them to the bag. "As long as I draw breath, you'll never be alone again. I vow it." He curved an arm around my waist, his hand resting on the spot of my mercy mark, his nickname for my scar from Terrence's bullet. In private moments, my husband often kissed that jagged line, followed by a whisper of thanks to the Almighty.

His words wrapped around me with just as much warmth as his arms. A rush of love surging through me, I stared at this man who'd given me his name and so much more. My mind drifted to my sister. Was she this happy and content in her marriage? I'd written her several letters with no response. Though this wasn't the time to cling to somber thoughts but embrace this moment. And it started with those pebbles.

"I felt impressed to bring these here. I wasn't sure why, but now I know." I reclaimed the bag and poured the stones into the brook, giving them a new home, a place of belonging. Just like I had with Warren.

Warren slipped his hand into his pocket and retrieved the pebble I'd given him almost a year ago. I knew he carried it with him, but seeing it again made my eyes glossy. "I want mine with yours." As if holding a pearl, he crouched and gently slipped it into the water. "Just as my place is always with you."

Last spring I hadn't dared hoped things would turn out like this. "I love you." This man had gifted me both sky and land. A place for my dreams to fly but also a steady landing place.

His arms wrapped around me, and his lips found mine like they always did when I'd say those three little words. Which were often. I'd once likened love to a crippling disease, but in truth, it was a cure. A haven for healing. With God's love within me and Warren holding me tight, my heart could soar to the highest heights.

Author's Note ───

WHEN THE TOPIC OF THE Roaring Twenties is brought up, most generally think of the defining elements such as women's suffrage, Prohibition, and the beginning of the Great Depression. But this era was also a fascinating period in aviation history.

Curtiss biplanes are nicknamed "the Jenny," derived from the model name JN-4 with the open-topped 4 appearing as a Y. This biplane was widely used in training pilots during World War I. It is a twin seater with both cockpits having sets of controls. During military training, the instructor would sit behind the student. About 95 percent of World War I trainees flew the Curtiss biplane. After the war the government had a surplus of planes and sold thousands of them to civilians for a fraction of their original price. Thus, the barnstorming era was born.

Barnstorming won its name simply because fliers would land on rural farms, negotiate with the farmer to use their open fields as a runway, then host an air show that day for the community. A lot of the small-town locals had never glimpsed an airplane, so these events were wildly popular. The barnstorming season ran from spring until late fall.

At the time, there were no government regulations on aviation. One didn't need a license to fly. In a way, it was every man for himself when it came to the skies. Pilots performed dangerous stunts to wow the masses. It was all the rage. Even Charles Lindbergh was a barnstormer. These shows would feature pilot tricks, such as loops, plunges, and barrel rolls. Also, flying circuses featured parachute stunts and wingwalking.

With the growing popularity of flying circuses, pilots seemed compelled to one-up other aerial acts, performing highly publicized dangerous stunts. Sadly, this bravado led to many deaths, forcing the government to pass laws regulating aviation in 1927. These new laws included safety standards that basically shut down barnstorming. For instance, most tricks had to be performed at low altitude so the spectators could see, but low-altitude stunts were no longer allowed. Also, the military stopped selling their surplus Jennys, so pilots couldn't easily purchase a biplane. This barnstorming era lasted less than a decade but made a huge impact on aviation.

In the story, Geneva mentions Ruth Law Oliver, a trailblazer for women fliers. She performed death-defying stunts all over the nation. One morning she was surprised to see a notice in the newspaper announcing her retirement. Her husband had submitted the bulletin, having grown weary of worrying over his wife's daring antics. The announcement coincided with the timeline of my story, and so I, of course, inserted a nugget about this amazing aviatrix.

While barnstorming was indeed dangerous, I also wanted to highlight the perils that could be found on the neighborhood drugstore's shelves. Arsenic complexion wafers were indeed sold in stores across America. The poison would destroy red blood cells in the skin, making the complexion fashionably pale. There were cases of women going blind from taking the product, as well as some instances of death through overdose. The wafers were still sold through the late 1920s. Oh, what women did, and still do, for the sake of beauty.

Another historical factoid would be the use of radio transmission in weaponry, namely bombs. This was accomplished through radio frequency—when the radio received a certain sequence of tones, the bomb would detonate.

The garnet is a mineral found in the Adirondacks, and I based the Hayeses's land off the Barton mine. The garnet is, of course, a dark-red gem, but mostly garnets are mined for industrial purposes, as its abrasive qualities are used in a variety of ways. That sparked my idea of a corporation branching out, utilizing the eagerness of small-town America while also manufacturing popular products.

Thank you so much for reading! If you've enjoyed this story, I welcome you to check out my other novels. You can find a list of all my books online at RachelScottMcDaniel.com.

Acknowledgments ———————————————————————————

THIS BOOK IS SPECIAL TO me, and one major reason is because of the people who've supported my journey. Here's my chance to brag on them. A huge thank-you to Kregel for believing in this book and to my editor, Janyre Tromp. Janyre, I will always say your friendship is the best thing that I've ever gotten out of Twitter.

I wouldn't be where I'm at without my agent, Julie Gwinn. Thank you for reading and championing my stories. My soul sister, Rebekah Millet. I can spend so much time gushing over how awesome you are. This book would be full of plot holes and ill-placed question marks if not for your genius touch. Thank you! To my favorite Marco Polo chat— you know who you are! I appreciate you ladies so much. Thank you for being there. Natalie Walters, this book—and my others—wouldn't be in existence without your generosity. You're a hero!

This story is different than my previous novels in format and content. (My first attempt at writing a married couple!) So I'm super grateful for early readers who helped me fine-tune this book! Thank you, Crissy, Joy, and Amy. Proverbs 17:17! As well as Ashley, Abbi, and Kim Ann. I really appreciate all your feedback!

To my husband, I know you've been getting teased nonstop for not reading my books, but here's your vindication. Because if not for you making me watch those intense prime-time shows, I would *not* have had the plot twist to this story. Thank you for helping me brainstorm

Acknowledgments

this book as well as my others. Oh, and for hero inspiration. I write romance, but our love story is my favorite.

A shout-out to my kids. Thanks for putting up with eating pizza and more pizza while Mama was on deadline. I promise to cook up some of your faves soon.

To Jesus—You're my everything. My words may entertain, but Yours give life.